With This Ring I Thee Bed

AN
EROTIC
COLLECTION
EDITED BY

ALISON TYLER

WITH THIS RING, I THEE BED

ISBN-13: 978-0-373-60555-2

For questions and comments about the quality of this book please contact us at Customer_eCare@Harlequin.ca.

Spice and the Colophon are trademarks used under license and registered in Australia, New Zealand, Philippines, United States Patent and Trademark Office and in other countries.

www.Spice-Books.com

Printed in U.S.A.

Recycling programs for this product may not exist in your area.

Contents

Contents

Dedicated
to SAM

Two human loves

make one divine.

Elizabeth Barrett Browning

~ introduction ~

"I do."

I said those words nearly fifteen years ago, in a sunny backyard ceremony, surrounded by friends and family. I knew Sam was the one for me from the start. In fact, *I* did the proposing.

"Ever think of getting married?" I asked after our first weekend together.

"Is that an offer?" he countered.

I nodded, he accepted and I bought the dress the next week. The ceremony took place in the spring, in a simple outdoor celebration. I wore white. He wore a suit. The handcuffs came later.

Marriage is revered in our family. My grandparents celebrated sixty-five years together, and my parents have been married more than forty. But we embrace an element of levity, as well. My folks got hitched on April Fool's Day. The "something blue" *I* wore was glossy midnight polish on my toenails.

But now I'm focused on my brand-new wedding. And you're invited. Don't worry—I'm not cheating, I'm talking about an anthology dedicated to all things bridal—from paper to diamonds.

With This Ring, I Thee Bed features tales of married sex, honeymoon sex, make-up sex, anniversary events and a seven-year itch. Couples experiment with new ideas, and (in some cases) new people. Lovers stoke the embers of passion as they fall ever deeper in love. In at least one instance, a gigolo is involved!

When I invited the authors to submit, I told them to toss the theme in the air like a bouquet—so that we'd all be scattered with petals as well as rice.

With This Ring, I Thee Bed takes the license for marriage from naked nuptials to brides in bondage. Naughty authors are registered at the Department of Kink.

Now, who else is ready to say "I Do"?

XXX,
Alison

P.S. Although a wedding book has been on my mind (and my hard drive) for years, I'd like to thank my best man, Mike Kimera, for giving me the title and escorting me down the aisle.

Now or Forever

Nikki Magennis

We should be halfway to paradise by now.

I look at Susie's blue kitchen clock. Just past twelve. The flight left three hours ago, heading to the Caribbean with two empty seats in first class.

The washing machine clicks over and I watch the clothes tumble around in the drum, soapy water sloshing from side to side. They're all too colorful. Bikini, sarong, sundress. Clothes I'm never going to wear. I'm washing them instead of burning them.

Our honeymoon was a present from Charlie's dad—one of the gifts that can't be quietly returned. It's not always possible to apologize. Some things can't be undone. And "sorry" isn't always enough.

I get another flash of Charlie's face. The way his eyes kind of flickered as I ran past him on the path, the way he looked almost as if he was smiling, the way he does when he's confused. He was a little pale, his freckles darker than usual.

Oh God.

It was all supposed to be a big white dream. We'd be like paper dolls cut out of a magazine. A pretty little church, the perfect lace dress, star-shaped flowers with delicate trails of ivy. Charlie would be nervous and I'd be trying not to laugh. We would kiss in soft focus. Bells would ring.

My phone goes—and it's playing the fucking Wedding March. My sister must have programmed it as a joke. I pounce on my jacket, scrabble through the pockets and find it, hit the cancel button before I look at the name.

Charlie. Of course it's Charlie. Did I think he'd just disappear? Six years don't evaporate that easily. Even if I've broken his heart and ruined his life, we're going to have to at least pretend to be grown-ups. I should call him back.

I don't. Instead, I pick at the lace of the bright yellow garter Susie made me promise to wear. It's a hideous thing—the color of crayon sunshine in a kid's drawing, with too many bows and ribbons sprouting from it—but for some reason I can't stop playing with it. Back when she gave me the garter—a hundred years ago, the night before the not-wedding—it seemed like a silly, joyous little joke. Now it makes me wince.

"The yellow ones are supposed to attract lovers. Maybe some of your good luck'll rub off on me, eh?" Susie had given me a big, theatrical wink, but I think she meant it at least a little bit.

Susie and I are best friends from high school. We've been through crushes, boyfriends, breakups and make-ups. I'd always been the one with the hectic love life, Susie the one with the steady boyfriends. Until I met Charlie.

My head snaps up as the doorbell rings. I don't want to speak to anyone, not the flower arranger, the dressmaker or the caterers, not friends and relations or in-laws. There's not a single one of the thousand people involved in the biggest not-wedding this century that I want to hear from.

The bell goes again. Maybe Susie forgot her key, I think.

Maybe it's not even for me. I tread nervously to the door and reluctantly open it a crack.

On the step is the one person I want most, the one I fear most. The door swings open and Charlie and I are facing each other over the threshold.

"Seb." It's his secret name for me. Silly, I know, but it makes me feel as if I'm about to collapse, like I'm a bicycle tire with all the air let out.

I'm shaking my head but I can't break my gaze, tear it away from those eyes the color of wet slate. Charlie is hard to read, but over the years I've learned his tells. Usually, I can pick up his quirking smile, some little giveaway angle of his eyebrow or how he tugs at his ear. Today, he's standing on Susie's front step with his arms hanging by his sides, and I can't tell a thing. Whether he wants to hold me or hit me. I close my eyes.

I don't know how to apologize.

"I just couldn't. I can't." My voice is thin, about to break. "Where do I start, Charlie?"

What I want most is to sag into his arms. He's my comfort, usually, my solace and support. I straighten my spine. No. Not now.

I stand back and let him in, taking a breath of his fresh-air-and-skin scent as he passes.

I follow him into the kitchen and it's easier, somehow, when we're not facing each other, so I turn my back on him and fuss with the kettle and the teacups. My hand shakes as I pour milk.

As the water comes to a boil, I turn and he's got the garter, that hideous yellow badge, and he's turning it round in his hands.

"You wore this?" he asks, a frown folded between his eyebrows.

"Susie asked me to." I want to snatch the garter away from him. I remember the sensation, tight round my thigh, the cheap fabric stiff and prickly. I stood there being prepped for the wedding and I remember having the sudden, violent urge to run away and rip it off and scratch and scratch and scratch.

Charlie nods slowly.

Normally, he'd crack a joke. Normally, this would be easy—being together, the easiest thing in the world, like everything's right and how it should be and…and perfect? I look at the yellow of the garter against Charlie's skin.

"It was all too good to be true," I say softly. Surprising myself.

He looks up and I can see for the first time a spark in his eyes. It could be dangerous. It could be promising. I take the chance.

"I'm scared, Charlie."

"Of what?"

"Of us." I watch his lips. I owe him honesty, at least. I take a deep breath.

"Of suffocating. I was standing up there at that altar and…"

"And what?" he says, his voice edged with flint.

"I don't want to hurt you," I start to say, before I realize what I'm doing. I start again. Look right in his eyes.

"I don't know if I can promise you so much. Just you, just me, forever." There's a rushing over my skin, and I'm running fast down a slope. But I can't stop now. "I saw my sex life flash in front of my eyes, Charlie. Do you understand what I'm saying?" I know I'm almost shouting.

Is that worse? I wonder. To have ditched Charlie in front of all his family and friends, to have left him awkward and alone at the church, or this? To tell him the truth, what I've been darkly afraid of all along? My lurid, cherry-red, heart-throbbing dirty secret.

How can I promise never to have another lover? Me, who's always been quick to get bored, and quicker to discard unsatisfactory bedfellows. Who's been first to try every practice and position, whose whole life is punctuated by sex—exotic and romantic and thrilling and brief and heartbreaking. Yes, I love Charlie, and yes, I love fucking him. But will I really be able to sacrifice every other man in the world—every other possible man?

I think about how Charlie is, and try and match it against the invisible future. I know it's wrong, but I'm trying to measure him. Testing, to see how I love him, how much and how far.

Yes, I love how his eyelids kind of slide down a few degrees, so he's giving me a snake's gaze, one that slips over my body in a prelude to his touch. I love how his mouth goes tight. How his fingers travel, how he takes mouthfuls of me.

And this. Yes, I'd forgotten how much I love this.

"Charlie?"

"Shut up."

How he is silent. How he pulls me to him and works his way from my wrist to my shoulders. Charlie is gentle. Most of the time. But he knows how to fix me in place. He's clever, too—sees immediately how he could take an ugly yellow garter and twist it around my wrists, how it would hold my arms behind my back firmly, but stretch enough not to dig in too much.

"What if Susie…"

He ignores me. I think this might be what I love most about us. He knows me so well, he can tell when to listen and when to just keep on going. Like now, as he strips me methodically, slowly, almost brusquely. He pushes the cardigan off my shoulders and lets it bunch at my tied wrists. Reaches for the buttons at my throat and lets the backs of his hands scuff over my breasts.

I'm biting my lip again, trying not to moan. For some reason, it seems important to match Charlie's wordless intensity. As though the only way I can apologize is with my silence, as though any more words would be too many.

He peels my shirt aside, bares my breasts and belly. He's holding my shirttails in his fists and he tugs me from side to side a little as he leans in to kiss me, letting me know how he can move me, how he can turn me.

And then we're kissing and it's too late for explanations. I forget why I left the church, I forget where I am and what my name is. All I can think of is the heat of Charlie's mouth, the scrape of his stubble and the hard pressure of his body against mine. The way he is kissing me recklessly, like a dare.

When he pulls away I'm breathing hard, as if we've been running.

"So I'm not enough for you," he says, and his lip curls a little. His hand drops to my breast and tweaks hard. I open my mouth but no sound comes out.

"You want more." His other hand, my other breast. I'm almost doubling over, and my nipples are burning beautifully as he pulls and pinches. When he lets go, I almost fall forward. In the sun-filled kitchen I'm gasping for breath—half-naked, disheveled and as ridiculous as the yellow garter.

Charlie knows how to tease, and today I'm wondering if he's playing out some kind of revenge. If he's going to teach me a lesson—how it feels to be left hanging.

"Please," I say, even though I think I shouldn't.

"You know what, Seb?"

He's leaning back and looking at me thoughtfully, as if I were a painting he's deciding whether or not he likes.

"I can understand you being chicken. I can even live with the thought of you fucking other people." His eyes flash. I look at him and the blush storms through my cheeks. He nods. "Yes, I am aware that you like sex, Seb."

He leans in close and whispers in my ear. "Dirty girl, aren't you? You think I didn't know that? You think I can't tell how hungry you are every time you walk down the street, shaking that tight little ass of yours? You think I don't notice how you stick your tits out when you're talking to a nice-looking guy? How you give all my friends the once-over, like you're just considering the possibility?"

I flinch. I really *didn't* think he'd noticed.

Charlie pulls back and sighs. He reaches, almost idly, to my trousers and flicks at the buttons. As if he doesn't care if they come loose or not. When he slides his hand into the front of my panties, he touches the tip of his tongue to his lip as if he's doing something tricky.

"What breaks my heart, Seb, is that you think I'm so stupid."

"I don't!" If I weren't tied up, I'd reach out for him. He curls his fingers inside my panties, cups my pussy in his hand and gives a little squeeze. It's like he's in control of my heart-beat now, as though each stinging pinch of my clit sends the blood running through my veins.

"You think I don't know you."

"That's not true," I say, although my voice is strained and cracking.

"It's not?"

I look up at him through the strands of hair that have fallen over my face. He meets my gaze, hard and direct.

"Seb, I know you. I know how you're torn."

While he talks, he keeps working at me, his fingers stroking my most intimate places, proving the truth of what he
says.

"You think that getting married is a death sentence. That
we'd be stuck fast together and we'd never be able to leave."

I bite my lip. I can't really deny this, not without lying.
He strums at me, turning the dial up toward orgasm. He can
make me come with a flick of his wrist. I rock on his hand,
lean on his arm so that he's virtually propping me up. I think
of his cock, how long it is and how full it makes me.

"Charlie," I say, losing the thread of our conversation. I
know I have to concentrate, have to hold back. But when he
tweaks at my aching nipple, I nearly give in.

"Nothing is forever," he says, his voice so soft it breaks my
heart. He tugs on my nipples, left and right, dosing me with
little shocks of pain.

"You like this." It's not a question, but I respond anyway.

"Yes. God, yes."

"And if you didn't want it? If you stopped liking it?"

I won't ever, I say in my mind. *Please don't stop.* He's alternating pinches of my clit and my nipples now, digging his
fingers into me, burying them inside me.

"Seb. Answer me."

I shake my head.

I whisper our pact, our long-ago agreement. What we discussed back when we were laying down the ground rules.
When we were still falling in love.

"I say the word. And it's over."

"Yes. You say the word. It's that simple."

He holds on tight to my clit, rubbing it between his fore-
finger and thumb until it burns. "Or," he says, "of course,
I can also say the word." His voice is low and creaky. Suddenly, I'm terrified.

I want to kiss him. I want to stop him from saying anything more. I moan and reach out for him, want his body slammed against mine, want him to rub against me, crush me, bore into me. Prove that he's here, with me and not lost.

"Charlie," I say, and there's panic sliding in my voice. "Please."

He cradles my head in the crook of his shoulder while he reaches to undo his jeans. At the same time he loosens the garter and throws it on the ground. Hands free, I grab for him.

We're swaying now, falling against the kitchen table and bumping into the chairs. I push my clothes roughly down around my ankles, still leaning into Charlie, nuzzling at him. He smells of the soap he uses, maybe a little of last night's whisky. I wonder what he did last night. Whether he slept. Whether he cried.

He turns me roughly and bends me over the kitchen table. Now I can't see his face and I'm even more scared—is this his goodbye fuck? Is he going to say the word, cut me loose, banish me from his life?

His hands are on my hips, holding me steady and firm, and I butt back against him, wanting him to be inside me, yes, but also wanting to be inside him somehow. I spread my legs, feel the head of his cock slip between my thighs.

"Come into me, baby," I say, tilting my ass up as though begging. His thighs are warm on the back of my legs. He pushes into me and I could weep again. My legs are shaking, about to start bucking and jerking against him, almost out of my control.

"Shhh," he says, stroking from the base of my spine to between my shoulder blades, dragging his hand over my body to soothe me. And it does—I rock slowly, taking a little more of him at a time until he's nestled deep in me and can't go any farther.

"More," I murmur, wiggling my hips from side to side. Charlie keeps caressing me, slow and steady. I hear him laugh.

"S'funny?" I ask, although I can't stop swaying against him, working myself up and down on his shaft.

"I'll give you as much as you want," he says lightly, while he withdraws in a rush and plunges back into me, making me gasp. "Whenever you want, however you want."

He punctuates his words with thrusts that get harder, more emphatic and blunter each time. His cock is thickening in me, corkscrewing deeper and deeper.

"And if you want me to stop…" He pulls out so that just the tip of him is in me, an unbearable loss. "You just say the word."

"Charlie," I say. He's hovering on the brink, I know it. The orgasm gathers in my fingertips, in my toes, rushes back and forth over me, crisscrosses from my nipples to my pussy and back to my mouth, my eyes, my heart. Just as I come, holding tight to the edge of the kitchen table, I get it. I get what he means. We'll be married if we want it, for as long as we want it, just how we want it.

Charlie slides forward, sinks into me, and gives me what I need. I rise up to meet him and we surge together, rocking, responding, fucking like we always do.

"This is how they fuck in heaven," Charlie said back in the first flush of our relationship, after six weeks of springtime courting and delirious sleepless nights. It was one of those embarrassing thoughts that spill out after especially good sex, and the way he said it—like a teenage boy awestruck and mad horny, made me blush. I remember we both laughed at the time.

Years later, and only after I'd managed to wreck our picture-perfect day, I realized he was right. It's why I wasn't all that unhappy that we missed the flight to Saint Lucia. Charlie and I know exactly how to make heaven on earth. We made it that afternoon in Susie's kitchen, with the yellow garter lying trashed on the floor and the sky outside turning a really pretty shade of pale blue, like shirts when they're fresh out of the laundry.

It was a strange day. We should have been brokenhearted that we'd created such a public disaster of our marriage. We were shipwrecked and empty-handed, and we probably both looked like fools. But in the space left behind we were free to make our own promises, say them quietly, in our own time.

There were no flowers, no speeches, no guests and no garter. Just me, Charlie and the words between us—the only ones that really mattered.

Racing to the Altar

Sommer Marsden

I eyed the billboard as my foot mashed on the gas pedal. The thought *cops hide behind big billboard signs like that* flittered through my head, but I mashed it anyway. My speed crept from 68 to 74. I was late. I was so fucking late it wasn't funny. I was racing to the altar. Hell-bent for matrimony.

Kelly and Tina and Tracy all awaited me at the church. No doubt pacing the small bridal room where they were to do my makeup and my hair. I could picture Kelly fretting as she ticked off the minutes in her head. How much time we had and what that would allow. Up-do with accent braids? Chignon? Traditional bun? She would kill me!

I shot past the sign advertising Rock Hard Gym and my stomach bottomed out when I saw the lights, my body tingling the way it does when I ride a roller coaster. The cherry lights atop the cruiser came on in a flash of crimson, and I gnawed my bottom lip.

Cop.

I pulled to the side of the road.

I didn't have time for a ticket. There was hair to be done, makeup to be applied, panic to be embraced. I had to go over my vows and make sure the seating arrangements were perfect and check the church to ensure that Uncle Sal was not next to Great-aunt Dot (or they would kill each other). I had too much to do. And at the end of it all, hopefully I would be lawfully married and not insane. Then Jackson and I would run off to Nova Scotia, never to return!

Okay, so we were returning. The point was that we had to make it through this stressful, heart-pounding wedding and reception before we could escape. And all I really wanted was to be with him. Somewhere quiet. Just me and him and our lips pressed together, making out like horny teenagers the way we did when we weren't tasting butter cream frosting or picking out dye to make shoes match dresses. I sighed, drumming my fingers on the steering wheel. In my head, I was already pleading my case. Figuring out what I would say to Officer Friendly to get off with only a warning.

"Do you know how fast you were going, miss?" he asked into my semi-open window. My heart shot up into my throat and my stomach dropped to my feet. I opened my mouth, but he cut me off. "I asked you a question, miss. Do you know how fast you were going?"

"Too fast?" It was all could think to say.

The good officer laughed. "Obviously, or I wouldn't be here, would I?"

His eyes studied me and I studied him. He'd pulled his aviator sunglasses down to peer at me, his mouth twisted in a wry grin. Bright blue eyes like an autumn sky, lush lips, peppering of dark stubble along his jaw. I thought it would be fairly easy to cut paper with his cheekbones, and I was struck, sitting out here in the bright October sunshine, by how utterly gorgeous he was. Nearly beautiful, to be honest.

"This section of road is zoned for 55 miles per hour, ma'am. You were going over 70. Were you aware?"

"No," I lied. He put his hand on the door and I rolled my window all the way down. My eyes went to his thickly muscled forearms, and my head felt swimmy. I'm a sucker for thick forearms. But I had a wedding to get to.

"I think you knew, and you were speeding anyway." He leaned into the window, crowding my space. He had a teardrop-shaped birthmark above his left thumb. I inhaled deeply and tried to think.

"I'm sorry?"

"Are you sure? You don't sound sure."

This officer, this man, this amazing specimen was nearly leaning headfirst into my window. So close to me and my jangling nerves I swore I could feel the invisible particles of his energy mixing with mine. It was downright dirty, was what it was, because my pussy was responding to the heady mixture of fear and excitement and attraction. "Yes, I am absolutely sure that I am sorry," I said, and any idiot could tell I was lying.

"I don't believe you," he said. He put his pad in his pocket and ran his finger along the seam of rubber that protected my lowered window. I watched that finger trace, and fought the urge to cross my legs. This was crazy. This was silly. I should ask for my ticket and leave. I should make him let me go right this instant. My bridesmaids and others would be foaming at the mouth by now. I. Did. Not. Have. Time. I didn't have time for this insanity!

"I assure you, sir."

"You're lying."

I felt a blush heat my cheeks. I blew out a sigh, trying not to think about church parking, place settings, snippy caterers and my betrothed's mother's insistence that we had some ridiculous disgusting red velvet groom's cake.

"I don't lie," I lied.

"Could you pull around next to my cruiser and step out of the car please, ma'am?"

Real fear sizzled through me then. My eyes found my watch and I almost cried. I was already a half an hour late to the church. In two and a half hours I was supposed to be saying, "I do." And then a party to rival all parties and then blissful, perfect alone time. Away from all the lunacy of a big wedding.

"Ma'am."

"Look, Officer, I don't have time for this. I truly don't." I smiled. He had to understand. He had to! I would make it all up, but right now I had to bolt. Hell, I pretty much needed a police escort.

"I don't recall giving you an option, ma'am." He smiled. That smile slid down my throat, snaked between my breasts, tickled over my belly button and stroked my clit like some living mystical thing.

"Um…please?"

"Please drive around and park next to my vehicle, ma'am. Then I would like you to exit your vehicle and wait."

I blew my bangs out of my face. Resistance was futile, as the saying goes. But I could just floor it. Mash my foot on the gas and take off like some bandit out of a seventies moonshine movie. God knows I'd seen enough of them. Even Jackson made me watch them! With a dad, three brothers and a car-crazed fiancé, I was pretty much a pro at car chases from the law.

He read my mind. "And, ma'am, if you try to run, you'll be sorry. Way sorrier than you'll be for lying to me now." He smiled again, all tan skin, white teeth and twisted humor.

I harrumphed, started the car and slowly drove to park beside the cruiser. To be honest, what I did was pretty much drift my big SUV next to it. The cherry lights were still looping but the siren was off.

I put the car in Park, eyed the time again. "Oh, I'm screwed. I am so, so screwed." But I knew from the set of that man's face I was not getting out of this.

I could hear his big boots crunching and popping over the dirt shoulder of the road. I shivered, rubbing my arms. I was crosswired. Unbelievably turned on when I should be begging and pleading.

"Step out, ma'am!" he barked, and I yelped. I opened the door and lowered myself from the SUV. Shit, shit, shit. I had worn my yoga pants and a tee to the church. Flip-flops to let my pedicure dry. I hoped my toenails didn't get dusty.

"Stand by the car, ma'am."

"I am by the car!" I worried my fingers together. I was so wet between my legs it was insane. I studied the fretting image of myself in his mirrored shades. I wished he'd lower them and gaze at me again so I could try and get a read on those eyes.

"*My* car, ma'am." He smiled and my nipples betrayed me by poking incessantly at the thin fabric of my ancient tee.

"Oh."

I walked to his cruiser as if I were going to the gallows. When I got there, I wanted to cry. Now what? Should I face the cruiser? Face him? I had no idea, so I stood in a stupid, cockeyed stance kitty-corner to him and the car.

"Face the cruiser, ma'am."

Damn. His voice was like hot caramel, melting chocolate, warm coffee on a cold day. It skittered down my spine and curled at the base of me. A steady wet echo sounded in my pussy. I was getting married in like…two hours!

"Hands on the trunk, please."

"But—"

"Now, ma'am." He walked closer to me and his energy pressed to me like an embrace. The breath shivered in my throat and a cool fall wind swung the loose legs of my yoga pants around my legs.

"But, in like two hours I'm—"

"Ma'am, if you disregard a direct order again, we're going to have a problem. A very serious problem."

I could tell by the set of his jaw and that stubborn-man look that this was it. I could obey or it would be ten times worse.

"Fine," I said under my breath. I put my hands on the trunk and hung my head, fuming. But when his hands settled on my hips and started to slide I was hot all right, but not from anger.

"I'm just going to pat you down for weapons, ma'am. Routine. You just keep your hands there on the trunk."

I couldn't really make noise with his hands on me. They glided down my hips, skimming my buttocks, caressing the backs of my thighs so gently they could have been an hallucination. My eyes drifted closed, my body going loose. My heart filled my ears and wet heat filled my pussy. I sighed. His hands slid around my bare ankles, which were a bit chilled in the early fall air. Then those hands were scooping back up the front, dancing over my flanks, my hips, the fronts of my thighs. His fingertips brushed the V between my legs and his longest fingers came precariously close to my pussy. I sighed again. Mostly so I could get some air in my lungs.

"Now where were you rushing to, might I ask." He said it right into my ear, his hot breath pouring into the shell, over the lobe, down my throat so goose bumps rose up like crocuses through snow.

"My wedding." I gasped.

His hands played along the wide waist of my yoga pants. Hot fingers dipped under the thin fabric, each touch searing my skin like a burn. I was a kiss away from getting married, and this man was making me nuts.

"Lucky guy, if you don't mind me saying." One hand had slipped completely into my pants and plucked and snagged at my tiny yellow (old!) panties. The other hand smoothed along the swell of my ass as if he owned me.

"Sir…um, mister? Uh, Officer?" I tried them all, but it was damn near impossible for me to think. That rogue hand had slipped down to cover my mound. My neatly groomed for my honeymoon, new-bride pussy. His fingers slipped along the ridge of my lips and pressed to my clit so that I shivered in his half embrace.

"Officer J. S. Monroe," he said.

"Yes, Officer Monroe. I'm going to be so very, very la—oh, God, right there." He had slipped a finger deep into my wet, pulsing cunt and he was just barely thrusting it. Just enough to make all the blood that slept beneath my skin hum like a chorus.

"You know it's dangerous to drive that fast," he said, his lips sliding up and down the back of my neck so that I shook as if I would come apart.

"I'm sorry. Really. I am so, so sorry that I endangered—oh," I said, because he'd slipped another finger into me and his free hand was yanking at my yoga pants.

I glanced around wildly. Someone would see us! Surely they would! Someone would notice us and this would end and…but no. Given how we had parked, how he had instructed me to park, we were blocked from sight on all sides. Barring an airplane, no one would see us. He had my ass bare to the wind, his dark blue dress pants pressed to my bareness. His erection pressed the crack of my bottom and his fingers continued to fuck in a slow, classic rhythm. Like a church organ or a hymn.

"Officer person Monroe," I babbled. "We really shouldn't be doing this. I'm going to miss—"

"You won't miss a thing, ma'am. You have my word. Why, I'll even give you an escort to your ceremony. Would you like that?"

His mouth slipped over my shoulder and even through my tee I could feel the humid heat of his breath. He cupped my breast, rolling the nipple between his fingers. I heard that other hand making busy with the belt and zipper of his blues. Was this really happening?

Then the warm, hard slide of his cock to my skin assured me it was.

"Yes, escort me. Hurry," I said. God, that sounded dirty.

"If you'd just bend forward a bit, ma'am, we can continue with the pat-down."

I bent forward, hands splayed on the warm white metal of the trunk. I pushed my ass out and he took his big knee and knocked my stance wider. There were his fingers again, slipping between my legs, into me, testing me. Then the head of his cock, pressing deliberately to my wet, wet opening. "Yes, Officer," I said.

My hair hung down and danced over the cruiser's bright blue numbers as he anchored my hips and slipped home, sliding into me from behind as if he belonged there. I held on to nothing at all. Only the tips of my toes touched earth as he started to rock and sway against me, his cock thrusting in and out, in and out with sublime friction. Officer Monroe steadied himself, his broad chest, decorated with various commendations, pressed to the back of my worn tee. His other hand snaked around my waist, making my belly muscles flutter and adding a rush of heat wherever his fingers touched.

"Is that nice, ma'am?"

I could only nod. I watched his long tan fingers, nicked from hard work and dealing with God knows what or who, track and dance along my skin. Down the small swell of my belly, the dip of my mound. I watched that teardrop-shaped birthmark dance above his thumb, and then his fingers found my clit even as he started to thrust harder.

"Is that a yes, ma'am?"

"Yes, oh, I'm going to be so—"

"Shh, no more," he ordered.

I bit my lip and gave in. Some vehicle whizzed passed us way too fast. Lucky for them, the law was otherwise engaged. And though I knew I shouldn't be doing this right now—not at all—I sank back a little farther, opened myself a little more and let him in as deep as he could go. His fingers painted circles on my clit, shivering every nerve ending to life.

"Oh, Mr—"

"Officer."

"Oh, Officer…"

"Yes?" His warm laughter filled my head as my toes and flip-flops struggled to find purchase, but he had me, swaying barely above earth. He had me, gripped in his huge safe hands, and I was coming. Coming apart, coming undone, coming as the early fall wind bit at my exposed skin. I was coming.

"That's a good one, ma'am. Good job." His hips started banging in earnest, the more gentle thrusts gone now, and excitement curled in my belly, bursts of excitement and the fear of being caught filling my chest, making my heart pound.

Another car whizzed by and he pushed me forward a little, so my belly, chest and head rested on the warm trunk, as if I was being arrested. Officer Monroe held my legs up and apart, driving into me hard so I would have scootched across the trunk if he didn't have me in his grip. I was open, exposed, so very, very bad. And I was going to come again.

"Oh, you're getting tight again. Do you have plans for another?" His voice had lost its silken texture. Now it was all grunting, panting, choppy words. I loved it.

"I might, if you, yeah, like that."

And he did it like that. And then he did it like that harder until he froze like a robber under a spotlight. Then a final jerk and he emptied into me as my cunt gripped around him tight, taking every little slice of friction he might offer.

My hair was a mess.

I let my heart come down a beat, and looked at my watch. Then I was scrambling across the trunk like a madwoman, hair standing on end or hanging in clumps, yoga pants nearly tangling me so that I went down in the dirt. "Oh, God! Oh, God! I'll never make it now!" I was damn near hysterical.

He took pity on me, bundled me up and put me in my car. Monroe pulled out into traffic, his cherry lights coming on and the siren screaming about as loudly as I wanted to right then. I could swear I saw him smiling in the rearview mirror as he escorted me to the church.

"Oh, my God! Where in the hell have you been! We are never going to—what happened to your hair, Fallon?"

"I, um…" They all stood staring at me. Kelly's toe was tapping the way it did when she was furious. "I had a flat and I had to change it and God! It was a mess."

It must've worked because they all rolled their eyes, threw up their hands and flew into action.

How Kelly made my hair go from trailer trash struck by lightning to damn near royalty is beyond me. But I was going to roll with it. The hushed presence in the church had the charged intensity you can feel in a room packed full of people about to yell "surprise!" The anticipation was palpable.

I'd done a quick cleanup in the bride's "facilities" and was powdered, perfumed, groomed and gowned. It was now or never.

Do or die.

No turning back.

The music cued and my stomach bottomed out. "Oh, God, I am going to pass out."

"Clench your ass! Clench your ass!" Tracy kept hissing in my ear. "It's what the fighter pilots do!"

But clenching my ass made me think of Officer Friendly and the frisking, and just as they threw open those big-ass doors to reveal the ivory-draped aisle, I got the giggles.

"Oh, no. She's freaking out. Good thing Jackson will think it's cute." Tracy blew out a sigh. Tapped my cheeks with the tips of her fingers, her version of a snap-out-of-it smack.

"You guys are so gross, how icky and in love you are." Kelly laughed. She nudged me and I stumbled forward a bit. Remembering the perfect feel of him. The feel of warm metal under my finger and—

"Go!" Tina said.

I went. I nodded and smiled and tried not to throw up. I kept my ass tense, no small feat when you are trying to walk gracefully to your betrothed.

He stood there, smiling. That perfect sexy-as-hell smile. In full-dress uniform, just for me.

In my mind, I was spread-eagle, facedown, being slipped and slid and used and—

"Fallon?" Reverend Scott said.

"Yes, here I am. Here I am," I repeated, and turned to Jackson.

Nervous? he mouthed.

I nodded. He smiled, took my hand for a squeeze, and I ran my thumb over the dark brown teardrop-shaped birthmark above his thumb. I raised it to my lips and kissed it.

In a few moments we would be man and wife. And then Jackson couldn't call me "miss" or "ma'am" when he played his game with me and made me damn near insane with want. Then he'd have to call me "missus."

Or "wife."

Forever Hold Your Peace

I.K. Velasco

This was supposed to be the happiest day of my life. It many ways it was. But I often wondered if I would never be satisfied, if I would always want what I could not have.

The mother of the bride, my sister—the maid of honor—and all eleven of my bridesmaids had finally left the small powder room to give me a moment of peace before the ceremony. The gentle rocking ocean waves and breezes outside the stylishly draped windows sounded like silence compared to the cacophony of a dozen women. I embraced the sound, burrowed under it as if it were down bedding, and allowed myself some refuge in the darkness behind my eyelids. I could feel the stress of the last few days ebb away with the tide.

It was really the stress of the last eight months. Planning a wedding was like leading a war, and I often felt like a general, my flagstaff held high, barking orders to the troops. "Those hydrangeas aren't quite the right shade of pink. You need to pick new ones. That fondant isn't right at all! I said the color of raspberry, not Pepto Bismol! I don't care if you're falling out of your dress, that's what duct tape is for."

And it was in many ways, but all I really wanted right this moment was to see him—my Jacob.

I hadn't seen him in thirty-six hours and the ache was palpable. I could taste it on my tongue, like an unquenched thirst, an unfulfilled craving. I knew it was only thirty minutes until I would be walking up the aisle, but I wanted to be with him right this moment, to share his space and breathe his air. I felt as if I would suffocate without him.

The door clicked open without warning, but it didn't startle me. I somehow knew it was him—my Jacob. He stepped up behind me and placed warm, familiar hands on my shoulders. Our eyes met in the mirror and he smiled a wide and goofy grin.

"You can't be in here!" I chided. "You're not supposed to see me before the ceremony. It's bad luck."

"Luck, schmuck." He tugged on his collar, uncomfortably. I wasn't used to seeing Jacob dressed in formal garb—white shirt, suit with no tie, charcoal gray, not black; since the wedding was at the beach, we'd wanted it to be more casual. The color darkened his eyes somehow—made them more gray than green, as they usually were. He looked devastatingly handsome. "Sixty percent of American marriages end in divorce. You're going to be a statistic in T-minus twenty-three minutes."

I frowned. "Don't say that."

Jacob squeezed my shoulders, his wry smile spreading. "Can't help it. Jaded, I guess."

"Well, I won't be a statistic. I'm very loyal. Nothing to worry about." I crossed my arms and pouted.

He laughed, reaching up to pinch my cheeks. "You know I love it when you pout! Plus those crossed arms are accentuating your voluptuous bosom." He straightened up to his full height, peering down at the tightly wound corset of my dress.

I feigned modesty, placing my palms over what I knew was ample, revealing cleavage. I'd chosen my dress precisely for that feature.

"I hate that you're seeing me when I'm not fully ready. I wanted you to see me later, on my father's arm, walking down the aisle...."

"See you when everyone else sees you? That hardly seems fair. I'm special, aren't I? More special than those people out there? I should get the first peek." Jacob reached up and lifted the layers of taffeta making up my train. He quickly found the lace between my legs, running his fingers along the edges.

I gasped, pushing at his hands. "Hey! Don't do that...."

He backed away, frowning. "I'm sorry. I thought you would want to..." His eyes changed again, from gray to black.

I reached for him, wrapped my arms around his waist and tucked my chin, pressing my forehead on his belly. "I didn't mean to push you away. I'm just... It's a big day. I want everything to be right. I'm nervous, excited." I felt his soft lips on my hair. "I'm sorry. Yes, I want this to be perfect for you." I leaned back and met his gaze. He bent down to kiss me, his mouth open and giving.

There was a fleeting thought about Jacob's kisses messing up my makeup, but that was soon forgotten when he lifted me out of the vanity chair, hands secure under all the taffeta and lace, and carried me to the nearby couch.

He lifted my skirt and bunched the fabric around my waist. His fingers clutched at the flesh of my thighs, pressing my legs apart. Jacob tore at my undergarments, ripping my panties aside and exposing the wet, pink folds beneath.

He leaned down and ran his tongue up and down my slit. I shuddered, clutching at his shoulders.

"Oh my...Jacob!" I murmured. "Please, harder, please..."

He acquiesced, cupping his lips around my sensitive bud and sucking. I came immediately, waves of pleasure pulsing from between my legs and out to my extremities.

I did not linger in this place of ecstasy, knowing we didn't have much time. I pulled Jacob toward me, crushing his mouth to mine. His weight was on me, his hips grinding between my legs. I bucked against him, gasping for air. I reached for his waistband and released his hardness, guiding him to my waiting pussy. He thrust up into me, and I welcomed the fullness of him.

"Oh baby, you feel so good," he murmured. He tilted my hips up and pulsed his cock deep into me and out again.

"Wait, wait," I begged, weakly pushing against his chest. "I want to taste you." I managed to sit up, and switched positions with Jacob, pushing him down onto the couch. I knelt before him, pulling his cock into my mouth. His eyes scrunched shut, and he pressed one cheek against the leather.

The sound started as a low whimper at the base of his throat. He mewled like a kitten. I could feel it building inside him. The pressure began at the bottom of his cock and flowed in gentle waves up to the tip.

The waves swelled his cock taut. I eased back on the pressure with my mouth, and I could feel him twitching up to the roof and down to my tongue. I smiled, reapplied the pressure and sucked him inside. He moaned.

I ran my lips slowly along the ridges, sank down until the tip rubbed the back of my throat. Building a steady rhythm, I rocked against him. His cries became urgent, his hands clenching as if he were reaching for some target just inches from his outstretched fingertips.

I felt connected to him like no one before. More than the physical, it was as if I was leading him up into some alternate plane of existence.

And suddenly, I lost him. It was as if he was the only one left in the world and I was lurking below, observing this massive writhing.

I continued to tug on his cock and the undulations swelled and peaked. The crest broke and he flooded my mouth again and again, the warm wetness flowing past my tongue and into my throat.

His trembling waned, replaced by a palpitation in his chest. Jacob was laughing, giggling beyond control, as if the rush of pleasure was bubbling out of him. I reached for his hands, knelt back and smiled as beatifically as possible.

"That was…" He laughed again. "Incredible, amazing, mind-blowing…"

"The best orgasm ever?"

"The best ten orgasms ever. I had no idea my body could do that. I had no idea your mouth could do that."

"I hope no one heard us," I said.

"At this point, I don't care. That was…amazing. Worth any embarrassment you or I would ever face." He shuddered again, shaking his head as if to clear the last threads of tingling.

I smirked. "I don't know about that." The image of my mother's displeasure passed across my mind's eye and I shuddered, too.

"Wow, it's sad, really," he said, sighing. "It'll never be the same again."

I nodded. "Yes, it will be different. That's life, isn't it? Ever evolving."

"I suppose."

I stood up, attempting to straighten my mussed hair. I would have to do my best to recreate the makeup job that my sister had done an hour ago. Hopefully, she wouldn't notice the difference.

Jacob tugged his pants back on, looking around the room for any leftover carnage from our lovemaking.

A beautiful, uninhibited chuckle suddenly escaped his lips. I looked over as he leaned down to the floor to pick up a swatch of white fabric—the tattered remnants of my lace panties.

"Oh my," I said. "I guess I'll have to go commando."

He laughed. "It'll be our little secret."

"Ready to go, sweetheart?" my father asked.

"Yes," I said, hoping to still the trembling in my voice.

Dad squeezed my hand, placing it on his arm. He smiled, a reassuring smile that could only come from a proud father. I squeezed him back.

We turned to face them, the crowd of family and friends sitting in rows of rattan chairs, each wooden leg nestled into the sandy beach. They stood when the music started, a lilting symphony so familiar.

I could barely see past the layers of white veil covering my face, but it didn't matter. I could see Jacob's shape to the right of the altar, standing beside his best friend, Michael. Both Michael and Jacob looked genuinely happy, and that made me happy, too.

The ceremony went by in a daze. We said our written vows, the classic "I do's," the exchange of rings, and then the minister said, "If anyone knows of a reason why this couple should not be joined in holy matrimony, speak now or forever hold your peace."

I had imagined this moment many times. I had even discussed it with Jacob, discussed the horrifying possibility of someone speaking up at this point in the ceremony. The memory of those discussions did not help me; we never did come to any conclusions. The reality felt surreal, a scene from a daydream or nightmare; which one, I couldn't decide.

I couldn't help it. I looked up over my groom's shoulder, at Jacob's place as the best man. Jacob's face was stone, his mouth a tight line. He looked back at me and I saw it, a gesture so minute, I was sure none of the one hundred forty-nine guests had seen it. I saw it because I was looking for it—the slight movement of his head shaking no.

I gasped, the air rushing through my nostrils so loudly it sounded like a last breath. I marveled at this silent conversation, the intricate exchange of glances. And the look that sealed my fate.

My groom followed my gaze, looked at Jacob and back to me again, the panic rising in Michael's face. Jacob smiled at him—that goofy, devilish grin—and placed a reassuring hand on Michael's shoulder. The crowd behind us laughed nervously, understanding the joke.

I laughed, too, hoping my giggles would help to conceal the true sadness of my tears.

A Lucky Wedding

Thomas S. Roche

Avery had asked for a few moments to gather her thoughts in the upstairs bedroom; Kris ushered them all out in a group— Mom, Vanessa, Kerri, Terri, Monette, Jane—and good riddance to them. Kris then mouthed, *"Twenty minutes,"* and winked and blew her a kiss before leaving herself.

God love Kris Keshanski, thought Avery. *Now that's a maid of honor.*

Avery locked the door, took a deep breath. It was all so intoxicating—her being the center of attention, which she hated, and being dolled up and beautiful, which she loved. She had barely even looked at herself in the mirror; she had looked, of course, sure, but not *looked*. For one thing, she didn't have her glasses on. Plus she'd been so distracted by all the bridesmaids and Mom and the hangers-on flittering about that she'd not had a chance to stand poised in the full-length, wood-framed standing mirror and get close enough to see, and say, "Damn, girl—you rock this."

She did. Her dress was white and traditional, maybe too traditional—gathered close at the hips beneath the tight cinch of the corset, which also jacked her breasts up improbably like hot-air balloons, until she looked as if she had a rack to salute to high heaven. She'd never had cleavage before, but she had it today—God's gift to lady surfboards, this lingerie.

The corset, in fact, was the one thing she had insisted on, but not just for the reason that it accented her moderate endowments. It also felt freaky good, being cinched into this thing, barely able to breathe, desperately wanting to swoon. Traditional or kinky? She'd never tell—let the guests think the white had been earned with long months of horny denial and chaste deprivation. It wasn't.

Avery gathered the dress up in front. She did not want to wrinkle it, but, she thought to herself, with sufficient care the crinoline could be smoothed down and she'd get a chance to admire herself.

Lord! Was she actually wearing that? *This* outfit was filth, pure and simple, raw savage depravity in white satin and pretty pink lace. She looked like a whore, which was kind of a turn-on, this being her wedding and all. And when, brightly, her mind filled with thoughts of dear Michael removing the twelve-hundred-dollar dress to find an eight-hundred-dollar see-through white thong with lacy pink flowers and a white, embroidered-rose garter belt, not to mention the seamed white stockings that said "Spread me" in the language of lingerie—when she thought of that, Avery Jacobsen soon-to-be-Vance went wet to the knees, put her hand where she shouldn't, and sighed.

It was true, then; she was a whore. Shameless, insistent... *Good God, that feels good.* She steadied herself against the mirror and rubbed faster, wondering if somehow she might get away with a quick one, spread wide on her back with the wedding dress gathered—no, no, fucking no, she'd just wrinkle it. She looked hungrily into her own eyes and rubbed herself gently—just a few more strokes, not a full wank or anything....

Oh my God, being shaved makes you sensitive, Avery thought as she struggled with whether she ought to come.

No, of course not, she decided: *Tradition.* Wasn't that the tradition? Get all worked up before the wedding, sure, but wait to come until your new husband fucks you. If it's not a tradition, it should be, right?

She'd been to plenty of weddings. Brides and grooms in the modern day seemed to change into jeans and T-shirts before hopping on Kawasakis or into rented Porsche convertibles for a honeymoon in Napa. Not so with Michael Vance's new bride; she'd been told in no uncertain terms she would be spirited away in a Holsman 1907 High-Wheeler reproduction, built from scratch for this occasion—with her very own crackpot inventor at the joystick. She was two-thirds convinced that the thing wasn't street legal, despite Michael's assurance that it was. The fact that he'd promised to follow that drive from the Jacobsen home to the Vance Bed-and-Breakfast with a bride's carry over the threshold if she was good—or a fireman's lift if she was bad—made her molten inside. Thinking about that cave dweller's threat-promise would have made her rub faster, if she hadn't already moved on, in her thoughts, to the growl of his voice at her ear, the warm breath on her neck as he told her with vigor what he'd do to her once he had her inside.

Vance Bed-and-Breakfast: in the family for four generations. Forest luxury. Redwood tubs. Steam showers. Four-poster beds.

Avery bit her lip, panting. Maybe just a quick toss. Just a quick one. Kris could smooth out the wrinkles, right?

Someone fiddled with the door.

Avery gasped. Her heart pounding, she removed her hand

quickly from the one place it should really not have been on her wedding day at 11:00 a.m., then adjusted her thong and pulled down her dress.

"Leave me alone, I'm getting ready!"

Whoever it was still fiddled. She could see the knob turning; they hadn't even knocked. Panicked, Avery checked herself in the mirror. Her dress looked okay. No signs of her recent adventures, other than the almost terrifying pinkness of her face and her cleavage, and the peaks of her nipples showing through the dress.

The door opened.

"Michael!" she cried. She seized a shoe from the nearby rack and threw it at him. He faced it down fearlessly as it struck the door next to him; she hadn't really been aiming, and in any event, with her glasses off her groom was mostly a blur. Damn that lost contact! She threw another shoe, which clunked at his feet. "Don't you know—"

"It's bad luck for the groom to see the bride—yes, yes, yes," said Michael, slipping inside. He closed the door and locked it. "But my dear, I've got bigger fish to fry."

"This *is* bad luck! It's tradition. Get out! You're dooming our marriage!"

Avery seized another shoe and threw it, half laughing, as Michael, grinning, closed in on her. He was a hell of an easy target, at six foot four with broad shoulders, but she didn't really want to hit him—black eye on his wedding day? She'd never hear the end of that one. Nonetheless, Michael got the message—as he'd gotten it before he ever opened the door: This was transgression, raw transgression, the breaking of an ancient taboo to which Michael himself had repeatedly proclaimed his devotion.

It was, therefore, more filthy than anything they'd ever

done. And after Avery and Michael's eighteen months together, there was some serious competition for that slot.

Michael seized Avery Jacobsen and very nearly slammed her against the wall. The feel of his muscles against her made her go loopy. He stooped low to kiss her, and she pursed her lips and turned her head.

"It's bad luck!"

"Is that right?"

"Yes!" Avery cried. "The worst kind of bad luck!"

"You don't say," murmured Michael, and put his hand into her hair, grabbing tight.

Avery gasped, looked up into his eyes, and watched as his full lips turned back in a sneering smile. Her own lips trembled with hunger. He pulled harder; her gasp became a whimper.

"There'll be lots of this soon, Mrs. Vance," he growled.

"Not yet, Mr. Vance. I could still change my mind. And some bright bird might object."

"Let them try." He grinned, shaking his fist as he looked into her eyes.

Michael kissed her.

She went limp in his grasp as his mouth savaged hers. She no longer resisted, exactly; her squirming struggles against his bulk were familiar and comforting, half weak and half fierce. It was really his hand in her hair that did it. In the weeks before the wedding she'd kept from soliciting his feedback; the comfort of their coupling came from the ease with which she assailed her femaleness, eschewing femininity whenever she thought it unnecessary. With her shorts and T-shirts, her little round glasses, her love of bicycling and her adoration of the works of Geoffrey Chaucer in the original Middle English—which she could recite from memory with a clarity utterly shocking to everyone except her and her professors—Avery was not a high-maintenance girl. She did not intend to be a high-maintenance bride.

Nonetheless, on the matter of her hair, she had craved Michael's opinion. *I think maybe up?* she'd mused one day out loud.

No, Avery, down.

Really? Down? she had asked him. He'd answered with his hand in her hair, pulling cruelly as he kissed her with enough ardor to shock Chaucer's merchant.

So it was that on this, her wedding day, she had surrendered to a sort of a tomboy-chic look, figuring traditionally prim bridal beauty could be forgone at her groom's request. Now she knew why: the son of a bitch had planned to kiss her like this from the first, to sully their marriage day with the— holy Christ, he was pulling her corset down.

"You can't do that," she whimpered. "Everybody's waiting. My parents…everybody."

He silenced her with his mouth, hard upon her, his tongue against hers as first one, then the other, teacup tit popped out with nipple already hard, responding to his thumb with goose bumps that went shimmying down her spine and deep into her sex. He thumbed, stroked, kneaded, pinched; she went loose against him, and when his lips left hers there was a string of spit stretched for a moment between them, just as in her favorite-ever movie kissing scene. Fresh, filthy, wet, sloppy—just like their sex life, forever.

"They've waited twenty-six years for this day," Michael said. "Let them wait fifteen minutes while I fuck their girl senseless."

"You may not," Avery declared, half convinced, half unconvinced, "fuck me senseless."

"Of course not," said Michael, and in moments she was

pulled back in his arms and splayed out on the bed, with a yelp. "You're *already* senseless."

"I'm serious," she panted deliriously. "You can't. They're all waiting. I won't let you do this."

"Then why are your legs spread?"

"Umm..."

Michael grinned savagely. "So you're a little whore for your wedding day, are you?" His hands went inside her slim, filmy lace thong, and in moments his fingers slid down her freshly shaved slit, finding her wet as a fountain and her clit throbbing hard. Newly shorn, her sex was exquisitely sensitive; getting dressed, she'd already begun to regret this planned wedding-night surprise, thinking she'd never make it through the day without touching herself. Now she gave it to him hungrily, feeling him explore her newly smooth sex, the smile on his face and the hard cock in his pants telling her everything she needed to know.

She grasped desperately at Michael's arms, first the one that still held her hair, then the one that was working inside her—holy shit, that felt good!

Avery spread her legs farther and rocked back and forth as Michael began to finger-fuck her. Desperately hungry, she clawed at the front of his tuxedo, cursing buttons and clasps as she fucked herself onto him. He gave her two fingers; when he brought his thumb into the mix, working her clit while her hips worked, her eyes rolled back and she all but tore his tuxedo pants open.

Michael's hard cock popped free; she went lunging for it, and his hand tightened in her hair.

"Say *please*."

"Pretty please," Avery responded, with not a hint of a smile on her face. This was serious business. "Pretty please, Mr. Vance. Pretty please, may I suck your big cock, sir?"

"My God, you're a filthy…" His epithet stalled in his mouth, because he'd loosened his grip on her hair and she'd lunged smoothly forward, her red-painted lips gliding down his full shaft before he even knew what was happening. With his left hand now free, Michael reached down to caress Avery's nipples; she squirmed and rocked on his fingers as she slurped, both hands circling the base and caressing his balls.

There was a loud knock at the door.

Avery's wet mouth came free. "Go away!" she called. "I'm still getting ready!"

"We can't find—" It was her father's voice.

Her mother hissed furiously, almost inaudible, "Don't tell her that!"

"But we can't find the groom," said her father, his stage whisper as inexpert as only a sixty-year-old man having kittens can produce. "Where's Michael?"

"He'll be here!" cried Mom. "Let's leave her alone!"

Long before that last statement, Avery's mouth had returned to her paramour's cock, gliding quickly up and down as she looked up at his brightening eyes. He worked a third finger into her, the tightness of her sex making him need to press harder to keep his thumb firm on her clit. She could not suppress the deep, throaty moan that made her lips tremble around Michael's cock.

"Careful. They're all waiting. They're downstairs in the garden. They can hear every moan."

Avery shivered all over, mounting quickly toward orgasm. She pumped onto his hand, thinking desperately, *They can. They can hear when I moan. They can hear it. Oh, God…*

Then she came, her hips going crazy as she shook all over, her moans stifled by Michael's cock deep in her mouth— so deep she would have choked if, expert that she was, she hadn't taken a breath before climaxing.

As the last of her orgasm pulsed through her body, Avery slipped her wet mouth off Michael's big shaft and, stroking it with her hand, looked up at him. "Fuck me, Mr. Vance?"

"Spread wider," he told her, and she did, relinquishing her grip on his cock and reaching down to steady her thighs as she held them wide open for him. Michael positioned himself, guiding his rod to her sex, plucking the slim, white lace thong out of the way, and looked deep into her eyes as he nuzzled his cock head up and down in her slit.

"Fuck, fuck, fuck, fuck, fuck, fuck." She could not stop saying it; her cunt was so sensitive from the explosive orgasm she'd just had that the gentle touch of his cock head against her opening was enough to make her shudder all over.

Michael grinned. He did not intend to stay gentle for long.

Avery's back arched; she lunged to embrace him as he penetrated her, but Michael's hand rested in the center of her chest, holding her at bay while he entered her fully. Her mouth opened wide and she shuddered in soundless moans, unable to find the breath to cry out as he fucked her. He held her, one hand on her chest, the other languidly grasping one knee, helping hold her open, exposing her sex as his hips began to work.

"I'm going to come again," she said softly, her voice all but ravished by pleasure. Michael withdrew his hand from her chest and put it on her clit, fingers splayed where her pubic hair had been. His thumb worked her clit in small circles, teasing gently at first and then harder, harder, rubbing fiercely as he pumped his cock into her, seizing her eyes with his own, looking deep into her as she trembled all over and came hard—and then Michael let go, fucking deep inside her and coming while she breathed a deep sigh and accepted him.

"Ready for marriage?" he asked as he withdrew.

"I'm not sure," she said. "Still got plans for that four-poster bed?"

Michael grinned and zipped up. He helped Avery to her feet and the two began working furiously to right her corset and her dress. It was not quite perfection, but after a touch-up of her lipstick, she looked rather like a bride who'd been crying.

"Just stick to the story," said Michael. "You're crying from happiness—not because you've been deep-throating cock."

"You're a savage," said Avery.

Michael cinched up her corset, bent her over and smoothed down her dress.

At the door, Daddy pounded desperately, in hysterics. "Av, we can't find Michael! He's nowhere to be found! Have you seen him?"

Michael winked, said, "Think eighties teen comedy," and his lean, six-foot-four frame went smoothly out the window. She heard him climbing the drainpipe and scrambling onto the roof. She thought, *Well, that's it, I'll be marrying a corpse.*

But there was no crash or thump, no great cry of a groom with a broken back—just the thunder of footsteps on the roof, and the climb down the far side; for fuck's sake, that man sure had *feet.*

If anyone missed the thumping sound of Michael leaping off the rear deck onto the gazebo, they were clueless—but then, this was her family.

When she opened the door to embrace her hysterical father, Avery really was crying—with a great explanation.

"I don't have anything borrowed!" she cried.

"Jesus Christ!" cursed her father, and she clutched him tightly, then winked at her mom—who, from the suspicious look on her face, knew exactly what she'd been doing in there.

Outside, she heard cheers and people crying out Michael's name. "Oh, thank God," said her father. "He's shown up."

"Look at that," said her mother. "He hadn't sped away in that goddamned jalopy of his, after all."

"Yeah, he was busy," said Avery, taking pleasure in her shamelessness; it still eluded her father, but Mom rolled her eyes—a mother knows.

Outside, Pachelbel's "Canon" was playing; tradition, right?

Avery kissed her father on the cheek. "Come on, Dad. Walk me down the aisle."

"With pleasure," he said, relaxing with a sigh.

She wiggled, straightening her dress. She felt suddenly lucky. She decided she had the best, the *very* best, kind of good luck.

Something Old, Something New

Sophia Valenti

I sighed softly as I lowered myself onto Justin's cock, relishing the familiar yet thrilling sensation. My eyes nearly fluttered closed as I savored that initial moment of penetration. I struggled to keep my gaze locked on him, and I was rewarded by the sexy look of longing etched on his handsome face. Although I could tell he was nearly consumed by lust, he didn't dare think of rushing me. He simply rested his hands on my hips, his fingers occasionally clutching my flesh, but otherwise holding himself still as I enveloped him with agonizing slowness. The anticipation was sweet and the wait maddening, but it only served to make us hotter.

Justin and I had been so busy orchestrating our wedding during the past few months—and, more recently, being gracious hosts to our out-of-town guests—that we'd barely had time to breathe, much less have sex. But finally, it was all over and we were alone—completely, totally and blissfully alone. I didn't need flowers, limousines or a frilly dress to be happy. All I needed was his hot shaft plunging inside me. I wanted to lose myself in the pleasure that only he could give me.

When I felt my bottom hit his plush sac, I let out a happy

little gasp and ground down against him, rhythmically shimmying my hips. Each sharp spark of friction against my clit was like a match strike, the sudden influx of heat inflaming my lust and inching me closer to orgasm. I bucked and moaned, stroking the dark hair sprinkled across his muscular chest. I was torn between wanting the moment to last forever, and being desperate for release. I could see the same lust smoldering in my husband's gray eyes. I was hopelessly lost in ecstasy, but as always, he knew what to do and how to take us over the edge.

Justin lifted me off him and positioned me on my hands and knees on the bed, so quickly that he made me laugh out loud. But that exclamation of mirth turned into a loud groan as he grabbed my shoulders and pulled me back against him, shoving himself inside me with one smooth motion. I glanced over my shoulder and smiled, knowing that I was in his very sexy and capable hands.

As I turned away from him, a flash of white caught my eye. It was the extravagantly priced French silk negligee that my maid of honor had insisted on giving me as a wedding gift. There it was, neatly draped over a nearby chair: a luxurious, full-length gown with a beaded bodice and delicate lace trim. I'd never even put it on. I had been considering slipping it over my head when Justin had stepped out of the bathroom, fresh from the shower. The sight of me standing there naked had been enough for him, and he'd immediately swept me off my feet and dropped me in the middle of the mattress.

Justin kept up his steady pace, pumping into me and occasionally leaning down to scatter kisses on my freckled shoulders. I tossed my head back and bucked my body against his, wanting him to thrust into me harder and faster. The slapping noise of flesh meeting flesh was hypnotic, sending me deeper into an erotic trance. Justin reached underneath me and cupped my breasts in his warm hands. His fingers danced over my nipples, making them achingly erect. He teased the tiny nubs, squeezing them between his fingers and thumbs until I gasped. The little bursts of pleasure-pain caused a rush of wetness to flood my pussy, and I began to corkscrew my hips as I continued to rock back toward him.

I may have begun our encounter with the desire to go slow, but that thought had completely flown from my head. I could hear Justin's erratic breathing, and I knew that he was also rapidly approaching his limit. I closed my eyes and concentrated on what I was feeling: the blissful sensation of fullness that was now coupled with his fingers strumming my clit. I was so slippery wet—and thrashing about so intensely—that I wondered if he'd be able to keep up his delicious actions. But I had nothing to worry about, because after only a few minutes of his determined circles against my puffy button, I felt weeks' worth of sexual tension disappear in a fabulous explosion of pleasure. I locked my thighs tightly together, trapping his hand and making an even tighter tunnel for his thrusting cock. Justin was clearly on the edge and didn't let me distract him from his goal. As I shivered beneath him, he bucked into me one last time. I felt his shaft pulsing inside me as he let out one final groan and then collapsed against my back.

Gradually, my senses returned as we lay entwined on the bed. I glanced out of the window of our little cabin and saw the inky blackness of the night punctuated by the glittering stars we were never able to see at home in the city, even from our apartment building's rooftop. The ship we were on was gliding through the Gulf of Alaska as we cruised our way toward fields of ice-blue glaciers. Most of our friends thought we were crazy, wanting to honeymoon amid snow-capped mountains, but Justin and I were never much for beaches, so we'd politely declined everyone's well-intentioned recommendations of resorts in Jamaica and Cancun and forged our own way.

Justin lay back with me in his arms, trying to catch his breath as I lost myself in my thoughts. Sex with him had been amazing from the day we met, but I did occasionally have nagging little worries. Would we still feel the same way—have the same desire for each other—one year from now? How about ten or twenty? I'd heard married friends complain about disappearing sparks and mind-numbing routine creeping into their beds. I didn't want that to happen to us, but I wasn't yet convinced of the possibility of lifelong passion. I wanted to believe that it wasn't a pipe dream. I knew there were happily married couples out there, and I hoped that Justin and I would be one of them.

Once we'd rested, we were both eager to rejoin the world. Well, the world as it was at that moment. Since we'd boarded the ship, we'd been hidden away in our tiny cabin. It was late and well past the official dinner hour, but we were ready to put on some clothes and explore what would pass as nightlife aboard our floating hotel. We weren't expecting much, to be honest, because we'd been warned by our travel agent that the vacationers who favored that particular tour were often considerably older than us. We'd confirmed that fact during our check-in, when we'd noticed that most of the people surrounding us were elderly couples and there wasn't a single child in sight.

I collected my tousled auburn curls, slipped on a dress and heels and headed out the door with a casually attired Justin, who led me through a maze of decks and hallways toward one of the ship's lounges. As we approached the doorway, I could hear the smooth notes of an old standard that sounded as if it was being performed by a live band.

We crossed the threshold to find a cozy lounge lined with red velvet banquettes and dotted with small round tables. There were a handful of sweet-looking older couples slow-dancing to the band's interpretation of an Ella Fitzgerald classic. Justin smiled and squeezed my hand as he led me out onto the dance floor. As I swayed in his arms, my eyes kept wandering to a handsome-looking man and woman who seemed to be greatly enjoying each other's company. They appeared to be much younger than the other people who were twirling around us, but they still had a good twenty-five years on me and Justin.

The man was tall and tan, and his dark hair was fading to gray at his temples. Every time he laughed, his eyes crinkled at the corners, and he'd occasionally lean forward to kiss his companion on the top of her silver-streaked head. His dance partner was a trim lady who was smartly attired in a stylish black dress that I envied, her bare legs looking as fit as those of a woman half her age. Her hair was styled in a chin-length bob that accentuated her high cheekbones and beautifully framed her face. They effortlessly danced across the floor, looking breathtaking and elegant, and seeming to have eyes only for each other. But it wasn't just their good looks that caught my attention. There was something about the way they interacted with each other that seemed so alive and af-fectionate: the way he'd stroke her cheek, the way she'd melt into his embrace. I actually wondered if they were newly-weds themselves. Don't get me wrong, the other couples also seemed like they were having a swell time, but I didn't sense the same sort of electricity sparking between them.

Justin pulled me closer, and we danced out the rest of the song before stopping for cocktails. As he handed me my drink, he noticed that I seemed distracted, and questioned me about it. I discreetly pointed out the arresting pair, who were still gliding across the floor. The man's baritone laugh mingled with her lighthearted chuckle, creating a sweet melody that merged seamlessly with the music.

"They just seem so happy," I said in an awestruck whisper, as I followed their every move.

"That'll be us in thirty years," Justin said, kissing me softly on the cheek. My eyes met his and I smiled. I was feeling more confident by the second that he was absolutely right.

Justin and I spent the next day enjoying all that the ship had to offer, and that evening eagerly dressed for dinner. After weeks of eating fast food on the run and dealing with seating-chart crises, it was luxurious fun to don formal attire and head off to the ship's dining room. It was as if we were going out on a dinner date for the first time in months.

We were to share our table with only one other couple, who had not yet arrived as we took our seats. I wondered which pleasant set of grandparents we'd be spending our evening meals with. At the same time, I saw the attractive pair from the lounge enter the dining room and stride toward us. My mouth literally dropped open in surprise, but I managed to regain my composure before they'd reached the table.

Rafael and Suze greeted us warmly and introduced themselves before taking their seats across from us. We announced that we were on our honeymoon, which made them both smile as they told us they were celebrating their twenty-fifth wedding anniversary. So much for them being newlyweds—although they could have fooled me! As we chatted throughout our meal, the depth of their affection for each other was even more obvious in such a close, intimate setting. I could sense their connection, and without either of them ever saying anything remotely sexual to each other, I just knew that sparks still flew between them. During our conversation that evening, Suze assured me that there weren't any deep, dark secrets to being a happy couple, aside from remembering to have fun and enjoy each other's company. It was as if the heavens had made our paths cross to allay all of my unspoken fears about married life.

For the rest of our weeklong trip, I looked forward to our dinner conversations. I found the two of them absolutely charming, and I eagerly listened to their stories. The entire trip was everything I could have wished for: plenty of alone time with Justin, the opportunity to meet new, interesting people, and awe-inspiring views of Alaska's sweeping vistas. However, Justin and I stumbled upon the most amazing sight of our vacation on the last night of our trip.

As much as I'd enjoyed our honeymoon, I was really looking forward to going home and beginning our life together as husband and wife. I was too excited to sleep that night, and I was sitting up and gazing out our window at the full moon. Justin wasn't having much success falling asleep, either, and since it had been unseasonably warm the past few days, he suggested we take a walk outside on the deck.

I slipped on a spaghetti-strap dress and a cropped cardigan, while Justin stayed in his drawstring pants and T-shirt. His black hair was cutely mussed, and I ruffled it with my hand as I passed him to fetch my sandals. He simply laughed and grabbed the key card for our room before we quietly made our way outside, being careful not to disturb our slumbering neighbors.

The night breeze was soothing—cool but not cold—and perfumed with the scent of the salty sea. Justin wrapped his arm around my waist as we strolled along the deck. Aside from the crashing of the waves against the sides of the ship, there wasn't another sound to be heard—until we approached a nook near the ship's bow. We soon realized we weren't the only night owls on board.

As we neared the corner, we heard voices—those of a man and a woman. They sounded like hushed, breathy whispers with a decidedly erotic edge to them. I stopped in my tracks and turned to look at Justin, my lips parted in surprise. I could easily make out his amused smile in the silvery glow of the moon. Silently, he cocked his head toward the source of the sound and urged me onward with a steady hand at the small of my back.

I was conflicted. The strangers' whispered words were becoming interspersed with feminine moans. Their encounter was escalating, as was the pace of my rapidly beating heart. I knew we were about to spy on a couple's most intimate moment. The rational part of me knew that it would be proper to turn away and head back in the opposite direction. But at that moment, the last thing I wanted was to be proper.

Justin and I hugged the wall, ensconcing ourselves in shadow as we approached the bend. My husband urged me in front of him, resting his hand on my shoulder as, together, we peered around the corner. There, in an oversize deck chair, were Rafael and Suze. He was sitting up and his wife was facing him as she straddled his hips. Her silky white robe was parted slightly, showing off her delicate shoulders, and her silver-haired head was tilted back as Rafael trailed sensual kisses down her neck. Her whimpers carried on the night air to our ears. The hungry, desperate sound of her cries made my own sex ache with longing.

Suze tangled her hands in Rafael's thick hair, her diamond wedding band glittering in the moonlight as her fingers roamed wildly. Rafael responded by pulling her robe off her shoulders, stripping her to the waist. Her teacup-size breasts were capped by already-erect nipples that her husband clearly found irresistible. His mouth slid downward to kiss and suckle each nub in turn. Her moans of pleasure increased in volume. It was as if they were in their own private world, even though that world happened to be in a very public place where they could be discovered at any second.

Of course, they *had* already been discovered, but Justin and I were careful not to make a sound. I was nearly holding my breath, feeling the dampness in my panties grow as I took it all in. I was hesitant even to blink. Their passion for each other was electric and inspiring, and I didn't want to miss a second of it.

Justin was resting his head on my shoulder, and I heard his gentle breathing grow more erratic. He turned toward me, and the hot puffs of air that he exhaled against my neck caused shivers to travel down my back. I wiggled against him playfully, and I wasn't surprised to feel his cock thickening underneath his pants. He swallowed a moan and grabbed my hips, both to still me and to pull me tightly against him. I kept staring at Suze, who was grinding against her husband as my own man began bunching up the sides of my dress to expose me to the night air. I silently thanked myself for being so lazy and forgoing panties; they would have only gotten in the way.

I blindly reached behind me to grope the bulge hiding in Justin's pants. With his help, I eventually managed to tug them down enough to release his erection. It popped free from the waistband of his pants, which were now bunched at his hips, and I wrapped my fingers around his warm flesh, stroking him gently and pulling him toward me as I watched Suze rise and reach between her spread thighs for Rafael's erection, which she'd freed from his shorts. I bent forward slightly, urging Justin to slip inside me just as Suze lowered herself once again, her head turned toward our hiding spot. It was almost as if we were in her line of sight and she were mirroring me, although I was fairly certain that we were still hidden in shadow and it was all simply a sexy coincidence— especially since Suze didn't seem startled in the least.

I bit my lip to ensure my continued silence as I rocked back against my husband, my ears full of our friends' moans and groans. Watching such a private, forbidden scene was thrilling, and the knowledge that we could possibly get caught ourselves excited me in ways I didn't know were possible. I'd never done something so daring before, and was fairly sure my husband hadn't, either.

Justin steadied me with one hand on my stomach and the other cupping my left breast. He gently toyed with my nipple as he kissed my neck and buried his face in my windblown curls. I, however, kept my eyes locked on the couple in front of us. Rafael had grabbed Suze's hips and was raising and lowering her on his cock as she threw her head back and moaned loudly. The two of them were gilded in moonlight, their figures glowing as though they were imbued with some sort of sensual energy that I could see as well as sense.

I braced myself with one hand against the wall as I reached between my legs with the other. My fingertips grazed Justin's cock the second before he thrust himself back inside me. I reached for his shaft again when he pulled out of me, to gather up some of my sticky wetness. He moaned at my brief touch, and I brought my slick fingers to my clit, too impatient to wait another second. Justin continued to thrust himself in and out of my clasping sex as I rubbed my puffy button in frantic circles.

Justin's dick was hitting me exactly where I needed it to in order to trigger my release. I struggled to keep my eyes on Rafael and Suze, but the sensual image in front of me seemed to shimmer like a desert mirage as my sense of sight was dulled by the ecstasy swelling inside me. I let the feelings overwhelm me as I spasmed in pleasure, squeezing Justin's thrusting shaft and sparking his release. He came with a whispered groan against my neck, holding my body tight to his.

Our friends' orgasmic cries were still ringing in the air as we caught our breath. Suze collapsed on top of Rafael's strong body, and from our hideaway we heard their breathless laughter, which inspired restrained giggles of our own. As they lay there together in an exhausted embrace, we straightened our clothing and sneaked off before we could be discovered.

As we rolled our luggage through the ship's lobby the next morning, we heard our names being called behind us. We turned to find our dinner companions, who wanted to say goodbye. Suze hugged me tightly as she congratulated me on our wedding one last time and wished me a lifetime of happiness. "Although something tells me," she said with a wink, "the two of you are going to do just fine."

Kiss the Bride

Lana Fox

"No, *lower*," said Jake, sliding my fingers down his side. His breath was warm against my cheek as he pressed me to the wall. "So I pull your veil off—" he mimed doing just that "—and throw it on the ground…like this…and now…" He cupped my face, leaning right in, and I felt my eyelids closing, felt his thigh brush mine. The smell of him filled me— a strong, herbal heat—and I parted my lips, ready for his.

"Just a stage kiss," I whispered.

"Sure." He opened his mouth on mine.

"So let me get this straight," I'd said, the night Dan offered me the part. "I have to screw this guy in front of—what?—a hundred people?"

Dan groaned across the phone line. "Sweetness, it's an *act*. Besides, the boy's hot. If he liked men, I'd be in there like swimwear."

"Do we have to do the sex?"

"Darling, it's amateur theater. Who's gonna come if there's no serious action?" Dan, who was training as a drama teacher, was required, as part of his course, to stage a play for adults. "Besides," he added, "they'll be generous on the feed-back forms if we make 'em hot 'n horny." He went on to tell me what *Kiss the Bride* was about. Two marriages—one that starts well and one that doesn't. "Two brides, two grooms," he said.

"So you wrote a play that has no gay characters?"

Dan gave a snort. "I'm obsessed with weddings, dollface. And it's not as if I'm ever gonna wear a veil myself."

I asked him how explicit the sex was going to be.

"Think steamy."

"Keith'll kill me," I said.

"Well, if *he* won't give you mouth-to-mouth the bastard can't complain."

Dan was right. Since the arguments had started, Keith and I had hardly kissed. We'd fight, get hot and bothered, then he'd turn me to the wall, enter me briskly and take me. It wasn't bad sex, but it was all about the fight, and he gave me no passion, no warmth. And the kissing rarely happened—even when I begged. Oh, many times, when we weren't fighting, I'd fall to my knees as if I was joking, pleading for a kiss.

"Me first," he'd say, pulling my head toward his groin. I'd feel his fingers running through my hair—and this, at least, was a kind of affection. Then I'd quickly unbutton him and take him in my mouth. His long groans of pleasure made me feel like I was wanted, and he'd slam his head back so it thumped against the wall, crying, "Terri, oh baby, go harder..." When he came, he'd ram against my throat, and though I'd gag, I felt like I was his.

But afterward, he'd laugh and take me in his arms, just for a minute before he drew away. "I should shower," he'd say, blue eyes crinkling. And I'd watch him walk off, buttocks perfect in those jeans, my lips tingling, an ache between my thighs.

Dan always said, "If 'wham, bam, thank you, ma'am' is his idea of tender, the guy isn't worth it. Let him go."

But I'd stand up for Keith. A medical student, he worked most nights, and I'd find him in the early hours, sighing over his books. Sometimes, in those moments, I'd come and kiss his head, and startled, he'd reach up and squeeze my hand.

"Dan, he's training to save lives," I'd say. "I have to give him some slack."

"Dollface," said Dan, who knew me too well. "No man who treats you badly is getting slack from me."

Jake, who was to play my onstage groom, really wasn't my type. For starters, he was fair, and I'd always liked them dark, plus he thought he was God's gift. Once, when he caught Dan eyeing his arse, Jake sauntered up, tipping him a wink. Dan laughed it off. "You're a prick-tease, love. You know I'd *eat* those buttocks!" And Jake grinned sexily, enjoying the attention.

Still, onstage the boy was sublime. He occupied the space with a pantherlike grace, touched my body easily without a single prompt. The first time we practiced the proposal scene, he fell to his knees and kissed my hand; the feel of his lips, so warm against my skin, and his breath on my wrist made me flush. For the first time, he gave me The Look— twisting his head, he glanced at me sideways, blue eyes glinting, smile half-cocked. I'd never been regarded with such absolute flirtation. As Dan directed from the seats below the stage "—Jake, hon, turn or we can't see your face—" Jake remained kneeling beneath me, my hand still in his. While he talked with Dan, he stroked my fingers, and I imagined those hands sliding down my body. A few inches closer and he'd be against my groin, unbuttoning my jeans with his teeth. I let go of his hand. He cast me a grin. Then, still replying to Dan down below, he idly touched my thigh. As he slowly caressed, I felt my breath give, and I arched against him, imagining his mouth.

"And Terri, love?" called Dan, from the row below us, his sandy-colored faux-hawk soft beneath the lights. "A touch more romance! He's inviting you to marry him, not ride him like a mule."

Blushing, I asked what he meant.

Dan flapped a pale hand. "More Audrey Hepburn, less Joan Jett. You're eyeing him up like he's sex-on-a-stick." And I'd notice, in that moment, Dan's wandering gaze, as he himself inspected Jake's superhot bod.

But Jake was now feeling up the back of my thigh, leaving a trail of heat. "Okay," I gasped. "Hepburn. I'll give it a try."

I liked Dan's idea for the sex scene. While Lee and Tina staged a fight to our left, Jake and I, to use Dan's phrase, would be "at it like bunnies." The sex was meant as the ultimate contrast—though our marriage started well, Lee and Tina's was doomed. As Jake and I stage-fucked, the classical music would build, and both scenes would come to a climax.

"Listen, cupcakes," said Dan one night. "Before we rehearse the sex scene, you two should prep it yourselves. Bring me something you've worked out already. I'll add my thoughts. Okay?"

"I forbid it," Keith had announced the week before. "No sex scenes. He so much as touches you, and you and I are through." This seemed unfair. After all, I'd recently caught

him with Ella Rogers in the beer garden at the Stony Swan.
It was December, and the garden was empty, the wooden
tables slick with ice, but there was Ella on the edge of one,
thighs parted, spine arched, knee-high boots jerking as Keith
pounded into her. She'd dropped back her head, eyelids
closed, scarlet lips glossed with saliva, and Keith was grunting
like a dog in heat, his hips thrusting, his hand on her breast.
As he grew wilder, Ella's eyelids fluttered and she cried, "Oh,
do it, do it…" and the table jolted beneath them, as her fingers gripped the wood. But I'd soon forgiven him, knowing
it was for kicks. Besides, Ella Rogers went with anyone who
asked.

Yet now he was jealous of a *sex scene?*

I felt my anger spark.

In our bedroom, as he was pulling on his socks, I told him
he couldn't stop me. "After the thing with Ella…"

"Sex is different for men," he said. "We don't attach like
you do."

"Tell me about it!"

He rose and grabbed my shoulders. "You wanna do your
sex scene? Fine. But I'll be there, so you'd better behave."

I blinked at him. "You mean I can get you a ticket?" He'd
never come to a play of mine before.

Softening, he smiled. "I'll be there, Terri, baby."

"To check on me? Or what?"

"I just want to see you shine."

But I knew the sex scene was still an issue, so backstage, I
told Jake we couldn't meet at my place. "My partner wouldn't
like it," I said.

Jake gave a boyish shrug. "Let's do it at mine."

We agreed to the following evening. He winked as he
walked away.

★ ★ ★

That night, in bed, I dreamed of screwing Jake, his body hard on top of me, his hands on my breasts. I could feel him filling me, warm between my thighs, and thrusting with a wildness I hadn't felt in years; but still, in spite of the vigor, he pressed his lips on mine, moaning into our kisses, drinking at my mouth. The more crazed his thrusting, the hotter our kiss, and I splayed my thighs widely, begging him for more. He worked me deep, plying me open, nudging at the perfect spot that Keith had never reached. But just as I was coming and our bones were jolting hard and the bed was rocking savagely, I woke quite suddenly and found Keith upon me, sweating like an animal, no tenderness, no kiss. I cried out, but he didn't stop rutting, eyes half closed in the darkened room. "Christ," he groaned, pelvis slamming down, as he came at my ear with a long, loud moan. At last he rolled off me, groaning with pleasure, and my insides twisted as I saw his proud grin. "See, baby?" he said. "We can screw when we're not fighting." And the saddest thing was the kindness in his voice.

The following evening, I stood in Jake's kitchen as he poured us amaretto. Aroused by our rehearsal, I'd chosen thigh-high stockings, and I kept on flushing at the thought that he might guess. "I'm serious," he said, with a shy smile. "If we don't have some alcohol, I won't be able to do it."

Amazed at his coyness, which seemed so out of character, I took the glass and asked why he was nervous.

"It'd be fine if you and I weren't attracted, but…" He shook his head, as if he'd said too much, then raised his drink and downed it. He widened his eyes as he swallowed. "Fuck it, you're hot."

I sidled in next to him and said I felt the same.

He laid a hand on my arm. "What would your guy say if he knew you were here?"

"He'd probably throw me out."

With both hands, Jake smoothed back my hair. "Because we're rehearsing a sex scene?" I nodded, smitten. "Can't say I blame him." His words smelled of almonds. "If you were mine, I'd be just as possessive."

I wanted to tell him what life with Keith was like—how the sex made me feel cheap, how we rarely shared affection—but the scent of the liqueur on Jake's warm breath made me lose my thread. It seemed like years since I'd kissed a man, like decades since I'd felt this way for anyone. All I could think of was his mouth on mine. "Why don't we start?" I asked.

"What? You mean, now?"

"Why not? We're in position."

With a boyish laugh, he began to walk me backward. "We need something to lean against, remember?" I felt the countertop behind me, felt him pressing up against me.

"That's better," I sighed.

"No warm-ups needed."

His thigh touched mine. His scent drowned my senses. His hands slid down my sides. "So I pull your veil off—" he said, miming just that "—and throw it on the ground...like this... and now..." But all the while, he held my gaze, and I pulled him up against me so I was sandwiched there. He cupped my face.

"Just a stage kiss," I told him.

"Sure," he said, and he kissed me.

His mouth was wet and sweet with amaretto. I leaned into him, sensing him there, firm beneath his sweater, warm against my chest, and when I felt his tongue I wasn't surprised, just grateful. Our kiss was seamless, and he moved with ease, raising my thigh, pressing against me. The sudden feel of him between my legs made my body jolt, and I gasped a little, astonished at my need. His hand slipped higher till he found my stocking tops, and then I felt him lunge against my core. The shape of his hard-on dug against my clit and I felt a sudden desperation. "I want you," I whispered, as he kissed along my neck. "Let's get it out of the way."

Suddenly, he stepped back, eyes jerking open. His hair was tousled, his cheeks red. "What does that mean, baby?"

I caught my breath.

"Are you saying once we've fucked, you won't want me anymore?"

"It's just there's all this heat between us! Keith need never know…. Once you and I have…*done* it…this won't be such an issue."

He held his head, turning from me. "Dan told me about your man," he said. "He doesn't deserve you. But I won't be a one-time screw. It's not the way I work."

"You're saying you want to date me?"

He spun around. "Of course I do. Why does that surprise you?"

I must have looked astonished, but he still strode up, pushing against me, his hands on the countertop behind. "Is this just an act for you? Being with me like this? Are you faking, like you do with that man of yours at home?"

I told him no. This was genuine. I wanted him.

"*How* genuine?" he said. "You wanna go to dinner?"

"Maybe," I said, but I was so damn wet that I foolishly added, "afterward, perhaps."

"You mean after you've used me."

"That came out wrong."

He lurched away from me, turning on his heels, walked to

the kitchen door and pulled it wide. "Tell you what," he said coolly. "Think on it. You want to date me, let me know."

I was floored. "But...our rehearsal?"

"This was never a rehearsal." The righteous anger in his eyes made me feel ashamed. Still hopelessly in lust, I walked from the room.

"I really am sorry," I said.

The following weeks, our rehearsals were steamy, not the least because of the tension that sparked between us. Returning to the drawing board, Dan marched us through the sex scene, directing each movement in detail. He'd tell Jake he was throwing the veil too far. "If it falls from the stage we're stuffed." And he'd urge him to be more tender. "Frankly, you look angry, hon...is there something wrong?" I was forced to endure Jake's body on mine, his fingers creeping up my thigh. My skirt would ruche when he raised my leg and pressed himself close. I'd sigh, eyelids heavy, as our bodies fell together, a stiletto dangling from my foot; and through my shirt I'd feel his free hand, clutching, slipping lower, gripping firmly....

"Dollface, that's perfect," praised Dan from down below. "But moan a little louder. *Project!*" And I'd suddenly realize I'd been trying to keep things quiet, worried that the others would guess I was aroused.

Worst of all was the thrusting. Jake would lunge between my thighs, both of us groaning, and I'd push against his hardness. I'd grow ever wetter, my sex burning up, the scent of him making me drowsy. The contortions I tried for just a moment of his hardness seem crazy to me now; and every time I felt his sex on mine, I'd gasp and slam the wall.

"Lovely, Terri!" Dan would shout. "Sweet Jesus, this is hot!"

When Dan first praised us like that, I realized Jake was laughing. "What is it?" I whispered.

"I've never received such kudos for a bit of dry humping."

Embarrassed, I said I was sorry.

He winked. "*I'm* not."

Then came dress rehearsals. Which meant undressing. The crowded little room behind the stage was dusty and lined with benches. We could hardly fit all four of us in, and there was no separate place for the women to undress. Plus we had several costume changes—from party clothes to wedding gear to party clothes again. "We'll act like pros" was Tina's mantra, as she ripped open her blouse and stepped into her dress. Lee would turn his back and change discreetly, while Jake and I pretended not to watch each other. Truth was, Jake smelled of this heavenly aroma, which flooded the room when he took off his shirt. He knew it, too, and would glimpse me sideways, watching as I tried to stop my tongue from hanging out. To make things worse, he'd strip off yet another layer—a smaller, tighter T-shirt that clung around his pecs—and beneath this, scented and bronzed, he'd linger as I stared.

But two could play at that game.

Hardly noticing Lee, who was changing behind me—and not worried about Tina as she struggled with her outfit—I'd strip right down so I was standing in my bra. Sure enough, as I stepped into my bridal dress, layers of net and satin pooling round my feet, I'd sense Jake's stare hot on my skin.

One night, he snapped, "Must you always stand there naked?"

"So you noticed?" I said. "I thought you averted your eyes."

Seeing his mistake, he flushed and said nothing, but

unbuttoned his jeans, pulling them down. As he straightened, I couldn't stop my mouth from falling open. There he stood, proud and tall, wearing no shorts whatsoever, his cock long and perfect, his buttocks bronzed and tight. Oh, what I wouldn't have done to feel him inside me, to have him thrust like crazy as I fondled that ass! When he pulled up his trousers, a smile on his lips, I began to wonder who was really winning here. He sent me a sly grin as he fastened his belt. It was I who was blushing now.

My home life was nothing like the play. Keith slaved away until two in the morning, scribbling notes at the desk in our room, scratching his head so his hair was messed up, groaning, "Anatomy's hell." I'd bring him mugs of coffee, massage his shoulders, tell him he was going to be a wonderful doctor; but he hardly said a thing, just sighed and carried on as if I wasn't there. My own course was in French lit, and I'd sit in the kitchen, reading alone, turned on by the sensual language. *Je t'adore. Mon plaisir. Oh, je t'aime, je t'aime.* And I'd dream of Jake—his hands, his mouth, his body firm on mine. At other times, I'd reach for my script, testing myself on the lines: *Of course I'll marry you. I feel you in my bones.*

When at last Keith and I would get to bed, I'd want to make love, but he'd turn away. I'd ask if he was sleeping with Ella. After all, he came home stinking of the pub. If his nights out were innocent, why wasn't I invited?

"Look, I love you," he'd moan, pulling the pillow over his head.

"Then why don't we kiss?" I'd ask, but he'd already be snoring.

He's coming to the play, I'd tell myself. *That's the important thing.* And when he reminded me to get him a ticket, I booked a front-row seat.

★ ★ ★

The final dress rehearsal was the toughest yet. Dan had decided our kisses were too quick. He made us practice the wedding scene over and over: Jake pushing back my veil, kissing me fiercely, his scent in my head, his hands sinking.... Then later, while the others performed their fight, we had to mimic sex. Jake smelled better than ever, was fiery when he held me, slamming me hard against the stage wall. The background music built in a rapid crescendo as I ran my hands across his chest. Just before he kissed me, with his fingers on my waist, he whispered, "See how well we'd work?"

And as he leaned in close, I said, "Oh, yes."

I was so wet I kept forgetting my lines. When we were meant to be romancing or arguing on stage, I was just dreaming of Jake's firm thighs, and the way I felt him harden as our bodies pressed together. Dan kept getting snippy. "Terri, *act* for heaven's sake! We've been through this often enough." And I'd try to focus, not only to save the play, but also to make Keith proud.

On opening night, we were nervous as hell. According to Dan, all tickets had sold. "Full house, darlings," he said as we waited on the stage. "Now come on, hold hands and gather in a circle." Dan told us to close our eyes, then guided us through deep breathing. "Let yourselves relax," he chanted. "We're all in this together."

Jake leaned in close and breathed at my ear, "I want your answer tonight. Are you my girl or not?"

"I wish I was," I whispered, my insides twisting up, "but Keith…"

"Fine," Jake muttered, letting go of my hand. His rage flared and he was beautiful; with his jaw raised and the pain in his eyes, I longed to be close to him again. But when I curled my fingers around his, he quickly shook me off.

I tried to tell myself this was for the best. Keith would be watching and I shouldn't get aroused. But in truth, I knew I longed for Jake and loathed that I'd hurt him.

An hour later, I was in the wings with Jake, who was straightening the cuffs of his dress shirt. Our first scene was a dinner party, and standing tall in a paisley bow tie, he was every inch the gent. Nervy, I asked for a hug, but he sighed and shook his head. "It's hard enough we have to fake sex when you've just turned me down."

Heart thumping, I glanced beyond the stage to the noisy audience. The seats were filled with students chattering and laughing, but where was Keith? When I'd bought him his ticket, I'd checked where he'd be sitting—front row, next to the aisle—and though we were late starting, the seat was still empty. "Where is he?" I said.

"Who?" asked Jake.

I bit my lip.

But Jake grabbed my elbow, twisting me toward him. "See?" he said. "He isn't gonna come. Terri, he's not worth it."

"He'll be here," I said, turning back toward the audience. "He knows it's important." But no—the lights were dimming and still no Keith.

Throughout the opening scene, I kept checking the empty seat. I even lost a line and had to be prompted. There was a moment between scenes three and four where I needed to rush backstage and change into my dress for my next grand entrance. Pausing by the mirror, I saw myself in white: pearls gleaming on my satin bodice, my skirts shimmering, my veil floaty... If Keith asked me to marry him, I knew I'd never say yes. Snapping from the dream, I grabbed my phone and quickly checked the messages. Keith had texted: Sorry, something came up.

Something came up?

Livid, I ran to position and entered the stage in my wedding dress, approaching gorgeous Jake with the carnation in his buttonhole. This was our marriage scene and I was the blushing bride, but my cheeks were flushed out of rage, not modesty. Dan, who was playing the vicar—his one and only role—gave me a warning look when Jake slid the ring on my finger. Dan was trying to remind me that our kiss was meant to be subtle, but when he said, "You may kiss the bride," and Jake pushed back my veil, it was I who dived in to kiss my groom. What was meant to be a gentle peck became a fiery clasp, and the audience whooped as Jake kissed me back. Our tongues slid together and he clutched my waist, as I ran my hands down his chest. He pulled away, eyes wide, and whispered, "Had a change of heart?"

Knowing that I had, I gave a nod.

In that moment, I'd worked it all out. Tonight I would pack my things and run to Jake. I had a vision of riding him in this white dress, our hips thudding as the netting crinkled around us. His smooth body arching, our rhythm growing quicker, the bedsprings squeaking in a building crescendo… He would rip off my veil, grab my breasts through the bodice, and I'd tear his shirt open, run my hands down his chest. All that muscle, just waiting to be felt! This dream made me so wet that I started rushing my lines. See, I needed our sex scene.

Now.

By the time Jake was pushing me up against the wall, and Lee and Tina were acting downstage, and the music was starting to build, I'd stopped feeling nervous and was enjoying Jake's touch. His mouth on mine was violent, his kiss wet and deep. He raised my thigh and I hooked my leg around him, pulling him onto me like never before. He groaned loudly and I felt him growing hard——a fact that made me gasp. As he rubbed himself against me, I reached between us and unzipped. I saw his eyes jerk open, saw him catch his breath; felt my sex burning, so thirsty for his. Then he leaned into my ear, breathy and wet, and whispered, "God, let's do it."

I glanced toward the audience, and though I couldn't see them—just a hundred silhouettes in a long, dark hall—I could feel their stares, could sense their growing pleasure, as we moved against each other. It was as if the whole room was holding its breath, swallowing, readying, leaning forward.

"Screw her!" someone murmured from a seat near the front.

"Is it real?" hissed someone else.

"Jesus," said a female voice from just below the stage. "This is really *hot*."

The music grew louder and faster. Jake grabbed my breast through the tight, boned bodice, and I reached down below again, guiding him inside me. He shuddered as he filled me, and the pleasure of his length made me arch, head falling back. How I groaned to feel him thrusting, feel his teeth on my neck, feel the shape of him inside me growing harder every time, feel the wetness of my clutching sex, my fingers in his shirt, as his warm scent rose.

"I've wanted you so long," he groaned.

I said I felt the same.

I saw him glance out at the noisy crowd, who were muttering and gasping at our obvious display. There were excited whispers, ripples of chatter. Somewhere near the front, a man gave a groan. Turning back, Jake grabbed my face and kissed me, while his hips thrust harder and I spread my thighs wide. I pulled his shirt open, laying my palms on his chest, and felt the quick pummel of his heart.

I tried to call him gorgeous, but only managed, "You feel..."

The heat in me grew heavy like a perfect weight, burning, working deeper till I figured it would give—but no, it kept building as we bashed against that wall, our kisses now wet as my sex. The music burst into a growing crescendo, building and building, dramatic and loud. When at last I was so aroused that the nearness of my coming felt like pain, Jake began to fuck me in a beautiful stampede, and we groaned together, long and deep, the pleasure rolling through us. Only when it died did I notice I'd been drooling, with saliva trailing down my chin.

The actors' voices behind us fell, and the lights grew dim. It was the end of the first act. The audience applauded, but Jake didn't move.

"That was quite a performance," I said.

He didn't return the joke. Instead, I felt him smoothing my hair from my face. "Don't tease me, angel. Say you'll come to dinner."

Gently, I told him I would. "We should go," I added, "before the lights come up."

I felt him slide from me, then raise me in his arms so I gave a little gasp of surprise. And humming an aria, he carried me offstage, my wedding dress loose, my cheek pressed against his lapel.

One Last Time

Saskia Walker

Why have you come back, Frank?

The last customer had left and I slid the bolts home, closing the world out. We were alone. Turning my back against the door, I stared across the pub at him. He sat at the bar as he had all evening, brooding and watchful. When I'd gone about my business, serving the other customers, he'd followed me with possessive eyes, making no attempt to hide the fact he wouldn't be leaving when time was called. I'd requested space and yet here he was, back again—and on a Sunday night when he knew it would be quiet and I'd be locking up alone. Frustration welled in me. Why did he have to make splitting up even harder than it already was?

As I walked back to my post I was unable to stop myself from noticing the breadth of his shoulders through his worn leather jacket, the way his thick, dark hair brushed his collar, and the outline of his buttocks through snug jeans.

"What do you want, Frank?" I stepped behind the bar, picking up the bar cloth as I went. Moving quickly, I rubbed it across the polished wood counter, trying to ignore him, but his hand shot out and closed over my wrist, halting me.

My back stiffened and tension beaded up my spine. His demanding grasp made my heart trip. I silently cursed myself, because this is what he did to me, so easily. I was aroused by this simple action—an action that merely hinted at the immensity of his power and self-control. My resistance faltered, as he knew it would. My hand fisted inside his grip.

"I want *you*," he whispered.

I tried to tug free, but couldn't. "I told you, it's over."

I'd told him that the week before, and he'd stared at me for the longest moment, then nodded and left. Not even a goodbye kiss. I'd shoved my emotional armor into place, but deep inside I was hurting, badly. And now, a week later, he was back. Did he want to say goodbye properly, or did he think I'd buckle and give in to him?

"Mel, you also told me that you loved me." His eyes blazed across the bar at me, so intense that I couldn't look away.

My chest tightened, my hand slackening inside his grip. I did love him, and I knew that would never change, but Frank's a long-distance trucker and he loves the road. "I need a man who is there for me at the end of the day," I responded, as levelly as I could, "not someone who passes through every couple of weeks to show me a good time."

"One last time, here and now," he said. It was a statement of intent, not a request.

Our eyes remained locked, and everything that had been between us surfaced in my memory. This man knew me, inside and out. He could tell what I was thinking, and his thumb stroked the side of my hand. Even though I knew it was wrong, heat pooled in my groin, my body anticipating him. I opened my mouth to object but my core clenched, showing me how much I needed him, and I couldn't deny it. Instead of words, I heard only my own labored breathing.

Taking charge, he pulled the cloth from my hand and cast it aside.

Reaching into his pocket, he brought out his handcuffs and put them down on the bar between us.

"Frank…" It came out on a whimper, because I knew that if he restrained me I'd be begging for him. That's how it was. I tried to level my breathing, closing my eyes for a moment, before glaring at him. He knew my weaknesses far too well.

When I looked back at him, he nodded at me.

I withheld a plea.

He clasped both my hands and drew them across the bar toward him, making me lean forward on my forearms. Threading the cuffs through the decorative brass rail that ran along his side of the bar, he made ready to tether me to it.

"You may think that you can deny this thing between us," he said, and I felt the cuffs slide into place. He paused, and I heard one click and lock, before he moved his attention to the other hand. "But I saw the way you were looking at me tonight, and I know that you want this is much as I do." He clicked the second cuff into place.

Frustrated by his ability to be so sure, when I was awash with doubt, I blurted out my feelings. "Of course I *want* this, but that doesn't mean *this* is good for me. *This* is stopping me from meeting another man, a man I could settle down and make a decent home life with."

He didn't respond to that.

Instead, he put his thumb on my lower lip to stop it from trembling. I glared up at him, half in anger and half in pent-up desire. One corner of his mouth lifted and he stroked his thumb over my chin in a tender, affectionate gesture. Then he stepped away, and as he walked the length of the bar and joined me behind it, I swallowed down the mental resistance, because I did want him. Badly. That was part of the problem. When it came to Frank, I was an addict.

Closure. This would give us both closure. I twisted my head and looked back at him. "Promise me, this is the last time."

"Promise." Brushing one hand down my spine over the thin material of my top, he sighed aloud. "You're such a turn-on."

Subtle, but it was enough to make me think about him, hard and thrusting into me. His presence looming at my back made me sway, and he grasped my hips, holding me still, taking charge. "What an invitation," he teased.

I hung my head, my hair falling forward. Positioned like this, with my arse sticking out and my chest against the bar, I was at his mercy.

Standing directly behind me, he leaned so that I could feel his body against me, including the hard shape of his erection pressed against my bottom through our clothing. He rocked his hips from side to side, and I had to bite my lip when I felt just how hard he was. Then he pushed my shirt up and pressed a kiss against my spine. The sensation of his mouth there tantalized me. The brush of his lips, so brief yet so suggestive, made me arch and sway again. Memories haunted me. One night he'd tortured me with love, securing my hands over my head and then kissing my body until I'd begged for release.

"Beautiful, as ever." He breathed along my skin, then slipped his hands under me, between my body and the surface of the bar. Cupping my breasts, he squeezed them through my top.

Unable to help myself, I moaned aloud. His palms seemed to know just how to hold me for maximum effect, making my nipples harden and sting.

"You were thinking about this, weren't you, when you were getting ready to close up for the night?"

"No," I blurted, shaking my head.

"I could see it in your eyes."

I hated him for being right, so I shook my head again, glancing back at him. "This makes it harder, every time we… It makes it harder for us to move on. You know that."

"Good." I caught his smile, just before he pulled my skirt up my hips, exposing my bottom.

Turning away, I silently cursed him. I could feel the weight of his stare on my exposed buttocks. Silence reigned, but for my heartbeat hammering in my ears. Then he sighed, loudly, and the sound ran ragged over my nerve endings. He slid one finger between my buttocks, before plucking at the G-string I was wearing. Squirming, I fought the rising urge to beg him to take hold of me. Conflicting needs assailed me. I wanted him, but I wanted this over with as well, because I needed peace of mind. Belief in my decision was getting harder to sustain by the moment. Reminding myself that I need companionship as well as hot kinky sex, I gasped aloud when he touched me again.

"You're very wet. Is this turning you on? Seems like it might be."

"Bastard," I hissed.

Laughing softly, he rolled my G-string down my thighs. When the scrap of fabric dropped around my calves and fell to rest over my high-heeled shoes, he touched my pussy from behind, riding one knuckle right against my entrance, teasing me.

"Oh, oh, oh…please."

His finger moved lower, under me, and stroked my swollen clit. Once. "Please what?" he asked.

"Please…touch me."

"Like this?" He plunged one finger deep inside me.

It was fast, and it shocked me. My head snapped back, a loud cry escaping my open mouth.

"Or like this?" He pulled out, and ran his now-slick finger over my clit. Back and forth, back and forth. Pleasure thrummed from his fingertip, fanning out through my groin. "Hmm? Which is it that you want, Mel?"

"I...I want you." Saying those words unleashed pent-up emotion, and tears blurred my vision. My hips undulated, my body pivoting against the point of contact, my climax closing.

"Good girl." His finger moved faster, and he was touching me with such confidence, such knowledge, that I was enslaved to it.

I came, and it was so sudden that I cried out and bashed one knee against the back of the bar as I rose onto one foot, pleasure washing through me. Hot liquid wet the top of my thighs.

That's when he thrust his cock inside me.

I hadn't even heard his zipper because I was gone on my climax, but the feeling of his hot, hard cock filling me and stretching the walls of my sex made me thankful I was tethered to the bar. The cuffs and my heels were barely holding me upright. It was Frank who was anchoring me—anchoring me by joining us together, deep inside. Tears smarted in my eyes.

"There's nothing like this," he said, and his voice was hoarse. Possessive hands stroked over my hips, holding me in place.

"So you say." I blurted it out, emotional and frustrated, and shoved my hips back at him, making a statement.

Swearing under his breath, he locked his hands on my

waist and rolled his hips back and forth—claiming me in deep, measured strides, showing me who was master.

"Oh, oh." My clit was still tingling, the heat in my womb making me want to roll and purr, and at the same time another climax was already looming. I was totally locked on to each thrust of his rigid cock inside me. And when he moved faster, I panted aloud and my sex went into spasm just as his shaft arched and swelled and jerked, over and over.

I felt his hand on my spine, knew he was seeking balance and connection. My forehead was resting on the bar between my tethered arms, my breath rasping into my lungs.

"I'm not done with you yet." He bent over me and growled the words against my ear, his hands roving my breasts again as he did so, making my hardened nipples sting. I didn't have the strength to ask what he meant. The action of his hands on me seemed to make my orgasm last and last, leaving me weak and trembling. My legs were all but buckling under me.

He reached over me and unlocked the handcuffs, then lifted me upright against him. After turning me around he locked my hands together again with the cuffs, keeping me captive.

I shook my head, shocked to the core. "You said one last time!"

"I did." He smiled. "I also said I'm not done yet." His eyebrows lifted and his eyes were dark with humor. Renewed lust was oozing from his every pore. He reached into his pocket. I was about to ask what he meant when I saw what he was holding. The blindfold.

Oh, no. I was done for.

I watched him moving the fabric between his hands, wishing I didn't want it quite so much. "You promised me, Frank."

He kissed me before he covered my eyes, and the touch of his mouth on mine made me lift my head toward him. "I hate you," I whispered unconvincingly, when I realized what he'd done.

"Hate me? Okay then, so you hate me… Now tell me you don't love the way this feels." He secured the blindfold behind my head, and then moved his hands lower, to cup my breasts again, and I could hear the teasing accusation in his voice.

I swallowed hard, wishing I had the strength to deny it. I couldn't. I loved the kink as much as he did. We were well matched in that department.

"Stay with me for a few minutes longer, Mel. It'll be worth it, you know it will."

It would. He'd done this once before, making me crazy for the sight of him. At the same time, he made me dependent on him, took me back to my flat and made love to me again. How could I not adore that?

Whispering words of love that I didn't know whether to believe or not, he lifted me into his arms. My head rolled against his shoulder. I was seeking his closeness. The smell of his leather jacket and his familiar cologne swamped me, making me drift on the moment. How long could I hold this inside me?

He took me out the back door, and I heard the lock click as the door shut behind us. He put me into a car, but when I asked where he was taking me, he didn't answer. A reassuring stroke of his hand quieted me, and I felt him put my bag down by my feet. He'd picked it up for me. That was thoughtful of him, I realized. Moments later he began to drive, fast. But not to my home.

I knew it was the airport as soon as we arrived, recognizing the noise, the procedures. I stayed quiet, listening, trying to work out what he was up to. When he parked, he got out of the car, came to my side and drew me out alongside him. I rested my back against the cold metal surface of the vehicle, wanting to run away. What was he doing? Taking the blindfold off, he let me get my bearings. We were in a car park and I could see the lights of the airport terminal beyond. A courtesy minibus was parked up by the gates, waiting for passengers to transfer. Was Frank leaving now? Was this the real goodbye?

After he unlocked the cuffs and threw them onto the backseat of the car, he reached into his pocket and held two passports up in front of me.

His and mine.

How the hell had he got hold of my passport?

Then he held up two tickets. I saw that Saint Lucia was the destination printed on them. "I had some savings. Seemed like a good time to use them."

"You think I'll fall back into line if you take me away on holiday?" He wanted to pour sugar on me.

"It's not just a holiday."

I couldn't quite latch on to his meaning.

He shrugged, somehow uneasy. "I've sorted it out with your boss. He's not expecting you back for two weeks. I have a suitcase packed with your gear. Your friends helped me…. Jackie got your passport and Louisa packed you a case." He nodded at the car. "It's in the back with mine."

There was something I'd never seen in him before. I tried to grasp what it was. He looked worried. Could it be true? Frank was worried about what he was doing? Doubt flickered in his eyes. It seemed as if the world hinged on this moment, and I wasn't sure why.

Fanning the tickets, he revealed a confirmation letter nestled between them. At the top of the printout I saw two words in large print—two words I never thought I'd see. I glanced away and then looked again. "Wedding package?"

"Yes. We can have the wedding right on the beach. In the surf, if you like." He was still tense as he spoke. "Mel, you laid down the law, and I decided. I want it all. I want to be everything that you need."

"I don't understand what you're saying." It was the truth.

"I want you to be my wife." His voice was soft, and somehow insecure.

Hope kindled inside me. A smile broke from somewhere deep in my chest. "You do?"

Above us, a jet roared as it took off.

He nodded. "I've traded in the truck, and I'll be working for a local haulage company when we get home, short haul only. I'll be home every night."

He locked eyes with me in that way of his, seeking my agreement.

I nodded, nestling against him. He was my anchor. He kissed me then, and it was long, slow and hungry for more.

"Now hurry up and pull yourself together," he said gruffly, as we drew apart, "because I have to get the cases out of the car, and we're late for check-in already."

I could hardly take it all in. "But I thought you said tonight was the last time?"

"It was. One last time, as we were." His eyebrows lifted. "I had to know if you really wanted it to end, or if you still wanted me. Your body always lets me know that you want me. It's a dead giveaway." That twinkle was back in his eyes. "I knew this was the right thing to do, back there at the bar."

That's when it hit me. Everything he'd said, and why he'd done what he'd done. I couldn't quite see him then, because my vision blurred. I bit my lip. A passing car blew my hair over my face.

He lifted the stray hairs away from my eyes and then rested his hand against my jaw and smiled. "Mel, next time I bend you over that bar, we'll be man and wife...."

Forsaking All Others

Janine Ashbless

We have two albums full of photographs from our wedding. The first is faced in cream satin printed with little gold ribbons and bells, and it lives in a tissue-lined box in the dining room cupboard with the good china, the set we use only on special occasions. All those photos are in colour. The second one stays in a locked briefcase under my side of the bed, and its cover is unmarked black leather. All the prints in that one are black-and-white.

They're the only albums in the house; everything else is stored digitally. I like to take both out and look through them. I like to feel their weight.

Here's the first album. Each laminated page turns under my fingers with a tiny sigh. The photographer we hired has embossed his name on the flyleaf in gold cursive script, which is sort of cheeky, but I forgive him. He was pretty good, I think; he had the right eye for arranging formal groups of relatives and friends, but he wasn't bossy or impatient. And all the pictures are flattering, thank goodness—at least to Roy and me. Each *snap-snap-snap* of the shutter was like a tiny round of applause.

Snap: Here I am in my wedding dress, stepping down from the limousine. My dark hair catches glints from the sun and the tiny silk flowers woven through my French plait shine like stars. It's a lovely dress, slim and sophisticated—rather than one of those frothy meringues—with a daringly steep plunge between my breasts that was held secure—*shh!* Keep it secret!—with double-sided tape that pulled at my skin. I was nervous as hell, but oh so happy that day. I remember how unfamiliar the clasp of the blue garter around my right thigh felt, as if someone was touching me.

Snap: Here's Roy in his gray tailcoat and high collar, looking so handsome I could kiss the page. We married because, after seven years living together, I suggested it was time we tried for a baby. Not that I have a desperately strong need to be a mother just yet, but we're settled and solvent at last, and I thought, *What if we don't take the opportunity while we still have it? What if we leave it too late and then I decide it's important? I don't want to regret that when I'm older.* And when I explained this to Roy, he smiled and said, "We'd better be married first then." That was how he proposed.

Snap: Here are Roy and Calvin outside the church. Calvin had to be best man, of course. Roy's known him since forever—or at least since college, which feels like forever. They share the cycling fixation and are off together for a road race at least once a month. It'd be annoying, if I didn't like him—but luckily, I do. He's fun, and I'll admit he's easy on the eye. We've gone on several cycling holidays together: Roy and me, Sylvia and Calvin, all around the Dordogne and Brittany and the Atlantic coast of Spain. Wine and winding roads. Calvin is three inches taller than Roy, with a big dirty grin that hides a determined business brain. He's a builder with his own company, one of those "work hard, play hard" guys. He's got his hand on Roy's shoulder in this picture, as if to back him up going into a fight. Roy, darker and slighter, with gray eyes that the photo has caught beautifully, looks tense but incredibly proud.

Snap: Here's me with Sylvia, my chief bridesmaid, in the grounds of the Waters Hotel, where the reception was held. She'd be the first to say that I look better in a long formal dress than she does; I've got the curves to make the most of it. Sylvia is a professional photographer herself—pretty famous, actually—and she looks exactly like you'd think a photographer ought: tall and tanned and lean, her blond hair usually twisted up into a knot on the crown of her head. She looks fabulous in khaki and cycle shorts and sports tops that show off her golden muscles. While Calvin is doing up decrepit barns on the Continent to sell as holiday homes to Brits, she roams the countryside, taking her art photos. Her specialization is close-ups of subjects so small you might otherwise miss their beauty. We've got one of her prints on our wall at home of a dragonfly resting on a rusted tractor, cerulean against the red, and it's just breathtaking. In this photo she's trying to look demure, but her grin is breaking through.

I hit it off with Sylvia the moment we met, the way girls sometimes do. I felt like I knew her instantly; we just meshed, even though we look so different and have such dissimilar lives. It was certainly a relief to the lads to find that their girlfriends got on so well. For the last six years we've all four holidayed together, visited each other at weekends and generally moved in the same orbit.

For the past two years we've been sleeping together.

It was Sylvia who started it all off. I was washing up in our Spanish holiday cottage when she came up behind me and slipped her arms about my waist in a hug. I wouldn't have been startled—she was always unselfconsciously demonstrative—except that I was only wearing a bikini at the time and her hands clasped my bare flesh. "Whoa," I said, bemused, as she stroked the curve of my hip.

Sliced olives afloat in the dishwater looked up at us like green eyes.

"You have such a great figure, you know, Debbie. You're really beautiful."

Blood rushed to my cheeks. I was actually more bemused by the compliment than the caress; I'd always thought of her as the beautiful one. "You think so?"

"Oh God, yes." She slid her hands up to my breasts and gave them a gentle squeeze. That was the moment I felt the first hot spurt of arousal, unexpected and primal, and I was so gripped by the sensation that I didn't move at all as she stroked the slopes of my cleavage, exploring the edge of my bikini bra. "You have the most gorgeous big boobs, Debbie," she whispered in my ear. "I've always been jealous." As she pulled the stretchy cloth aside to bare my nipples, I giggled breathily. "And Calvin couldn't keep his eyes off you out there."

I twitched. "I'm sorry, Sylvia—"

"Don't be. Do I sound pissed off? I was just thinking, if the guys were to walk in right now…"

"Uh…"

"D'you think they'd like what they saw?" She circled my nipples with her fingertips and teased them to stiff points, which she pinched. I could feel the soft pressure of her thighs and belly snuggling up against my backside.

"I think they'd love it." My voice sounded funny, not like my own at all.

"So what would you do if they did see us, Debbie?"

"I…I don't know."

"Would you let me lick your beautiful tits in front of Roy and Calvin?"

"Sylvia…"

"Would you lie back and let me eat your pussy? Would you get off on them going all hard watching us?"

The pleasure of her fingers and the thought of our two guys getting massive boners watching her and me play together—that was enough to make me moan. My bikini gusset was filling with wet.

"Then," said she, "let's do it."

There was quite a lot more discussion, but in the end that's just what we did that night, after getting back from dinner at a local restaurant. Both of us girls had worn our tightest, most low-cut dresses, and we'd piled on the teasing and the flirtation over the meal. As we walked back to the cottage Roy's hand was already on my ass, but I didn't intend letting him drag me off to bed just yet.

"We've got a special treat for you two," Sylvia announced, drawing Calvin into the living room. "Come on."

We sat them down on the sofa and stood before them. Both men looked intrigued, catching our mood of giggly promise. I was so dizzy with excitement and anticipation that it hardly seemed real, and I just let Sylvia take the lead, slipping her arms around me and kissing me full on the lips. She tasted sweet and felt surprisingly soft, not like Roy's hard and bristly embraces. Our kiss was slow and sensual, punctuated by little breathy smiles. When we broke at last I looked over at the lads. Roy was sitting forward with his mouth open and Calvin, slumped back with his knees sprawled, had a monster grin on, but their delight was shared and undisguised. Bottles of beer dangled forgotten in their limp hands.

Sylvia's hand moved to my back and pulled my dress up, all the way to my ass. I could feel the cooler air contrasting with the heat under my skin and between my legs. Gently she eased the stretchy fabric up my torso, over my breasts and off. I stood there, blushing a little to be so exposed in my undies—a lacy, magenta thong-and-bra set picked especially for this moment because it showed off my curves. I caught my breath then. This was the moment when Roy would object, if he was going to at all.

He didn't. How could he? Wasn't this every man's fantasy? And we made sure that for both men this was like Christmas and their birthdays coming all at once. We kissed with lots of tongue showing, our sighs and squeaks of pleasure unrestrained. I worked Sylvia's top down over her shoulders to reveal that she wasn't wearing a bra, and then she undid mine and our bare breasts met. Stroking and exploring each other with gentle hands and hungry lips, we stripped ourselves of the last of our clothes. Sylvia flung my panties cheekily into Calvin's lap and he jumped as if he'd been electrocuted, then wound them round his fingers. She backed me up against the breakfast bar. Sliding to her knees, she gave the two men an uninterrupted view of my nakedness as well as her own out-thrust ass. And then, wriggling that ass with delight, she pressed her hot mouth to my slit and ate out my pussy.

God, I was so turned on by then that there was no question of simply putting on a show. This was for real. The two men were motionless, pinned by the sight before them, but their avid expressions said it all. I could see the bulge of Calvin's erection just about threatening to split his jeans. I could see Roy's hand in his lap, squeezing the swollen length of his cock through his pants. Watching them watching us just about sent me into orbit. And as Sylvia's tongue danced on my clit, I leaned back against the bar and lost all self-consciousness as, squealing and bucking and with my breasts bouncing, I came.

We both went off in our separate couples afterward, and Roy fucked me over and over again for hours, like a man possessed.

The next day, as cautiously at first as if we were approaching a dangerous wild animal, we had sex as a foursome for the first time. It was the most fun I think I'd had, like, *ever.*

Since then we've been…what? Fuck-buddies? Is that the right phrase for it? We've kept it quiet, of course. We've never tried to involve anyone else. Sometimes we swap partners and I'll have Calvin pump me full for the night, while Sylvia gives Roy a thorough workout. Sometimes we'll do it all together. There's no pressure, no tension, no jealousy. We're just four friends who enjoy each other's company, in and out of bed. It's not like I'm ever going to be tempted to run off with Calvin: he's not enough of a tender romantic to satisfy me. And Sylvia would find Roy's steady nine-to-seven job in the same town all year round utterly stultifying. Not to mention the fact that we all love our own spouses.

Snap: Here's a picture of the four of us in front of that big fountain in the grounds of the Waters Hotel. It's my favorite in this album. Roy is holding me and Calvin is holding Sylvia. We all look so happy, and so good together.

Snap: Here's one of Calvin making his best man's speech. He'd warned me teasingly that he might drop a sly nudge-nudge line just for the fun of seeing me blush, but in the end he was absolutely discreet, coming out only with a mild innuendo about getting off with the chief bridesmaid.

Snap: Here's one taken much later on during the reception, after we've eaten. It's not posed; Roy and I are leaning on the marble balustrade overlooking the rose garden, champagne glasses loose in our hands, just talking. The photographer must have taken it from the promenade below while I was preoccupied. I remember my feet in their white satin shoes were starting to ache, and I'd become pensive for a moment.

"It feels strange, don't you think? To be married?"

"Actually, I don't feel that much different." Roy put his arm around my waist and kissed my temple. "We're still us, and I still fancy you even if you are my missus." His grip tightened. "You look hot, Deb, you know."

"But we are going to be different, aren't we?" I was trying to grasp my nebulous feeling of unease without raising my voice above a murmur. "I mean, we'll have to be a bit more grown-up now."

"You can buy me slippers for Christmas."

I gave him a poke with one finger. "I mean…you know. We'll have to stop messing around. Like, playing with Calvin and Sylvia."

"Really? Why?"

"Well. We'll have responsibilities. If there's going to be a baby around…"

"It's not on its way yet."

"But we will have to stop sometime. It can't go on forever. You know that."

Roy frowned a little. "Actually, I was imagining us still at it when we need Viagra and walkers. And maybe, you know, a nurse to help us get into position…."

"Oh, be serious!"

"It's my wedding," he said mildly. "The only thing I intended to feel serious about today was the 'I do.'"

"Not the 'forsaking all others'?" We'd had a traditional church wedding for his mother's sake.

He shook his head, his eyes twinkling. "I sort of saw that as 'forsaking all those except the ones my wife gives me permission for.'"

At that moment one of my aunties came up to talk to us, and the conversation ended abruptly.

Snap: Here's me in my reception dress. My going-away dress it would have been, except that we weren't leaving on honeymoon until the next week, and were staying in the hotel's bridal suite that night. It's a nice frock, sea-green and turquoise and silver, which sounds garish, but it's beautiful in actuality, and I'd matched it with some stunning silver jewelry. I'm keeping the ensemble for other party occasions—maybe for Sylvia and Calvin's wedding, if they ever get around to it. Sylvia's always said that if she does get married it'll be the simplest register office affair. Roy is down to shirt and trousers and a dangling bow tie by now. It's late, the disco is in full swing and the supper buffet has been ransacked. We're waving goodbye to our guests, leaving them to dance and make their own way home or to bed. The bride and groom can't be the last to leave.

That's the last photo in this album.

We went upstairs to our suite, where my wedding dress and veil lay out on the bed as I'd left them, but a big pile of fluffy white towels and a couple of bottles of champagne had made an appearance. Roy took me in his arms, just as he had done so often that day. But this time it was different. This time he kissed me slowly and deeply, the way that always gets to me, breaking down my barriers. This time he wrapped his fingers in my hair and tugged my head back, and the almost-threat of his grasp sent a spark of arousal right down my spine and through my belly to ignite a glow at my clit. This time his cock started to get hard. His other hand pressed me to him, squeezing my ass, and I writhed my hips.

When we broke apart I was breathless and already warm.

"Want to go to bed?" he asked.

"Hmm." I nipped at his lower lip. "I believe I do."

"You can come out now," he called over my shoulder. That was when Sylvia and Calvin came out of the bathroom, grinning. She was holding her own camera.

This is where the second photograph album starts.

Snap: I'm kneeling, out of my dress but back in my veil. It hangs down over my face and torso, so sheer that it doesn't hide those big breasts of mine cradled in their beautiful lace La Senza bra, or my wide-eyed expression as I gaze out at the camera. The two men either side of me are faceless and fully dressed, only their midsections visible in this print. Each has one hand on my shoulder, pushing me down to my knees, and the other hand tight around one of my wrists, holding it up. My fingers are curled helplessly, my lips parted in anticipation of what's to come.

Snap: Head-and-shoulders shot. My veil is flipped back now. I'm kneeling between two sets of bare male flanks and two cocks, erect and angled toward an apex, like swords held at a salute for when the bride exits the church. I've got one cock in each hand and my head is turned toward Roy's— you can tell it's him because of the dark pubic thatch and the hairier thighs—and my lips are wrapped around his bell-end, sucking hard.

They're amazing pictures, the textures of flesh and fabric rendered so finely that even just looking you can almost feel them beneath your fingertips.

Snap: Closer yet, the two cocks are almost touching over my head. Champagne foam escaping from a newly opened bottle oozes and slops down their flushed shafts and drips into my open, eager mouth waiting below.

Snap: I'm topless and pantieless now, leaning back against a male chest, breasts upthrust. Champagne is being poured down my torso from the bottle tilted over my tits; it gushes in runnels off my erect nipples, sluicing over my belly to run into the shaven split below. You can see bubbles freckling my skin. Calvin's sandy head is between my thighs and he's lapping champagne and sex juices from between my spread pussy lips. He said it was the "best fucking cocktail" he'd ever tasted. God, we got champagne everywhere. On the towels, on the carpet, on the coverlet...everywhere.

Snap: My back is to the camera, the veil hanging down to my ass cleft, my spine a shadowy, sinuous line under the transparent fabric. I'm sitting astride Roy's lap as he perches on the edge of the bed. With one hand he's holding my wrists cruelly together at the small of my back, and with the other he's twisting my head sideways so I can suck Calvin's cock as he stands beside us.

Snap: Just my spread thighs, poised over the smooth column of the champagne bottle's neck as if I'm about to impale myself upon it. My thighs are glistening with moisture and my sex lips visibly unfurled.

"Can you take it?" Roy whispered in my ear as he held me.

Snap: Yes, I could. All the way.

Snap: My breasts fill the frame, ripe as fruit, my hands supporting them and squeezing them together to make a cleft as I lie back on the bed. Two cocks lie along the valley of my cleavage, one entering the frame from above and one from below. They snuggle up together, cushioned by the mounds of my flesh. They're both so turgid and glistening that they look as if they're molded from rubber.

Snap: From behind, Roy's ass and spread thighs, his hanging ball sac silhouetted between them in a halo of hair. My chin and lips just visible, out of focus, below. He's got big balls by any standards, and I love to paint myself with lipstick and suck them.

Snap: Me on all fours on the bed, getting spit-roasted.

Roy is behind me and Calvin is fucking my mouth. I'm still wearing my satin shoes and my wedding stockings with their ivory lace panels, and the blue silk garter around my right thigh. My upthrust ass looks round and voluptuous, and Roy's fingers are dinting it as he grips tightly, shafting me with obvious vigor. From the angle of my head, it looks as though Calvin's cock is going all the way down my throat. My eyes are heavy-lidded, my mascara starting to streak as the tears well up.

Snap: I'm bent forward and Calvin's thick cock is halfway into my ass. It amazes me that Sylvia could get this angle for the picture. The contrast of skin textures makes my mouth water. My puckered asshole looks like a licked chocolate.

Snap: Trench warfare. Calvin's cock in my ass from above, Roy's chin below, prickly with stubble, his tongue licking up to touch me. Between them my pussy gapes, a glistening no-man's land of dark furrows and swollen ridges.

Snap: My face, as I'm racked by orgasm. Tendrils of hair cling to my hot skin. My lips are spread in an O but every other muscle is locked with strain, my eyes squeezed tightly shut.

Snap: Close-up on a double penetration. One cock where it should be, one in my ass. It looks oddly neat: all holes filled. My skin appears smooth as vellum, contrasted with the textures and corrugations of masculine flesh. Calvin's scrotum rides high, a wrinkled bulge almost one with the underside of his shaft, while Roy's balls are more distinct and bulging. Oh God, I'd never tried it before my wedding night; they'd been conspiring to serve it up for the special occasion, it turned out. And it took us some time to get into that position: lots of lube and easing of muscles, lots of working fingers in first. Sandwiched between their bodies I was held absolutely immobile, at their mercy. They soothed me and stroked me and forced me to come with terrible, ruthless patience.

Snap: A head-and-shoulders shot again. My hair is in wild disarray by now, my veil askew where it's fallen off and been pinned on again, my makeup smudged. Between me and the camera two heads, one dark and one light, suckle at my breasts. You can see my hands gripping the backs of their scalps, my nail varnish shiny, my new wedding ring very visible; you can't tell what they are doing to me below, but you can see from the look of tormented concentration on my face that I'm about to come yet again.

Snap: I'm riding Roy on the bed, cowgirl style. Well, sort of. Calvin stands behind me holding my arms stretched up and pinned over my head, so I'm one long line of tension as Roy thrusts up from below. My breasts are caught by the camera midbounce, weightless balloons.

Snap: My left breast just as a hand smacks it, the shock wave billowing through my flesh.

Snap: My butt, upraised, my pussy facing the lens full-on again. There are four hands on and in it. Fingers delve into my cunt and into my anus, competing for access. I'm very open. My clit shines like a cherry stone. Just visible on one ass cheek: the imprint of a slapping hand, fingers spread.

Snap: My eyes are closed, my swollen lips parted, my face tilted back and ecstatic. I look like the model for a saint at prayer—except for the pale splashes of spunk all over my chin and cheeks, dewed in my eyelashes and dripping down my throat.

Snap: The two men are reclining against the pillows, both gleaming with sweat, both grinning. You never saw anyone look so satisfied with themselves as those two. Between them I lie with limbs askew, my face hidden and my hair fallen across Roy's thighs, exhausted and replete and as happy as

I've ever been. You just can't capture my muffled, disbelieving giggles in a photo.

That's the last picture in the album. It's the perfect wedding memento. The perfect present.

There goes the doorbell now; quietly, I lay the books of photographs aside. That'll be Sylvia and Calvin come to pick us up. I can hear Roy heading down to answer the door. We're going away on a cycling weekend at a hotel in the Lake District.

And just for now I'll put off growing up.

Mother of the Bride

Cheyenne Blue

Since when had dove-gray defined who I was? Dove-gray and lilac.

The dress laid out on the bed was...elegant. It was tasteful and refined. It was mature. When had I become mature? I picked at the lace that adorned the neckline, thinking absently that it would itch like hell. It matched the trim on the huge floppy hat. The hat simply screamed "Mother of the Bride"; it looked like a drooping satellite dish. I'd have to stand in the back row for the photos or it would obscure half the wedding party.

The wedding party. The bride and groom. The mother and father of the bride, the mother and stepfather of the groom, the father and stepfather of the groom. Five bridesmaids, ranging in age from thirty-two down to two, and five groomsmen, all supposedly of adult age. A best man, a matron of honor. And cousins, aunts, uncles, all with their husbands, wives, partners, live-in lovers, fuck buddies and "good friends," plus endless, mostly annoying, children.

I hated it. Jonas, my partner, hated it. But the bride—Skye, our daughter—loved it all. She had picked the dress out for me, told me it looked perfect and wonderful. Skye loved it, and that was what mattered. Wasn't it?

Jonas appeared naked from the en suite bathroom. His long gray hair was already tied back in a neat ponytail and he'd obviously just trimmed his beard. A whole inch was gone from the bottom. Droplets clung to his sparse frame, a trickle ran down his lean leg, winding through the still-dark hairs. He turned to the closet and his skinny butt jiggled, just a little.

When he came over to the bed, his hands were full of charcoal suit, silk shirt and purple tie.

"I still can't believe we're doing this," he mused. "How did we acquire such a traditional daughter? When we were her age, we were backpacking around Europe."

"Drinking too much."

"Sleeping on beaches."

"Squatting in that Victorian terrace in London."

"Doing drugs that wrecked our heads and should have wrecked our livers."

"Voting communist. Saving the whale. Campaigning for Greenpeace."

"Free love. Free Nelson Mandela."

We'd had this conversation hundreds of times and the gist of it was always the same.

"When Skye was little," said Jonas, "we were living in the commune in Arizona. She ran around naked in the dust—"

"We all did that."

"—she was vegan, she went on spirit walks, she had never watched television."

"Now she lives in a condo in the city, eats out five nights a week and sets her TiVo to record three or four TV shows each night. Dear Goddess, she's even an *accountant*. She talks about her IRA."

"She has an IRA, which is more than we do. The only IRA we knew were the Irish freedom fighters."

I sighed. "They say that children do the opposite of their parents, but I never thought it would happen to us. I thought she'd be even wilder."

Jonas put down the suit and came up behind me, wrapping his arms around my waist. "She's a conformist. Before you know it, you'll be cuddling your two point five grandchildren."

"Not too soon, I hope. She's too young. I'm too young."

He touched his fingers to the strands of gray threading through my dark brown hair. "It's the way she is."

"I know. And I'm happy for her, truly I am. I just wish... I just wish she could be roaming free, as we used to do."

"Maybe she did her roaming with us. Not many kids have sailed around the world by the time they were six. Or lived on an ashram and a kibbutz."

"She says she was happy. But I think she would have preferred a settled childhood."

Jonas's hands wandered around my waist, stroking my skin. His touch still had the power to move me, even after all our years together. I clasped his hands where they rested on my waist. Strong hands, strong man. Truly my soul mate.

"We can do the navel gazing another time. But right now, Penny, we need to dress for our daughter's wedding."

My mouth turned down. "Dress."

"I know you hate it, but Skye picked it."

"It's not *me*. It's matronly. I'm not matronly...am I?"

"Never. You're still my lover and soul mate, and to me you'll always be my rainbow girl, in the tie-dye and Birkenstocks you wore to our commitment ceremony."

I turned in his arms and kissed him, my lips sliding over his to briefly suck on the lower one. "That was a day to remember. The closest we've ever come to doing what Skye is doing now. I wonder why she feels the need to make a legal bond. We never did. Our affirmation was enough."

"Just us and some friends, under the sky, in the Rockies in Colorado, the sun on our faces, nature around us."

"We exchanged woven anklets instead of rings. Skye and Owen have traditional gold bands, the exact symbol we rebelled against."

"Henny Penny." Jonas turned and leaned his forehead against mine. The pet name fell warmly into the space between us. "How blessed I am to have you in my life."

"Blessed," I echoed, and reached up with seeking lips.

His hands rose and wound themselves into my long, gray-streaked hair—the hair that Skye had wanted me to dye and style for her wedding. The silver strands stood out against his tanned hands. His lips moved with assurance, caressing mine, deepening the kiss until our tongues tangled in a slow, wet dance.

When the kiss reached the point where we had to move it forward into something more than a kiss or stop, Jonas broke off. His forehead rested against mine again for a moment, our breath mingling in the space between us.

"Not now," he said. "We can't tell Skye we missed her wedding because we were having a skin celebration of our own."

I smiled and let my hand drift down his side. "Later."

"Later," he echoed.

The traditional stone church was mostly packed with traditional smart people. There was a small knot of bright clothing, flowing hair and beards—some of our friends whom Skye had invited. They stood out like dandelions on a sleek, manicured lawn. Like the rest of the congregation, I stood as the organ swelled into the "Wedding March," and Skye glided down the aisle on Jonas's arm. Her face was obscured by the long veil. I remembered how, mildly, I'd pointed out to her that she wasn't a chattel to be "given away" by her father. That she didn't have to wear a white dress; even our traditional daughter wasn't a virgin.

Skye had smiled her sweet but determined smile, her endearing smile, the one that usually got her what she wanted. "I know," she'd said, taking my hand over the breakfast table, "but it's what I want."

What she wanted. We'd raised her unconstrained by the shuttered thinking that said women couldn't do this, or nice girls didn't do that. We'd encouraged her to be open and free, taught her that sex was a gift and a pleasure, not a sin, not something to be hidden. And here she was, age twenty-two, binding herself to a staid traditional world.

The words of the Christian service were unfamiliar to me. Behind me, I could hear my friend quietly repeating the words of a handfasting ceremony. And suddenly it was over, and Skye and Owen were kissing, and then they were returning down the aisle to stand outside in the watery May sunshine, hand in hand, confetti in their hair and clinging to her peachy skin.

"My back aches," I grumbled to Jonas, interminable hours later, as we were shunted into yet another photo lineup.

"I'll rub it later."

"Later" came after the photos, the cocktails, the congratulations, more photos, the dinner, the first dance, the last dance. And finally, Skye and Owen disappeared to change, and then left in a welter of hugs and good wishes. She'd hugged me and Jonas, a long, tight clasp, that spoke of a farewell far deeper than the two-week honeymoon in

Jamaica. I thought I could feel the echo of the little girl she had once been.

As the younger people settled back in for another round of drinking and dancing, I slipped my hand into Jonas's. "Think we can leave now?"

He hummed in affirmation, and together we slipped out the door of the ballroom, down the long anonymous corridors of the hotel, up to our room on the third floor. The lights were off when we opened the door, but I'd left the drapes partially open. When I turned on the light, I saw the bouquet of flowers on the bed. Skye's bridal bouquet. I picked it up and turned it over in my hands. The only tradition she'd omitted was throwing her bouquet. Now I knew why.

Her note was simple and to the point. "Because I love you, and because you loved me enough to give me the wedding I wanted, not the one you wanted for me."

Tears pricked at my eyes, and I handed the note to Jonas. "Obviously, we didn't hide our feelings too well."

"I doubt we could have kept them from her. She's very astute."

Carefully, I set the bouquet on the bedside table and reached for my partner again.

His hands moved to the top button of my despised lilac-and-gray dress. Working swiftly, he slipped the buttons, pushing aside the cloth, moving it down my arms until I stood there in my simple cotton bra. Bending, he set his mouth to my nipple, warming it through the fabric. The dress pooled around my waist.

In a glissade of motion, we moved to the bed, dropping our clothes as we went. We'd moved like this a thousand times before. We knew each other so well. No need for a slow striptease that night, no need for the ritual undressing of each other. This time was all about us, and a celebration of our life together. And a celebration of Skye, as well; our daughter, made in love, who today was leaving us for her own love and life.

We lay on the bed, facing each other. I stroked the long gray strands of his hair, reaching behind to release his ponytail, combing out the strands until they flowed free over his shoulders.

He growled at me, biting my nipple playfully. "I should let you be. Maybe I'll go and have a drink at the bar. A fine bourbon, some good company…"

"You wouldn't dare," I said, and wound my fingers tightly into his hair, tugging as he tongued my breast.

I treasured these moments, lying together in bed. Whether it was the afterglow, or a slow buildup to intimacy, the warmth and the loving were the same. Even when we didn't make love—when he couldn't or I wasn't interested—we still held each other, and stroked and played and cavorted like puppies, softly warm and playfully tender.

He pretended to think, his hips undulating into my groin with casual disregard. I could feel him swell slightly against me. I tried to feign indifference, but my gasp gave me away.

"Maybe I'll join Owen's mother and stepfather. I'm sure they appreciate a fine drink."

I caught his lips with mine. "Too staid for you."

I kissed him slowly, feeling him engorge further as he wriggled against my belly. I knew he was aroused, but I wouldn't give him the satisfaction of rolling over and letting him drive into me until we were both sated. No, I liked to tease.

"I told them I'd meet them at the bar later." Another stalling tactic. He'd said no such thing, and I knew it.

"Liar."

His lips settled on the curve of my neck, and his hand crept up my side, insinuating between our sticky bodies to find my nipple. It bloomed into his fingers, peaking softly between his finger pads.

I smiled at the touch of his hand, and grasped him by his hair again, dragging his head back, forcing him to look into my face.

His expression was not one of sly manipulation; not like when he talked me into letting Phoebe, his sister, come and stay with us. Phoebe intruded upon us, claiming Jonas, trying to drag him away from me. When Phoebe was coming, Jonas's expression was one of trickery. But this time, his expression was content. He rolled me over so that he was on top, and parted my thighs, pressing down into the cradle of my hips. The tip of his cock rested at my opening. I was slick and wet with desire. He rocked toward me, his erection growing, pushing through my outer lips, damp and warm.

I lifted a thigh, still slender, but without the tautness of muscle I had when Jonas first met me. He stroked its softened surface with his fingertips. I was still his Penny; he didn't love me less. My fingers teased between his legs, stroking the seam where his sex met his body. He responded and the tip of his cock slipped inside me. I rocked forward to meet him, and he slid home, sheathed in my liquid heat.

I cradled his face in my hands. "Just love me," I said.

He rocked with me, in the rhythm we had perfected during our years together. His movements made me moan a little, and I clasped him tight, keeping him deep within me, close against my skin.

We were closing our world around us again. For twenty-two years there'd been three of us: him, me and Skye, and now, while she was still part of our circle, Skye was stepping away into her own life. The sadness I'd been suppressing welled anew, and the sky fell, just a little.

Jonas's fingers touched my lips. "I know," he said, and his eyes were rueful. I waited for him to continue, but he was silent again, moving gently within me.

We lay together, and our hands communicated what our voices could not. He stroked my hip, I grasped his hair and pulled his head to my breast. Our love was as strong as ever. He seemed to sense my uncertainty, and opened his mouth over my breast, biting softly, leaving his mark on my skin.

My hands stroked up to his shoulders. "When Skye was little, I often dreamed of her being happy with a partner," I whispered, "just as I'm happy with you. Our child's happiness, isn't that what every parent wants? So why do I feel so sad?"

Jonas raised up on his hands so that he could better see my face. "One part of our lives is over. It's been a great part, raising Skye, but she's flying free now. We'll still be parents, but it's different."

We lay there entwined, and thoughts of our daughter wove through my head. With a sigh and a mental shake, I came back to the here and now. I started to kiss Jonas again, a longer deeper kiss, a demanding kiss, rife with the sort of desperation I had felt in our early days as lovers, when we were proving something to ourselves as well as each other. I wriggled, breaking the kiss, and guided his mouth down to my nipples.

He's always said he loves my breasts. Too small, I've thought, but Jonas said he loves their size, their pertness, their sensitivity. For a moment, I remembered Skye's wispy head at my breast, but then Jonas bit gently and Skye's image vanished. I stroked my way down between Jonas's legs, teasing with knowing fingers, spreading moisture and fluid, running my fingers around where we joined. He started a thrusting, pounding rhythm, fierce and needy.

I climaxed in a soundless clench around him. His eyes were squeezed tightly shut in concentration, but I saw the moisture in the corners. And he came as well, deep inside me. We held each other afterward and I knew that Skye still held our hearts, but maybe they were now just a little emptier.

I kissed Jonas softly. "I love you so much," I told him.

He knew, of course. How many thousands of times had we said those words during our three decades together? He laid his palm against the side of my face, and I could see love—and relief—in his eyes. "I'm glad you're able to let her go."

"Of course. I'm not a clinging mother. It's what I've always wanted for her—that she chooses her own path in life. And that's what she's done, proudly and confidently. She'll be okay. She and Owen will be fine."

He smiled. "And we'll be okay, too. We still have the love. It's there, woven through our life together. I love you. You love me."

"I do," I said, and my words were almost like a vow.

I Married a Gigolo

Jax Baynard

We had a heat wave in February. There was definitely a Mark Twain thing going on—the hottest summer I ever had was a winter in Plum. There was some debate about whether this was caused by global warming or natural climate fluctuation, the kind of debate no one can win because no one really knows the answer. You say tomato, I say fuck you. Whichever it was, it was hot and people were a little confused about the season. Plum winters are not what you'd call cruel, but it does go down to freezing on occasion, and sometimes below, so the 78 degree temperature was out of the ordinary.

I live in a small town. I think it must be the habit of humans everywhere to name their places after what they destroyed in order to live there. In our case it was plum trees. The valley was full of them for a time, but there aren't many to speak of now—just the old, ragged trees in people's yards that bear small, bitter fruit. The kids pelt each other with them in the summertime, and the passing cars of the tourists, driving too fast. We have tourists. The town is too picturesque not to. The buildings are from the turn of the century and look like livery stables and general stores because they used to be livery stables and general stores. Now they hold shiny things for people to buy.

I'm a field biologist for the National Park Service, an expert in native grasses. Try to make small talk out of that one. There's a fifteen-acre field behind my house and it's like my own private laboratory. I don't own it. The guy in the white ranch house next to me owns it. George thinks I'm crazy, but he likes me, so he lets me poke around in the field. We met one night when he sauntered out to ask, 1) why was I in his field, and 2) had I lost something? Because I was walking around with my head bent down. I was counting grasses. There are more than thirty species in my field, although only about three of them are native. That's the state of things in the world. I watch them battle each other for acreage. People think grass just sits there and grows, but there's a lot more going on than that. It's really kind of exciting. The only one I really hate is the tarweed (nonnative variety). Everyone has a bane plant—not henbane, but bane-of-your-existence—the plant that makes you want to pour Round-Up all over it, even though you know Round-Up is poison and Monsanto is a corporate terrorist.

I go to George's house for tea occasionally. It's decorated from the Sears & Roebuck Catalog circa 1952. The wallpaper in the living room has ducks flying over the marsh. I'm not even going to describe the paper in the bathroom. The other reason he came out was because of the way I look. You know the famous painting of the woman standing in the clamshell? That's not me. That is my hair, however. People cannot get over it. Also I'm pushing six feet tall and everything else is in the right place, so there's always someone looking. It's never true love, though.

Speaking of which, I met Tom at New Year's. Strictly speaking, I met him when he moved to town. We were introduced and then proceeded to ignore one another for a year and a half. I don't know what happened at New Year's, but somehow his big, sexy pillow lips were all over mine and I had no objections at all.

There was alcohol involved.

When I sobered up, I still thought it was a fine idea, but Mr. CPA had anxiety written all over him even before our first date—which never actually happened, because he panicked and canceled it. So there I was, hormones in full bloom, and if I wore panties, they'd be in a twist. Mr. CPA, by the way, is not my usual type. I tend to like sturdy, dark, amusing men, and he is tall, lanky, blond and hairy all over. He walks like a man who was a bear in his previous life, and whose previous life occurred recently. I just couldn't get over the way he kissed, and the battling grasses were being edged out by fantasies of exactly where on my body those lips would feel best. His name is actually Tom Doe. There have been plenty of jokes about that. His full name is Thomas Haymore Doe III, which sounds impressive, but then he came west and here he's just Tom Doe. He has family money somewhere behind him. His grandfather owned a factory that made buckle tongues. Not buckles, just the little tongue piece that goes in them. Who knew there was money in that? He's six foot six, wears size 15 shoes and his cock is enormous. Go ahead, ask me how I know.

Even through the hormone haze I could see that there wasn't going to be a relationship—there wasn't even going to be a date. That left one thing: steamy, casual sex. Since he clearly wasn't going to invite me to his house, that left his office. It's not an easy prospect, being a corner office with one door and two windows situated between the environmental consultant's and the herb shop. That's not a lot of privacy. I did have one or two things in my favor: February is tough for the tax guys, because they're already swamped, and he'd been sleeping alone for a while. Like I said, it's a small town. So one afternoon during the heat wave I put on a cleavage-enhancing sundress and meandered over there. He looked happy to see me. He always looks happy to see me—for about two minutes. Then he gets nervous. So I figured I had a two-minute window to get some action going. Not a lot of time for a girl to work, so I just walked in and sat down on his lap and nuzzled up to him in a friendly way. Ever since we evolved our big brains we like to use them all the time. But sometimes language is only a hindrance. I kissed his neck and licked inside his ear, and he laughed like he does when he's nervous and doesn't know what to say. But I rolled my hips and wiggled my ass against his cock, and he stopped laughing.

I had just decided I was going to have to suck on his ear all day when he turned his head and—finally!—gave me his mouth. You would not believe the way this man kisses. It's better than ice cream and chocolate and heroin and crack all put together in one big Happy Meal, and at the first slide of his tongue against mine, I went wet and ready. He seemed to have come to a decision, surging against me and pressing himself tightly to my ass. I would have done him right there in the chair, but he jumped up to lock the door. The shades were down, barring the afternoon sunlight. On his way back to me, he stopped, a comically horrified expression on his face, and slapped his palm to his forehead. "I have an appointment in twenty minutes with the head of Sustainable Land Use Today."

I stayed right where I was, splayed out in his chair, dress hiked up, the slick shine of my cunt clearly visible. At least I assume it was, because he looked down and licked his lips and forgot all about his appointment. The phone rang. "Jesus

Christ," he whispered, looking like a man harassed beyond
all endurance.

"Let the machine pick it up," I suggested, and lay back on
his desk with my thighs spread wide. "Come over here and
kiss me again." He did, saying he wanted to have his lips on
every part of my body. So thoughtful of him. But I recom-
mended he start with my clit. I was worried about the time.
When I wouldn't stop groaning, he moved his face from my
crotch and covered my mouth with his. The thick, hard slide
of his cock shut me up. It felt large and perfect and he was
naturally good with it. He fucked like he kissed: with a lot
of enthusiasm and exuberance and natural talent. It made
me want to smile, except that I was so close to coming I
couldn't. Just at the end he let me take all his weight. He had
one hand behind my head and his tongue in my mouth and
his hand on my hip, holding me down to take it. There was
a lot of it to take. I couldn't breathe, but who cared? He let
my mouth go at the last moment, when he felt me clenching around the wet length of him inside me. "Come. Come.
Come," he whispered in my ear, and I did, arching my back
and jerking my hips as close to him as I could get. There was
the wet gust of the two of us combined, and later I would
think about his paperwork, and how much of it got ruined.
But right then I was limp with satisfaction. It passes even
faster than the orgasm, but that feeling of utter peacefulness
after coming is stronger in a different way, and with him it
was very strong.

But he was already standing up and straightening his
clothes and looking at his watch again. He helped me stand
and straighten my clothes. He combed my hair back from
my forehead, running his fingers from the scalp all the way
to the ends, and kissed my forehead and was sweet, but I
knew he wouldn't call, later or ever, and I felt sad. I didn't say

anything, just unlocked the door and let myself out. I passed his two o'clock appointment outside. "Is he ready for me?" he asked, and looked perplexed when I burst out laughing.

"I don't know," I told him honestly. "I think I may have worn him out."

I should have let it go then. You chalk it up to experience and move on. But I just couldn't do it. I woke in the middle of the night from a dream in which he was saying my name, certain that if I just knew the secret, he would accept me. In the daylight, we passed on the street and I smiled and pretended nothing had happened, because he did. I got tired of feeling bad. It occurred to me that I was way too available, way too willing. A man like him did better with someone to chase, someone to convince. I got a little obsessed with the CPA, I will admit. Then I did something inadvisable.

I didn't mean to hire a gigolo.

I was surfing online for someone else to date, and I somehow ended up in the gigolo area. I don't know how that happened. His looks were the clincher. Tall, blond and handsomely sculpted in a Greek god kind of way. He looked perfect for making Mr. CPA jealous. He would be the one thing Tom wasn't: totally obsessed with me, and the fact that I was paying him to be obsessed was a fact that would hopefully never come to light.

After an intriguing phone call, I drove to San Francisco to meet him. Honestly, I liked Val right away. He was funny, for one thing. When I explained my requirements, he perked right up and said, "I love it when I get to act." He gave me a break on the fee, as well, reasoning that he wasn't actually going to fuck me, just parade me around town and look like he'd be fucking me later. And he paid for the coffee. He's one of those people who stops traffic, but he himself seems to view his looks as an asset for his job and nothing more. In forty-five minutes, four people tried to pick him up, and I was right there the entire time.

His coffee cup arrived with the barista's number on it. Instead of being pleased when he noticed it, he merely seemed pained. *Poor guy,* I thought, *he must get it all the time.* I put on my best suit of indignation. "Excuse me!" I hollered at the girl, who was, I have to admit, pretty fetching. "Please stop trying to pick up my boyfriend!" She turned bright red and a general titter ran around the room. "Sorry," I said cheerfully to Val. "My tongue gets away from me."

He wasn't perturbed. "Wingman," he said approvingly. "I like it."

The taxi driver chatted him up and then refused to take the money, which is unheard of. "He is bi," I told him, "but we don't have an open marriage."

"Now we're married?" Val asked, smiling, once we'd reached the sidewalk.

"Anything to help out," I said magnanimously. The salesclerk at Saks (Val needed a tie for dinner) slipped him her number on the receipt. "I'll take that," I snapped. There was a ring right on her finger. "Can I have your husband's number so I can call him?"

This one didn't even blush. "He's busy," she said dismissively. "He won't miss me."

"Jesus Christ," I said outside. "Is this your life?"

"More or less." Val shrugged fatalistically. "You get used to it."

"I wouldn't," I said flatly.

He looked at me thoughtfully. "With that hair, you must have."

I was still staring at him in startled amazement when the traffic cop handed him a blank ticket with her number on it.

My friend Clyde thought the whole thing was crazy—not euphemistically crazy, really crazy. You can tell how far out you are by the reactions of your friends, and from Clyde's reaction, I could tell I was pretty far out. I trust Clyde. I tried to explain. "I'm not done with Tom yet."

"No problem, crazy lady," Clyde said, and ordered another beer. The thing about Clyde is that he can say horrible things that don't sting at all. Clyde started a glassblowing studio in the old livery stable. When I ask him how he is, he says, "If I have to make another unicorn, I'm going to swallow the gather." The gather is the molten ball of glass you pick up on the rod before you blow it into something—in Clyde's case, a unicorn. Or a paperweight. They're big with the tourists. When he drinks too much, he gets morose and compares himself pejoratively to Dale Chihuly, and I point out that Dale Chihuly only has one eye (therefore no depth perception) and hasn't blown his own stuff in years. We have a good time.

"Bound for trouble," Clyde said. "Can I hang out with you guys? I've never met a gigolo before." I assured him he could. I was looking forward to that rumor—me, Clyde and the gigolo in a three-way. That was going to disgust a few people and make a few people really jealous. Clyde and I amused ourselves for a while designating who was going to be which.

By the time Valentine showed up, a few days later, the heat wave had ended. It was winter again. I don't think Valentine is his birth name; he swears it is. In my opinion, it's much more *Miami Vice* to parade around with your gigolo in the sunshine, but the best laid plans of mice, men, desperate women, and so forth. Sunshine is also preferable for hanging out behind the recycling Dumpsters waiting for the CPA to come out of his office for lunch so you can prominently be tongue kissing the guy you hope he thinks is your new squeeze. "Your lips are turning blue," I said to Val. "Should we leave?"

"All in a day's work," he replied easily. We chatted desultorily through stiff lips. He told me about his date. "She liked the tie, thank you." (He let me pick it out. I chose one with leaping frogs on it.) "Sometimes they want dinner first. Sometimes they just want fucking."

"Anything kinky?" I asked hopefully.

His eyebrows went up. "Are you kidding me? It's all kinky." He sighed. "I'd be thrilled with missionary."

"Ever take it up the ass?"

"Man, woman or object?" He sounded a little bored. I guess it was shop talk to him.

I pressed on. "Any of the above."

"Nope. I'm a top."

"You're laughing at me," I accused, and he agreed by laughing some more. It's hard to give a guy a hard time when he's trying not to shiver. I tucked his hands into my armpits, under my coat.

His eyes closed. "Thank you, Lord."

I jumped. "Oh, shit. There he is."

"Action," Val murmured, and took my hand in his. "Which way?"

My guess was the diner, so we headed in that direction, keeping Mr. CPA in sight. Maybe Val's little prayer had some effect, because just before the diner someone flagged Tom and he stopped about twenty paces in front of us. Val put his tongue in my ear, a not unpleasant but so unexpected sensation that I yelped.

"Hussy," he growled. "You love it." Then he dipped me and put his tongue down my throat in what I will have to say was a very genteel manner. It is a small town. Right then, the ridiculousness of the situation—a situation entirely of my own making—struck me. Here I was, on a public street, making out with the gigolo I hired to make the CPA I made out with jealous. Clyde was right. I was crazy. Tom didn't give a damn. If he did, he would have been with me, and I'd spent a chunk of my small savings on a bad idea. I was hard put not to throw up my hands and cry uncle. On the other hand, it takes a lot of man to dip a woman my size and hold her there and kiss the piss out of her, so I put some effort into kissing Val back. The CPA saw. Everyone in the diner saw, which meant it would be all over town well before dark.

Val set me back on my feet. For a talkative man, he'd gone suspiciously quiet. I waited, feeling like all kinds of a fool. "Oh, God," Val said. For a self-professed heathen, he invokes the Lord's name often enough. "I want you," he said wonderingly. "I would love to fuck you—for free, I mean. You wouldn't have to pay me." He turned bright red. "Forget I said that. That was crass. I apologize."

I stared up at him. He has very blue eyes. For the first time in two months there was not a thought of the CPA anywhere in my entire brain. That was worth all my savings alone. And whyever not, I thought, salvage something from the sorry situation I had created? I reached for Val's hand. "You come with me."

Reader, I fucked him.

I took him to the potting shed behind the livery. If the gardener came in, he was going to get an eyeful, but I figured with the glass furnace and the yelling and the testosterone, Clyde and the boys wouldn't hear a thing. Val looked around assessingly, as if we were thinking of buying.

"I'm your present," I said to him patiently. "How would you like it? From the front or from behind?" He had that lovely glazed look in his eyes and his tongue had clearly gotten disconnected from the dictionary part of his brain. He spun his index finger in a circle and I obligingly turned around. I was wearing a skirt and silk long underwear and hiking boots, an outfit I'm not going to explain at the present moment. Val slid his hands up under the skirt and pulled down the long underwear, and since I don't wear panties, there I was. I heard his zipper go down and thought wistfully, *Foreplay, I'll have to get some sometime,* and reminded myself that I was Val's present, he could unwrap me any way he wanted to.

There was a long pause. Apparently, he was one of those people who take a long time unwrapping a gift. Just the thought of having to wait made me twitchy. Suddenly, I didn't want to wait. Val reached around and placed my hands on the galvanized countertop and pulled my hips back against him. He wedged his cock into my ass crack and moved his hips a little. His breath was uneven. "Can't catch anything from me," he huffed in my ear. "The women I sleep with, their doctors go over everything with a fine-tooth comb."

I arched my back a little. "Me, either." Foreplay was a great idea, but when it came right down to it, I didn't seem to need it much. *Please,* I thought. *Pleeease.* But I was his present. He put his cock between my legs and got it wet and slid it back and forth, the fat head of it butting into my clitoris on every stroke. My knees started to buckle and he bit my neck.

"Stand up," he ordered, so I did, holding on until my knuckles turned white. He used his knee to spread my legs farther apart, and surged into me, a long glide that had me groaning. "Hold on," he commanded, and began to thrust; strong, controlled thrusts, when I just wanted him to go faster. He stopped moving and now I was the one to take the Lord's name in vain. He leaned forward, blanketing my back with his chest, and forced his thumb up inside me, alongside his cock. My breath escaped in a hiss. "Easy," was all he said. He put his index finger on my clit, and every time he thrust, his thumb pressed hard on my G-spot and his fingertip rolled over my clit.

I came, if you could call it that. It wasn't like any orgasm I've ever had. It was a body-gasm. Every single cell in my body contracted inward as far as it could possibly go and then exploded. I don't remember being moved, but when I was aware of the world again, I was lying on my back on a wooden table. Val was standing between my legs, still pole-hard inside me. "Did you come?" I asked, and he nodded.

He watched me, looking like a very serious schoolboy. "I like you," he said shyly.

"Well, I like you, too," I said weakly. I waved a hand. "Don't stop on my account." His whole face lit up and he moved, thrusting in and out slowly, a dreamy, concentrated expression on his face. His hair had gone damp with sweat and was sticking to his forehead, masking the blue of his eyes. I certainly wasn't going to come again, but I was kind of enthralled by Val, and a little sorry I'd missed his first climax, and looking forward to the second. I found enough strength to raise my legs and press them against his hips, logistically possible because he'd cleverly stepped inside the band of silk around my ankles. "Those boots have to go," he said, and I laughed softly.

All this sex was making me happy.

It was like being rocked on the ocean, but after a while he made a vee of his fingers and placed one on either side of my clit, low down at the base, where it's not so sensitive. Then it was like being ridden, those relentless fingers clasping me on the outside and his cock working me on the inside. "Val," I said, pleading.

"No." He was easygoing in temperament except, apparently, during sex. Was now really the time to find out? "Wait and come *with* me."

I started grinding my hips into the table to get them lower so his fingers would be higher, and thought, *Splinters!* And nothing else. I tried sitting up and he just placed one big hand flat on my chest and pushed me back down and pinched my nipples until I tried to bite him. I spun out a bunch of dirty talk to try and make him come faster.

"Heard it all," he muttered, and finally I gave up and lay back with one arm over my eyes and let it build and build and build. He slowed, moved his fingers and picked up again. I lasted maybe two strokes and dissolved with him, as requested.

"Bastard," I said when I could talk. "I'm *not* paying you for that."

He'd joined me on the table, and while it doesn't sound cozy, it strangely was. "Too late, Cass," he said smugly, his hand resting lightly over my pubic bone. "I already cashed your check."

All's well that ends well, they say.

The CPA and I went back to ignoring each other. Clyde got a showing of his high-end stuff at a fancy gallery in the city, and he's making unicorns and paperweights with joy in his heart. I went back to the battle plans with the Tarweed and tea with George.

Valentine is an ex-gigolo. The ring on my finger says so. He only gets kinky with me now, and once in a while, when he's lucky, I let him do missionary.

Strippers and Cigars

N. T. Morley

Jason had told Mike and Paul a thousand times, in a thousand different ways: no goddamn strippers. Really. None. Nada. Nyet. Nein. Not a single stripper. Not one. Not even if she was really cute.

He'd fucking *told* them.

Sure, Annie had encouraged him to have a bachelor party—hell, she had practically *demanded* that he have one—but never once had she said the word *stripper,* and Jason hadn't had the guts to bring it up. When Paul and Mike had said they were handling everything, he told them unequivocally: no strippers.

They had hemmed and hawed, argued and bellyached, explained to Jason in as many different ways as they could manage why it wasn't *really* cheating to get a lap dance from a college student in a G-string, why they were totally sure that Annie wouldn't mind. They'd tried to figure ways around his rule—what if she didn't strip, but showed up naked? What if she didn't strip, but just undressed? What if she stripped, but she wasn't a stripper—she was just, you know, a secretary, sexy maid or schoolgirl?

When that hadn't worked, they'd complained about how he was ruining everyone else's fun, about how now that they were all married with kids, they *never* had the time or money to go to strip clubs. He was the Last Man Standing; hopefully this would be the last bachelor party for a hell of a long time. Was Jason really going to deny them their one chance to give him a royal send-off?

None of those arguments swayed Jason. And even though they encouraged him to ask her, he wasn't about to bring the matter up with Annie.

So it was decided, unilaterally: a little party at Mike and Mary's house, guys only, a few TVs scattered around the room playing washed-out DVD porn as a weak homage to their vanishing youthful sexual exuberance. Maybe some cards, Cuban cigars, stag gifts, dirty jokes, that short of shit. And lots of fine tequila.

Which was where the trouble really began. Because by the time the stripper showed up, Jason was hammered. He hadn't drunk tequila in years, and he'd forgotten how good that burn felt going down your throat, how intense the salty taste of lime could be mingled with Cuervo. *Stripper? Did I say I didn't want a stripper? Wait, I did say that, I don't want a stripper, but hell, another shot? Sure!*

But Jason still would not have crossed that line; he was all about Annie, and there wasn't enough tequila in the world to make him go elsewhere for his stimulation. But what the tequila *did* do was make him think the best of his friends when they shuffled him out onto the sundeck to check out Liz's flower garden. "Flower garden? Sure, I guess…" said Jason, and he was out.

He should have known. Like Mike or any of them gave a flying fuck about his wife's flower garden. Of course, Mike was extra sure to close the sliding glass door and take Jason around the far side of the deck; when they came back in, the door to the bedroom was closed.

He figured it was some kind of a cheesy gift—who knows, an inflatable penis or something? His friends would never fuck him over and trick him into cheating on his fiancée—would they?

But then, after another fifteen minutes of tequila slammers, Mike leaned close in the smoke-filled room and said, "You ready for the main event?"

"No," slurred Jase drunkenly. "Oh no you di-int."

"Don't try to talk like a twenty-year-old black girl, Jason. It's undignified."

"You didn't."

"Did."

"No. No. You're not hearing me. You didn't."

"Yes. Yes. I'm hearing you. We did."

"I told you *no,*" he said. "Stripper, no no no."

"Tequila, yes, yes, yes," said Mike. "And stripper—"

"No," said Jason.

"Relax, tight-ass. We checked it out with your betrothed. She said it was fine."

"Bull *shit,*" Jason said. "Really?"

"I swear it on the grave of my virginity. She said to get you liquored up and let some stripper slut leave perfume on your crotch. She said some other stuff…not yet rated. She's a pistol, that one."

"Excuse me, what?"

"Hey, don't blame me," Mike said, "if your girl's a potty mouth."

The other guys were cackling like biddies, telling the one about the blonde painting the porch ("It's not a Porsche! It's a BMW!"). Jason muttered something about sexist pigs, stood up and stalked over to Paul, who was puffing drunkenly on his Cuban.

Before Jason could say a word, "You're welcome," Paul said. He kicked a chair over and pushed Jason toward it. "Now sit there and enjoy your stripper."

"Annie really said it's okay?"

"You believe this guy?" Paul groaned.

Jason sat down guiltily.

"Now, as you know," Paul said, as if he were reading from the Bible, "our good friend Jason Samuel Carson III is about to kiss his bachelorhood goodbye and spend the rest of his life dragging around the best-looking, sweetest and most kind-hearted ball and chain in the western United States."

"Fuck you," slurred Jason. "Ball and chain, fuck you. Best in *all* the States. Fuck you."

"But before you do, Jason, we'd like to send your un-grateful ass off with a little gift from your best friends in the world. One last sultry night of unspeakable delectation with the lusty temptress of all married men's fantasies—Trixie."

The partygoers erupted into hoots and howls, clapping furiously, making fools of themselves as best they were able, now that the tequila had taken its toll. "Strip-*per,* strip-*per,* strip-*per!*" They started chanting like sex-drunk frat boys, until Paul shut them up.

"Now, I don't mean to encourage temptation, Jase, because I know you're the most faithful fiancé there is, but there's one piece of information that I'd like to tell you. Well, two, actually. The first one is that because this is a private party, there is no need to worry about that liquor-and-G-string crap. That's right, boys, Trixie's G-string comes off."

The drunken chants came: "Pink! Pink! Pink! Pink!"

"Christ, did you guys eat a box of old *Penthouse Letters?*" Jason grumbled.

"And the second thing," Paul said, "Trixie doesn't usually do full service. But tonight—"

"Full service? No. No!" moaned Jason miserably. "Not interested."

"You haven't seen her."

"I don't need to see her."

"I think you do."

"I really don't."

"You really do," Paul said. "And besides, she's already been paid."

"You might want to get your money back."

"So, Jason, just let nature take its course. We all know you love Annie, but once you see Trixie—trust me, you will not resist this girl. You are duty bound to take her in the back room and—"

"Please, my virgin ears," Jason said sourly.

"I even changed the sheets!" Mike howled.

"Disgusting." Jason sighed. "Look, I'll let her dance for me, but—"

Paul got down in Jason's face. "Wait until you see her, Jase. Those tits! Those hips! That ass! She's got a great ass!" He was bellowing. "You'll change your tune! Let's have her out!"

"Thank you, Nicholas Cage," Jason said with a frown.

A slow, grinding techno rhythm pulsed through the room. Mike turned it up louder and louder until the whole room was vibrating and Jason could feel the beat in his breastbone. The roomful of guys clapped, shouting and chanting rhythmically, except that they were so drunk they all started chanting different things, some of them "strip-*per,*" others "Trix-*ie!*" still others "hoo-yah, hoo-yah, hoo-yah," as if reliving their Navy days, which to Jason's knowledge none of them had ever experienced.

"Don't you have neighbors?" shouted Jason.

"Shut up and cheat on your girlfriend, bitch!"

Paul dimmed the lights as the door to the bedroom opened; Mike had rigged a photoflood as a makeshift spotlight, illuminating the unbelievably hot female form standing there: *Trixie.* Jason's eyes went wide. Christ, she really was gorgeous! Long, raven-black hair, pale skin, full lips painted whore red, knockout body displayed in a tight spandex minidress that laced up the front so tight that her tits were spilling out everywhere. Her nipples were evident under the spandex, hard despite the oppressive heat in the house. The dress clung to her hips and was decent by perhaps an inch. Her magnificent thighs were almost totally revealed, and she didn't have stockings. Instead, she wore knee-high patent leather laceups, pointy-toed with impossibly high heels, but she stood on them gracefully—as if she'd had an awful lot of practice.

Jason knew right then he *did* want to fuck Trixie silly—right on Mike's bed. It would serve Annie right! Every face in the room was turned toward him as the music pounded. Jason turned a million shades of red and buried his face in his hands as the place erupted in shouts, cackles, guffaws and applause so loud it almost drowned out the deafening music.

"He likes her!" someone shouted. "He likes her!"

Trixie came for him, her hips swaying with every step; she wiggled her tits and ran her hands down her tightly clad body.

He racked his brains, momentarily trying to remember if he'd ever gotten hard in front of so many other guys before—certainly not in a strip club, that was for sure. This time, though, his cock sprang to attention instantly as Trixie closed on him and let her hips grind with the music. Her body undulated in a smooth rhythm; she twirled and pumped in a come-on.

Mike had cleared the heavy wooden coffee table. Trixie used it for her platform; she jumped up on it, started writhing. She was not an expert dancer; as a matter of fact, she wasn't even very good, but Jason didn't care. He wanted her; he was fiercely turned on, and wanted to see more. She began to toy with the laces of her dress. *She's really going to take her clothes off!* Jason thought. Which was what strippers do, so it shouldn't have surprised him—but holy shit, she was really doing it. *What the hell,* he thought. *Let 'em look.* She tugged open the dress and popped her full, round, firm and perfect breasts out.

The guys all hooted. Trixie's eyes flickered over the front of his pants and—yeah, she knew he was hard. She smiled. *Good God, those things are perfect,* thought Jason.

Trixie descended from the coffee table; she didn't do it very gracefully, but to him it looked gorgeous. Trixie sashayed to him, leaned over and called out, "Hands at your sides, cowboy!" over the music. Jason obediently put his hands at his sides and Trixie lowered her breasts into his face, almost to his lips. He leaned his head forward eagerly, opening his mouth to capture one of those perfect, hard pink nipples. But Trixie pulled away just before his lips could make contact. She made a no-no-no gesture with her finger and shot him a wry, seductive smile. She sat down on the coffee table and spread her legs wide, aiming her crotch at Jason; he could see right up her skirt to the snug G-string beyond.

His friends were shouting, "Take it off! Off! Off!" Her black G-string was mesh and practically see-through; he could catch the contours of her pale pink lips beneath it and admire her glorious ass. Trixie wriggled the skintight minidress down her body. It slid easily down her thighs and she dangled it from one toe before tossing it straight at Jason.

The dress hit him in the face. Even over the reek of tequila and cigars, he could smell the perfume of her sweat and the faint hint of her sex.

"Give me that!" shouted Paul, and snatched the dress off Jason's head to toss to the cheering men. They passed the dress around, huffing it.

Hey, let 'em smell, Jason thought. *I get to taste.*

Now Trixie was naked except for her G-string and boots. She had her booted feet tucked under her ass, with her legs spread. She lifted her lower body off the coffee table, pumping in time with the music. It looked as if she was fucking someone, and the rhythm was familiar to Jason—so much so that it made his cock surge. Her fingers splayed between her legs, stroking her mesh-clad pussy up and down with one hand as she played with her tits with the other. Her magnificent curtain of black hair swayed back and forth very close to Mike and Dave and Simon, her tits within easy reach—but everyone kept their hands to themselves.

Trixie eased off the table, swaying over to Jason, the dancing awkward, even forced, but the girl nonetheless irresistible. She faced away from him, planted her booted feet firmly on either side of his and spread her legs wide. She pushed her ass into his face. His hands came up and rested on her hips, and that first touch between them was electric. When he leaned forward, he could smell her pussy. Trixie lowered her ass into Jason's lap.

The smooth cheeks of her ass rubbed against his hard-on. She rocked back and forth in time to the music, and Jason knew he would shoot in his pants if she kept that up. But then she sat squarely in his lap and lifted her feet off the ground, propping her legs over the arms of the chair as the guys around the room cheered. She leaned back and Jason could smell her again, sweat and a faint hint of perfume, an unfamiliar scent that made his pulse quicken. Trixie's face came close to his as she rested her head on his shoulder, her raven hair tickling one cheek as she reached back with her hand to caress the other.

"Fuck me?" begged Jason. "Fuck me now? Please?"

Trixie responded by grinding her ass quicker, jiggling her body and rubbing his hard-on dangerously close to orgasm. He closed his eyes and felt her all over him, smelling her, wanting to taste her. He was going to come.

But Trixie seemed to sense the exact instant when his climax would have erupted. She pulled herself off him at the very last moment. She stood over him and smirked at him as she draped her tits in his face; this time she didn't pull away when his lips closed over her nipple. She let him lick, then straightened up and laughed flirtatiously.

Then, that final moment came—the promised moment that never happened in clubs. Trixie slipped her thumbs under the sides of her G-string.

"Let's go commando, shall we?" she cried over the pulsing music.

Jason drooled.

Her hips swayed back and forth as the music pulsed through her. She tugged the G-string down just a little—just a tiny, tiny bit—then let it inch back up. She turned around and showed Jason her ass, that glorious ass that had just been pressed against his cock. She bent over, squirming, as she took the G-string down an inch—two inches. Then, over her ass, down her thighs, over her calves. She stepped out of it.

Trixie picked up her G-string and turned around, covering her pussy with one hand as she inched closer to Jason, dancing. He stared at her, transfixed. Still covering her sex, she leaned close and draped the G-string in his face.

He could smell her pussy strongly now; the G-string was soaked through.

Someone chanted, "Pantie sniffer!"

Trixie sat in his lap, facing him, her perfect breasts in his face. She wrapped her legs around him, hugged him tight and ground her crotch against his hard-on.

"Please don't make me come," he begged over the music. "I want to put it in you."

"Do you?" Trixie asked flirtatiously. Then, tenderly, she bent down and gave Jason a kiss on the lips—dry, no tongue. It was the most exquisite kiss he had ever received.

Trixie's hand went between them. Her finger slipped between her pussy lips, came up glistening. She slid it between Jason's lips and he thought he would explode. She moved it deeper and he tasted her—sharp, salty, musky, strong.

"Please let me fuck you," Jason said.

The music ended.

"Congratulations," she whispered. "Your girl must be so open-minded."

"Don't I know it," he said, his ears ringing.

Trixie took his hand and pulled him up, leading him toward the bedroom. The guys all chanted different things, some "Consummate!" some "Fuck her!" someone "Sex her up!" (Huh? thought Jason.) Trixie led him to the bedroom and dragged him inside, slamming the door.

Mike had changed the sheets, all right, but they never made it under the covers. The second the door was closed, Trixie had Jason on the bed and was atop him. Naked except for her gorgeous, kinky boots, she spread her legs over his crotch and draped her breasts, full and lovely, in his face. He suckled one nipple into his mouth as she groped desperately at his belt and zipper, as if not getting him inside her in an instant would drive her completely insane. She moaned as she took out his hard cock, started sliding her mouth up and down on him. He closed his eyes and moaned as the sounds of the party got going again in the living room. Trixie moved up gracefully and spread her legs around his head, dipping her pussy onto his face as she descended on his cock again. His tongue delved hungrily between her lips. She devoured his cock as her hips pumped in time with Jason's tongue. He found her clit and greedily licked it, but he was so fucking close.

"Please don't make me come yet," he gasped.

"Oh," she whimpered, pouting. "But I want to."

"Fuck me," begged Jason.

"Not yet. Lick me," purred Trixie, and ground her pussy down onto his face. He started working her clit, his tongue seething against her rhythmically. He felt her lower body pumping against him as she got closer—and then she came, her whole body shuddering on top of him as he kept licking her desperately.

Still shaking, mad with lust, Trixie turned around and spread her legs for him, sliding his cock up to her pussy and fitting it between her swollen lips.

"Congratulations," she breathed as she sank down on him. "And many happy returns."

She was dripping wet; her snug sex gripped him tightly, still clenching rhythmically from her orgasm as she began to fuck Jason. Her lower body rose and fell as she pinned him down and worked him hungrily, cradling his head and guiding his mouth to her breasts. He sucked her nipples and tried to hold still, but couldn't; he started pumping up into her, meeting each stroke. Then Jason cried out, climaxing, coming inside Trixie, so loudly that his friends outside started cheering. *Well, they asked for it,* he thought. He panted heavily as he finished, looking up into her gorgeous face and wanting ever more of her.

He rolled her onto her side, his cock popping out of her as he caressed her face.

"You little vixen," he said. "Now all my friends have seen you naked."

"Yeah, so they have," she said. "What was I supposed to do? You said you didn't want a stripper," said Trixie. "And you can tell from my dancing that I'm not one."

"You did great," breathed Jason. "More."

"Oh, I'll dance for you, cowboy," she said, stroking his face. "I'll dance for you plenty. Once that ring is on my finger, there'll be a lot of dancing."

"Is that right?"

She purred and thrust herself on Jason, kissing him.

"Every night, cowboy. Every night."

Something Blue

Shanna Germain

"Oh, for fuck's sake, Mom. Quit with the perfume. I smell like a bouquet of dead flowers."

My mom *tsked* her tongue in that way only Italian mothers can, and waved the crystal perfume bottle at me the way I imagine mothers have waved things at their daughters since we evolved into opposable-thumbed creatures. And possibly before.

"Nonsense," she said. "You smell beautiful. Like lilies. Lilies for my Lily."

"Oh, Ma…" I groaned at her words, then lifted my arm and sniffed at the recently sprayed skin. My nose wrinkled without me telling it to. "You're right, I don't smell like dead flowers. I smell like flowers *for* the dead. Just perfect."

The only good thing was that I hadn't got my dress on yet. Instead, I was standing in the bedroom that Thad and I shared, wearing the only set of pure-white lingerie I'd ever owned, letting my mom ease her prewedding jitters by pulling various beauty implements out of her Mary Poppins-like makeup bag. She'd already scrubbed my face and neck with some rose-waterish gel, then tried to pluck my eyebrows, proclaiming, "You could be so beautiful if you just took more time." And now she was making me smell like dead things. If I didn't know this was probably the most important day of her life, at least since her own wedding thirty-some years ago, I'd think she was trying to sabotage me.

It was still two hours before the wedding, which left me plenty of time to wash the scent off. If I could just keep her from spraying the lacy bra and panties, that was.

As she looked at me, my mom's lids got pink around the bottom, the way they sometimes did. I guessed she was thinking of my dad, a lithe, energetic man with a wicked sense of humor, who'd died four years too early to see his daughter married off. We both missed him—and I know he would have liked Thad, even though that old adage about marrying your father hadn't come true; they were nothing alike.

My mom sniffed and then spritzed me with another dose of lily-scented perfume, either so she wouldn't cry or in the hopes that she could sink it so deep into my skin that I'd never be able to get it off. I ducked my head just as her finger hit the trigger, and the spray caught me in the corner of my mouth, a gagging mist of scent that choked any words of comfort right out of me. Not that I would have comforted her, truly. I was actually thinking of saying something along the lines of "I knew we should have eloped."

But by then my mom was already going full torrent on to the next phase of her project, having abandoned the perfume bottle on the dresser for a mascara wand, which was bearing down on my left eye.

I caught her wrist just before the wand made its way to cornea-scratching distance.

"Ma," I said. "I'll do it. I'd like to have both eyes to see as I walk down the aisle."

Her Italian came out at most weddings, anyway. Now that it was her daughter's big day, the accent and the worry were in full force. *"Bella…"* she said. "I just want it to be perfect. And you—" she threatened my eye with the mascara wand again "—to be perfect."

I gently wrestled the black-tipped dagger from her perfectly pinked nails. "I *am* perfect, Ma. Thad thinks so. That's what matters, right?"

She tugged on the corner of my panties with two pinched fingers—the oddest sensation ever, I have to admit, having your mother's fingers on your underwear—pulling them down off my hip just so she could pull them back up.

She gave another little *tsk* at my words, but this time her reaction was fake. The Italian equivalent of warding demons away from a beautiful baby girl by naming her Ugly One That No One Wants. My mom liked Thad. She had since the day he met her, when he sat his tall, wide-shouldered frame at her dining room table, put his napkin in his lap and ate four helpings of her sausage-packed lasagna. Never having to say a word—his actions, and those baby blue eyes of his beneath his pale bangs, melting my mom easy as butter. "You know, if you dump this one, I'm going to keep him in the family and disown you," she'd told me on the phone the next day.

I had no doubt she meant it.

Of course, she didn't know Thad like I did. Which meant that she didn't know his vision of me as perfection had nothing to do with white dresses or lilies or whether I'd let her attack me with makeup implements. Thad liked me dirty, the messier the better. In leather, not lace. Trussed up in black, lipstick smeared, and kneeling at his feet. He didn't care about dresses or cakes or flower girls. He'd said so to me once; in the middle of another endless discussion with my mother about cake colors, he'd pulled me into the hall-way, pressed me hard against the wall with a loud enough thud that I was afraid my mother could hear two rooms over. Whispering his lips along the curl of my ear in that way that made his short whiskers rub sharp against my cheek, each word punctuated with a drag of his hardening cock along the fabric between my thighs. "Lil, let me marry you all trussed up… Cuffs. Collar. My fists in your hair. My cock in your throat. No one else has to come.…"

I'd had to moan before I could answer—the kind of moan that arises out of nowhere, conjured as much from his words as from his actions. A moan low and aching in my throat, one I tried to swallow back even as it rose, unbidden, into the air between us. I followed it with a laugh, a shake of my head, a whispered tease. "If we got married like that, I'd hope we'd be the only ones who'd come."

God, that wicked, wicked grin of his. The way it starts at the edges of his cheekbones instead of his lips, spreads inward to his mouth, knife-sharp from his knowledge of what I want. A hand burying itself in my dark curls to tug my head sideways. "Oh, yes," he said, pushing forward so that his hard cock dug into me, seemed to bruise my very center. "We both would. More than once… Lil, let's just skip all this. I'll wrap your wrists in leather, fuck you till you scream 'I do.' That's good enough for me. Please…"

His words made me want to say yes. He so rarely said, "Please." Usually it was me begging that word. *Please fuck me. Please let me suck you. Please, yes,* when he reached into the closet for his favorite long crop. *Please, harder,* with his nails at my nipples.

From the other room, my mom had cleared her throat. The sound pulled me back to the hard roll of Thad's hips against mine, the hand still fisted in my hair, the shuddered exhalation that was slipping through my lips. I shook my head, despite his grip in my strands, cocking my chin in the direction of my mom, sitting in the kitchen by herself debating yellow daisies versus purple-blue irises. I'd voiced my preference for the purple, but I could already tell I'd be getting butter-yellow.

"We can't," I said, whispering for no reason at all. I wanted to. Oh, I wanted. But it wasn't just about disappointing my mom, my whole family. It was also that I found something appealing about the whole miserable white wedding drama. The whole thing was so pure, so perfect and pretty and wholesome, and I was none of those things. I had this image of me, dirty and soiled, skin bruised by his hands and leather, all hidden inside the white folds of lace and silk. Like a perfectly frosted wedding cake that, when you cut it open, revealed not a sugary-sweet vanilla, but a darkly spiced chocolate, soaked in rum.

"I know. The pure wedding for my impure slut," he'd said, and I knew that, like always, he understood exactly what I wanted. He gave another thump of his erection into my hip, hard enough to send a shiver up my spine, his voice hissing into the hollow of my ear. "Let's go tell your mom the daisies are fine. I'll decorate your ass with enough blue blooms to make up for it when we get home."

He had, of course, done as promised. The flat of his hand sinking into the curves of my flesh with that repetition that I love. The sound of my skin pinkening and then purpling. My fingers on my clit when he said I could. His voice in my ear, whispering through his teeth, growling, "Lil, Lil, Lily..." as I came.

Now, my mom, unswayed either by my plea or by my stealing her tools, was setting to work laying out more weapons of torture—this new set designed to tame my unruly brown curls into something resembling what a woman more innocent than myself might wear. Flattening iron, curling iron, six kinds of hair spray, four kinds of mousse.

She recited the litany of steps as though she'd had to memorize it. "Mousse first, then flat, then curl, then spray." The mousse came out of the can in a huge, pink lump onto my mom's palm. We both looked at it for a moment in silence as it seemed to shift and settle, some creature out of the Pink Lagoon.

Then I couldn't help it. I started laughing. "Oh my god, Ma," I said. "Enough. Enough."

"But your hair. It's all—" she gestured around her head with her unmoussed hand "—wild."

"I know. It's okay. Why don't you take a break? Go make some coffee. Fuss over Grandpa or something."

She looked uncertain, holding up the moussed hand. "What do I do with this?"

I tried not to grin. She'd spent two months planning this event down to the last detail, and now she was so nervous she couldn't handle basic functions. I swept the mousse off her palm and rubbed it into the ends of my hair before pushing it all off my face into a loose bun. "There," I said.

"It's still..." Unable to resist, she pushed her fingers into my now sticky strands, sending hair every which way.

I gently pried her off and turned her toward the door, a hand on each shoulder. "Go. Now. I'll be fine. Just, please, send Thad in."

"But you're in your—"

"I know, Ma. He's seen me in my undies before."

She uttered a tiny squeak of protest as she slipped out the door, but she must have passed the message along, because a few minutes later, there was a knock on the door. Thad peeked his head in, blue eyes filled with an impish glint. Cocking a brow at the white-on-white pantie and bra ensemble, he slid his whole body inside the room in one fluid, easy movement. I was glad to see he wasn't dressed up yet, either—still in a T-shirt and jeans, my favorite leather belt looped around his waist.

He took one look at me...and laughed. The bastard. "Holy coif," he said, his blue eyes bordered with a thread of dark mischief.

"Save me," I said, laughing myself, holding out an arm for him to sniff.

He smelled my skin, and I could feel his lips brush it, soft as a wing. "You smell like a funeral parlor."

"I know. Isn't it awful?"

"Yes." With that single word, his voice hardened, that delicious rasp that changed everything between us, that took away the equality and turned us into what we truly were. Master. Slave. And beneath his word, another sound—his fingers clicking the bedroom lock closed.

Yes.

Click.

I shivered in my pristine undies, wrapped my arms around my body to hold myself still, watching him.

"You know, I can't have you like this, right?" He took another step forward, until I could smell his skin even through the mist of gag-me-lilies that surrounded me. He smelled of pine sap and shaving cream and leather, always. I could catch a whiff of any one of those scents, anywhere—the grocery store, a restaurant, on a walk through the woods—and I would instantly want to be on my knees, drawing my tongue along the length of Thad's cock. When he was here, all three combined were enough to make me instantly wet. I could feel the moisture already coating the white satin between my legs, ruining the fabric.

He stopped in front of me, crossing his arms over his chest as his blue eyes slowly rose up my body, a trail of goose bumps following in the wake of his gaze.

"I'll tolerate you all pure on the outside, in the white dress and white undies and the—" he reached and fisted his hands over the loose bun, giving a tug that sent my hair tumbling about my shoulders and drew prickles of mild pain along my scalp "—almost tame hair. But…"

He leaned in, bit the thumping pulse at the side of my neck, held it in the soft grip of his teeth for one beat, two beats, before he let go, his words whispering along my marked skin. My nipples puckered at the heat of his breath. "I want you dirty and dark on the inside. Bruised and naughty. Like you really are…"

"Oh…" I said. I thought he'd tell me to go down on him. I could taste him already, the salted caramel of his arousal, could feel the curve of his cock against the roof of my mouth. "Yes, yes, please…"

But he didn't. Instead, he turned me, using his grip on my hair to make me pirouette like a doll until I faced the bed, his hips sinking forward into the curves of my ass so I could feel his cock, canting to the left, the already throbbing pulse of it pressing through the skimpy satin.

"Take hold," he said, using his free hand to move one of mine to the bedpost, showing me how he wanted it, the other still buried in my hair, pulling my head back, curving my spine the way he liked it, until my whole body was a soft C, all hips and ass against him. I put both hands on the post, wrapping my palms around the wood as I would around his cock, my thumbs softly stroking its curves. He gave a low grunt of approval at my position, then stepped back. My ass felt cold without his pressure there, and I wiggled in protest.

The sound of his belt stopped my movement. No man I'd ever known before Thad could make me nearly come with that sound alone. I'd once joked it was the real reason I was going to marry him. He did it one-handed, the other still buried in my hair. The sound of the buckle first, metal jingling against leather and flesh. Then he did this slow, slow slide, leather hard against the denim, one loop at a time. So slow I ached for the sound of the next pull, the next loop, ached to hear that final tug that meant the leather was in his hands and would be against my ass.

He bent over me, chest to back, threaded the belt through my legs, catching the white satin and my own shaved heat, pulling upward so that I squirmed against the thick strip of leather, trying to ease my ache.

"Dirty," he whispered in my ear. And I was. I wanted to be.

Pulling the belt along my cleft, he replaced the material with two fingers, digging beneath the fabric, sinking them into me without warning, so hard I cried out at the feel of it.

"Hush," he said, and his voice, the low crack of the belt, the curl of his fingers, all landed at once. My skin broke open everywhere, bloomed with a pain that made me want to shift away from his stroke and lean into it all at once. The next pain followed only a second after, then the next, mixing together until I couldn't tell which was which. He kept at it, fingers scissoring inside me, the strokes of the belt moving across my ass, never landing the same place twice, each pain a new and pronounced pop against my skin. My palms were sweating, wetting the wooden headboard, and I gripped tighter, trying not to slip. His thumb angled up, circled the tight point of my clit, making it beat a stuttered rhythm of want that matched each fall of the leather.

When he finally stopped—just with the belt, not with his fingers—I could hear us both panting. My head was down, the black that seeped into my vision keeping out all light, reducing me to little more than a tiny pinpoint of pleasure.

"More?" he asked between breaths, with that broken edge to his voice that I loved to hear.

I panted, a low wheeze of pleasure that rose from deep in my throat. "More," I begged.

"Sorry, baby," he said. "Not now."

I tried to protest, but he turned me, as quick as that, steering me back by the hair until my ass was pressed against the footboard. Every sting and bruise and welt came back to life as he held me to the wood, pushed me along it until I was down on my knees. By the time I was all the way down, he had his jeans undone and the base of his cock in one hand, the long shaft pulsing in his hold.

"Suck me," he said. "Say 'I do' with your mouth...."

Lifting my chin, I coiled my tongue along the smooth head, into that place just beneath the ridge that made him growl low in his throat and push harder between my lips. I took him in, the way he'd taught me once, so long ago, tilting my throat back, letting him inch deep and deeper, swallowing against his tip. I love it like that, when he goes slow, when I can feel the veins, the smooth curve of his head sliding...sliding over my lips, along my tongue, against the ridges of the roof of my mouth. He tasted of salted fig, meaty and sweet.

"Ah, fuck, Lil," he said, his fingers buried in my hair, hips speeding up as he began to fuck my throat. The way he says my name sometimes, like when he's fucking me, or when he's just looking at me with that wolfish grin, I'd swear it was enough to get me off. I had to sneak a hand down, sink it into the silk, two fingers curling to replace where his had been.

"Oh, no. No you don't," he said, the fist in my hair pulling my mouth off his cock, my tongue snaking out into the widening distance, trying to lap at him. "That's my job." He's grinning down at me with those blue eyes, not master now, but equal. Wanting like a boy. And then we were both laughing as he lifted me by the shoulders and spun me, the next step in our ever-changing dance.

He laid me facedown on the bed, and followed me, lifting my hips with a hard clasp of his fingers into the skin, the tip of him already butting against my heat. I leaned hard into him, wanting him so fiercely that I could already hear myself begging, a low whispered plea that chanted from my lips.

"Please, what?" he said, centering his tip against me, teasing and teasing with that soft curved skin. Every time I arced back into him, he leaned back, too, keeping himself poised there. "Please, what, Lil?" His fingers traced my curves, his touch too light.

I dropped my forehead to the bedding, my cheeks hot. He knew what I wanted—he always knew. Why did he make me ask? I shook my head. I wouldn't.

But his fingers were circling and circling, dropping down my curves to center over my clit, just one hard flick against the sensitive skin. My nerves sang and I parted my lips with a ragged groan of pleasure. I knew that I'd always give him what he asked for, what we both wanted. "Please fuck me, please, please…"

He slid into me on the first "please," filled me until I couldn't breathe, pulling all the way out on each backward stroke, thrusting to the hilt again on each of my words, his rhythm low and hard. One hand still worked my clit—flick and circle, flick and circle—and the other swung against the bottom of my ass. A careful hit—the sound of the slap dulled by his flattened palm—but each sting on my already marked skin made me bite the bedding, trying to quell my rising howls so the whole house wouldn't hear.

He switched suddenly, the hand at my ass digging in, nails piercing my skin, pulling me back, while the one at my clit folded, his fingers falling onto the peak of skin with a hard slap that sent sharp-edged streamers through me, paper cuts of pleasure that slid beneath my skin. My orgasm opened like a dark bloom, spread outward in petals and thorns. "Fuck, Lil," he said again, his voice tight through his clenched jaw, and then he came with a low groan; his hips bucking hard against my curves, filling me.

It was a long time before I could speak again, our fast breaths the only sound in the room. My ass prickled and burned from the way he'd worked me with the belt and his hands. And I could feel my hair, wildly tousled, sticking to my face. The room—and my skin—smelled of lust and leather and come.

He pulled from me, a movement that left me empty. A few fingers stroked the curves of my ass, pushed in against the hot spots, made a bruised ache spread beneath my flesh. I knew it wouldn't be long before my skin was mottled and purpled, flowering bruises shaped like his hands and belt and nails.

"My dirty slut bride," he said, and the thrum in his voice made me want to fuck him all over again. I rolled over, facing him, and he leaned down to kiss me the way I liked—mostly teeth and the hard push of his mouth, as if to eat me up.

My mom got her wish in the end—her daughter, all decked in white, my hair tamed into a low bun at the back of my neck, wearing tiny pearls in my ears and a bit of mascara on my lashes.

I got my wish, too, truly. Walking down the aisle slowly—partly because I was afraid I would fall in my high heels, but mainly because I wanted to savor every moment. The way Thad's blue eyes looked at me, at all of me, knowing what was beneath the white, and wanting me anyway. The scent of sex and leather beneath the odor of lilies. The way my panties pressed, damp and coated, between my legs. And with every step I took, the brush of white satin over my bruised ass, sending blooms of pleasure and pain over my skin. My hands clutched a bouquet of white daisies, but I knew the real bouquet was underneath, planted on my pale skin, a testament to love and lust and what it really means to say "I do."

Speak Now

Heidi Champa

When the oversize envelope came in the mail, I knew right away what it was. That didn't stop me from burying it under a pile of junk mail and bills, believing the old adage—out of sight, out of mind. It didn't work. Despite the layers of paper hiding it, the wedding invitation was fresh in my mind every minute. Trevor and Jessica were finally tying the knot. I knew hiding from it was childish, but it was the only thing getting me through the day.

It's not like I didn't know it was happening. They had been dating on and off since college. Plus, I'd heard through my mother's ever-vigilant grapevine all the details of their engagement and the lead-up to their wedding. Since I hadn't settled down and given her the chance to play mother of the groom, she had no choice but to covet other people's good news.

"Greg, did I tell you, Trevor and Jessica are having their reception at the country club?"

She told me with as much gusto as she could muster, trying to get me to commit to coming home for the blessed event. My mother had called me no less than ten times, wondering why I hadn't responded to the invitation. I knew I could avoid it, make an excuse not to show up. Distance was on my side. But I had to go.

Before I could change my mind, I dropped the response card into the mailbox. It was done. I was driving five hundred miles to watch the man of my dreams marry the woman of his. I packed up the car, carefully hanging my freshly pressed suit in the backseat. Shaking my head, I pulled away from the garage, leaving behind the city, my apartment and clearly, my sanity.

I hadn't been home in almost a year. And I hadn't seen him for nearly two. Trevor was a doctor, and his dream of a small-town family practice had come true. All he needed for his perfect life was the perfect wife. Jessica fit that bill to a T.

The first time I met Trevor was when he waltzed into my homeroom senior year of high school. He didn't wait for the teacher to tell him where to sit; he just plunked down next to me and smiled.

"I'm Trevor."

"I'm Greg."

"Good to meet you, Greg."

That was it. I was hooked. Our friendship grew quickly and easily, just like my crush on him. He started climbing the tree outside my window a few months after we met. It was the perfect height, a huge branch reaching right to the edge of my windowsill. Even when there was no reason to sneak in, he would forgo the front door for the chance to scare the crap out of me by appearing at my window. He would tap out a slow, repetitive rhythm until I came and let him in. Most of his visits would last only a few minutes, long enough to leave me wanting more and feeling even more conflicted. How could I be in love with my best friend?

Nothing ever happened between us. I was too scared to try and change our relationship. Until one night the summer after his freshman year of college. I didn't go to school, choosing instead to get a job at a newspaper, while Trevor stayed local at the state university. Once the summer came, we were inseparable, neither of us having much to do but hang out every night.

We had both begged off attending the annual Fourth of July fireworks display, content to sneak beers out of my dad's secret stash and watch crappy movies on the tiny television in my room. We slouched on my beat-up futon, munching on chips and sipping warm Miller's right out of the can. I never drank much, and I was feeling fine after just three beers. But more than that, I was feeling brave. Brave enough to do something truly stupid. I let my head fall on Trevor's shoulder. Holding my breath, I waited for him to shrug me off. He didn't. Instead, he shocked me by wrapping his arm around me, his fingers gently grazing my shoulder. My heart jumped on contact. It was the first time he'd really touched me, outside of playful punches and shoves. I relished every second of it. But I wanted more. I put my hand on his leg, a couple inches too high to be casual. Again I waited for him to flinch or throw my hand off him, but he didn't. He covered my hand with his, pushing it higher still, until his cock was only a few inches away.

Awash with liquid courage, and thrilled by his encouragement, I turned my head to look at him. He gazed straight ahead for what seemed an eternity, then finally turned and met my stare. Our mouths were inches apart, but I was frozen. Luckily for me, Trevor was willing to give us a push. His hand slid from my shoulder to the back of my neck, his fingers lightly tugging at my hair. He smiled one last time before covering my parted lips with his. Every part of me was shaking, my hands gripping his T-shirt.

We pulled apart after a few minutes, both of us breathless. I was expecting Trevor to freak out, but he just smiled. His voice wobbled a bit, making me love him even more, when he said, "What took you so long? I thought I was just going to have to jump you when you weren't looking."

I never got the chance to answer. I was distracted by his kisses and his hands on my belt. There was nothing in my head, no words with which to object. Despite my fears, my questions and my doubt, I let him open my pants and reach inside. My cock was almost painfully hard, over a year of unrequited feelings driving me mad. Trevor closed his fist around my dick, gently moving it up and down. I gasped into his mouth, my fingers digging into his wide shoulders. Dangerously close to coming, I felt moisture dripping from my slit. His thumb passed over the weeping head, making my muscles contract. Releasing my mouth, he pushed me back onto the thin mattress, sliding my pants down my legs. I rose up on my elbows, looking up at him bathed in the blue glow of the television. His smile damn near killed me.

"Trevor, are you sure?"

"You worry too much."

That mouth, the one I had just tasted for the first time, closed around the head of my cock. My back arched, my hands instinctively going to Trevor's head. His hair was like black silk, softer and finer than it appeared. His mouth kept going lower, until I felt his nose hit my belly. I heard the crackling and popping of fireworks exploding across town. They grew louder and louder, the show climbing to its crescendo. Trevor grasped my hips, sucking me hard and

deep. My mind was still swimming, my body on complete
overload. Riding the edge, I knew I was close.

"Trevor, I'm gonna come."

Instead of speeding up as I expected, he eased his tempo.
His tongue swept up the underside of my cock, his fingers
making a tight ring around the base. Everything moved in
slow motion, boom after boom echoing outside my window.
With one last stuttering stroke from Trevor, I was finished.
My hands tightened, my hips jerked, my cock squirting
into his warm, wet mouth. The ceiling was littered with
red, green and yellow flashes, the same colors that had just
erupted behind my eyelids. Soon, everything was quiet. The
fireworks inside and out were finished. Sitting up, Trevor
was waiting to kiss me, both of us still shaking in the dark.
We never did finish the movie.

After that first night, his knocking became a regular oc-
currence. We would lay in my single creaky bed, our hands
and our mouths exploring, never getting enough. To the
outside world, we were still the same friends we always were.
But in my room, we were free. Until Trevor met Jessica.

When my car hit the state line, my stomach tightened just
a fraction. Even with hours to go, it still felt too close. Jessica
had always been around, moving on the fringes of our group,
just a nice and pretty girl. At least, that was all she was to me.
Trevor saw her differently. As much as I tried to ignore it,
to tell myself it was just my imagination, he liked her. A lot.
Their relationship blossomed right out in the open, while
ours was still stuck in the shadows. His trips to my window
grew infrequent, our nighttime meetings close to nonexis-
tent. It was hard not to feel like a substitute, when his only
appearances coincided with fights with Jessica.

But I told myself it was enough. When we were together,

it felt as real as any public kiss shared between any couple. If it had to be a secret, I could live with it.

My foot sank down on the accelerator, my heart pounding just thinking about Trevor. Scenes from our past ran through my mind like a movie, including the last time he'd rapped his knuckles against the ancient glass of my window. It had been weeks since he'd shown up at all. Even longer since I'd kissed him.

"Hey. Can I come in?"

I stepped out of the way, letting him throw his legs over the ledge. He shoved his hands in his pockets, looking everywhere but at me.

"How've you been, Greg?"

"Good. How about you?"

"Good. You know, same old shit. It's been a while."

"Yeah, well. I know you're busy."

"Pre-med is a lot worse than I thought. And Jessica's been hounding me about everything."

Something in me snapped, my words coming out before I could stop them. "I really don't care, Trev."

He looked stunned. More than stunned, he looked hurt.

"What's gotten into you?"

"Nothing. Maybe I don't care about you and Jessica."

"Ah, now we're getting somewhere."

"Don't tell me you're surprised, Trev. I'm tired of being second best. Something you do when no one's looking."

"I can't help how I feel, Greg."

"About her or me?"

We stood looking at each other, both of us with our arms folded.

"I know you don't want to hear this, Greg, but I can't keep doing this."

"This? Tell me, Trevor, what is 'this' to you? Because, to me, this is love."

"I'm not sure anymore."

He looked down, and his silence said it all. I looked at the futon, and all the visions of Trevor and me hit like a tornado. My heart broke, the bed catching me before my legs could give out.

"I'm sorry, Greg. It's time for me to move on. You'll always be my friend. But I can't give you any more than that."

He seemed to wait for me to say something, to do something. But I couldn't. I didn't. There was nothing to do. I could still picture his face as he climbed out the window. That was the last time I saw him.

My eyes finally refocused on the road. Miles had flown by without my even noticing. Familiar surroundings were closing in, and so was my regret at saying yes to this wedding. The wheel almost turned itself as my old house came into view.

The room was still and dark, but I couldn't sleep. I wasn't used to all the peace and quiet. Living in the city had changed my brain somehow. I needed the noise, the ever-present sirens and voices and squealing car brakes. I could barely make out the tree outside my window, the close branches blocking out what little moonlight there was. Lying in the inky black, with no streetlights to cast any shadows, all I could do was think. And all I could think about was Trevor.

After years of me avoiding birthdays, christenings and family reunions, Trevor had managed to bring me back to the old house. But nothing was the same. My old room had been totally redone. His wedding invitation was sitting on the brand-new dresser, my pressed suit hanging in plastic in the new cedar closet. My old trophies and posters were long gone. A blue-and-white floral pattern covered every surface, every detail a perfect fit. I hardly recognized the place. When I tossed and turned, the brand-new bed didn't even give a squeak. Every spring on my old bed had creaked, registering the slightest movement. I missed that noise, too. Anything to break the overwhelming silence.

As I was drifting off, I heard it. The light tapping against the old glass panes was as familiar as ever. I nearly jumped out of my skin. My first thought was that I'd imagined it, until it happened again. Easing out of bed, I crept over to the window and saw him. Hesitating just a moment, I pulled the window open, my hands suddenly trembling in the dark. Damn him and that smile.

"Hey, Greg. Can I come in?"

"Trevor, what are you doing here?"

He didn't answer me, just put his leg over the windowsill and stepped inside. I could barely see him, but I knew every inch of his face. He produced a flashlight, pointing it straight up under his chin and grinning like a fool. Before I could say a word, he turned the light on the walls, taking in the tiny blue-and-white flowers.

"Nice wallpaper."

"My mom finally redecorated."

"I can see that. It doesn't really work for me. I miss the old green walls and those bad posters you had."

"I'll let her know you disapprove."

He smirked, setting the flashlight on the dresser. The circle of light gave the room an eerie glow. He ran his hand over the back of his neck, his unease obvious. I sat down on the edge of the bed and watched him pace around the room.

"So, what are you doing here, Trevor? Don't tell me it's cold feet?"

"I had to see for myself. That you were really here."

"You knew I was coming. I sent in my little card."

"I guess I just thought… I don't know what I thought."

He picked up the invitation, looking at it as if he'd never seen it before. I watched his eyes moving over each word in silence. Tapping it against his hand, he looked at me. Even in the dim light, I could still see the apprehension all over his face.

"It's been too long, Greg."

"Well, you know. Life has gotten a little complicated."

"Tell me about it. I understand now why people elope. It is amazing that people get married at all."

He walked toward me, sitting down gently on the brand-new double bed. I could smell the alcohol on him, but he didn't seem drunk. I decided to placate him, despite my churning stomach.

"I know you and Jessica will be happy together."

"How can you be so sure?"

I looked at his face for the joke, but I found his expression serious and stern. He looked scared. I didn't know what to say to him.

"I just assumed you were sure before you asked her."

I tried to laugh, but it died when his arm draped over my shoulder, our hips touching as we sat on the fluffy duvet. Trevor turned and looked at me, but I didn't return his gaze. I couldn't. I didn't trust myself to see his eyes in that moment. He leaned closer to me, his lips right by my ear.

"Can I tell you a secret, Greg? Right now, I'm not sure at all."

His breath was hot, but not as hot as his tongue, which swept across my earlobe, shocking my mouth right open. Trevor, always one to take advantage, pulled my open mouth to his, kissing me deeply. I knew I should stop him, push him away, but I just let myself be kissed, let my tongue swirl around with his. Finally, reason took over and I managed to get free from Trevor's strong grip. Standing up, I tried to quell the panic rising in my throat.

"Don't, Trevor. Don't."

He followed me, not letting me go easily. His hands pulled at my waist, trying to get me back in his arms. I resisted, edged away. But I only ended up against the wall, Trevor pinning me to the freshly changed wallpaper. It smelled of plastic and I willed my mind to focus on that—anything but the feel of Trevor's hands.

"Greg. Greg, look at me."

I gave in, gazing into his eyes, and I saw it. The same look I'd seen the day we met, all those years ago.

"Come on, Greg. Don't be mad at me."

"You said this was over. That we were over. You're about to be a married man. Don't fuck with me, Trevor."

"You could always do that. Make it all sound so easy. It's not, you know."

"It may not be easy, but it is simple. You love her, don't you?"

"She has nothing to do with us."

"She has everything to do with us."

"I know what I said to you, but it's not over. At least, it's not for me. You left, but I could never get you out of my head. Or my heart. Tell me it's over for you, Greg. Tell me you don't love me anymore."

"I can't do that, Trevor."

"So ask me to stay." He smiled at me, his face softening at my encouraging words. But I couldn't give him what he wanted.

"I can't."

He straightened up a little, bracing before he spoke again. "Then tell me to leave."

"You know I can't do that, either."

His fingers traced down my cheek, his thumb pressing my bottom lip. My mind was being torn apart. The man I loved wanted me again, but I knew that come morning he'd be gone, standing in a tuxedo at the front of the Lutheran church. While my brain screamed for reason, my heart leaped in my chest.

"What do you want me to do, Trevor? Tell me what to do."

"Kiss me, Greg."

It wasn't easy or simple. I knew it. But I shut it all out as I leaned forward, our mouths meeting in a fury of emotion, making up for every missed opportunity. Clothing started dropping and flying, our mouths staying firmly attached. My hands reached for his zipper, my fingers fumbling with the easy task. He rescued me, easing his jeans down the rest of the way before making quick work of my flannel pajama pants. He led me by the hand to the bed, finally big enough for both of us. Our hands kept moving, but our eyes stayed locked.

"Trevor."

There were a million things I wanted to say, but I couldn't express any of them. Only his name came to my lips in a choked whisper. At that moment, it seemed like enough. He took my hand and slid it down his chest, his own nerves evident as his stomach twitched under my fingers. I hesitated before wrapping my fist around his cock, the feeling so familiar even after so long. Our feet fought with the blankets, trying to make room for our twining legs. I took a nipping bite of Trevor's neck, his tendons standing up as he arched toward me.

Letting my tongue follow a crooked path down his body, I paused to reexamine the landmarks I'd traced so many times. The scar that lived a few inches above his navel, the trio of moles that formed a perfect triangle on his left pectoral muscle. I tweaked his nipples until they were hard, his moans stifled by the corner of an overstuffed pillow. When I reached his thick, hard cock, I drew in a deep breath. I admired the full length of it, from the long, slightly curved shaft to the thick, flared head.

My hands eased his thighs apart, my tongue slowly tracing the ridge of the glans, taking my time to explore every inch. I teased his slit, tasting his salty flavor for the first time in ages, and forcing a delicate cry out of his mouth.

He twitched and jerked as I slowly swept my tongue over the sensitive ridge. I closed my mouth around the velvet-smooth head and slid my way down. I could feel the blood racing under the skin, his veins pulsing as I sucked him off.

"Greg, oh God."

He put his own hand over his mouth, keeping himself quiet. I pushed and pulled him in and out of my mouth, years of want swelling within me. The way he said my name always shot a bullet right through my heart. Pulling me up, Trevor brought our mouths back together. I slid up the bed next to him.

"I want to fuck you, Greg. I need you. Please."

I didn't need to answer. I just kissed him hard, one last time before I rolled away, so my back was facing him. I heard him fumbling with something on the floor, his hands digging in the pockets of his discarded jeans. When he produced a condom and lube, my smile was impossible to hide.

"Pretty confident, weren't you?"

His laughter vibrated against me, then his tongue was lightly licking my shoulder and his fingers wandering over my hip. By the time his big hand wrapped around my dick, I was hard. I felt his other hand move down my rear, gently easing my cheeks apart. Suddenly, the cool wetness of his lubed finger pressed against the tight pucker of my hole. His teeth gently rasped over my earlobe, pulling and sucking it into his mouth. At that moment, I let him inside, his finger gently pushing into my ass.

One finger became two, and slowly I relaxed against his thrusting fingers. I heard Trevor tear the condom open and for a moment his hands left me. I looked at him over my shoulder, and his eyes met mine. His lips curled into a smile before kissing me deeply. I felt the head of his cock pushing me open, his hand back on my shaft. I moaned as he eased in, just the tip of his dick filling me, stretching me. I pushed back against him, letting myself relax as he inched inside a little farther. I gasped as the pressure gave way and he slid deeper and deeper.

Before he started moving again, I felt him pulse and grow inside me. Not wanting to wait another second, I eased away from him, feeling the pull of his thick cock. He fucked me slow and hard, his tongue flicking gently over the back of my neck. It was nearly impossible to keep silent, and our labored breathing sounded like shouting in the quiet room. His hand slid back up to the head of my cock, his fist twisting around me. I looked back at him through fuzzy eyes, my ass pushing hard against his bucking hips. I was lost, completely.

"Greg, oh Jesus, Greg."

His voice ringing in my ears shattered the last of my control. Trevor fucked me faster as my come shot into his waiting hand, the hot, sticky liquid rubbing all over me as he continued to stroke.

With a fierce series of thrusts, I felt him come, his twitching cock squirming inside me as he bit my shoulder. When he withdrew, our kisses kept us together, and we devoured each other until our fatigue slowed us down. We separated, our heavy breathing still punctuating the deep silence.

"God, I'm going to miss you, Greg."

It was meant as a compliment, but all I could hear was the meaning behind it. My wounded heart knew this was the last time we would be together. Once he was out that window, he would be gone for good.

He dressed, his tousled hair making him look just like he had on that first night. That night on the futon, a million years ago. If only we could go back and stay there in that warm, hazy moment of perfection. I stood near the edge of the bed, watching him. His eyes breezed over the invitation one last time as he picked up his flashlight and turned it off. In the dark, our words felt different.

"So, I'll see you tomorrow?"

"Sure, wouldn't miss it. And I promise to forever hold my peace."

His smile was resigned, his hands around my back holding tighter than before. Our lips met, both of us aware of what came next.

"I better go. I have to be up in a few hours."

"Be careful getting down that tree. The branch is looking a little weak."

"I always am."

His body was almost all the way out the window when he turned to me, pulling me into one last kiss.

"Greg, I…"

"I know, Trevor. I know."

I wasn't in the church the next morning. My mother bought my flu excuse and left for the wedding without me. As soon as she was gone, I loaded up the car and took off.

As I made the familiar left turn onto Landow Street, I heard the bells clanging in the calm air. I pulled over, stopping just long enough to watch a billowy white dress emerge from the stretch limo. Reality smacked me hard in the face. I stepped on the gas, flying toward the interstate faster than the speed limit suggested.

The next week, my mother called. Along with all the details about the fairy-tale wedding, she casually mentioned that a branch had fallen off the old oak tree. I knew without asking which one it was.

Wedding Crasher

Rachel Kramer Bussel

To put it bluntly, weddings make me horny. Not the idea of a wedding, me in a frilly gown and veil, walking down the aisle with the mythical man of my dreams. I leave that stuff for other girls, ones far more traditional than me. I can get through all the schmaltz, the bad dresses, worse food and even dismal music, as long as I can find someone to make my night a little more interesting. It can be a man or a woman— or both at once. I've had some of the best sex of my life at weddings, and I think the reason is because even the cynics among us can't help but get lulled into the sense of love and companionship in the air at a wedding. We want someone to celebrate with, even if we're not breaking in the honeymoon suite.

My friends know I can be counted on to make a scene, at least, if anyone catches me in the act. That's happened once or twice, when the groom has gone looking for his best friend and found him receiving a blow job from yours truly. These days, I try to keep my comings and goings a little more discreet, but really, everyone's entitled to a little fun, and the bride and groom shouldn't hog all of it. Actually, I think I often get more action than they do, because I haven't been through the ringer. All I have to do is show up and look pretty...and suggestive. It's a fine line, because you don't want somebody's grandmother to come up to you and tell you you're a floozy.

My most recent wedding adventure was perhaps the hottest of all. Instead of just one guy, I scored a sexy couple. They were also newlyweds, but what I liked about them was that they weren't dressed like everyone else. The reason I knew they were newlyweds was by the discreet rings they wore, their lovey-dovey looks and little kisses, and by asking. I was curious about them, since Mara was dressed in a low-cut fuschia top and long black skirt with a slit up the side, plus patterned fishnet stockings and sexy black boots, her short black curls swinging around her head. Tom looked hot, but not too formal, in fitted dark jeans and a white-and-blue checked shirt.

Mara and Tom, I knew before they even told me, were the type to have an alternative marriage. The three of us wound up chatting away and pretty much excluding everyone else at the table, all of whom could probably tell where our night was headed by our increasingly risqué conversation. When Larissa, the bride, came over, she had a knowing look in her eye. "Jackie, what are you up to?" she asked me, seemingly amused by my antics. I know she counts on me to liven up any party I attend, and her wedding would be no exception.

"Nothing, just some innocent conversation," I said, winking at her. She just laughed and gave me a huge hug. "Have fun...and don't do anything I wouldn't do!"

Well, those were fighting words, because before Jackie up and decided to get married, she was as much of a wild wedding-goer as I was. In fact, she and I had once ended up in a threesome with the best man.

I stood near Mara and Tom as the toasts were made, but as we consumed several more glasses of the sweet champagne, something changed between us. Her laugh was a little louder, and they were becoming a little more touchy-feely. You'd have to be watching closely to notice—and I was. At one point, during a lull in the conversation, she just looked at me. The question was plainly in her eyes: was I in or was I out? I was in, for sure. I'd already scoped out the eligible men and there was nobody I wanted to bed more than these two.

We made our way back to their room, and I could tell we were drawing stares. As drunk as wedding guests tend to get, at this soiree at least, we were the only trio making a hasty exit; it's hard to do that invisibly, but what did I care? Their room was close by, which was a good thing, because all the champagne had made me even more horny. I'd forgotten how hot the energy a couple radiated during a threesome could be. I'm mostly a guy's girl, and I love to bend over and have a man take me from behind, love running my hands along his chest, love the carnality of a man in the throes of lust. Still, there's a magical sensuality for me when I meet the right woman, one who's as daring and horny as I am. Mara was just such a woman, I could already tell, and I was eager—eager to see what she'd do away from prying eyes, eager to watch her fuck her husband, and eager to share some of their powerful sexual energy.

When we got to their door, Tom fumbled with the key and Mara grabbed my hand. Her skin was soft and the pressure of her touch made my pussy pound. I truly hadn't come to the wedding intending to get laid. Drunk? Yes. Laughing with my formerly slutty friend as she marched into the bonds of marriage? Yes. A hot and heavy makeout session? Yes. But I never anticipate postnuptial nookie. It kills my buzz, since if it doesn't pan out, I feel let down. I like to wait and see what unfolds. So Mara's hand in mine reminded me that I was a lucky girl, indeed. Who needed her own wedding reception when she could have a wedded couple to share?

Soon we were in their room, which was dominated by a king-size bed. There was none of the awkward tension that sometimes happens when people who barely know each other are suddenly thrust into a sexually charged room together. Instead, we moved like we were long-lost lovers. They began taking off my clothes, Tom's hands easily unzipping my dress while Mara reached first for my shoes, then peeled down my stockings. "You're beautiful, Jackie," Tom said. "Isn't she, Mara?" She stood then, so close her nipples brushed against my breasts as I stood there in only a pale pink see-through bra and panties.

"Yes, she definitely is." Mara's voice was soft and husky, and then she leaned forward and kissed me deeply, while Tom's tongue traveled along the back of my neck. He stepped closer so I could feel his erection against my ass, nudging me, letting me know he wanted to be inside me. I had thought I'd be watching them, but I couldn't refuse their silent invitation. I'm a voyeur, but I'm also not one to shy away from an opportunity to play with a beautiful lover, let alone two. Mara bit my lip softly, and I grabbed her hips, pulling her close. We were as far from the pomp and circumstance of a wedding as possible, ready to get out of our elegant outfits and into ones that fit us much better—our birthday suits.

"I told Mara when we first sat down and saw you that I thought you'd be the perfect after-dinner snack," Tom said. His corny line didn't bother me, especially because he'd taken out his cock and turned me around so I could see it. He'd shaved his pubic hair, and the extra-large dick in front of me made me lick my lips in anticipation. Suddenly, I was back to being fully in the moment, not caring about happily ever after, just about happily right this very second. And so I did what my instincts told me to do, but what the more proper guests would never dream of: I got on my knees and started sucking the cock of a man I'd met only hours before. I shut my eyes and focused on the dual sensations of power and submission, of offering myself up to him while making sure he knew just how much pleasure I could give him. In only a few seconds, Tom was whimpering. I glanced up, my eyes full of mischief as I let his penis part from my lips.

Mara walked toward us, looking down at me with both lust and tenderness in her eyes. No, the three of us weren't committing to anything beyond the next few hours, but that didn't mean we were simply indulging in pure carnality. Rather, we didn't need words to convey the bond we'd so quickly formed.

"Jackie," Mara said, transforming my name with her husky voice. I pictured her as a bride, walking down the aisle, her slightly chubby cheeks glowing much as they were now. I pictured Tom carrying her away and then throwing her down on the bed.

Then her hand came up to my head, grabbing my hair and yanking it back. I had thought I was in control, but maybe I'd been her puppet all along, a quiet mastermind. Or maybe I *had* been in control, emphasis on the past tense. Either way, hearing Mara say my name and seeing the look in her eye let me know that she was the bridezilla here, so to speak—she was running the show, and I was going to do whatever she wanted. Tom looked at her with the same reverence I felt. "Don't leave me out," she said, pulling harder on my hair. A noise escaped my lips—a whimper, a moan, a plea, a thank-you? I'm not sure what it was, but she took it to mean I was hers, and promptly shoved the fingers of her free hand into my mouth. Ah, so that was it—she wanted to play with me, too.

"I have a cock in my suitcase. I was planning to use it to fuck Tom, and I still may do that. But I think first I need to fuck your sweet little mouth, don't you?"

I couldn't answer her, at least not with words, while her fingernails curled against my tongue, but I opened my eyes and nodded as best I could. She was wily, that Mara. I never would've seen it coming, but I know from experience that surprises can be the sexiest things of all.

"Get the strap-on," she snapped at Tom. I know for some men, hearing a woman talk like that would wilt in an instant any arousal they'd had, but Tom leaped at her command. Maybe they'd simply been playing coy and flirtatious, when they'd been the predators all along, I thought as my eyes scanned his body when he emerged from his rummaging with a sleek silver, glittery harness and a giant red cock. It was molded to perhaps resemble a penis, but it didn't, not really. It was thick and long and hard, but a shocking bright red, the hue a wild girl might dye her hair or the color of a sassy summer dress, the kind that would never be appropriate at a wedding.

It was a girlie cock if ever there was one, and Tom proceeded to smoothly undress his wife and then get her into the harness with a practiced ease. Clearly, they weren't new to any of this; maybe they were just as much the wedding crashers as I was. Whichever—there was a beautiful red cock before me and I'd have been highly disappointed if Mara hadn't done what she did next. "I'm not going to fuck you with this unless you show me that you can give me just as good a blow job as you did my husband," she sneered.

I liked this side of Mara, and my body instantly responded, the space between my legs clenching, wetness building as I went to work. Tom approached but simply watched, his light breathing sounding louder than it should have as I shut my eyes against the brightness of the dick. Mara softened, or so it seemed. "That's it, just like that," she murmured, stroking my hair as I sank my lips down until the head of the toy pressed against the back of my throat. It wasn't bigger than the biggest cock I'd ever sucked, but it was close. Mara was a tiny girl, but she made up for it with the sword she wielded, and soon her stroking grew more frantic. I heard noises and felt some movement, and when I looked I saw that Tom was fucking her with his fingers while I went down on her dick. She was getting my submission and his, two for the price of…well, simply for being her.

This was new for me. I'd had threesomes, but there was always an air of naughtiness, as if we were doing something wrong or decadent or outrageous. These two made it seem like we were just having fun, and indeed, we were. We didn't need to defy anyone—except maybe our hosts—to enjoy each other. My oral fixation meant that every time the cock dragged along my tongue, it was like activating my G-spot. Mara came, shuddering against me, leaning her hand on Tom's shoulder as he finished her off.

Then she eased back, pulling out of me and offering her dick to him. He must have an oral fixation, too, because he scrambled to fit it all in. Tables weren't just turning, they were getting thrown across the room, and I loved it. Mara watched him suck and slurp and bob up and down, before digging her nails into the back of Tom's neck.

"Now what?" hovered in the air, but nobody dared to say it.

"You sit here," Mara ordered Tom, placing his ass up against the headboard of the bed, a pillow behind him. His dick was extremely erect by now. She positioned me on my hands and knees and then directed my lips to his dick. This time, though, I was doing it at her behest.

But when I started, she was behind me, nudging my entrance with the head of the toy. I struggled to stay steady as she entered me, but I was so turned on it really wasn't a problem. We drifted into a rhythm, her thrusts pushing me down, his dick plunging deep into my mouth. He kept reaching forward to play with my tits, but it wasn't really the time for that. Her thrusts were too firm and steady, and I focused on enjoying them while giving Tom my all. Soon I wasn't focused on anything except the warmth and wetness of my sex, the way Mara would sometimes slap my ass, Tom's gentle strokes of my cheeks and neck. We heard noises outside, loud cheering, and I smiled momentarily. Whatever we were missing couldn't be as exciting as what was going on here.

"I want to see you come around my dick," Mara said. It sounded like a request, but I knew it was an order. She pinched my clit hard to confirm this, and I pulled away for a moment to lick Tom's balls. "Isn't she pretty?" Mara asked him, and something about that set me off. It told me she was looking at me—at my ass, my pussy, my most intimate parts. She was looking, and she liked what she saw, enough to comment. I was giving her pleasure, even if it was indirect.

I smiled softly up at Tom and he groaned when I then took one entire ball in my mouth. He grabbed my face and started slapping his cock against my tongue, then jerking off onto me. I stayed still and let them each use me for their pleasure, which turned into my own. Feeling those first drops of hot come hit my skin set me off, and I squeezed the dick so tightly I was amazed Mara could keep it steady inside me.

I couldn't scream, because Tom shoved his cock right back into my mouth. That was probably a good thing, because when I scream, it's loud. I didn't mind causing a bit of a stir among the wedding party, but I didn't need everyone to clock my orgasm down to the second.

When Mara's dick eased out of me, I was a little sore, but I liked the reminder. I shifted to the side, then stood, looking vainly around the room. Was that it? Should I be on my way? I had nothing to cover myself with except my dress, which was now crumpled on the floor. Mara inched her way up to Tom, straddling his face, and he licked my juices off the toy, then removed it as easily as he'd put it on.

They kissed and I watched, suddenly hungry for what they had. Not marriage per se, or even love, but true passion, the kind that was only bolstered by sharing it with someone else. But instead of banishing me, they welcomed me into their arms, their bed, dare I say their marriage? At least for the night. And the next morning. And with an open invitation to visit them whenever I wanted.

By the time I was on the train home, I felt as if I'd truly gotten a glimpse into the meaning of love. Maybe it sounds sappy for a girl who's more used to causing a stir than catching a bouquet, but it's true. Mara and Tom gave me a new kind of wedding adventure, one I didn't, unlike the others, share with the bride over a post-honeymoon gossip session. This one was a little more special, something I borrowed, something new; I'd leave old and blue for the real brides.

I did write Larissa a thank-you note, after I received hers. She didn't pry, and I like knowing that whatever she did on her honeymoon, she'd be hard-pressed to top what I did right after it. But I also learned that it's not a competition, an either/or choice. Who knows, maybe someday I'll even walk down the aisle, but only if I can do it with someone like Tom, who knows that marriage isn't about closing doors, but opening them.

Blushing Bride

Bella Dean

"There's the lovely Mrs. Loma." Boyd buried his face against the back of my neck and I shivered. An entirely lustful rush of want ran from the nape of my neck to my virginal white panties.

"Here I am." I breathed. I glanced around as his lips traveled lower, his tongue touching wetly to my right shoulder blade. I moaned and then the crinkling of cellophane filled the small, quiet corner of the ballroom we had managed to find.

"Molly," Boyd said, with a laugh. He tried to sound stern. "What is that sound I hear?" He wrapped his big arms around my substantial white gown and his laughter rumbled through me. I continued to wrestle the Baggie out of my garter.

"Shut up, Boyd. I am having some stress." I had quit smoking three months before the wedding. I had to keep up my fitness for modeling. The money was good, but the pressure to be thin was excruciating. I had to pick a doable addiction. Something I could burn off if I really tried. Something fat-free, portable and easy to smuggle. My new addiction was Gummi Bears. I didn't light up; I chewed. I bit off little green heads, red arms, orange legs while the weight of wedding stress nearly crushed me flat.

Boyd guided one hand to my generously hoisted breasts and stroked me through the beadwork and lace. My eyes drifted half-closed even as I popped a green bear into my mouth. "Oh, God," I said. Both to his touch and the bear.

"Tell your husband what's wrong," he said, swaying me with him to the music.

"My mother keeps telling the waiter to say 'fillet mignon.' You know, where 'fillet' rhymes with 'billet.'"

"Did you tell her filet rhymes with bay?"

He kissed my shoulder and I pushed an orange bear into my mouth. The burst of sweetness on my tongue and the curl of heat in my panties commingled into a pleasantly doped sensation. "She said that the English say it. Fillet, fillet, fillet." I changed it, wishing my mother would behave for just one day.

"But we're not in England," Boyd said. He rubbed my hips with his hands and my dress whispered secret things to us. There was entirely too much fabric between me and my groom.

"Ah, I tried that."

"What did she say?"

I popped a yellow bear. "She said we're not in France, either. So she can say fillet."

"Ah. That makes sense."

"Do not defend her." Green bear, red bear, white. All in one mouthful.

Boyd turned me and I swallowed. He kissed me softly, fingers stroking over my waist. "I'm not. I'm just trying to calm you down."

"And Uncle Jobie is drunk as a skunk singing 'Margarita-ville.'"

"But they're playing The Spinners."

"I know!"

"Molly, he gets drunk at every event."

"Still." Kiss, kiss, kiss went my groom. His tongue ran lightly over my bottom lip and my pussy went wet in my little white bloomers. "I just cannot breathe with all the stress."

Boyd backed me farther into the murky ballroom corner. A fake plant shielded us from the insanity that was our re-ception. "If the bride and groom would join us on the dance floor, we'll do the garter business!" The DJ's porn star voice boomed through the ballroom.

Boyd's tongue stroked over mine and he pulled me flush to him, my crinoline complaining, his hard-on riding the tender place between my legs. My breath stalled out in my throat and my chest buzzed. Then I groaned. "Damn them all!"

He laughed. "Easy, Molly. Be easy. Let's go show off those pretty toned legs."

I shoved the Gummi Bears into his pocket, since my smuggling place was about to be removed and tossed to some drunken male attendee. My fingers brushed Boyd's cock on their way out of his pocket, and he exhaled fast, with a bark. "Oh, baby."

"Margaritaville!" cried my uncle in a drunken shout.

"Oh, God. Oh, God!" I said, anxiety swirling in my belly. I reached for Boyd's pocket to grab the bears and he stopped me. He twirled me and gave me a sharp smack on the ass to propel me forward. Even through all the fabric the smack left a crack of pain on my bottom and I blushed. "Boyd!" I yipped.

"Go on, girl." He laughed. "Go on, Mrs. Loma. Go get 'em!" And he smacked me again.

"Give them to me." I pushed my hand into Boyd's pocket and he cruelly arched his hips and gave me a handful of cock. I laughed. Hard. I snorted, actually. I had him wedged there in the mirrored corner of the elevator, and somehow, miraculously, we were alone.

"No bears for you! No bears. But if you want something in your mouth, I have something in mind." He pulled me close and my breath slid out of my lungs. I smiled a half-drunk, goofy smile and kissed him. His five o'clock stubble scraped my carefully applied makeup.

"I want the bears."

"Behave."

"Please." I breathed. I kissed him harder, pressing my pelvis to his despite the padded barrier of miles of white dress.

"No."

"I need them. I am…" The truth threatened to come out, so I bit my lip.

Boyd pulled back to look at me. He slid his warm finger along the arch of my cheekbone. Touched my lip gently. "What?"

"Nothing." I dropped my eyes and leaned against him for his warmth and his strength. I heard the crinkle of the candy bag, but didn't want it anymore. Panic welled in my chest and I tried to relax. I tried to remember how to breathe.

"What? Tell me, Molls. What's wrong?" Now he looked serious and concerned and all the things he should not be on his wedding night.

I swallowed hard several times to stave off the tears. I tried so hard to ignore the tight crawl of emotion in my throat and the way my heart was flip-flopping as if I might die. "Nothing, nothing. It's fine."

"You're going to cry? Oh shit, are you sorry you married me? Do you regret me?" Real pain flashed across his handsome face, and I had never felt like a bigger ass in all my life.

"God, no! I'm sorry, Boyd. I'm just having a little..." I fanned my face.

"A little what?" He pinned me to the wall, big brown eyes intent. Worried.

"Anxiety. I'm having anxiety," I said to his flushed red lips. My lipstick stained him in places, and I put my lips to the really red spots. Boyd pulled me back.

"Why?" His fingers twined in mine and his big rough thumb rested over the pulse in my wrist. Marking every jump of my freaked-out heart.

"Our babies?" I said it like a question.

Boyd grinned. That grin that had gotten me into this wedding dress in the first place. It smacked my heart with a resounding whack and then shot straight down past my belly button into my pussy. I moaned. He could not turn me on while I was scared. It was unfair. "What about our babies?"

The elevator pulled up short, rocking us on our feet. I gasped and then walked forward like a drunk across the deck of a ship caught on stormy seas. Boyd steadied me, laughing at my instability. "Just come on, Boyd," I said, getting angry. When he walked I heard the crackle of the Gummi Bear bag in his pocket.

"What about our babies, Molly?"

I staggered down the hall. "Nothing! Be quiet." My fear had turned to annoyance that he simply would not let it go. Didn't he know that if I said it out loud it would probably come true? Or some stupid superstition like that.

"Mol!" He was laughing and I heard him running up the hall. A delicious mix of what felt like fear and arousal swirled through my nether bits, making my cheeks flame and my heart beat faster. I jiggled the suite handle. Stupid wedding gown, no pockets for a key! I turned, straining for air, my back against the smooth wooden door. I yelped when Boyd caught me up in his arms, his smile somewhat feral now. "Tell me."

"I can't." His mouth came down on mine and his tongue pressed hard to my tongue. My knees went wiggly, and Boyd pushed past me with one big forearm and swiped the card key.

"You will," he growled, walking me backward. His knees were pushing against the full, imposing skirt of my gown, but I felt it slip between my knees and my cunt went wet for him. God. I wanted to forget my anxiety over the future and just fuck.

"No. Please. Fuck me. Don't make love to me, Mr. Loma. *Fuck* me," I said against his bottom lip. I meant it, but I was also kind of hoping for a bit of distraction.

Boyd let out a low sound and walked me back faster, so that I staggered a bit. Then he dropped like a stone, coming up with handfuls of crinoline and satin and fluff. "Tell me."

"No," I breathed. What was he doing?

Boyd jostled me, so I turned. His hand found my bottom. The panties, the garters, the old-fashioned white stockings I had let him pick out for kicks. His big palm slid warm and sure across my buttocks and I closed my eyes, liking the feel of his hands on me. My husband's hands on me.

"Tell me what you're scared of, Molly. I'm your husband. You need to tell me and I'll make it not scary anymore." His teeth found the back of my neck and I shivered. His fingers danced over the edge of my panties, stroked the elastic garters. He slipped a finger under my stocking. I grew wetter with each second that ticked by. With every beat of my heart I wanted him more. Boyd nipped me again and said in a warning tone, "Come on, Molly."

"No," I whispered. "Please just—" That was all I managed, because fire erupted along my flank. My ass blazed with sensation even before I heard the resounding slap.

"Tell me," he said in my ear.

I was gobsmacked. Shocked. Irate! I… "Do that again," I managed to gasp.

"You need to tell me."

"Please."

Boyd laughed. "You have it backwards. You're supposed to be a brat and I punish you. But you want me to do it. So let's do it this way. You tell me and I'll do it again. What about *our babies,* Mrs. Loma?"

The stinging pain had warmed my skin and it throbbed, no doubt dull, red and flushed. I dropped my head and my voice. "They'll be a mess," I confessed. One big, dark fear released into the quiet bedroom.

"Oh, baby." He laughed. And then his hand came down on my other butt cheek and the pleasure that rushed through my pelvis was staggering. Even as the white-hot flashes of pain traveled through my skin, my pussy grew ready for him. I wanted him so badly, but I wasn't ready yet. Not ready for this new sensation to end.

I shook my head, held my breath, paid attention to the sinuous pleasure in my cunt. "They'll be scarred for life, our kids." Another fear dropped like a little poison seed at his feet.

"No way, no how," Boyd said, and cracked hard and fast across the very bottom of my ass, his big blunt fingers landing close to the wet entrance to my body.

"They'd be on *Oprah* before their tenth birthday," I said, sobbing just a little.

Boyd sat on the bed and pulled me over his lap, all too fast for me to process. Three blows in a row accented his firm tone. "That is crazy."

"I'm scared we'll break them," I confessed, squirming on his lap.

His large hands smoothed over the flesh of my bottom. They kept time with my pulse and I felt like one big heart-beat. It throbbed in my breast, my ears, my cunt, my ass. I squirmed on his lap, feeling his hard-on press the bodice of my dress. I wiggled some more to feel it again. It was for me, that hard-on.

"No more. You're wrong about all of it, babe. We will be awesome. My blushing bride." He laughed, touching my hot, smacked skin. "Don't be scared," he said. He pushed a finger into me, slow and soft. Sank into me one millimeter at a time, so that I stopped breathing so I could pay attention.

"How can you know?" I yelped. Then I moaned and pushed back to meet his probing fingers. He added a second and stretched me, making my pussy slippery and primed.

"Because I believe in us."

"We'll wreck them. Oh my God! I fall down all the time. And you! You can't pick your socks up. And—" *Crack, crack, crack!*

I wiggled again, gasping. Boyd's hard cock rubbed my left breast and I closed my eyes, biting my lip. "Stop, Molly."

"I drink too much coffee and you eat *way* too much meat! They'll be little high-strung carnivores right out of the womb."

Three more blows and I felt his hips arch up as if he was thrusting. Here we were, me in my gown, him in his tux, in our hotel room because our flight didn't leave until morning.

Here we were in some swirling column of fear, arousal and spanking. "Boyd!" I yelped.

"We are not going to mess up our kid, Molly. You are very creative, I am very strong. We both are very smart."

"I burn oven mitts because I forget to take them out of the oven."

Crack, crack, crack! "That's a matter of common sense, not intelligence. So, we just don't let you use the oven when I'm not home."

"You wash all the clothes together and turn all the whites pink!"

Crack, crack, crack! "So he'll wear pink clothes. Real men wear pink." Boyd growled. His fingers thrust into me faster and I bucked my hips, riding his fingers.

"Oh, Boyd," I said, hanging my head so all the blood rushed into my face. It still didn't feel as fiery and tender as my bottom.

"Can you be done with that now, Molly? No more." He rolled me to the bed and set about getting my dress off.

"I should have changed, like every other bride." He was patiently undoing dozens of cloth-covered buttons.

"Shh, I like it. It's like opening a present that will last forever." Boyd slid a finger beneath my bodice and stroked each nipple. I was dizzy with wanting him and the constant thumping reminder of my spanking. I squirmed, growing impatient for him. For his cock.

"Do them faster," I said. I squirmed some more and Boyd pulled my bodice down gently so that my breasts popped free of the bustier and then breached the barrier of my white gown. My nipples stood up like two ripe, perfect berries and he took one in his mouth.

"Patience. You need patience. We're going to get started on that family. We have a lot of messing around to do, so we need to get cracking on them babies." He let the West Virginia twang creep into his voice and I giggled.

"Stop torturing me."

He abandoned the buttons and pushed up the enormous skirt. "I'm going to fuck you now, Mrs. Loma, future mother of my emotionally stunted children. In your dress. In your stocking. If you have any objections," he said, his voice husky and filled with want and humor, "speak now or forever hold your peace."

I spread my legs for him, watching his big brown eyes on me. I had never loved him more. My heart beat faster and my ass thumped in time. When he ripped my panties on each side and whisked them away, I managed to gurgle, "Keep those for the scrapbook!"

He laughed. He was out of his tux in record time as I watched, loving his hard, tan thighs, loving his hard cock, loving all of him more than I ever had in my entire life. "I want a whole passel of kids with you," he declared. "We can lead them all onto the *Doctor Phil* set and they can tell the world how their mother sings too loud and off-key."

"Boyd!" I swatted his arm as he kneed my legs apart to get me wider. Put his hard cock to me and rubbed my soaking wet slit until I arched up, impatient and demanding.

"We'll tell the world about the time you forgot to take off your socks and got in the shower." He thrust into me quickly and I grabbed his shoulders, bit him hard.

"Oh, God, Boyd." I laughed, feeling no breath at all in my lungs as he started to move.

He pressed his lips to my hair, fucking me hard so that we slid slowly across the duvet on the satin of my dress. "We'll tell America how you burned the green beans that time and then set the pot on the counter *and* burned the counter to boot!"

"I thought the counter was heat safe." I whimpered. I was going to come. His hard length filled me and his wet skin kissed my clit with each thrust. I hooked my legs around him and he touched my face. Kissed me.

"I'll tell them how you bought me women's underpants once. And they were purple."

"They said boxer briefs and they were royal-blue." I giggled, my cunt tight to the point of blissful agony. I thrust up so he could fill me more. All the way. Take me over. I wanted to not know where I began and he ended.

"They said *boy shorts* and the color was Royale."

"Apples and oranges."

"No. Ladies' panties."

"Baby," I said, coming. The orgasm swelled in me, until I felt hot and cold and perfect. My welted skin, marked by him, kept time with my racing heart, and it was one more perfect point of joy in my body.

"Yes, ma'am."

"I came."

"I know. I liked it." He put his hands under my ass and angled me just so. His cock brushed the perfect place then. As good as the other place had been, this was better. His fingers plucked at my bruised flesh and I felt another orgasm inching toward me. "And I want you to do it again," he said in my ear.

I kissed him. Kissed him for every stupid thing he had teased me about. For the spanking and for knowing just how to push me. For fucking me and loving me and marrying me and all of it. When I had kissed him as hard as I could, I kissed him harder.

"Jesus, Molly," he said, and pinched me once, hard on the ass. His breath rushed over my ear as he came, small gasps that sounded like prayers coming out of his mouth. I followed right behind, with another small, perfectly sweet orgasm rolling in to fill the void left by the first one.

"I love you."

"I love you, too, Mommy Dearest." His laughter against my throat was the most beautiful thing I had ever heard.

"Was that better than Gummi Bears?" he teased from the far side of the room.

"Way better than bears," I said, feeling somewhat calm for the first time in what felt like months.

Boyd hung the dress up as I studied myself in the mirror. My bottom was flushed red and pink with a fingerprint visible, part of a palm print. A welt here, a purple streak there. I pushed and probed, relishing each sweet bite of pain. He came up behind me and hugged me, staring at my eyes in the mirror. "Come on, wife." He pulled me from my reflection toward the bed.

"What?" I teased.

"We're having a whole brood. We have to get a move on making them." He kissed my shoulder, cupped my breasts.

"Mmm. What if I say no?"

Crack!

"I was just asking," I said, and let him pull me to the bed.

Anniversary Waltz

Portia Da Costa

Oh my giddy aunt, I didn't realize I'd spent quite *that* much! I knew there was that new dress for the Spencers' party. And the garden furniture. And the replacement items for the dinner service. And my Day of Beauty at Cleo's Spa… Oh God, how could I not work out how much all that would add up to?

I'm in for it now. And on our wedding anniversary, too. Maybe I should hide the statement? Pretend it got lost or hope that in the fond glow of this special day, my dear husband won't even think about it? But that won't work. Julian's nothing if not meticulous, and he knows the statement always comes on this day of the month. And even if I don't show it to him, he'll check it online, anyway.

My heart thumps. My stomach feels all fluttery. I feel weird in a million different ways. And not all of them unpleasant. In fact some of them are quite pleasant indeed, and I feel more wicked because of that than any amount of overspending.

I can already see Julian's expression in my mind. Cool. Stern. But with that look in his eyes. That strange twinkle that not even his aura of displeasure can hide. I've let him down again, moneywise, despite all my pledges and promises to keep my self-indulgence under control. But he knows me so well. He was probably anticipating that I'd fail...yet again.

I'd better prepare for that, as well as our quiet celebration dinner, for our anniversary. My hand shakes as I leave the statement on his desk. There's no way that that I can sidestep him looking at it. And the damning total might as well be printed in inch-high letters of flaming red.

The house is very, very quiet. I could hear the proverbial pin drop as I stand in my dressing room, deliberating over suitable clothing. All around me there's a sense of an ominous brooding readiness. It seems to press down on my skin, activating secret trigger points of excitement. I'm shuddering and Julian hasn't even seen the statement yet. I'm quivering in my plain white cotton underwear.

He likes me to look nice, look sexy, a bit daring sometimes. But on occasions like this it's old-fashioned sobriety all the way. The quiet, obedient, sensible wife act. Not me, really, but it's performance, a game, a challenge. Smooth cotton lies against the skin of my breasts and bottom, cool and tantalizing as I run my finger along the rail, flicking the hangers, pondering the outfits on them. The suitable ones are all at one end, not worn often, or out of the house. I pull out a very good, cream-colored vintage skirt. It's long, elegant and knife-pleated. Perfect. One of my husband's favorites. And with it a white rayon blouse, softly tied at the neck.

Sensible. Demure...

Submissive.

Yes...

I twirl before the mirror, letting the pleats spin out in a last wild whirl of frivolity. As they settle back into place,

I'm just as he'll want me. Dressed to fill the bill. The big, fat, credit card bill. My head goes light, still floating as I study my reflection, and see myself as Julian will see me. Smoothing my fingers over the stuff of my blouse, I image they're his fingers, and they're assessing the layers beneath. The firm bra holding my breasts in a custodial grip. The prim top of my old-fashioned full slip. No skimpy plunge-front underwired confections for my Julian tonight, nothing transparent, nothing abbreviated. It's all sturdily made. I lift my skirt and check… My knickers fit smoothly, but not too tightly, untrimmed, full cut, no nonsense. My garters and stocking seams are straight as arrows, superneat. My heart flutters again and my hands flutter, too, at my throat, the perfect fantasy good little Fifties housewife.

Trying to calm myself, I comb my hair, touch a little bit of rosy color to my lips.

Later, Julian arrives, kisses me fondly and hands me an exquisite bouquet of flowers. Which obviously I don't deserve, given my irresponsible extravagance. He eyes me with that hawklike look of his. He knows. I don't have to say a thing.

When he goes to change for dinner, I hear the snick of his study door first, and I'm holding my chest again, as if I could stop my heart bouncing. The statement is sitting there, in the center of the blotter on his desk, and he'll read it, since he never leaves important matters unattended.

Dinner is delicious, though I do say so myself, and Julian praises me for this domestic virtue at least. Our chat is light, amenable, comfortable in a way. We've had sufficient anniversaries for them not to be quite such a big deal these days. But he doesn't mention the statement or its horrendous total. We don't settle our differences and our difficulties over the dinner table.

But as he rises from his seat, he gives me a long, assessing look.

"Shall I see you in five minutes then?" For just a split second, his tongue sweeps out and licks his chiseled lower lip. "Or do you wish to wait until another day, given that it's our anniversary?" His handsome face is straight, benign, composed, but in his blue eyes there's a demon happily dancing.

"I'd prefer not to wait, dear, if you don't mind." My voice is as level as his, and steady, but in my chest the butterflies whirl and flutter, and my lower belly is all heavy, wild turmoil. He nods and I watch his retreating back, my hands clenched in my lap, knuckles white with the effort of keeping them there and avoiding doing other things.

I love that he's so cool and imperturbable. No screeching destructive rows for us, no seesaws of resentment, then easy reconciliation, or long angry silences. We do things a different way. An orderly, quiet, civilized, almost stately way. And when we do get uncivilized, it's all the more delicious....

Not that I'm feeling stately, quiet or calm now. I look normal, hopefully, but my pulse is racing as if I've been whirling again, pirouetting. And my crotch, oh my crotch is hot and moist. Part of me really *does not want* this appointment in Julian's study in five minutes time. But most of me is counting the seconds, wishing them done and past so I can race up there. To him.

In my bathroom, I give in to the shakes, grabbing on to the side of the basin as I hunker down on the toilet, trying to relieve myself. Best go now, rather than need to later.

I must be serene, I must be quiet, I must behave; that's my mantra as I step into a fresh pair of knickers and smooth them up over my hips and tummy. The others were sticky with excitement....

"Come in." Julian's voice sounds clear and strong as he calls out on hearing my knock on the door of his study. There's a quality of youth in it for a moment, too, even though he's of an age where distinguished gray has already appeared in his thick dark hair. He sounds happy, full of anticipation but in his familiar, controlled way.

Obeying the summons, I close the door as quietly as I can behind me, then take my customary place on the fine Persian rug before his desk.

Julian appears to be making annotations in his journal, his handsome face impassive and unrevealing. No trace of the suppressed excitement I thought I detected just a moment ago. The credit card statement has been moved from the blotter and now lies in the wire basket, ready for paying. He'll probably use the online system. Afterward.

Me, I'm feeling that dangerous turmoil in my nether regions, and emotions surge and billow in my chest. I have to keep myself rigid so as not to do something incredibly stupid. Like touch. Reach out. Grab. Hurl myself forward. Julian is so good-looking, he's regal almost, with his beautifully groomed hair and his glowingly dark eyes. His body is athletic, and his hands narrow and scholarly. His is the strongest arm I've ever felt.

"Oh, Amanda…" He looks up from his writing, his expression mild and a little resigned. "What on earth am I going to do with you?"

Almost having to bite my cheek to try and remain solemn, I smile my inner smile. His question is patently absurd. He knows—and I know—*exactly* what he's going to do with me. This show of almost avuncular bemusement is simply a facet of this dance we do. One of his favorite figures, in which he always, always leads.

"I don't know, Julian." I keep my voice small. As if I'm afraid. Which I am, in a way.

"This can't go on, you know." He reaches over and taps the statement. "I thought we agreed to discuss any large purchases. To—" he pauses, significantly "—*negotiate* them." That emphasis, oh so subtle, makes me flex my fingers against the pleats of my skirt at the thought of previous "negotiations" and the radical effects they produce.

"And now I find *this*." He points, as if to a figure, although he's really looking at me, not the items on the statement. "And *this*. And *this*." Again, not the sums, just me and my face, which is already blushing, and my body, which must be visibly quivering with excitement even though I'm trying not to let it. "It does seem that you've forgotten what we agreed."

"I guess I must have," I whisper.

"I'm certain you must have," counters Julian firmly. "So I think we'd better see to it that your memory is better from now on, don't you?"

"Yes…I suppose you're right."

"There's no 'suppose' about it, Amanda." His eyes are dead level. He's a brilliant actor, but the fire's there; even he can't hide it. "We both know there's only one way."

I hang my head, not really ashamed of my extravagance at all. In fact I glory in it. The only thing that I can't face is the intensity of my husband's glittering gaze. It makes me weak, weak at the knees. Knees I want to tumble to so I can crawl around the back of the desk and reach for…

"I think you'll find what we need on the sideboard, Amanda." He goes on in the face of my silence. I'm not even supposed to speak at this juncture. "I wonder if you would be good enough to fetch it."

With slow steps, and eyes still downcast, I walk over to the polished antique sideboard and look down tremblingly at the object that lies there.

I hardly dare touch it. I raise my hand, then withdraw it, feeling dizzy again as if I've been waltzing in his arms for half the night.

"Amanda," he prompts softly, and with a leaping heart I pick up the leather strap.

It's not an ugly thing, in fact far from it. The leather's a rich, very, very dark brown, not unlike the color of Julian's hair, and the intricate filigree tooling in white is a little bit like the elegant threading of gray that he has. If it wasn't for its purpose, I'd consider the strap an object of rare beauty. But as it is, its awesome purpose fills my imagination with breathtaking resonances.

"Place it here," he instructs, pointing to a spot toward the edge of his desk. "Then you may clear the usual space in readiness."

Leather upon leather, I set the strap on the desk's black hide inset, then begin my ominous task. Files, ornamental inkwell set, Julian's favorite pen, his PDA and mobile phone; all these I arrange to one side, so the center of the desk is quite empty. When all is ready, I glance toward my husband for my next cue.

"Very good, my dear." His voice is quite kind, approving. "Very neat. And now, I think you know what to do next?"

It's intoned as a question, but again, underneath, it isn't one. I know exactly what to do, and blood rushes around my body as I comply.

Carefully, and with as much grace as I can muster, I arrange myself facedown across my husband's gleaming desk, my head facing the side where he's sitting. Folding my arms, I lay my face against them, and the skin of my cheeks feels very hot.

"Nicely done, my dear," Julian murmurs, coming around to stand directly behind me. His long supple hand settles lightly on my buttocks, touching first one then the other, the contact quite distinct through my layers of clothing. "Now, let's get you ready, shall we?" It's as if we're having a perfectly normal conversation as he takes hold of the hem of my skirt.

Julian is a very graceful man, very methodical, and in this, more than anything, he pays attention to every tiny detail. First, he rolls my conservative, pleated skirt carefully to my waist, then he tucks my slip over it to secure it. There's a pause, while he seems to consider the arrangement, deliberating, assessing. Then I feel him catch his fingers into the waistband of my white cotton briefs and peel them slowly down my quaking upper thighs. Rolling these, too, he makes a little bridge between my knees—just as he edges my legs apart, momentarily pressing his calf against mine.

That bridge of white cloth pulls taut.

I gasp. I can't help myself. I can't contain myself. The soft, wet folds of my sex are on show to him now, and the thought of him seeing them only makes those folds get wetter. It's a strange thing…. He's my husband, and he's been seeing every inch of my body for years and years. He's totally familiar with it, and I'm familiar with him looking at it. But *this* exposure—in delicious shame and the anticipation of punishment—is completely different.

"Are you ready, Amanda?" Julian's voice is ineffably polite, yet somehow deeply charged. I know it wouldn't make a halfpenny worth of difference if I said I *wasn't* ready. It's too late now to stall our momentum, to break the pattern.

There's a rustle of cloth, Julian taking off his jacket, and a pause after that while he rolls up his sleeves. Any second now I'm going to pay for my extravagance with the household credit card, pay dearly in the way my husband likes. *Really* likes…

The dreaded moment arrives with a whistle, a crack, and after a second's delay a huge blank white pain in my bottom. I hear a piteous cry, and even though I know it's me, it sounds like a weird and birdlike stranger. I'll never get used to this. Never. It's like a swathe of flame blasted across my flesh.

"Hush now." Julian presses a fingertip against the single first weal. I gnaw my lip and bury my face against my arm to stifle more cries, all the time loving his severity and deeply fearing it. "Try to keep quiet, Amanda," he urges. "Try for me. Please? A punishment is far more memorable borne with dignity."

What's dignity? I certainly haven't got any. No matter how much I'd *like* to have it. As the polished strap cracks down on me with unrelenting frequency, I howl and wail and shout despite my husband's cool and patient admonishments. Each stroke finds a new way to burn me; each leather kiss discovers fresh and virgin skin. Within minutes, my entire backside feels as if it's been flayed, roasted, blazed on a spit. The muscles of each burning buttock seem to drum.

"Oh, please…" I moan, but I'm not quite sure what I'm moaning for.

I'm begging, but for what?

Stop?

Continue?

Harder?

More?

Wrapped in red mist, my mind has stopped working.

Julian, however, chooses to hear those last two words. He redoubles his efforts, moving down now to lay the lash across my thighs.

In a cleansing rush, I cry freely, the teardrops wetting the white sleeves of my blouse. The suffering in my thighs is soon a match for the torture in my bottom. But even that isn't my lesson done, not by a long way.

One final harsh refinement still remains.

"You must help me now, my dear," whispers Julian, leaning over me. "I know this hurts you, but believe me, I mean to do you good."

With an overtheatrical sniffle, I unfold my arms. I can't tell if I'm experiencing genuine reluctance or just feigning it. I can't tell the difference. But pressing my face against the leather blotter, I reach behind me.

"That's it, my love," praises Julian. "Be brave now, my darling perfect girl."

The touch of my own fingertips against my hot bottom makes me gasp and groan and then hiss long with pain as I pry the groove wide open.

What follows is a blur of tears and torment. In a show of skill and marksmanship, my husband whips my tender anus, letting the leather dance over its target with each stroke.

I complain. I howl like a she-cat. I swear inside, silently cursing him and telling him I can't bear it, yet at the same time swirling my hips to court his blows and invite their impact.

I'm not quite sure when I pass the hidden frontier, but somewhere along the line a great flame has begun to burn…a conflagration that's wildly raging, between my legs.

"Are you sorry, my dear?" Julian inquires eventually, letting his fingernails take a turn across my agony.

"Yes! Oh yes, Julian, forgive me," I choke out, unable to contain myself. Blind with lust, I grind my belly against the desk.

"I do, my darling, I do," he says, and now at last his voice is hoarse and low, vibrating with hunger. As he speaks I hear a swiftly running zip.

And now, at last, oh God, oh yes!

Julian's thick penis slides deep into my sex and his rough belly hair makes me whine again as it grazes my sore bottom.

"There, my darling, isn't that better?" His breath catches as he inclines over me, shoving with lithe, powerful hips. "Have you enjoyed your anniversary treat?"

"Oh hell, yes," I agree, thrusting back at him.

Loving the pain. Loving the pleasure. Loving him.

I Will

Erastes

You never really expect to marry your childhood sweetheart, because, God, what a cliché that is! But that's what Mark is, was and always will be. It doesn't matter to me that his eyes are not the bright intense blue-green they once were, that age has dimmed their shine just a little, because I still love them. They remind me now of cool seaside caves, where we once kissed in secret. It doesn't matter that his hair has thinned at the top and sides, and that he's no longer that sun-kissed Adonis I ran with, chasing endless Frisbees on endless summer beaches in the seventies. He's a man now, not a boy, and he's had life hit him sideways. Life that does that to all of us, and it shows on him. But I watched every line grow, and every flaw on his face and on his body are signs of the life he's led. With me.

Of course, when we met, I couldn't say I knew I was going to marry this man. Why? Because I was six and he was five (and three quarters). We shared a desk, and I spilled milk over his painting. He hated me that first morning, but we made up again at lunchtime because I had chicken sandwiches and he had Spam, and we shared a love of Mars bars.

I find it amazing sometimes that I can remember that so clearly, and yet if Mark were to ask me what I gave him last Christmas, I'd find it hard to recall.

And that's how it started, crayons and milk and Spam. I'm grateful to the Spam company, despite the fact that neither of us like it much; we still buy it now and then, two silly old queens laughing over a secret joke no one will ever share.

All through school we slotted into each other's lives, Mark and Jim. Rarely apart, even our names were synonymous. "Have you invited Mark 'n Jim?" "Where's Mark 'n Jim?" We sat together, did the same subjects, cheated abominably in exams. We both knew that neither of us would go to university without the other.

I don't think there was even a time when I realized I was homosexual, because Mark was there, and I was there for Mark. We never dated, never talked of women—but then one day he turned to kiss me and my lips were there, as if they'd always been waiting for his. As it should be. Perhaps that's not entirely true; perhaps there was never a time when I doubted I was anything else? It doesn't matter. It may have done to others, I know it did to some, but it never did to us.

I'm making it sound simple, and it was anything but. We had all the problems that teenagers in love have, but for us, obviously, they were a hundred times worse. Homosexuality was legal—barely—but certainly not for boys our age, and once we kissed, once I'd held him so close to me that our very breath combined, I knew—just knew—that nothing in the world would stop me spending my life with him. Of course, my parents had other ideas, and once they and Mark's parents found out, any thought of university was out of the question for both of us.

Life wasn't easy, even in a big city like London, but jobs were the least of our worries. We soon found those, Mark in a bank and me in retail. With the "never darken our door again" money that Mark's parents gave us, we rented a flat, a home of our own. And when the doors were closed and the curtains drawn, we could be ourselves, luxuriating in the castle we'd built. Someplace where we could pull the drawbridge up and send the world back out of our fairyland.

Life threw rocks at us for a while, big rocks. Mark's parents tried to reconcile, but only if he'd give me up. It was a nasty time, and they used some pretty vile methods to do it, made it a real smear campaign. We lost our flat, I lost my job, and things were so rocky for a while I turned to drink. Mark stood by me the whole time, facing down every threat his parents made, working all the hours he could to get us a new place. We made good friends during that period, despite how bad it was, friends we still have today, friends with floors and spare rooms, open ears, open minds.

Finally, Mark's parents gave up for the second, and thankfully last, time. Mark helped pull me out of the bottle, with his characteristic gentle patience. Helped me dry out and got us back on track.

Yes, life hasn't been easy, but I can't imagine having lived a minute of it without him.

I came home last night to find him quiet, and only half listening to my complaints of rip-off dry cleaners, while his eyes were lost in some other place or time. I rambled on, because I know my man; he doesn't want to be cajoled with "what's wrong?" He wants to tell me, but only when he's ready. It's taken us years to find this groove; it's a circuitous route, but it works for us. It wasn't until I was checking his case—he was off to stay in the hotel; we're nothing if not traditional—that his arms went around me and he leaned against my back, his breath soft and warm against my ear.

"You smell like the city," he said. He kissed my neck and I had to deliberately close the case and slide it onto the floor. He was still, after all these years, just as capable of melting me with kisses to that part of me (any part of me, actually, but I don't want to swell his head too much) and I didn't want to crush the case and contents under our combined weight.

"Well, don't smell me then," I said, turning in his arms and kissing his chin. It was one of my biggest regrets that I'd never grown as tall as he had, but it had its compensations, like now, when I could rest my head on his shoulder. "I need to shower and you need to clear off. I'm not having you here after midnight. It's bad luck."

"That leaves me several hours, but—" he caught hold of me as I attempted to wiggle free "—I need to ask you something."

There was something in his voice that made me stop. His quiet abstraction caused my heart to contract in my chest. "Anything, love," I said, with a lightness I didn't feel.

"I was thinking today, how long we've been together."

"Forever," I said softly.

"And I know that we've done this, but I want…" He stopped, frowned.

I was panicking now, and my mind went to the problems I could foresee. I'm always the one who immediately turns a crisis into a disaster, and all I could see was chaos, and the way his words could ruin tomorrow for a hundred people, starting with me. But his arms were still around me and he looked puzzled, not like a man who was about to ruin my life, so I hung on, desperately. "You want?"

"It's just… It's just I know we've done this, but it was at the restaurant, and we never talked about it, and the families got involved—and the guys…" He pulled me tight. "Because I want you so badly, Jim."

"You've got me, you plank," I said, my words muffled on his shoulder. "What's brought this on? It's natural to have doubts, I hear." I never had, didn't think he had, but he wasn't making himself clear.

He turned and, for an answer, pulled us down on the bed, cushioning me with his body. I'm ashamed to say that we bounced once and there was a fair bit of scrambling before we were in place, wrapped around each other, each part of us a perfect fit, made for each other in every way. His mouth sought mine, warm but scratchy skin rubbing against my face. Even after all the time we'd been together, sex with Mark never felt routine. We might do the same stuff again and again (and dear Lord, again, please) and there was little we could do to each other that would surprise us, but it was never dull. The touch of his hand on my stomach, inching its way under my shirt to find my hardening nipples, it was heaven, familiar heaven.

"I love you," he murmured against my ear.

"I know—" I started, but it was hard to concentrate with his fingers running circles around a nipple. He knew it drove me mad, and would often do it until I ended up assaulting him.

"No, you don't," he said. He shifted, moved on top of me, taking his weight on his elbows, and looked me deep in the eyes. His expression was dark and so unbearably handsome that I melted as certain parts of me hardened to the point of aching. He started to undo my shirt, teasingly slowly pushing aside the fabric and kissing my nipples one by one, his tongue swirling around the nubs and his chin scratchy and delicious on my chest. "I've loved you all my life." The vibration of his voice, mixed with the cool teasing tongue, was wonderful torture.

"Not—" I managed to gasp "—when I spilled milk over your painting."

He laughed, a chuckle against my chest, which I felt all the way down to my balls; I fumbled with his jogging bottoms, pushing them down as far I could, reaching for the warm, lightly furred skin of his thighs. "No, not that morning," he said, kissing me in small dipping motions, like sexual push-ups, each one bringing his erection into contact with mine, but frustratingly, through too many layers of fabric. "But it seems like every moment since. I love this—" he kissed my mouth "—and this—" my chin. "And this particularly." The hollow of my throat.

"Mark..." I gasped. "Please." My hand slid between us, seeking his cock. If he was going to torture me, at least I could do the same. But he caught my wrist and brought my hand up to his mouth and kissed my palm, in the way that drove me wild, teasing his tongue around and around, then drawing my fingers into his mouth with such prurient and obvious pleasure and innuendo, while never taking his eyes from mine, that I wanted that moment to freeze forever, just to see him look at me that way for the rest of my life.

We undressed each other, slowly and sensually. He was surprisingly gentle and deliberate. He punctuated each movement, each garment removed with a reward: a touch, a kiss. Every reward was graceful: light to begin with, then deepening in pressure. I closed my eyes and let him take the lead, because despite the fact that we were horizontal, the treacle-slowness of his motions against me, the patient viscosity of every movement, it all felt like a dance, a slow endlessly cyclic dance where our legs and arms could tangle with each others' and never make a false move. I pushed my hips against him, seeking some relief, but somehow he kept his lower body out of my range until he pulled my trousers from my legs.

Even then he had no mercy. I lay entirely at his whim, no longer able—no longer even wanting to seek him out. I felt like a banquet laid out for his tasting, and all I wanted to do was please him. He dropped his head to my stomach, tickling the hairs there with his nose and tongue. The delicate sensation seemed to set fire to everything below it, and the entire area from my knees to my waist felt electrified, and in some way separate from me. If I'd been able to float above and look at us on the bed, I had a mad, fanciful idea that I'd see sparks flying from me, enough to light the room.

Finally naked and looking deep into my eyes, he took my cock in his hand, waited until I'd done the same to him, and we began our mutual, blissful climb. Each stroke of our hands taking one more step up a dizzying ladder of pleasure. Every now and then, his long fingers would graze gently against my balls, causing me to gasp and thrust hard into his hand. I lost myself in his hands and mouth, his hard shaft warm and pulsing in my palm, endless kisses, our bodies turning slick with sweat. Finally, I cried out as the pressure turned to heat that spasmed through every inch of me, and all I could do was let the tide of sensation pulse in his hand.

Gradually the tide ebbed; my hand was damp with his come and I opened my eyes to find him smiling like a huge smug cat. I grabbed a sleepy kiss and he pulled me into his arms, then kissed my temple, as his fingers circled the back of my neck. "This is how I planned to ask you," he said. "Not in the restaurant—I meant to do it later when we came home, but the others found out, made it impossible not to ask. But this is where it should have happened. With nothing between us, no table, no friends."

"No clothes," I said, chuckling.

"That's a bonus. So are you ready for the question?"

I nodded; I had a lump in my throat, and I couldn't have spoken for anything.

"James Alexander Mitchell, I love you, and I always have, I always will. So tell me, this time just for my ears—will you marry me?"

I swallowed, feeling for a moment like that little boy who had seen his new friend smile at chicken sandwiches, and said, "Yes. I will. I meant it then, and I mean it now. I will marry you. Tomorrow."

He kissed my forehead, and I felt him exhale, as if he'd been holding his breath. I was asleep in moments and, when I woke, late into the night, he'd gone. On the bedside table was a little box, with a simple gold ring in it.

As I sit on the edge of our bed, my heart is beating like a drum; now the morning is well advanced, the house is full of drama. The doorbell rings constantly, and I've had to hide for a moment as our extended family and lifelong friends gather to help me get ready for what they say will be the most important day of our lives. I can hardly believe it myself, that after all these years we have come to this moment, a moment I thought would never happen in our lifetime.

It's time, and I stand ready to open the door and go and greet my friends and family. But I pause just a moment, sitting and looking at the gold ring he left me; it warms in my hand the way I always do in his. It's like him. Solid. Constant, enduring.

It's too big for my finger, but then, it's not for me. It's for me to give back to him. And *I will.*

A
Vow for a Vow

P. S. Haven

A new guy started at work about a couple of months ago. Derrick. Young guy. Fresh out of college. Athletic. But not a jock.

I watched him every day. He didn't know it. Or at least he pretended he didn't. From my cubicle I had a direct line of sight to the copier, the copier Derrick managed to jam at least twice a week. And every time he jammed the copier, he would open the doors and pull out the tray and then stand there and stare at the thing without a clue. The doors came up to his waist and he'd stand just inside them, so that someone could theoretically be on her knees in front of him and no one would be the wiser.

He certainly wasn't the only guy in the office I found attractive. He wasn't even the most attractive, really. But there was something about him. I didn't quite know what. Maybe it was the fact that he was obviously attracted to me. When we were introduced, he'd been damn near paralyzed by my cleavage. Or maybe it was his youth. Maybe it was that lean torso of his that I just knew was ridged with tight muscles under that button-down shirt. Or maybe it was how nervous he always seemed in the office, still not quite accustomed to the world of grown-ups and eight-to-five workdays and paper jams. Or maybe it was his hands, running through his hair as he stressed so hard. Big hands. Tanned hands. Weathered past their years, as if they'd known a farm tool or two. Maybe it was how pitifully lost he seemed, here in Metropolis, as it were. Overwhelmed by it all. Bright lights, big titties.

Derrick jammed the copier again today. And just like every other time, I finally got up and walked over and cleared it for him. Like every time, he thanked me and laughed that embarrassed, "aw shucks" laugh of his. Right then and there I decided that today was the day.

I could feel him staring as I bent at the waist to push the paper tray back in place. I knew he could see the triangular impression of my thong imprinted on my too-tight skirt. I had bought them just for him, those panties. Panties I would have never bought for Stan. Tiny panties. Just for Derrick.

I asked him if he liked them. He didn't answer. I didn't expect him to. He scanned the office and told me to get on my knees. This I had expected. I lowered myself to one knee, hidden completely between the open copier doors. I had undone the top two buttons of my blouse the moment I'd heard the crinkling paper, and now Derrick was gazing down into the deep canyon of cleavage formed by the push-up bra I'd bought for him. My newfound confidence lent my hands a dexterity they hadn't always possessed; his belt, button, zipper, tucked-in shirt, underwear posing no obstacle. His erection was insistent and throbbing between my lips. He was mouthwatering. I sucked it, but just barely. I was not going to give him this blow job. If he wanted it, he was going to have to take it from me.

I watched him for a moment, his eyes darting frantically

around the office, then down at me, then around the office again. I wondered what he was more afraid of, getting busted or crushing the high school sweetheart he was still charity-dating. Whatever it was, it evaporated and he thrust his hips, sank his cock all the way in. He forgot all about his girlfriend and our coworkers. They were all at lunch, anyhow. Well, most of them.

I had to remind myself to breathe. Before I could pretend to resist, he was fucking my face. In. Out. In, in. Out. He told me this is what he'd wanted all along. What he'd been waiting for. I wanted to tell him I knew, but he wouldn't take his cock out of my mouth long enough to allow it. My name tumbled out of his mouth in an endless whispered chant in that deep, ragged voice of his. He told me over and over again how good it felt, how good I was, how hard he was, how ready to come I was making him.

He reached down and took the lapels of my blouse and gave a swift tug, the buttons popping off in series like a string of firecrackers. I unfastened my bra just in time for his shaft to smack wetly between the soft mounds of my breasts. He clasped each in a big hand, smashed them together tightly and forced his cock through the snug tunnel they formed, fucking my tits. I watched, focusing on the glossy head as it crested and then disappeared into my cleavage. Finally I caught it between my lips and began to suck again.

He nearly collapsed, bracing himself against the copier, the heels of his palms banging against the controls and prompting a steady march of crisp white papers to issue forth. He was ready. I was ready, too. Ready for him to come. Come in my mouth. And the thought of that made me feel so fucking dirty. I was going to let him come in my mouth. The words echoed in my head, the mantra: *Come in my mouth. His come in my mouth. Come in my mouth.* And he tangled those farmer's hands in my hair and did exactly that.

I prairie-dogged up over the copier doors and looked around to see if anyone was watching, half hoping they were. I felt a little bit high. Almost giddy. Derrick staggered away, drunk on endorphins, stuffing his shirttail in. I stood, wobbly on the heels I had worn for him. I sauntered back to my cubicle, slowly, smiling, savoring.

Two down, three to go, I said to myself.

I had been an adulterer for less than a month, and I liked it.

Stan was eighteen when he told me he loved me. I was nineteen, and it took me two weeks to say "I love you" back. We were each other's first lovers, and through eight years of dating and twelve years of marriage we were each other's only lovers, or so I thought. I know Stan's brother teased him mercilessly about the fact that he'd been with only one woman, but I felt it was just punishment for talking to his brother about our sex life in the first place. Besides, it was a fact I was fiercely proud of.

I saw Stan's cock for the first time on the one-month anniversary of our first date. I gave him a blow job on his great-aunt's love seat while the rest of his family sang "Happy Birthday" to his grandma in the kitchen. He didn't want it at first. Tried to shoo me off. Said he was scared we'd get caught. But I did it anyhow. Of course he'd wanted more later that night. So much more. But I made him wait. And he did, patiently. And for the next two decades his patience was rewarded.

But this isn't about my first cock. It's about the cocks that came after. I went twenty years before my second cock. Derrick was my third cock ever. And the easiest yet. With

Derrick, the only real hurdles had been logistical ones. De-
termining the right place, the best time. But with Stan there
had been the same time and place issues, only magnified.
We were both still living at home with our parents, and I
had a fairly brutal curfew even at nineteen years old. Our
only real time alone was spent in my bedroom with the door
mandatorily open and my father doing the crossword in bed
just down the hall, my mother snoring beside him. Even at
Stan's grandma's birthday party, the problems of time and
place seemed totally trivial next to my daddy and my own
fear and guilt and insecurity and the promise I'd made to
Amber Randall in eighth grade that we'd both wait until we
were married to our respective Mr. Rights before we ever
did anything remotely sexual.

The second cock was even harder. In a lot of ways the
second cock was more like my first than my first was. The
first cock was all but a forgone conclusion. I had always
known there would be a first cock. And then I had known it
would be Stan's. It was inevitable. But I had expected never
to see the second cock, and was perfectly happy with that.
Proud of that. Protective of it. The second cock was a complete and utter surprise. The second cock was the start of all
this. And that second one posed a lot of the same problems
Stan's had. Even if I was no longer scared of my daddy finding out, all my feelings of fear and guilt and insecurity were
still there, only now they were ten times worse. As bad as the
fear was (I was scared to death that I would slip up and leave
a clue), and bad as the guilt was (on more than one occasion
I came within a bitten tongue of blurting out a tearful con-
fession), the worst of it all was the insecurity. In my entire
life I'd performed fellatio for exactly one man. And he loved
it. He thanked God for it every time. But conversely, he had
received fellatio from exactly one woman. He had nothing

to compare it to. Maybe I was decidedly mediocre. Maybe I was workmanlike at best. I rarely did it anymore, so what if I was out of practice? Maybe the second cock wouldn't be quite as impressed as Stan was. Perhaps the second cock had been serviced by many women with far more talent than me. But before I sucked that second cock, I promised myself that what I possibly lacked in skill I would more than make up for in enthusiasm.

The second cock belonged to a complete stranger. I still don't know his name. He was from out of state, so I'll probably never see him again. Which is good, and sad, too, because he was sweet. He wasn't even mad that I rear-ended his car. It was some kind of classic, too. The kind that guys like him freak out over. Blue, lots of chrome, a little too loud. He called it something with a bunch of letters and numbers. A GT-something or other.

It was late, close to midnight, and I was on my way back from my sister's apartment, playing midwife to her wiener dog, which was having pups for the third time in two years. The car guy and I had been sitting at a light that steadfastly refused to turn green, despite our combined efforts to convince it otherwise by periodically creeping farther into the intersection. And on one of those creeps, my phone rang. And I reached for it. And I nudged up against the back bumper of that blue GT-whatever. It wasn't a hard hit. Not at all. In fact, we could barely find the scuff mark it had left. But I was rattled.

Mr. GT circled his car and knelt to examine the chrome bumper, gravel crunching under his boots. He had stubble the color of concrete and wore those kind of jeans. You know the kind. Like they'd been faded by a couple summers of sun and sweat and asphalt and oil. Like the only time they left his body was when they'd fall from him into a pile at the edge of his bed, where they'd stay while he slept in the nude, slept through his alarm, and woke up in a rush and pulled them back on again.

I offered my insurance information, but Mr. GT promised me it was no big deal. He said he could buff it out, said it was nothing to get excited about. But even if his bumper wasn't, those jeans were.

My stupid phone rang again. I answered, ready to explain to Stan where I'd been, what I was doing out so late, what had just happened. Before I could begin, he was doing the same, giving me some story about the alarm system at work and promising he'd be home no later than an hour from now and hanging up before I could hear if he was still at the strip club or already back at the motel.

I was shaking, as much from my anger at Stan now as my anger at myself for hitting this poor man's car. And the poor man stepped to me and held me by my shoulders and fixed my eyes with his own blue ones and promised me it would be okay.

I didn't even know how to hold his cock at first. I had only held Stan's, and had never given it much thought, really. But Mr. GT's cock was different. The way I was laying across the passenger seat of his car, body curled around the stick shift, forced me to try a couple different grips before he finally lost patience with me and pushed my head down. And for the first time in my life, I was sucking a cock other than my husband's.

I don't know if I assumed all cocks were the same or simply never thought about it. But GT's cock was nothing like Stan's. It was bigger. A lot bigger. Longer. Thicker. Which excited me and frustrated me at the same time. I couldn't get as much of it in my mouth as I could Stan's. But it was hard, straining up from his lap as if trying to push further through my lips, and I swelled with pride at the thought of making this big cock hard, as if bigger cocks took more talent to get erect or something.

The head moved into my throat every time, choking me, making my eyes well up. I covered this by pulling free every few strokes and gasping to him how much I loved it, how good he tasted, just like I'd seen the girls on Stan's tapes do. Hoping it would make me seem like a pro, like a woman who knew what to do with a cock, not a pretender obsessing over the details: Was I using enough tongue? Was I moaning loud enough? Should I stick my ass out? Like the first-timer I was, I cared.

GT told me he was going to fuck me in the ass. Eye for an eye, he said. I'd rear-ended him, now it was his turn. I simply crawled into the tiny backseat and waited for him on all fours. He coiled his body through the seat backs and unfolded himself behind me. I heard the tinkling of his belt buckle, and then, almost before I realized it, he had jerked my pants around my thighs.

He stopped for a minute just to look, and even though I still had most of my clothes on, I felt as exposed as I ever had. It doesn't get much more naked than knowing someone is staring at your asshole. I spread my legs, spread my ass, showed him more. And he liked it.

He gazed at me, the backs of my thighs, the split halves of my ass, the puckered asterisk between, and his cock bounced and twitched with eagerness. He laid his hands on the swells of my ass and I pushed it into his palms, and he squeezed and clutched and kneaded. He pushed the halves together, smashing them into clenched bunches, then spread them apart so widely it hurt, my asshole expanding and opening to him.

He lowered himself onto me, pressing his lips against my back, tracing the tip of his tongue onto my ass, gliding it down between my cheeks, deeper still until his tongue flickered over my anus. Impatiently, I pushed my hips back against his face, and he took the cue, burying his face in my ass and sealing his mouth over my asshole, giving it a long, deep tonguing.

I asked him to fuck it. Please. I felt his fingers dip into my soaking cunt and then work that wetness into my asshole, loosening and dilating it. He told me to beg, and so I begged. He told me to tell him what I wanted him to do, so I told him I wanted him to shove his big cock in my—

I bit at my sleeve to keep from screaming. Slowly, carefully, calculatingly, he worked it in. It felt as if my body was swallowing up his cock, absorbing it. I was his now; we both knew this. I would do anything, anything, just as long as he kept doing this. I could feel his cock moving into my ass, pushing, forging new territory. I took it all, every inch, as if my ass was made for it. Any hesitation, any fear or guilt I had felt dissipated, and all that was left was the dirty thrill of being entered there. In my head I heard *one down, four to go.*

Once he was completely inside me, he fucked me. He fucked me like the stranger he was, with zero regard for my own pleasure. He fucked me until the muscles in my legs turned to jelly. He fucked me as if he had stolen me. He called me a whore and I told him I liked the sound of that. He called me his filthy little slut, his dirty little fuck-toy. And I told him I loved that.

I could feel his sweat dripping onto the small of my back. I braced myself against the armrest, stiffening my arms and arching my back to get the most of his cock. I cried out, yelling to the empty intersection that he was fucking my ass so good. The interior of his car filled with our noises and scents; his snarls and grunts, the creaking of the ancient vinyl seats, my strangled gasps, the sweet smell of naked skin and perspiration. I was almost weeping as he filled me with his cock, accepting it completely, ignoring the ache that came and went. I sobbed on every entry, my ass contracting helplessly around his shaft. I masked my struggles by moaning like the whore he said I was. I looked over my shoulder at Mr. GT, his face glowing eerily green, then yellow for a few seconds before finally turning an angry red. He watched his cock going in and out of my asshole. When he came, he was all the way inside me, somewhere deep, his cock snapping and coiling like a snake on hot pavement.

I dropped my head onto the cool vinyl of his backseat and tried to remember how to breathe.

Tanya, my little sister, has been a cheater her entire adult life. She'd never had a husband or boyfriend she didn't fuck around on with some other guy. She'd never had some other guy she didn't fuck around on. But she was angry with me when I'd confessed my newly acquired marital status to her. She told me that I was supposed to be the good sister, the role model, the thing she tried to be, even if she knew she never could be. She recoiled at the idea that I would choose to begin cheating on Stan after twelve years of marriage. She said she could maybe understand it if it had not been premeditated. I countered that only the second and third guys had been premeditated, that the guy I rear-ended had been spur of the moment. As spur of the moment as anything I'd ever done, in fact. And besides, I argued, how is it less reprehensible if it's unplanned?

Of course she couldn't answer that. She didn't even try. She was too busy warning me against the dangers of using adultery as a weapon. Cheating as revenge, she said, was totally fucked up. She was right, for the most part. I had been using it as a way of getting back at Stan, picking men that were his opposite; tall men, strong men, men who knew what they wanted and didn't sneak behind someone's back to get it. And I explained all this to Tanya, and she nodded and said she understood. But it didn't keep her from being mad at me.

Even my best friend, Kris, was disappointed in me. And Kris hated Stan. She knew he had this coming, knew he deserved every orgasm I gave someone else. She even admitted as much at lunch today. I called her a hypocrite when she requested the smoking section. She hated cigarette smoke and its culprits almost as much as I did, but she had spotted a pair of straining biceps on a waiter in the smoking section when we'd walked in.

He was French, it turned out, and Kris and I both were old enough to be his mother. Well, I was, anyhow. Which would've made Kris his meddlesome aunt. Every time he reached to fill a water glass or retrieve an emptied plate, the short sleeves of his tight black shirt would try to strangle the life out of those bulging arms. And every time, Kris's eyes would be glued, even as she chastised me about the moral and spiritual implications of straying.

Between rounds of sleeves vs. biceps, it dawned on me that I had become not unlike the smokers Kris and I sneered at. Adultery and smoking were both bad for you. They were each bad for those around you. Both could prove to be prohibitively expensive. And both could most certainly ruin your life. Yet, like a lot of smokers I knew, not only could I not quit, I didn't even want to. Because despite the ostracism, despite the risks, despite it all, I liked it. Plain and simple. And like a lot of smokers I knew, I felt I was now part of some kind of outcast club of bad boys and girls. Like the cool kids who sat in the back of the bus. Like somebody with a dark side. Like a rebel.

I did my best to explain this to Kris. She called me a
whore. Only this time it didn't make my pussy wet, like it
had with Mr. GT. I wasn't a whore, and I told Kris that,
even as our too-young, too-French waiter leaned across me
to fill my water glass yet again, brushing my forearm with
his pressed black slacks that contained, I knew, a too-young,
too-French cock that would fit perfectly in my cunt.

And it did. Even as the door to the walk-in storage cooler
was sealing closed behind us, garçon was on me, locking
limbs, pinning wrists, mounting. A burst of grunts, wet
noises, gurgled moans, my expelled gasps condensing to fog
in the thirty-five degree air.

He bent me over a pallet of cases of frozen peas, raised my
skirt, took down my panties and thrust away. In his thick
accent, he told me I was a bad girl, and I told him he had
no idea. He told me I needed a spanking and I asked him
if he was man enough to give me one. And he showed me
that he was. A startled yelp slipped out of my mouth the first
time he brought his hand down across my ass. I started to say
something, *not so hard,* maybe, but my voice died in my throat
as he grasped me by the hips and snatched me back to him,
running me through with his cock, forcing the breath out
of me. Again he struck me and I glanced over my shoulder
to see a scarlet welt rising across my cheek. Instinctively, my
hands flew back to clutch at my bottom, desperately trying
to rub away the sting, made so much worse by the frigid air
of the cooler. The waiter grabbed my wrists with one hand
and pinned them firmly to my back. I could feel my naked
cheeks clenching in fearful anticipation as again he raised his
hand and took aim, bring his palm down across my backside,
my glowing red cheek jiggling ridiculously. He murmured
something in whispery French, and thanks to Mrs. Binoche's

eleventh grade class, I believe he was comparing my ass to a soufflé.

I squirmed beneath him as he fucked away. It was like he couldn't get deep enough or drive hard enough. It was as if his mission was to punch his cock into my womb, and he faced an obstacle: my ass. He couldn't go around it. He had to go through it. I wanted him to turn me around, to fuck me while facing me. French kiss me while he did it, even. But garçon didn't want this, and where my wants conflicted with garçon's, my wants were disregarded. I pictured his cock being long enough to run through my entire body and protrude from my mouth, like a pig on a spit. And with that, I hurtled into a raw, hoarse orgasm. And another.

Three down, two to go.

On the way home from the restaurant, as I ignored Kris's jealous scowls, I expounded upon one of those revelations you have half a lifetime after everyone else has it. No doubt Kris had known since before she could vote that cocks come in all different shapes, sizes and flavors. But I had no idea until I became a cheater. I explained to Kris how Mr. GT's cock seemed so big, the shaft straight and thick, the smell of gasoline and sweat filling my head as I sucked it. I told her how Derrick's cock was smaller than GT's and was curved like an archer's bow, and how when I swallowed his come it tasted like the saltwater my mom used to make gargle with when I had a sore throat. Garçon's cock was squat and bulging, like the muscles in his arms, the head round like a knob.

Kris told me to shut up.

Two months ago, Stan admitted that he had cheated on me. With five different women. Why he came clean, I have no idea. Maybe he thought I was onto him. Maybe he couldn't bear the guilt and paranoia any longer. I don't know. And I don't care.

In those first few days of reflexive outrage, I threatened to leave him, threatened to divorce him, ruin him. I felt utterly deceived. I demanded to know names and places, demanded a timeline. Even though I really didn't want them, I demanded details, if only to put Stan through the humiliation of having to recount his dalliances to his wife. His shame, his tearful apologies were not enough. They would never be enough. We both knew this. But I slowly came to realize two interdependent things: neither of us wanted a divorce, and because of this, I now had a blank check.

Within six weeks I had fucked three other men. To be completely honest, I could have stopped there. While I had enjoyed each one at the time, part of me felt as if Stan and I were even. Mainly, I think, because I felt no remorse. As if my lack of guilt over what I had done lent each transgression more severity. But there was a different, bitter part of me that wanted the numbers to match, wanted to fuck the full five I had planned upon when I first decided to do this. After a mental tug-of-war that lasted days, I finally decided that if the fourth fuck was the present itself, I wouldn't necessarily turn it away. If it did not, so be it. I would keep that fifth and equalizing fuck forever in the future, indefinitely in reserve, keeping the balance of moral power tipped in my favor.

In a way, this was crueler than just going through with it, and I realized that. But I really didn't give a shit.

In the days and weeks that followed I caught myself, on multiple occasions, on the lookout. Not for that fourth cock, necessarily, but for kindred spirits. Cheaters like me. Other adulterers. I imagined them everywhere. That man in front of me in line at the pharmacy counter. He was probably buying those condoms to keep from knocking up his tax advisor, I'd think. The bank teller smiled at the loan officer. I bet she blew him under his desk this morning. That couple getting into the car together? No doubt they were racing off for a lunchtime quickie.

But I hadn't been looking for that fourth fuck. It found me. The same time the fifth one did.

It was Danny's idea, all of it. He'd called me, said he'd talked to Tanya the other day when she'd phoned to ask where the alimony payment was. He told me he'd asked her how Stan and I were doing, and Tanya had told him the truth. I told Danny we were working things out, in our own way. He told me I was a bigger person that he was, because he still hadn't gotten over my sister fucking around on him. Said he still felt like he owed her one.

When Danny opened the door to his apartment, Jamie, his older brother, was standing behind him. I really don't think either of them expected to fuck me tonight, much less simultaneously, but Danny's just naive enough to have called Jamie to come over, and Jamie is just stupid enough to figure it was worth the trip.

Danny asked me if I remembered Jamie, and I told them both that I did. There had been no other pretense, no fore-play. They were hard and I was wet. It was simply time to fuck. The first position we tried was me on my hands and knees, Jamie's cock in my mouth, Danny fucking me from behind. Jamie held my head as he worked his cock in and out of my mouth, humping up against my face, alternating entries with Danny's thrusts, causing me to bounce back and forth between the two of them. Danny dug his fingers into my soft hips and drove into me. I tried to moan, but Jamie's cock was lodged in my mouth so completely that all that came out were muffled whimpers.

After a while the men switched stations, and again. Then we rearranged ourselves, Danny on his back with me riding him, Jamie standing beside me while I sucked him. We changed again, this time me on my back, Jamie kneeling between my legs, eating me, while Danny straddled my face and tried to fuck my mouth, slipping out more often than not while I contented myself to lap at him while he jacked it in his hand, pushing it wetly all over my face, before finally snaking it back through my open mouth. Over and over again they used me, sticking their cocks in whichever hole happened to be available; pussy, mouth, ass, they didn't care and neither did I.

Then we were rolling, Danny off me, me away from Jamie, and we instantly rejoined, weaving limbs and hands and fingers, six arms, six legs, three mouths, two cocks, one cunt. The choreography, while sometimes awkward, was never hesitant. They had done this before. Almost before I realized it, they had manipulated me onto all fours, Danny under me, Jamie behind me, and were entering me in concert, Danny in my cunt, Jamie in my ass. The three of us pushed, pulled and slid, writhing and grinding until we were fully interlocked, the domes of their cocks separated by the membrane inside me.

And then the fucking began in earnest. I felt everything. I felt their cocks, insistent and relentless, moving in unison inside me, pushing against one another. I felt their aggression and also their restraint, their barely checked urges to fuck me as hard as they could even if it meant they'd rip me open. I felt my body, the spaces inside being filled and emptied. I could feel their gathering momentum, infectious in its buildup, both of them past the point of no return now. I felt my own overwhelming need for this. I couldn't have stopped now had Stan walked through the front door.

I fucked with my mouth clamped over Danny's, with my fingers crawling across his scalp. I fucked with my breasts smashed against Danny's sweating and heaving chest. I fucked with my ass squirming and thrusting back against Jamie's plunging cock. I fucked with all my feelings of shame, anger, betrayal, regret and guilt.

My entire body buckled, my orgasm shooting through me like a bolt of electricity, paralyzing me. I was jammed between both men, immobilized, my body quivering with a series of tiny spasms neither man perceived, both cocks still pistoning into me, oblivious to my moment.

And they came. My God, did they come. Danny was first, which seemed to set off Jamie, like sticks of dynamite with their fuses twisted together. We lay on the carpet for what felt like the better part of an hour, all of us spent. The room was still, the only sounds our gradually normalizing breathing, until even that couldn't be heard. It was so quiet you could almost hear the vows break.

Five down. None to go.

After that, I quit. For a few weeks I acted as if it had never happened. Not Stan's five. Not my five. None of it. We went about our lives like a happily married couple. Naturally, every now and then, there would be a character on TV with the same name as one of his whores. Or there would be a story on the news about a cheating husband. And Stan would just freeze, literally holding his breath, even his eyes unmoving. Then I would ask him what he needed from the grocery store next time I went, and he'd exhale. And we'd get on with our lives.

I never told Stan the method I'd chosen to deal with his infidelity. I guess he simply assumed he had married the most forgiving, understanding saint of a woman on the planet.

Yet I missed it. I missed the way my heart pounded when I thought I might get caught. I missed the discovery of each new man, the hunt for what he liked, the search for his weakness. I missed the cat and mouse of it all. I missed being a part of that club. But most of all, I missed having a secret.

For months afterward I kept a constant vigil on Stan's cell phone bill, checked his pockets daily for incriminating receipts. Lipstick on the collar. You name it. But nothing. I really do think he had stopped cheating. And I think it disappointed me.

Seven Year Itch

Kristina Lloyd

They say your life flashes before your eyes when you're about to die. When I stepped in front of that bus, I think my life flashed before Jim's eyes, or at least our married life did.

"Liss!"

The bus horn blared over his cry. I saw not my life, but windows flashing by, a passenger in a red hat, thick black tires, trees touched with green and in the gutter, the book Jim had been consulting, *A Rough Guide to Paris*.

"Fuck's sake!" Jim yelled. "Gonna get yourself killed!"

I stumbled onto the pavement, Jim's grip on my wrist. He was livid, his cheeks flushed crimson, his mouth making words that wouldn't quite reach me. The bus was gone but the noise remained, a horn filling my ears punctuated by the wild thud of my heart. I stared at Jim, watched his tongue leap like a landed fish in his mouth, wisps of sandy hair rippling across his forehead.

Even in my dazed state, I knew his anger was born of sheer, blind terror. He sometimes yells at the kids this way and so do I, desperate to alert them to the dangers of sockets, juggernauts, running with scissors and that bad-tempered terrier at number twelve, which I suspect has a bad case of fleas. But the kids were at their grandparents, and it was as if, in lieu of their presence, I'd been put in Lola's size-nine Hello Kitty shoes and was on the receiving end of a massive, fatherly bollocking.

Traffic whizzed by. Jim's fury barely registered, nor did anything else very much. I'd almost shuffled off this mortal coil, yet it was as if someone else had experienced the drama on my behalf, their attempts to communicate its significance being relayed to me via a dumb show. And instead of understanding the episode in all its potentially tragic immensity, my awareness and emotions were channeling toward one small and pure point, to the pressure around my wrist where Jim's fingers clutched, the force of him twisting my skin and near enough crushing my bones.

You haven't touched me like that in years, I thought.

Jim flung my arm away, then jerked me into an embrace, squeezing me so tightly I fancied he wanted to draw my body into his.

"Oh Christ, Liss," he muttered. "Christ, you fucking scared me." He stroked my head vigorously, smoothing down my hair over and over. "Liss. Liss."

My shoulder throbbed from where he'd yanked me back from death—and my wrist burned as if sore from rope. The thought looped in my head: *you haven't touched me like that in years*.

"Watch where you're going, okay?" Jim squeezed my upper arms, giving me a little shake.

"I'm fine," I said. "The driver saw me, anyway."

"One day he won't," Jim replied, as if I'm always stepping in front of buses.

Oh, I know my head's in the clouds at times, but Jim likes to make out I'm witless. He exaggerates my errors and any disastrous acts of rashness to shore up his belief he's the epitome of competence in a world of fools.

"What would I do without you?" I muttered sourly, but my words were lost on him as he stooped to retrieve our *Rough Guide* from the road.

Jim waggled the book at me. "Better this than your body," he said.

Later, back in our hotel room, I lay on the bed in a towel, freshly showered in advance of our evening meal at a small restaurant in Saint Germain, while Jim sat in an armchair by the window reading an English newspaper. Whenever we go abroad, he regularly buys a day-old English newspaper, although he rarely reads one at home. *Better this than your body,* I imagined him thinking. Better this than lips, hips and breasts. Better the sports pages than your cries of bliss. Better the crossword than making love in Paris.

I sat up, rubbing moisturizer on my freshly shaved legs, wondering if he'd notice I'd made an effort. Seven years ago to the day we'd said "I do," me in pistachio-green silk, Jim in a morning suit of the most perfect slate-gray. But prior to that there'd been another date we would celebrate, the anniversary—now superseded by the official one—of the night we first got together. Perhaps because Hallmark doesn't make cards declaring "On the Anniversary of your First Fuck," we no longer commemorate that event, although my memory of it is crystal clear. We were psychology students and I'd listened, rapt, to Jim's seminar presentation on Freud's theory of the death drive. I hadn't done my reading, so was fascinated to hear Jim contend Thanatos, archenemy of Eros, wasn't merely a wish to die but rather an impulse toward stasis, peace and calm; toward the comfort of oblivion in a deathlike state.

Marriage, in other words.

After the seminar, I complimented Jim on his talk and we wound up drinking far too much in the student bar. When he walked me home, we stopped to kiss in a shop doorway and I found him unexpectedly and wonderfully forceful. He pinned me to the wall, spanning my forearms with thumbs and fingers as he ground his body against mine. He kissed and groped me, and when I made a resistant move, he saw its insincerity and pushed me back to the wall again, his hand firm on my shoulder, teeth nipping my neck in rebuke or warning, I couldn't tell. Arousal plucked at my cunt, deep and sullen like the chords of a double bass; and so, feeling my knees were about to desert me, I took Jim home to have my suspicions confirmed. Here was a guy who had what I treasured, a sexual confidence bordering on arrogance and greed, an assertiveness I'd hitherto experienced only in bed with extroverts, sporty types and men who seldom visit the library.

Before long, I was regarding Jim as The One, but that was back when I believed in The One. Now I think there are any number of people we might make our life with and The One is no more than a one whose path happens to cross your own at an amorously convenient time. Oh, don't get me wrong; I love the very bones of Jim, but sex is not what it was. And there are times when, were a bullish Romeo to come swaggering by, I could be swayed into believing seven years of marriage constitutes an amorously (and yes, adulterously) convenient time.

I don't believe our failing is due merely to the ring on my finger or being shattered by parenthood (although exhaustion, admittedly, does tend to trample one's libido). No, I believe love got in the way of us, plain old love. Because once, when we cared less, our sex life resembled a crazed experiment with Jim eager to make me suffer and me hungering to surrender. We were gleefully abandoned, both thrilled to have found the yin to our yang. We invested in some odds and sods—cuffs, blindfolds and a rubber-ball gag I'm now embarrassed to recall—but the real high was from the interplay between us, a connection so fluid and profound it was as if, in preparation for this moment in our lives, we'd been studying the shamed secrets in each other's brains since the onset of adolescence. I felt I could show Jim everything and I did, and the compliment was returned a thousandfold.

But somewhere down the line, tenderness and affection smoothed away the rough edges of our dark delirium. The postcoital gentleness in Jim's eyes was no longer merely postcoital. He loved me. I became more precious and therefore, to Jim, more fragile. Similarly, I lost the ability to cast him as a devilish bastard determined to have his way with me. He hurt me less often and with less intent, until we were having what I can only describe as efficiently romantic sex where we frequently stroked and kissed, hoping to disguise the truth of what sex had begun to feel like: goal-oriented, mutual masturbation; happy and loving but lacking that head-spinning buzz. The arrival of the children served to bind us within the family unit, leading us to where we are now, so steeped in domesticity and familiarity that our marriage, with its sporadic fumbles under the duvet, is practically functional incest.

Seven years ago I'd said yes. Lying on that blank hotel bed in Paris, I ached to say no. I wanted to be someone's whore, worthless and wanton, crying "Stop fucking me, please," and "I hate sucking cock, don't make me, no." And he would hold me down, snarling, "Whores can't say no, it's not their word, no such thing as no for a whore."

My groin felt giddy and trifling, almost as if it were happy. Impossible, I know, but that's how I perceived the sensation.

We'd been in Paris for two days but, getting high on my desires, I felt we'd finally arrived. We were on holiday, normality suspended. I could taste freedom and it tasted precisely like that moment before the first sip of a cocktail at five in the afternoon.

"Jim," I ventured. "Seven years ago today…"

"Christ, I know," he muttered from behind his paper. "Young, weren't we?"

I bit my tongue because even as I was thinking *well, what's that meant to mean?* I was agreeing with the sentiment. Marriage years feel like dog years, seven for every one (yet the kids grow so fast it's as if they're siphoning off our energy) and it seemed a lifetime ago we were united in joy. I knew I ought to count my blessings, be more grateful, but dissatisfaction had become my default, grumbling like a low-grade pain. Jim didn't seem to care that the two of us simply ticked over, but oh, I yearned for more. I wanted my happiness back and I knew something needed to change, either the situation or my perspective on it. The trouble was, which?

Well, I'd been grappling with perspective awhile and it wasn't damn well working. At home, I wouldn't have dared do it, but hotel rooms bring out the stranger in us all, and that five o'clock cocktail was an inch from my lips. Summoning up my courage, I flung off my towel, rose from the bed and crossed to kneel naked at Jim's feet. The curtains were open, our tall windows overlooking a narrow street whose shabby, folded shutters suggested permanent Parisian sleepiness.

We'd booked the break as a seventh-anniversary gift to ourselves, eschewing the traditional option of wool (well, you would, wouldn't you?) for romance and adventure. And now I knelt before my husband, hungering for a passion akin to the soul-swelling glory inspired by the city around us; by its subterranean catacombs, bloody revolution and high, shimmering fountains; by that crazed whirl of traffic circling the Arc de Triomphe, lovers in cafés and a history littered with whores and bohemians. All of this I wanted to come pouring into me as love and lust, releasing my heart so I could thrive once again.

Jim tipped down a corner of his newspaper, eyeing me with puzzled curiosity.

"Hurt me," I whispered.

"Liss," he replied wearily, as if being pestered by the kids.

He snapped his newspaper back. In truth, I think he was embarrassed. Well, so was I. Mortified, in fact. I knelt there, humiliated, alone, and seething with shame. I read a headline: Angry MPs Hit Back. And another: Sunshine Adds Years To Your Life. My nipples were sharp, goose bumps prickling on my thighs, that anticipated cocktail thrown in my face.

How can you know someone so well that rejection ceases to have meaning? Because wasn't that it? My being turned down was on a par with Jim looking in the mirror and thinking, *Hmm, hair could do with a trim*. It appeared Jim and I were so enmeshed, he thought I was him; thought I was beyond being wounded by a snub.

Well, I wouldn't stand for it. I snatched at his paper, the crash as it crumpled detonating in the silence, a bomb blast in the numbed contentment of our marriage.

"Hurt me!" I sobbed. "I nearly killed myself today. I could be dead right now. Dead! Or, oh God, maybe I am. Maybe… Hurt me! I want to know I'm alive! Fucking hurt…"

Jim stared. Perhaps he was contemplating how to hurt me, but the delay of no more than two seconds infuriated me. So I knelt forward and slapped his face, another bomb. Stunned, Jim glared at me, the flush of my handprint rising in his cheek, a lick of displaced hair hanging over his freckled forehead.

For several seconds, the world was on hold. All the clocks stopped, traffic froze, birds hung in the air, poised midflight like picture-book birds, and the population of China didn't increase. Then Jim drew breath, restarting the world with a jolt. His hand was flat and fast and he struck me hard across the face, knocking the room sideways and flinging my hair about the place. I heard someone laugh, a low, dirty, triumphant laugh, and realized it was me. The room righted itself and my cheek flamed, the buzz of disorientation percolating from my brain down to my groin.

I gazed at Jim, exhilaration lifting my heart. As ever, anger made Jim doubly handsome, but despite the intensity smoldering in his eyes, confusion shadowed his fury. For one terrible moment, I thought he might turn tender and smear regretful kisses across my forehead, holding me close as he promised to make love to me more often, perhaps tonight after dinner, when we were both slightly hammered.

He squared his shoulders, his stubbled neck pulling tighter as he raised his chin. Being on holiday, he'd allowed himself to shave less often, and the pale peppering on his jaw enabled me, with a little imaginative will, to cast him as a nefarious villain or ruthless brute. He looked down his nose at me, eyes narrowing as they focused on mine. I hardly dared breathe. A man and his wife, lost together in a room in Paris. Jim's nostrils flared fractionally before he spoke, a single word whose tawdry thrill came charging down the years to ignite a remembered fire in my cunt: "Slut."

I smiled, unable to conceal my delight. With measured slowness, Jim put his newspaper aside. Leaning forward, he angled my face toward his, tilting my chin with a featherlight fist. In a softly menacing voice, he said, "Something amusing you, is it?"

My pulse raced, an answering throb drumming between my thighs. I was alone in a foreign city, meeting a man I used to know. I opened my mouth, but he cut in with a quietly vicious, "Shut up."

I swallowed hard, feeling nervous and uncertain, much as I had in our early days before habit set in. He stood, moving the chair away and leaving me isolated on the carpet, with no nearby furniture for security. Strange, but he seemed so tall, taller than I recalled. I remained on my knees, keeping perfectly still as, with ponderous and authoritative strides, Jim circled me. I could feel his eyes on my flesh, and when he walked out of my range of vision, his gaze seemed as tangible as a touch, his fingertips scooting across the width of my shoulders, then sliding down my spine to linger on the curve and crack of my buttocks.

"Clasp your hands behind your head," he said.

I did, opening up the stretch of my belly and breasts to exposure. Knowing I was under Jim's scrutiny rendered me awkward and shy, and the folded shutters beyond the window didn't help, either. My armpits seemed to tickle themselves, while breath from no place floated across my skin. I wanted to brush something from my stomach but there was nothing there, not even an itch. All the air around my flesh made me feel insubstantial. Half fearing I might fade and disperse into dust motes, I squeezed my locked fingers for ballast. I had an urge to sit back on my heels, clamp my hands to my breasts, curl up in a ball and hug my solidity. But, no. I had to tough it out, had to ride the waves of vulnerability as Jim turned me over in his mind, prowling while debating what to do with his slut.

At length, he returned to stand in front of me. I was

hyperaware of my nipples, both so hard an invisible mouth might have been sucking them to erection. Jim bent to tap me under each breast, his touch efficiently brisk as he set my flesh jiggling. "Look at you, all on show," he said. "So obvious."

I glanced at his face, not wanting to meet his eyes in case it broke the spell. I could tell he was still mad at me for the slap, and consequently, I didn't know if he was acting out of lust, love, resentful obligation or even hate. I wondered if perhaps he was going along with this to deny me any conjugal complaint and earn himself a victory. It wouldn't be the first time. But I'd be able to tell. When his heart's not in it, Jim fucks like a martyr.

"You ought to be ashamed," he said. "On your knees, begging for a fuck."

I shook my head. I liked this game. "I'm not begging," I murmured. "I don't want it." I struggled to get the words out, embarrassed to be role-playing after such a lengthy absence. "You're forcing me, making me kneel."

"That right?" asked Jim, haughty and cynical. He's always been better than me at dirty talk and role-play, able to turn the act off and on much as he's able to turn sex off and on. He stooped and reached between my thighs, finding me wet and swollen. "Well, your pussy tells me a different story." Crouching down before me, he fingered my folds as he examined my face. "Tells me it wants fucking. You're soaked down here, Liss. Can't pretend you don't want it when your pussy's dripping wet."

In a whisper, I said, "You made me wet. Forced me. I don't want—"

Jim drove two fingers into my hole. I groaned lightly, my juices clicking in the room's silence as he thrust up and down. "You don't want it?" asked Jim. "Don't want fucking?"

"No," I breathed.

"Gonna have to do something about that then, aren't we?"

Jim withdrew and stood. My cheeks were hot, my body taut and tingling. Jim's buckle clinked, leather hissing through the hoops of his jeans as he whisked off his belt with a snap. My cunt flared at the sound.

I gazed at Jim's bag by the dressing table, seeing him in the corner of my eye and expecting him to double the belt for a nostalgic thrashing. Our flight number was still attached to his bag and I thought how odd and yet ordinary it was that Jim and I were at once this—a couple locked in their game-playing privacy where two invent the world—and also that—numbers among the thousands passing through Charles de Gaulle Airport, day after day, year after year, not a trace of us remaining save for a bunch of pixels on CCTV.

Jim didn't double the belt. Instead, he wrapped it around my upper arms and fastened the buckle behind one shoulder. "There," he said, sounding satisfied. "Collared your body."

The words alone were enough to excite me, but the feeling was something else. My arms were trapped by my sides, the brown leather forming a strap across my breasts, my nipples jutting below. Clasped in that leather embrace, I felt at once safe and defenseless, the security of being held working in curious harmony with the assumed cruelty of my captor. Well, I wouldn't get that from a bullish Romeo, I thought, and felt momentarily guilty for all the times I'd considered such a trite alternative to our years of love and trust.

Jim jerked the tail of the belt and I lurched sideways. He laughed, evidently pleased with his new powers. "Come on," he sang, pulling on the belt. "This way. Good doggy."

On my knees, I shuffled after him, my bound arms making me feel not unlike a penguin. My comic lack of dignity perturbed and embarrassed me, and yet as ever, that very ambivalence, that excruciating humiliation fueled my lust for shame-tinged pleasure. Jim led me to the bed where, with a tap of his foot on my bottom, he indicated I should climb up.

"On your back," he said, unbuttoning the fly of his jeans. "Legs spread."

His eyes shone, all his attention on me, no part of him reserved for listening out for the kids. Likewise, he'd captured my attention, too, transforming the hotel room into our everything and our everywhere. I wobbled and wiggled into position, hampered by my inability to balance, while Jim released his hard-on. He has such a strong, handsome cock and the sight of its flushed tip peeping through his fingers had my juices pooling in readiness.

"You don't look like someone who doesn't want it," Jim sneered. The mattress bounced as he sprang onto it, then positioned himself between my thighs, cock at the ready.

"You ordered me," I countered, but my voice was a whisper. "I've no choice."

Jim hitched my buttocks higher and rubbed the heavy end of his cock along my crease, slicking himself with my wetness. I was wide open for him, my bound arms distorting my sense of my body and turning my cunt into my most significant physical feature, a giant blossom pouring a slow, warm waterfall between my thighs. I felt myself a cocoon or enormous grub, my flesh no more than a necessary backdrop for the cunt he sought.

Jim nudged at my entrance. "Ah, but you want it," he taunted. "Don't you? Want to feel this inside you?"

And I did, oh God, I did. I wanted him with an urgency I hadn't felt for a long time. "No," I protested, getting bolder. "No, you're a bastard. I don't—"

Jim drove into my depths, filling me with his meaty weight, then clamped a hand to my mouth. "Shut up," he said, hips lunging in a frenzy. "Don't care what you think. Just gonna use you. Use this body, use your holes."

His nastiness made me reel and I panted into his hand, my breath making his palm hot and humid. I wondered if he was still mad at me for the slap, if anger was fueling his lust. If so, then I would hit him more often. Below the sleeves of his T-shirt, the freckled hills of his biceps flexed and tensed, and I adored that he'd kept his clothes on. Our nudity has long been commonplace and our lifestyle doesn't allow for impulsive, frantic, fully-clothed sex. Or perhaps that's what we told ourselves.

"Slut," he gasped.

He released my mouth, grabbed hold of the belt across my breasts and pulled. My upper body curled forward and he held me that way, using the leather as a handle or harness, his fist by my cleavage as he fucked me hard and fast. With my trapped arms, I was utterly at his mercy, a rag doll jerking to his rhythm. The belt chafed my nipples and he fucked with such jackhammer ferocity it sent the blood soaring to my head. Before long, I fancied my consciousness was trying to escape my mind and I cried out, dizzy and delirious, the bumping of my clit making my pleasure coil quickly.

I came in a whirl of sensation, my cunt clutching and rippling as white pinpricks of light danced in my dizziness. Jim gave a brief, smug smile, but he didn't let up, his cock ramming thrusts into my thick, swollen flesh. Then he released the belt, snatching himself free as I fell back onto the bed. Knees either side of me, Jim shuffled up my body, pumping his cock, his bright, greedy eyes fixed on my breasts. Heat colored his face, tendons taut in his neck as his fist shuddered. My body shook with the vigor of his movements, the rumpled bedclothes growing uncomfortable beneath me. He seemed to be taking a while, glancing up from my breasts to the wall, then down again. Much as I love to see the spray of his orgasm and revel in his pleasure, it was the friction of the bed linen against my skin that made me wish he'd hurry up. Plus we had a table booked for eight.

"Come on me," I said.

Jim grunted appreciatively.

"Come on my tits," I said. Again Jim grunted. Encouraged, I continued talking dirty, something I generally shy away from. "Come hard, shoot over me," I urged, my tongue loosening. "Give me your come. Your…your hot come. Drown me in it."

Jim peaked with a dark, guttural cry and the soft rain of his orgasm spattered onto my skin. It felt wonderful and fresh, its tangy scent filling my nostrils. Jim panted for a few seconds, then slid a hand across my belly, smiling down as he smeared his liquid over my skin. His silky, sticky fluid was a soothing contrast to the itch now prickling on my shoulder blade, an irritation heightened, of course, by my disabled hands. I could see a gray woollen blanket had escaped the cotton sheets, and I rubbed my shoulder, seeking to scratch myself against the fabric that was the source of the problem. It only made matters worse.

I gave Jim a little more recovery time, then, when he rolled onto his back, I blurted, "Jim, I have this damn itch. Will you get it for me? No, don't untie me! Just scratch. I can't bear it. My right shoulder. Down a bit. Down, down. In a bit more. Yes, now up. Just…yes! There! Yes!"

Jim scratched me as hard as he would scratch himself, his clawed fingernails scrubbing my skin. I groaned in blissful relief, sounding unintentionally orgasmic, then laughed at the sound of Jim laughing at my noise. And then our laughter grew, bubbling and sporadic, one sparking the other off until we were laughing for no reason except laughter itself, riding the high of how we'd delighted and surprised ourselves by having sex the way we used to.

When Jim unfastened the belt, he printed kisses where he'd scratched me. *Passion doesn't die,* I thought as I flexed my shoulders. *It simply settles into something else.* And instead of obvious, flashy excitement, there's the steady glitter of mineral veins in the rocks that sustain us. And there is this, too, the easy laughter, the comfort of his arms, and dinner in Paris on the evening of the day I nearly got hit by a bus, but he saved me. I slipped a hand under Jim's T-shirt, nuzzling up to his chest, and over and over I told myself, *I am lucky, I am lucky.*

Rites of Passage

ADR Forte

He looks around the room, at the curtains moving in a breath of air disturbed by his entrance. They're new. He doesn't register details, but he notices the light, dim and golden. Cloth that matches the curtains is draped over the furniture. The material is smooth, shiny and dark, some shade of red.

Behind him, footsteps click on the floor.

"Like the decor?"

He turns to see her standing there. She shines in the dimness like a white candle: white dress and pearls and shining pale hair twisted into a knot. The joke he wants to make about the wedding being next week dies on his lips. Instead he clears his throat.

"It looks… It's great," he says as she takes a step closer. He can smell the light perfume of her hair, feels the hair on his arms rise at her proximity. From habit, he reaches out to put his hands on her waist, but she catches them halfway, shakes her head.

"No," she says with a reproving smile.

He hasn't heard them come in, but other women have materialized: her sister. Her best friend, who let him in not five minutes before. Five minutes before and she was wearing jeans, carrying a wine bottle and a cell phone, looking every bit the slightly frazzled hostess. Now she glitters in red, like the curtains and the room.

Another face, another friend.

They're all in red, and none of them smile. Their faces are those of the women he knows: ordinary girls, pretty girls, yes, even girls he thinks of as hot. But tonight... Tonight they're more than that. They're sexual, feminine.

He swallows, and looks back at the face of his fiancée— this woman he knows so well, that he plans to spend his life with. She lets his hands go and he lets them fall to his sides.

"This is my special night," she tells him. At that, they all smile.

"I want you to be there," she'd told him.

"But..." he protested, not sure what his reasons were for objecting. He'd searched for some, because she was looking at him expectantly, waiting for an answer.

"It should be your night out," he said. "With your girls. For you to—" he'd waved a hand at the hair neatly coiled on her head "—let your hair down one last time. Go wild."

She'd laughed.

"And why would you want me tagging along, anyway?" he added. "You're gonna be stuck with me forever."

He'd been teasing, but something in her eyes had unsettled him just a bit, as it did from time to time—in those moments where they were alone and she was silent, like after they'd made love, lying exhausted but sleepless among tangled sheets. The way she looked at him as if staring right through muscle and bone to some other part, something even he couldn't see. He liked to joke that she knew him inside out, but deep down some part of him knew it was more true than he could ever imagine.

Really true. Scarily true.

"I know," she said, and it felt like cold water hitting his back, leaving him short of breath and tingling. He'd looked away to mask it, to keep his composure because they were in public. A noisy, crowded café where they'd sneaked away from lives and jobs to have lunch, because even twelve hours apart was too much.

"Bring Tom," she told him. "So you won't feel so out-numbered."

He'd rolled his eyes at her and smiled, but he knew he'd be going to the damned bachelorette party.

He exhales. Anticipation warms his stomach. *Don't kid yourself,* he thinks. But he can't help it. He cracks a smile, raises an eyebrow, but the flippant words won't form. Silence keeps its hold on him as her matron of honor, Diane, steps around and takes his hand.

"Come on over here," she tells him, as if they're all just getting together for drinks and dinner, instead of the five of them alone with him, the atmosphere so charged with sexual tension he wonders if this is no more than a seriously perverted dream.

In heels, Diane barely reaches his shoulder, yet he lets her lead him to a silk-draped chair. He tries not to think about the small fact that she's the *matron* of honor as he sits, and his gaze strays to the neckline of her dress. It plunges far lower than anything he's ever seen her wear, far lower than anything he would ever have imagined her daring to wear.

He forces himself to look up, ignoring the thud of his heart and the surge of arousal in his crotch. This has to be a test, just a test. Something they've read about in some damned magazine to see "how does he handle temptation" or some other fucking nonsense. Or maybe they're just doing this for their own amusement, for a good laugh at his expense, to see if he can deal with it.

Either way, he's failing miserably. He knows it as they form a half circle before him and he sees light shining through flimsy cloth, revealing a curvy hip here, a narrow one there. Slender waists and delicate breasts and full, lush ones. His dick wakes up fully and enthusiastically, and robs him of any ability for rational thought.

His bride-to-be stands directly before him, between his knees.

"Dearest," she says. There is laughter in her tone, teasing, and her gaze is turning him inside out again. It takes him a few seconds to realize she's unbuttoning the neck of his shirt. Before he can say "wait," before he can ask questions, she pulls it up and off with Diane's help. His T-shirt follows the polo, yanked over his head, whisked from sight. It happens too fast even for disbelief.

Some part of his brain that still works finds it amusing he can be bare-chested and still feel as if he's sitting in the middle a furnace. Well, in a way he is. Funny that.

Her sister steps between the others, glasses of wine in hand. She gives one to Diane.

"And this one for you, Sean," Emma says, holding it out to him. "We thought we ought to get you a little drunk first."

The glass is almost full and as her fingers brush his, wine spills. He looks down, expecting to see the cold drops sizzle, because he's burning up. But no, they only trickle down his chest, and one drop falls to his stomach, just above his navel. He looks up to see them exchanging glances.

"Go ahead," says his fiancée to her sister. She steps back, her hand swept outward in a gesture of invitation. Making a gift of him.

He opens his mouth to protest, but what the hell exactly is he going to protest? And in God's name *why?*

His future sister-in-law kneels between his legs.

Blond hair and red sequins flash for a second and then thought evaporates at the feel of her tongue, wet and cool, on his skin. It heats up as she licks the spilled wine from his chest, as she licks her way down skin with no wine at all on it, down to the single, stray drop.

He realizes his muscles are taut to the point of pain only when her tongue completes its exploration of his navel and she lifts her head. He exhales, wincing at the discomfort of his pants being much, much too tight across the front now, and laughter tinkles all around him.

Someone nudges the glass in his hand.

"Drink up, lover boy."

Obedient and dry-mouthed, he does, draining half the glass—a good thing, because his legs are abruptly forced wider to make room for another perfumed, satin-clad body kneeling at his feet. Aislynn this time. Aislynn who's incredibly fucking hot and very married.

He swallows the tart aftertaste of wine and feels the tug on his zipper, welcome relief from the pressure on his dick. He closes his eyes, retaining the barest thread of concentration to keep his glass upright as hands free his erection. As other hands pull pants and underwear down.

Jesus Christ. They're undressing me. No, they've fucking undressed me. I'm naked in front of them all, and two women I have no right to even look at are playing with my dick. Jesus. Fuck.

He opens his eyes and takes another swallow of wine.

"Chug it!" a voice, soft and wicked, teases at his ear. *What the hell,* he thinks. He drinks it all, and as quickly as a hand takes the glass from him, a soft mouth touches his, sucking, tasting, nibbling at his lower lip. With his free hand, he reaches out, his fingers tangle in short, baby-fine hair and he pulls her closer, kisses her harder. Flor, his beloved's best friend. Nearly a sister, too.

But then, what does it matter, when he feels tongues sliding wet along his hard-on? When he feels one warm mouth sheath his dick and the pressure of another on his scrotum. He groans against Flor's mouth, but a hand on his chin pulls him away, turns his head.

Long nails scrape his neck and the scent of Diane fills his head as her tongue finds his. Going by instinct, he reaches out and his fingers find cloth over warm, yielding flesh. Still kissing him, she guides his hand inward. He pushes the low-cut material back, feels her nipple rub against his palm as he caresses her.

Need rises in his crotch and he thrusts upward into the warm mouth sucking on him.

Laughter.

"Easy, Emmy. We don't want him losing it yet."

Her mouth releases him.

Emma. Dear God, *her sister's* been sucking him off. Well, if he wasn't going to hell before, he is now. Comforting that if he dies tonight, he knows where he's headed, and at this rate, they just might give him a coronary.

Diane bites his lower lip one last time and steps back. Hands tug at his dick and he sees Aislynn wrap the band of rubber around it, around his balls, cold and alien against his aroused flesh. They giggle as they snap the ring closed.

"We want to keep you up all night, Sean."

Oh God. He *is* going to hell *tonight*. There isn't any way he can survive this.

But there's more at stake than that. He looks up, over the sacrilege being carried out against his private parts, and finds her standing just beyond the circle. Watching.

He pleads silently. *Tell me if I'm failing you. Tell me if I'm losing you forever because of this.* But her eyes are in shadow and her perfect face like a magazine cover. She gives nothing away.

Angry desperation boils through him. He sits up, pushing their hands away, tries to stand up, but Flor's hand on his chest shoves him back.

He sees *her* brows draw together and she shakes her head. "Don't fight us, dearest," she says.

Diane slips something cold and clinking down over his head. He feels it tighten around his neck and he pulls, tries to turn, but looks back at the sound of *her* voice again.

"It's fastened to the table. And you can't take it off."

His pulse pounds in his throat, under the metal around it, and he lifts his hand anyway to test the clasp, to find the lock—a real lock, a hardware store lock, and nothing that he's going to break.

Flor runs her fingers down the side of his face. He feels them brush perspiration away.

"Come on," she says. "Give me your hand." He feels smooth, hot skin and silky hair curling around his fingers. He takes a deep breath and turns to look at her. Smiling, she moves his fingers farther under the skirt hiked up over her narrow hips. Sticky softness between her thighs, flesh so hot he feels answering heat creep into his face.

Biting her lip, she closes her eyes and leans one knee on the edge of the chair beside him. Forcing himself to breathe slowly, he moves his fingers just as carefully, finding her, making her squirm. A hand touches his dick, caressing the shaft. Another runs down his chest and over his stomach, cups his balls. Bare breasts touch his arm, his leg.

Kisses distract him. Kisses everywhere: from his mouth, to his shoulders, to his scrotum, to his calves. His other hand is seized, commandeered, dragged across taut nipples or between soft thighs. He doesn't have the skill to manage both hands, to drive Flor to the edge and keep track of which other woman's tits or pussy he's being forced to stroke. He can't think with the hands stroking him, the lips kissing him, with the incredible, insanely maddening tightness that builds between his legs, a sensation he's never felt before.

The fucking cock ring. Dear God. And the wine is taking effect, blurring the edges of control.

He focuses on Flor, pinches her clit, pinches the nipple in his left hand. Elicits moans of pleasure from both women. He glances around to see Aislynn, one hand between her legs, the other using *his* hand to pleasure her breasts, her head flung back in delight.

Oh, fuck this.

He closes his eyes and prays to whatever gods of carnal delight there are for help, giving in to pleasure, moving his hands and his hips in mindless rhythm. And that sadly outnumbered, still-sane part of his brain tells him he's crucified between their bodies: collared and bound, arms outstretched, legs spread. Fucking Jesus. Seriously.

And *she's* watching. Watching him.

Laughter fills his throat. He thinks he might be just a tad delirious.

He'd proposed one night as they sat on the garden swing in her backyard. The full moon turned the diamond in the ring a bright, opaque shining white. On her milky skin it looked like magic, and he felt dizzy when she kissed him.

"Are you sure?" she'd asked after a moment, spinning the band over and over on her finger.

"How can you ask that?"

"Because I have this tendency to demand the impossible," she
said, half-sarcastic. *Mostly serious.*

*So he'd kissed her again, his head so light with euphoria he might
as well have been stoned out of his mind.*

"I don't care."

"I'm gonna hold you to that."

He'd just laughed.

Flor slides a leg over him. She's shed her dress, and her
naked skin is damp against his. Bracing her knees against
him, she arches up over him. He catches her around the waist
with one hand, the hand he's been using to pleasure her, and
holds her in place, glad she's so tiny. But his other hand is
free now.

Free to help guide his straining dick into Flor's wet pussy.
He's past worrying, past second-guessing. He's nothing but a
machine now, and he functions at their will.

Hands still hold his legs down, spread apart, and the act
of thrusting his hips upward from this position is killing his
back, but he does it anyway. Fucking the girl in his lap until
she comes. And he doesn't.

Not with this goddamned ring.

They take him one by one, each of them different: wanting his mouth or his hands, wanting nothing but his hard
flesh pumping between their legs. Emma straddles him and
grinds against his length inside her. The pressure is impressive and insane, making the blood pound in his head.

She slaps his face, nails stinging like tiny needles on the
flesh under his eye, and he snarls, furious, digs his fingers
into her soft ass as punishment, thrusting up roughly. She
laughs and yanks the chain backward, slamming his head
against the chair.

The pain courses through him like a shot of liquor, and he

nearly sobs with the need to come, to let his frustration, his aggression explode. But he can't.

They're too good.

They know when to slow down, when to go still, when to inflict pain with sharp nails on his scrotum or his face, so that he shudders uselessly, unable to push himself just that fraction further, to find release. They torment him with soft hair and sweet nipples and cunts so wet he has to bite back cries of agonized pleasure with every thrust.

But at last they are satisfied. The silk chair drape is crumpled, soaked with sweat.

Diane takes the chain and yanks it forward, sending him stumbling from the chair to his knees on the ground. The impact jars through his bones, and he grinds his teeth. His dick is bruised, raw, a dull ache of unsatisfied need, but there's nothing he can do about it. Nothing at all.

He doesn't even think about trying to free himself of the ring. He knows an exercise in futility when he sees it, and more than that, he doesn't *want* to.

That's what surprises him most of all.

Fingers run through his perspiration-damp hair, drawing it back from his face. The same hand pushes his head up. Aislynn stands over him.

"You okay, lover boy?"

He nods. Yeah, he's okay. No idea why, but he is. She rubs a finger along his lower lip and shakes her head.

"I'd love to use this mouth, but we have bigger plans for it."

He doesn't know what that means, but he refuses to even try to guess. A machine, or a slave, doesn't wonder what or analyze why. He only expects to be used again. So he sits perfectly still as the blindfold goes over his eyes, and he feels Aislynn move away. He waits.

Then he feels *her*. How he can tell, he doesn't know, but even before she speaks he knows her touch on his shoulder, her hand sliding down his back.

"You've done so well," she says at his ear, voice soft and caressing now. "I want you to do one more thing for my pleasure."

Anything.

Anything but this.

He pulls back, every inch of him panicking at the scent of male cologne, the velvety smoothness of male skin brushing his lips. He shakes his head, a blind, mute protest. Hoping she's there and she'll relent. But he knows she won't. The chain is yanked up, bringing his mouth up against that smooth, hard cock again, and he turns his head aside. But he hears the other man's gasp, senses his sudden movement.

Christ. This poor son of a bitch before him has no idea, either.

And then it hits like a shit-ton of bricks.

Bring Tom.

They can't have.

Yeah, right. By now, he knows better.

"Tom?" He's afraid of the answer, turning his face up as if that will help confirm what his eyes can't.

Silence where each heartbeat drums in his ears.

Then just one word, shocked realization as Tom adds it up, just like he has: "Shit."

Sean tears at the blindfold, loosening it enough that he can drag it off.

His best friend, his best man, stands above him like a colossus—naked but for the cuffs pinning his arms behind him and the chain snaking down to the cuffs on his ankles. And a blindfold.

Sean looks away. He can't do this. Even though it means breaking his promise. Even if he's failing her.

"Boys," says Emma in an amused, scornful tone. "Don't be difficult now. You'll make me have to whip both of you and I'm *tired!*"

Female laughter from all around, reminding him.

"Suck his cock, Sean."

"Like hell," Tom snaps, but his dick is still rock hard, despite the lack of a ring. Despite the fact Tom's military, married and straight, and they've been friends since Little League.

Sean tries not to think about all that, but even with his gaze on the floor, he knows it. Knows how close their bodies are.

He looks up, searching, and finds the one face he's looking for. She's standing to his left with the end of his chain in her hand, still wearing her white dress, and his stomach goes cold. For a long, long moment, they stare at each other.

"Sean?" It's Tom's voice.

Without looking away, he answers. "Yeah, I'm here. I don't think we're going anywhere until we do what they want."

"Bullshit."

But Tom doesn't make any attempt to move, and Sean knows his own long-suffering dick is hard, too.

He won't think.

He doesn't think.

He just closes his eyes for a moment, takes a deep breath and lowers his head.

Tom's cock fills his mouth. So like a woman and so not: same soft skin, but hard muscle and flesh. He can taste the salt of perspiration, the tang of arousal as he slides his mouth down the shaft, and his eyes water as the tip touches the back of his throat. He gags, but Tom's hips nudge forward, and his own dick moves in response. Wanting.

Turn it off. Turn off the guilt and the freaking out and the what-the-fuck-am-I-doing. Just suck.

They've always played off each other, guessing the other's moves on the court or the field. Shouldn't be surprising that they find the other's rhythm now. No surprise at all that he tastes precum on his tongue, or that Tom is moaning, grinding his hips.

Just like every woman he's fucked tonight. *Guess this is what being a slut feels like.*

He can't breathe. Tom fucks his throat hard and vindictively, but Sean refuses to slow down, to give his aching jaw a chance at rest. Saliva drips down onto his chest, and all he can hear is the roaring blood in his ears, the harsh rhythm of Tom's breath. He grips Tom's ass and pulls his hips forward, ramming his friend's dick down his own throat.

He's gonna make the bastard come. Because he can.

Because he has this power.

Because he just doesn't give a damn, and what does it matter anyway and fuck it all…he wants to.

He wants this, but he doesn't know why. Swallowing Tom's cum, watching Emma take off the blindfold so Tom can see him on his knees with Tom's cock dripping cum on his bruised lips, seeing the proud smiles of the girls—so pleased at how well their boys have behaved—he wants all of it.

Every humiliated, tormented, sexy second of it.

The others withdraw, Tom to be rewarded for his compliance and the coven to indulge their inhuman appetites yet again. In the sudden stillness and silence the exhaustion of Sean's body catches up with him, turning the light in the room fuzzy and surreal, making him aware of each breath he takes. But *she's* still there—sharp as a diamond, just as beautiful.

Flor and Diane have stayed behind, too. They stand to each side of her and as he watches, she lets the chain slip from her hands to clatter against the floor. He holds his breath as they undress her, stripping everything away but heels and pearls. They undo her hair and it spills down her shoulders in a cascade of soft gold that sets him aching all over again.

Diane leaves, but Flor lingers a moment longer. He watches them kiss, watches Flor stroke her breasts and pinch her nipples, sees her bite her lip just like she does when he touches her that way. Then, once she's ready, anointed with arousal, Flor gives them both a smile and slips away.

And at last they're alone: bride and groom.

She crosses to where he still kneels, and sinks to her knees. She unhooks the chain, but she leaves the collar on as she lies back on the floor, drawing him down on top of her. A shiver of lust runs through him.

He catches her wrists and holds them down on the floor to either side of her body, arching over her. She lies still, waiting, but he feels the tremor in her limbs, the tension in her thighs under his. Slowly, he lowers his head to the valley between her breasts, feels the heat of her skin on his cheek, the ripple of reaction as his lips press against one soft curve. He can hear her heart beating fast and frantic.

Never releasing her wrists, he pulls her hands downward as he kisses his way from her chest to her thighs. She parts her legs silently, but at his tongue flickering over her clit she sighs a little, a tiny protest. He feels her thighs flex inward.

She's so sensitive there, so easy to tease with nothing but his tongue and his lips until she explodes…but not tonight. Tonight she'll come with him inside her.

With her taste on his lips, and in his head, mingled with

the taste and the smell of every lover he's served tonight, he stretches himself over her once again, releases her wrists long enough to position himself against her. He expects to feel the room shake when his dick slides into her soft flesh, an earthquake generated just by them, just because of how badly he wants her. So bad it's sheer agony. But it's sheer heaven, too.

Her face is flushed, red staining white and gold as he fucks her. He watches her tits jiggle each time he slams into her, hears her breath rasp, sees her sink her teeth into her lip. He's distancing himself from all of it, from the demand of his tortured dick. Lasting long enough to see her start to shake, to watch her hair moving like liquid across the polished floor as she tosses her head from side to side. Long enough to hear her cry out and feel her pussy clench around him.

He lets her wrists go, braces himself on his hands and gives in to the need. Movement becomes a blur, his head is spinning, and then pain and sensation flood his groin and he registers the rubber of the cock ring flicking his balls as she undoes it. Sets him free. Emptying himself into her. Bodies locked together endlessly.

For a few breathless seconds, he thinks this orgasm might well kill him.

But it doesn't.

He lies on the floor for a long time, staring at the distant ceiling. The whole room feels steeped in red now, sated and exhausted and transformed. Finally he feels her shift; he turns to look at her and she meets his gaze, silently, steadily.

The corner of her mouth tilts upward and she reaches out to draw one soft finger down the side of his face.

"Husband," is all she says.

And even in the dim light he can see himself reflected— *held*—in her eyes.

Naked Nuptials

Alison Tyler

"God, you're sexy," Wes said. Once again, I'd tried to make the bed while naked. And once again, Wes had found it far more interesting to muss things up.

"I'm almost finished," I told him, leaning across the mattress to stretch the corners of the scarlet satin sheets as flat as I could get them. I knew this position made my ass look amazing, and I added an extra little wiggle to my hips as I focused on tucking in the far corner of the sheet. "Just let me—"

"Sure, I'll let you," he said with a laugh, pushing me forward, so that I was spread out facedown on the still-rumpled ruby-red comforter, and then pressing against me from behind. "I love when you do the chores naked," he continued in a soft, sexy growl. What he meant was that he likes when I *try* to do the chores naked, because rarely am I able to *finish* any of the tasks I begin. If I start trying to dust, or vacuum, or pay bills while in my birthday suit, Wes jumps me. Of course, I wouldn't have things any other way.

"You look so good when you stroll around like that," Wes continued, nuzzling my ear and then lifting my long wave of wheat-blond hair up in one hand and kissing his way down the nape of my neck. I shivered at his touch, losing myself in the warmth of his lips against my bare skin. Wes chose the perfect locations to leave his kisses, alternating on either side of my spine as he worked toward the dimples of my rounded rear. As he moved, I could feel his body against mine, his strong torso, muscular arms holding me where he wanted me.

As usual on the weekend, Wes was naked as well, and he let me feel exactly how aroused he'd been to find me straightening up in the nude. For several delicious seconds, he kissed my back, making all my nerve endings hum with anticipation. Despite my best intentions, I had no more thoughts of straightening the sheets. As I held my body still, I only had fantasies about what Wes was doing to me—and dreams of what I would soon be doing to him.

Without a word of warning, he slid one hand under my body, stroking my sweetly shaved pussy, discovering the abundant wetness waiting for him. In spite of my earlier faux protests, I'd been hoping he'd stroll back to our bedroom, hoping we would be engaged in a similar position before too long. My man always knows just what I want. He slid his fingertips in crazy circles up and over my clit, and then thrust two fingers inside me, prepping me for what was to come next.

His cock. Oh, God, how I love his cock.

To let him know that I was ready, I arched my hips, and Wes took this as an invitation to slip inside me with one firm thrust. Any last lingering thoughts of making the bed vaporized from my mind as my man began to fuck me in earnest. I closed my eyes, feeling his heat spread to mine, his hard body pushing forward, thrusting over and over.

My sexy wetness enveloped him, and he responded to the welcoming embrace of my pussy by continuing to slip his fingers up and around my clit. With each thrust, and each luscious rotation, he pushed me farther forward on the bed, until we were back in the now-tangled sheets, rutting against one another in perfect tandem.

"I love catching you naked," Wes murmured as he slammed inside me, and I smiled to myself. The only thing I had on was a pair of high-heeled mules and my engagement ring, which sparkled in the lazy summer sunlight. As usual on Saturday mornings, I'd been doing the chores naked in hopes that he would catch me back here, that he would do just this. I'd folded the laundry naked, vacuumed the carpet naked, and then moved on to making the bed before he found me.

You see, in my opinion, there's nothing sexier than…well, nothing. *Wearing* nothing, that is. Based on the sheer number of fashion magazines on the stands today, as well as many of my friends' admitted addiction to *Project Runway,* I realize many other girls must feel that clothing is the best way to express themselves creatively. But I like showing all—not simply teasing with a peek of skin, a cutout here, a deep slit there. I adore slicking myself all over with some sparkly scented lotion, then sprawling out on our soft, rose-colored carpet in the living room wearing only my birthday suit. Luckily for me, my fiancé feels the same way. Of course, we don't parade around town naked on a daily basis, not like that naked man in Berkeley I read about. For us, it's not political—it's sexual. Whenever we're on our own, we're stripped down.

Now, as Wes's fingers continued to make the most sexy rotations around my clit, I could feel the climax building, and I moaned and arched my hips against him, giving him space beneath my body to touch me with more ease. Wes did precisely as I hoped, stroking me expertly, rotating his knowing fingers in dreamy circles within circles until I couldn't help but cry out with the pleasure. Wes knew just what the husky sound of my voice meant.

"Come for me, Chelsea," he urged, and I did, climaxing hard and fast one beat before my man. He rode the wave of my climax, bucking his body against mine, fiercely thrusting into me as his pleasure peaked, and then falling forward on top of me, so that I could relish the sensation of his weight against me.

"You planned that," he said in a mock accusation afterward, still holding me to his chest, where I felt so safe.

But I would admit nothing.

"You *knew* if I came back here and saw you stripped down that I wouldn't be able to control myself."

My grin gave me away. Wes knows by now that being naked while engaged in normal activities is my favorite aphrodisiac, and it's Wes's, as well. I love watching my tall, handsome man stroll through our apartment in his altogether. He is extremely sexy, with his thighs well-muscled from weekly long-distance bike rides, his abs flat from an addiction to sit-ups, his pecs like something out of a muscle-man magazine. When I observe him from the rear, my legs go weak, simply from the sight of his finely sculpted ass. And if he turns around and catches me looking, then I'm rewarded with the added thrill of seeing his fierce cock grow even larger from my constant admiration. Because it does grow, every time he feels me watching him.

We are the perfect match in this way. As much as Wes likes to be the center of attention, he also gets off on viewing me when *I'm* naked. He most appreciates my body when I am revealed, randy and ready to go.

At home, I do everything in the nude—I cook naked, read the paper naked, make the bed naked—or try to.

★ ★ ★

Our naked fixation explains why we decided that for our wedding, we wanted to be married in our altogether—all together with our favorite bare-all buddies, that is. After only a little bit of online research, we discovered the ideal environment, a luxurious tropical island retreat created for couples exactly like us, duos who adore lounging in the nude. The risqué resort actually *encourages* naked nuptials, and the concept of being married outdoors and undressed fitted our lifestyle to perfection. But because I am what Wes has called "a superstitious sweetie," I still wanted to follow a few of the standard traditions. Every bride cherishes a few preconceived notions of what she'll look like as she walks down the aisle. Yet something old, new, borrowed and blue takes on whole new meaning when you're not planning on wearing a wedding dress, garter or any of those expected accoutrements.

This became my focus for several weeks prior to our wedding. How to meet the traditions in a nontraditional way. For old, I would have the ring—an heirloom passed down for generations in Wes's family. For new, I was planning on wearing a pair of dramatic chandelier-style earrings, diamonds Wes had given me the day he'd proposed. Borrowed would be a veil from Leann, my best friend. But blue. Blue stumped me.

That's when Leann told me about the latest wedding rage in Manhattan. Creative brides, who didn't want to wear tacky blue garters or sport bright blue Gothic-inspired toenails, were having the curls on their delta of Venus dyed instead. What an unexpected solution! Several days before the wedding, I headed to a salon in an absolute burst of excitement. I am a natural fair-skinned blonde, and I keep the area between my thighs well cropped. But I'd never even thought of decorating this triangle before. At the high-end salon, I learned that I could have the curls between my legs sculpted into a heart shape, and then dyed the most beautiful cornflower blue. This went off without a hitch.

The problem after that was keeping the secret from Wes. I wanted desperately to surprise him on the day of our wedding with my heart-of-blue. Yet because we are so often naked together—nearly *always* naked together—this turned out to be far more difficult than I would have expected. To ward off bad luck, the groom isn't supposed to see the bride on the night before the nuptials. But I had to hide my delta of Venus from Wes for three whole days!

"What's up with you?" he asked when he spied me wearing knickers at home. This is something I never ever do. As soon as I return to our apartment from work, I strip down, often leaving a trail of clothing for Wes to follow if he arrives home after I do. A stunning silk blouse here. A sheer stocking there. One patent-leather shoe pointing in the direction of the bedroom. But now, I was standing by the mantel in our living room wearing a scarlet bra and a pair of matching satin boy shorts while I casually went through the mail.

"Nothing, just thought they were pretty," I told him lamely.

"Take those off, Chelsea," he insisted.

But I wouldn't. And that turned out to be more arousing than I might have expected. For four years, Wes has seen me every day without my clothes on. Every moment that we're together, we are naked, and we've always considered this one of our biggest turn-ons. Now, Wes was watching me with clothing on, while *imagining* me with clothing off. I could practically see the concept working in his mind. He stood by my side, his hands roaming over my body, touching my breasts through the fabric of the bra, then cradling my ass through the lacy red boy shorts.

"Wait until the honeymoon," I teased, swatting his hand away when he tried to pull down the panties. "Then you'll get to see me naked once again."

Wes remained floored by the concept. It was as if I'd all of a sudden turned old-fashioned on him. As can be expected by our lifestyle, I'm no prude. I have always taken great pride in my body, and it shows in the way I walk, stand and even make love. I hold myself regally whether I'm naked or dressed, and I arch my back ever so slightly to show off my ripe, round breasts. Being naked so often has given me a confidence about my body that shows whether I am stripped down or dressed up. But now that I insisted on keeping the private parts of myself private, Wes found himself going out of his head with lustful desires. All he wanted was to slip my shorts down my long, shapely legs. And I kept telling him "No."

"Seriously, Chelsea," he said, "if you won't take them off, I'll do it for you. You can just stand there and let me undress you." I could tell how turned on he was by the gleam in his deep brown eyes. "It'll be fun. You don't even have to move. I'll do everything."

"Uh-uh." I grinned. "Not for seventy-two more hours."

Wes's dark brows furrowed. I could feel his eyes on me, watching me twitch my hips as I walked away from him, and then he pounced after me, pulling me into his firm embrace.

Face-to-face, he asked, "But why?"

"Chalk it up to superstition," I told him, and for a moment he seemed to accept this explanation. But only for a moment.

"Let me taste you," he begged next, knowing damn well how much I like his tongue teasing me between my thighs. "Come on, Chelsea." He still had his hands around me, pulling me against him, so I could feel that he was harder than steel. I closed my eyes for a moment, reveling in the sensation of his ready cock pressed against my panty-clad pussy. It was unexpectedly arousing to me to feel him through that satin barrier.

"Through my panties only," I insisted, and he pouted, but ultimately gave me what I wanted, lifting me in his strong arms and carrying me down the hall to our bedroom. He set me on the bed, then lay down and gazed up at me, licking his lips in anticipation. I could tell that he thought I would fail in my endeavor to keep my pussy under wraps, but I held strong.

As anticipation beat within me, I straddled his face and he ran his tongue along the red satin of my boy shorts, before sucking my clit through the fabric, making a sexy wet spot with his mouth. I pushed hard against him, loving every second of the sensation. Wes knows all the special ways to please me with his mouth, but it had been years since he'd dined on me through my panties. We are always skin to skin. With his hands on my hips to hold me steady, he began tracing shapes up and over my pussy through the panties. I rocked my hips against him as I grew even more excited, pressing my pussy to his lips, then backing off, pressing harder still, then pulling away again.

Oh, it felt amazing. Wes does the most spectacular tricks with his tongue when he eats me. He presses the flat of it against my clit. He uses the pointy tip to trace letters and numbers. To spell out words like *I love you*.

Finally, he nipped at my clit through the barrier, and I moaned and closed my eyes, on the verge of climax so quickly I could hardly believe it. Taking advantage of my arousal, Wes tried to trick me into letting him roll down the waistband of the shorts, but I refused to allow him access, and finally he gave in, making me come with his tongue on the outside of my panties only. I was in ecstasy, my head back, my body shaking, my secret still safe.

"Let's take a shower together," he suggested the next day, finding me once more in a bra and panty set and giving a sad little shake of his head when he saw that yet again I wasn't naked. This set was a pale lavender, with peekaboo holes cut at the nipples and a flutter of ruffles on the rear of the panties. It was extremely sexy in my opinion, but not at all what Wes had in mind. He prefers nothing. Frilly little panty sets make him want to shred the fabric into bits, leaving an explosion of former underwear spread around us like colorful confetti.

"You know you want to, Chelsea," he cajoled. "We'll get all soaped up together and then I'll fuck you against the wall."

Ooh, that sounded good. I love when we do it in the shower. There's almost nothing more erotic than being all wet and hot together, nothing sexier than feeling Wes taking me against the cool blue tiles, his cock as wet as I am as he slides inside my waiting, willing pussy. But I shook my head. "No, baby," I said, "not until Friday night."

He grabbed me up in his arms and pressed his mouth to my ear. "I've been thinking about you all day long. I need to see your body. I need to see you naked."

As he spoke, he thrust forward, once again letting me feel how hard he was—so fucking hard—and I finally agreed to soaking in our condo's hot tub, wearing a cute gold thong bikini and tiny bandeau top. Wes had a difficult time controlling himself, and when we got back to the apartment, we did it against the wall in our entryway, with him sliding the bottoms of my bathing suit aside and thrusting deep inside me.

I remained facing the wall, knowing that he wouldn't be able to see my pretty surprise, losing myself in the way he took me, demanding, desperate.

"I have to see you undressed," he insisted on the morning before our wedding. "Don't be such a tease, Chelsea. Let me see you."

It had now become something of a game. Wes wanted to make me lose—and I wanted desperately to win. To my great relief, we had to rush to catch the plane, and I was able to keep my secret undercover. I wondered what he would think when he finally saw my sexy reveal. I was almost as excited by this as I'd been on our very first time together.

Leann was my maid of honor. She and her man helped us on our big day, with Ken keeping Wes busy while my best friend assisted me with my own preparations. Staging a naked wedding meant that we didn't have to worry about renting tuxes or ordering carnation boutonnieres. Mostly the men went around discussing the music with the band and telling the caterers what type of champagne to pour for the first toast.

After much consideration, I decided to use body paint to complete my non-outfit. We hired a talented artist available through the hotel, and she came with an array of paints. Just as every girl dreams of her wedding day, I'd always had an image in mind. I described the style and Melody went to work, creating a lattice of lace and decorative designs, while leaving my nether heart totally blank.

My nerves were jangling as I got ready to walk down the aisle. When I met Wes at the altar, he couldn't keep his eyes off me. His eyes swept up and down my body, drinking me in, draining every drop that he'd missed for the past few days. Our vows were lovely, but luckily brief, and then the two of us retreated for a bit of private time before the party.

Once off on our own, he got down on his knees as he had when he proposed, but this time he pressed his mouth to my mound, his tongue flicking between my pussy lips. I gripped his shoulders and shuddered, the sensations flooding through me.

"You tease," he said, touching the blue curls with his fingertips.

"I wanted to surprise you—"

"And what a surprise." He grinned at me.

"Something old was the ring. Something new were the earrings. Something borrowed was Leann's veil. And something blue…"

Wes continued to trick his tongue up and down between my pussy lips until I had to tighter my grasp on his shoulders to keep myself steady. I would have fallen down, collapsed in a heap on the floor. Unable to stand. To move. To think. But I realized, as the pleasure flooded through me, that I'd learned something new. Being on display is sexy as all get-out, but keeping myself under wraps for three days had been an erotic game of peekaboo that I knew Wes would never forget.

Love, Honor, and Obey

Rita Winchester

"Have we got some man meat for you!" Sarah threw back her head and laughed. Sarah has red, red hair and big green eyes and she loves to look at men. Okay, so I was mildly terrified.

"Really, Diana, it's no big deal. Don't worry. Some men shaking their, uh, stuff in honor of your nuptials." My very best friend, Wanda, smiled. "Don't look so panicky. We're taking you to a private beefcake show, not the gallows."

I have to be honest. I'd prefer the gallows. I'm not much of a beefcake kind of girl. I tend to prefer my beefcake in my bed or in my shower or in, uh…me. And I prefer his name be Nick, because that is the cake of beef I was marrying day after tomorrow.

"Woo-hoo! Bring on the liquor!" my high school friend Lisa crowed.

And then in unison. "Lick her? I barely know her!"

Okay, so it could be worse. I wasn't much for a male dancing revue, but it was all my favorite women and some drinks and food and all that jazz. I had no plans of being titillated, turned on or sexually involved.

So it should be fun, right?

★ ★ ★

"We have the bride, bring out the boys." My God, Sarah could be loud. They plopped me into a chair decorated with garters and inflated condoms, and someone had put up a pair of purple fuzzy handcuffs. Another someone shoved an icy glass in my hand and the lights dimmed.

I dumped my purse on the floor and stuck my cell in the pocket of my swishy, girlie skirt that Nick said reminded him of a mermaid. If he called, I could sneak out and talk to him. It was cheating, but who cared. I'd rather be with him than almost anywhere in the world. Including The Proper Send-off, the premiere club for brides-to-be.

"Ladies and gentlemen. Oops, no gentlemen," the mistress of ceremonies teased. "Only the ones on display. We are here tonight for the ladies' pleasure. A hand-selected array of heart-stopping good-looking men here to strut their stuff."

Hand selected. I tried not to giggle but failed. The point was to have fun, after all.

"See that?" Lisa nudged me. "Hand selected. Damn. Wish it had been my hand. Why did no one ask me to be on the selection committee?"

"Because they needed them unmarred and unmolested?" I teased.

"Oh, picky, picky." She winked at me.

The MC was still talking. I envied her gorgeous black satin gown, and was that…yes, it was. A whip. She had a whip. Now where was the lion? I grinned.

"We'll be bringing the gents out soon enough, ladies. In the meantime, tell your server what you'd like to drink."

My server—my hand-selected (so they say) server, Blake—was huge. Huge! Tall, dark and handsome. Shorn head, dark brown eyes, rippling man muscles but not overdone. Just enough muscle to make you take notice. "Hi, there. What can I get you?"

I opened my mouth to answer and my phone vibrated in my pocket. I flipped it open. "Say yes," said Nick. His voice was rich and familiar in my ear and I felt that tug that had plagued me all week. I just wanted to be with him, not at this crazed premarriage lunatic ritual.

"I—"

But he had hung up. *Say yes?* Odd. "I'll have a big, big, giant, um…margarita?" I wasn't much of a drinker, but felt I could use a bucketful.

Blake nodded, leaned down so we were face-to-face. "Strawberry, peach or regular?" His lips were a fraction of an inch from mine. So close I could feel the warm tickle of his breath on my mouth. I shivered. Was he crazy or just intense? Either way, it managed to unnerve me.

"Peach?" I liked peaches, so what the hell.

"You're the bride?"

"I am." He was still there. Big brown eyes pinned to mine, mouth so close barely a wisp of smoke could have snaked between us. "I am—" I cleared my throat "—the betrothed." Shit, how stupid did that sound?

"Will you do me the honors of a kiss before I go?"

I waited for him to grin. Or for the punch line. Or for the men with butterfly nets to come in and claim me. Instead, I had a faceful of handsome, patient, waiting-for-an-answer Blake. In my mind I heard Nick. *Say yes.*

I felt a bit like Alice down the rabbit hole but I nodded. What the hell, right? "Yes?" I said.

And he kissed me. He leaned in, soft, plump, manly lips crushing to mine. He put his order pad on the table and put his hands in my hair. He hauled me forward, gently but firmly, all the while his tongue slipping over and around mine, so that my toes curled in my sleek red boots and my mind went soft and white around the edges. He kissed me harder and my pussy flooded with heat and liquid want. Then he pulled back, kissed me once more softly on the lips, and stood. "I'll be right back with your order."

I turned to see my friends staring, stunned and wide-eyed, as I ran my tongue over my lips and tasted Blake on my mouth. I shivered again; had it gotten cold? Or was it hot? And then I shrugged. "Sorry. I don't know what…came over me." I didn't know how to explain Nick's call, so I wouldn't. I was the bride, after all. Now, where was my drink?

"We know you've been patient, ladies, so it's time for your reward!" The MC was back, her long sleek hair tethered high atop her head in a ponytail that reminded me of a circus horse. She was wildly beautiful, like an animal, and I couldn't help but stare. "Here are the boys. Enjoy the view!" She ended with a flourish and disappeared as a herd of handsome, huge men hit the stage. I was relieved to see that no one was oiled up, shiny or wearing any kind of thong.

Thank God for small favors.

One stood out above all others, though. He looked like Nick. Dark chocolate hair that streamed lime-green, bright blue, hot pink from the swirling overhead lights. He wore faded busted jeans and work boots, and when he danced he did not hold a maniacal smile on his face like some performers, but a cockeyed, knowing grin. My eyes went right to him and riveted. I knew it wasn't my Nick, but damn.

My phone vibrated and I popped it open. "Good job on saying yes, baby. I liked watching that guy want you. But not get you. Nothing more than a little kiss," he whispered in my ear.

I looked around wildly. Amid all the gyrating men,

beautiful people, caterwauling girlfriends and flashing lights, I was a small, nonmoving force. No Nick. Anywhere. I glanced up on stage and the guy was coming toward me. The one who looked like Nick. The one with the jeans and work boots and cockeyed grin. The one that made my heart speed up and my panties wet. Here he came.

"Nick, where—"

"Shh. Just listen. Do it again, okay? Say yes. Do you understand, Diana?"

"Yes, I under— Well, not really. I mean…"

He was right there, edge of the stage, barely dancing. More like moving so slightly to the music that it couldn't be cheesy or gross, but was somehow inexplicably, incredibly sexy and hot. I shook my head, confused.

"Do, it, Diana. Say yes," Nick growled, and then hung up. Again!

"Oh my *gawd!* He is checking you out!" Sarah wailed, twirling that wild red hair around her fingers and bouncing like a madwoman to the techno beat. I wanted to crawl in a hole. Or punch her. I wasn't sure. Instead, I kept my gaze focused on the Nick double who was coming down off the stage. *Say yes*… What the hell did he mean? A clawing panic filled me, but then I remembered I trusted Nick. I'd do what he said. Even if I didn't understand just yet.

Nick's double came toward me, smiling. He leaned in, pushing me gently in the chest with tented fingers so I sat down almost against my will in the red, crushed velvet, padded chair. "So, bride-to-be, would you like a lap dance? Can I dance just for you?"

"N—" I stopped myself. Was this what Nick meant? Surely not. He wouldn't want this person gyrating all over me days before we got married. I was still recovering from Blake's hot kiss! And all the bits of me south of my border had not recovered at all. My pussy still ached, my nipples still rose indignantly inside my lace bra and my head was still swimming. And now the sexy doppelganger from hell was in my face, wanting to shake his moneymaker to the beat. For me! "Yes." I sighed.

He grinned. "Good girl," he said, sounding so much like my man. He pressed his body close to mine, hovering but not touching my lap. He was huge, and if he sat on me...what would happen? Would I get squished, broken or worse... God...horny? Too late! I was horny already. Completely turned around and backward and confused. That was how I felt. But I also felt this big, strong, warm man dancing so close to me that his chest brushed my hard nipples through the thin fabric that separated us. But just barely. His fingers grazed my hair, so soft that at first I thought I had imagined it. The tips trailed along the lines of my body but never really touched me. It was as if he was stroking the air above my skin. I felt the tingle of his energy and the heat baking off him in waves as he moved ever so slowly, like something wild and dangerous. "Jesus," I said, not thinking.

"Close. Jess. Nice to meet you, missus. You are the one to be wed?"

I could only nod as some very minuscule part of him touched some minuscule part of me, but only for a fraction of a heartbeat. Not long enough to draw a breath or register a location. All of me tingled and shook. All of me wanted to get up, go find Nick and fuck him until he forgot his name. "Yes," I managed to reply. That seemed to be my word for the night.

"He is a lucky man," Jess said. I picked up the soft, slight and nearly unnoticeable cadence of some foreign accent. His dark hair slid into his eyes and he grinned, his fingers dancing along the contours of my face, one fingertip barely touching my lips. Just long enough for my heart to stall and my cunt to twitch. I needed to get laid. Like…yesterday.

"Time for the bride to come up and say a few words!" It was the commanding voice of the MC. And just like that, Jess was gone, and I was in the chair alone, shivering, a horny, mussed-up bride-to-be. I rose as gracefully as possible, trying not to blink and strain to see in the weird lights. I stumbled forward with an urgent intent to listen.

My phone gave another jumping buzz and I opened it. "Don't say 'say yes' again!" I hissed. "I need you. Badly. So, just don't say it. Got it?"

Nick's almost malicious chuckle made the hair on my neck raise up and wave. "Okay. I'll say *just do what she says* then." And he hung up. He. Hung. Up.

Damn!

With the help of the mistress of ceremonies, now done up in royal purple with a pinup-esque hairdo, I stood on stage as a crowd of women and servers clapped. "Are you all ready to do the deed, Diana?" the MC asked.

"Yes. Yes, I am. I am ready." I smiled. I had to pee. My nerves were doing the jump and jive in my belly, along my spine. Why was I up here and why were they torturing me and why was she looking at me like that? The MC has huge green eyes and full pink lips. A small mole above her upper lip made me want to touch it with the tip of my finger. A beauty mark. Truly.

"Good, glad to hear. How many years have you been with your man, honey?"

"Nick? Ten. Ten years. And he said a solid decade is too long to wait, but we were only seventeen when we met and—"

"And now he's gonna make an honest woman out of her!"

Lisa yelled, and gave me the thumbs-up. I snorted and then blushed.

"I say we give you an appropriate last hurrah. The way we do things here at The Proper Send-off. I want to give her one spank for every year she's been with her guy. What say you, ladies of the audience?"

Oh. Dear. Holy. What?

"I, um...I'm not sure that..."

But no one was listening to me. Which is why I hate bachelorette parties. But they were all out there roaring and clapping, hooting and hollering like some backwoods jug band gone haywire. I rolled my eyes, anxiety making my stomach dance and dip. The MC turned to me and smiled, her teeth impossibly white in the flashing black light. She sat on a throne that two big, burly men wheeled out and locked into place. Then she patted her lap and said, "Belly up to Bonnie, baby. It's time for a spanking."

"But I really don't do that kind of th—" *Just do what she says.*

I sighed, glancing around again for Nick. I knew he was here. I could feel it now, him watching me. Orchestrating all of this to make me crazy. And it was working. Nick always joked with me. "Love, honor and obey, baby. I love to watch you obey."

That thought set my body on high alert. My senses sharpened and a pulse beat between my legs, one that would eventually drive me mad if I didn't find Nick and have him. But the thought that he was watching me from somewhere was enough to make the whole spanking thing seem that much more dirty, that much more kinky. I climbed onto the small throne, draped my belly over her knees, my fingers trailing over the toes of her patent leather fuck-me boots, and raised my ass in the air. She pressed her knee to my pelvis and I felt the pressure on my clit, in my pussy. I bit my lip, trying to focus on the fact that: a) I was the bride; and b) I was on a stage in front of lots of people.

The women went wild, but it was all a dull roar to me. All I could think about, worry about, wonder about was Nick. And where he was. The MC bent down and whispered, "Bonnie will do you up right, darling. And that man of yours, he's a keeper." Her breath smelled like cantaloupe and I could smell her purple leather skirt and perfume. I hummed and the vibration seemed to rock through the core of me. I'd give a million dollars for Nick to drag me off and fuck me. For now, I would jump through his hoops.

"I plan to keep him." I sighed, as her hand ran along the swell of my ass cheek. She was gentle, but that would change. And knowing Nick, he had told her all. Told her that, yes, I could go for a hard spanking once in a while. And by once in a while I meant as often as possible.

"Good girl," she said, the term of the night, it seemed, and the first blow landed.

"One!" yelled the crowd in unison

The vibration of voices and the sharp crack of the blow filled my womb with fire. My pussy was molten. Ready. Missing only one thing—Nick.

When the mistress of ceremonies hit ten, the crowd went wild. I moved and wiggled in her lap, trying to focus on my crowing, dancing, drunken friends. My bottom stung, hot and throbbing from my ten blows, and my eyes darted wildly, trying to find Nick. She took pity on me, stroking my ass with feathery, soothing touches that made my eyelids drift shut for a second or so. Bonnie leaned in and said, "Behind the curtain. Go through the slit, turn right. He's watching from back there, honey."

She tapped my ass gently and helped me stand. I didn't

think, just bent down and kissed her. She held my face, kissing me a beat longer than I had intended. I meant for it to be
a thank-you peck, but her tongue touched mine for a brief
second and all my nerve endings sizzled and sang. "Ever
kissed a girl before?" She laughed, releasing me.

"No."

"Go on and cross that off your bucket list, then."

I grinned. "I'm sure he saw that, too."

"No doubt. Go on. Go find him." She tapped my ass with
her handy-dandy whip and I scooted off.

I didn't have to look. I pushed blindly through the long
red curtains and crashed right into a wall of man and muscle.
Nick. He grabbed me up, mouth smashed to mine, kissing
me. We staggered back, hit a door, bounced into a room and
I shoved my hands in his hair, tugging so he hissed and bit
my tongue. "God, you tortured me." I yanked again and
slipped my pussy along the hard line of his cock through his
jeans.

Nick kicked the door shut. We were in someone's teeny
tiny dressing room. God, I hoped they didn't need it. And
then I didn't care, because he was tugging the buttons on
his fly and I was wrestling with my panties, my skirt flying
up around my middle like some colorful bobbing jellyfish
in an invisible tide. "Love, honor and obey, Di. You did
good, baby. You did so fucking good. Above and beyond."
He shoved my wayward skirt up almost to my breasts, then
yanked up my hundred dollar tee to get at my breasts. His
hot mouth started sucking and licking, until my head lolled
back and hit the small, peeling mirror.

"I always obey," I lied.

"You lie." Nick hooked my leg up around his waist, sliding the hot, pebble-smooth head of his cock to my pussy. "I
wanted to see you obey. Be a bad girl for the night."

"On your orders," I managed to answer, arching my hips so my body could take him in. But he made me suffer. Made me wait. He stood there, kissing me, pawing me, hands everywhere—demanding and pulling at me. But he did not slip into me. He stayed poised and ready while I quivered and shook, my teeth actually chattering from need.

"Yes. I asked and you obeyed. You love me." He slipped in an inch.

Just an inch and nothing more.

My body worked up around him as if my pussy could draw him in by sheer will. "Yes."

Nick grunted, kissed me softly so that I made a desperate heady sound. "You honor me." He laughed and slipped into me another inch, stilling like some maddening Zen sex master.

"I do. I do. I honor you. I love you and honor you and oh, God, Nicky give it to me," I begged. I didn't care anymore. All I had wanted all night long was to be with him. Right like I was now. And all I wanted was for him to fuck me.

He hoisted me up so my ass hit the weathered lip of the makeup table we were draped across. Bottles rattled and fell, and I would have to remember to apologize to whoever got ready in here. He pushed hard and his cock filled me so that I groaned and clutched at him.

"And you obeyed me, baby."

"Yes, yes, I did, Nick. And I deserve a reward." I gasped, throwing my legs wider for him, pulling at him with greedy, frenzied fingers.

Nick laughed, slamming into me. His mouth suckled and kissed and licked along my jaw, my throat, my collarbone. He dipped his tongue into the hollows of my clavicle until I shimmied in his arms because it tickled. "You're the best wife-to-be ever, baby. I love you."

His voice had gone dark denim and his eyes sparkled like a dark sky full of stars. He was going to come. My hair whispered along the antique mirror, and out in the noisy other place that was not here, people cheered. I gripped his shoulders, my pussy growing tighter, my heart growing bigger. This was my reward for loving and honoring and obeying Nick. I wanted this reward until I was very old. So old that I forgot how much I loved when Nicky fucked me. Which should be…never.

"I love you, too," I confessed, biting at his lips as his fingers pinched my spanked-red ass cheeks. "I love you, too. So much," I babbled.

We came, together, man-and-wife to-be. The mirror beating out a dirty Morse code on the old theater wall.

"I will reward your obedience for—" He stopped, dark eyes hooded with his recent orgasm.

"For…?" I prompted, gripping his cock with my pussy so that he rolled his eyes and groaned.

"Forever, or as long as you'll have me, baby. As long as you'll have me." He fingered my voluminous skirt. Tucked my breasts back in my soft cotton tee.

"Forever it is," I said, and kissed him again.

May the Best Man Win

Kate Pearce

April hesitated outside the hotel door and checked the number against the one written on the back of her hand. Okay, so she'd turned up a couple of days early for her own Vegas wedding, but she was sure Tex wouldn't mind. She stared down at the pointed toes of her lucky red cowboy boots. He'd be pleased to see her, wouldn't he? She swallowed hard. So why the hell was she still standing in the hall like a fool?

She knocked on the door and heard Tex's familiar booming laugh. She fixed a smile on her face as the door began to open.

"Hey, quiet down in there, I gotta get this!"

April stared at the expanse of Tex's muscled chest, her smile dying as she registered his shocked expression and his instinctive move to slam the door in her face. And no wonder. Sprawled on the bed behind him were two blondes, naked except for their pink cowboy hats and matching thongs.

Tex stepped into the hallway and shut the door behind him, tried to kiss April's cheek. "Babe, you weren't supposed to get here until Saturday."

April pretended to sigh. "God, Tex, you're right. This is *all my fault,* isn't it? How dare I turn up when you're having fun?" She narrowed her eyes. "And how dare you fuck those two tarts when we're supposed to be getting married on Saturday?"

Tex scowled and ran a hand through his thick black hair. "Babe, they don't mean anything to me, you know that. It's just that I get lonely without you…."

"*Right.* Ever thought about using your hand and the hotel porn channel? What do you think I do?"

April yanked off her engagement ring, grabbed his hand and dropped the diamond into his rope-callused palm. So much for love, so much for marrying the boy next door. Since Tex had become a rodeo star he'd changed, seemed to think he was God's gift to women and had a right to fuck anyone he wanted to.

"I told you last time that I wasn't going to listen to any more of your excuses," April said. "So I'm done. We're done. Goodbye."

"Babe…"

April walked away, half hoping he'd come after her, but knowing he wouldn't. He was way too full of himself these days and would assume she'd come running back whenever he snapped his fingers. But that wasn't going to happen anymore. As she turned the corner, tears filled her eyes. All those years of her life and her career, wasted on that asshole. He'd been so sweet when they'd first met, so in love with her, so willing to please….

"Hey, hold up, honey."

April jumped as she realized she'd walked right into the checked shirt of another cowboy. This one smelled of leather and sandalwood rather than beer and cheap perfume like Tex. She raised her head and stared into the amused brown eyes of Ben Carlton, an old rodeo friend of both hers and Tex's. His expression changed and he dropped his hands to her shoulders.

"What's up, April? I didn't think you were due in till Saturday. Isn't that the big day?"

She hastily wiped her eyes. Ben was as tall as Tex, but bigger all over. Despite his size, he had a gentle way with horses April had always admired.

"Nothing much. I just realized that my ex-fiancé is a dumb-ass, two-timing loser."

"Your ex-fiancé? Shit, what did he do?"

"What do you think? Put it this way, he wasn't exactly pleased to see me."

He sighed. "Not those two blondes? They've been all over him this week."

She frowned up at Ben as he walked her toward the bank of elevators. "You don't sound very surprised."

Ben pushed his Stetson back on his head. "Jack and I tried to have a little talk with Tex the other night, but he didn't want to hear us. I'm sorry, April. He's acting like a complete jerk."

She forced a smile. "I got that, but thanks for trying to set him straight."

"Hell, honey, me and Jack know how much you care for the bastard, and how much you've given up for him. You could've been a barrel racing champ in your own right if you'd paid less attention to Tex and more to your career."

"No need to rub it in, Ben. I've been a fool."

He put his fingers under her chin and kissed her nose. "You're no fool. How about you get a room and meet me in the bar for a drink?" He winked. "I'm certain Jack and I can take your mind off your troubles."

"Are you sure? I don't want to interrupt, and I know that you and Jack are..." *God, how could she put this delicately?*

"More than just best buddies?" Ben's smile was as sexy as hell. "Do you think I'm gay, then?"

Dammit, she was blushing, and she guessed he was enjoying watching her squirm. She'd definitely wondered, and had often regretted it, as well. Ben was far too fine a specimen to lose to the gays.

"Jack and I have an arrangement," Ben said. "He likes to be fucked, and sometimes I'm willing to oblige him, but I'm not gay." He studied her intently. "Do you still want to come and have a drink with us?"

She smiled at him. "Absolutely."

"Great, you have my cell number, right?"

"Yeah, I do."

"Then call me when you're set, and I promise you won't regret it."

The elevator pinged and April stepped inside, kept watching Ben until the doors shut and she was taken down to the lobby. Shouldn't she be in tears now, rather than contemplating an evening out with two of the nicest, sexiest guys on the rodeo circuit? Her engagement was over, her career was in ruins, and all she felt was a huge sense of relief, as if all the doubts and fears of the past year had evaporated. Had Tex really brought her that low? Did that explain her reluctance to even knock on his door?

April pushed aside her confusion and headed for the registration desk. With a bit of extra eye contact and a fine display of cleavage she managed to get a room on the fifth floor. She had no idea if Tex would come after her, and asked the hotel clerk to block any calls from his room. She didn't want to deal with him and his tantrums right now. She wanted to enjoy her evening and forget he'd ever existed.

She dressed in her shortest denim skirt and a blue silky halter-neck top that matched her eyes. High-heeled silver sandals and lashings of mascara and red lipstick did a lot to restore her confidence and set her thinking. If Tex saw her in that bar with Ben and Jack, there was no way he would ever think she was missing him. She intended to be the life and soul of the party.

When she walked into the crowded bar, she paused and looked around. Because it was finals week, the place was crawling with cowboys, some the real deal, others the dime-store variety. Before she could call Ben, he waved at her from the bar and she made her way through the throng. His smile of welcome was enough to make her glad she'd had the courage to stay in Vegas. Even in her high heels he still topped her by about six inches.

"Hey, April." Ben touched the shoulder of the guy sitting next to him. "You remember Jack Delano, right?"

"Of course I do. How're you doing?"

April smiled at Ben's companion. He was tall but slender compared to Ben, his black hair and tanned skin reflecting his South American heritage, his blue eyes hinting at something more European. There was a quietness about him that had always intrigued April, a stillness that few men in her world possessed or valued. But he noticed everything and was the quickest to react to any problem. In the years she'd traveled around the country on the rodeo circuit, she'd never seen him lose his temper with an animal or a person.

"I'm doing good." Jack touched her arm. "Sorry to hear about Tex being such a fuckhead." He nodded at the far corner of the bar. "He's here with the dumb blonde buckle bunnies. Me and Ben thought you'd probably like to go somewhere else."

She smiled at them both. "That sounds good. As long as

there's beer and dancing, I'm happy." God, she really was. The thought of not having to worry about what Tex was getting up to without her, waiting for him to call, hating it when he forgot, listening to him tell her the same lies over and over and over...

Ben took her hand. "Then let's go."

He pushed a path through the throng toward the exit, and Jack stayed close behind her, one hand riding casually on her hip. April let out her breath as they emerged into the golden pillars of the hotel lobby. Her smile faded as Tex appeared from the direction of the restrooms. He stopped right in front of her, his handsome face flushed, his gaze darting between her, Ben and Jack.

"Where the fuck do you think you're going?"

"Out with my friends," April said.

Tex swaggered a step closer. "The loser and the gay? Is that the best you could do?"

Beside her, Ben stiffened, and April put a hand on his arm. "Nope, two guys I grew up with on the rodeo circuit. Guys who still like me for who I am and haven't turned out to be a worthless dick like you."

Tex's smile wavered and he pointed at Ben. "You've always wanted to get in her pants, haven't you?"

Ben shrugged. "Hell, yeah, who wouldn't? Even Jack wants to bang her. Your loss, buddy."

April stifled a smile as Tex's expression turned mean. She didn't want any fighting, didn't care if Tex thought she'd come back to him if he beat the other guys up. It was definitely time to go. She linked her arms through Ben's and Jack's.

"Night, Tex."

She kept moving until they were out in the hazy evening heat and the constant roar of the Vegas traffic. Her shoulders tensed in case Tex decided to follow them. But even he wasn't quite man enough to take on Ben and Jack.

"Do you really want to get in my pants, guys, or did you just say that to annoy Tex?"

Ben stopped walking. "Honey, come on, you know I've always carried a torch for you." He smoothed a hand over the front of his Wranglers. "A big one." He winked at her and then at Jack. "And Jack's willing to pitch in if we need some variety."

April stared up at Ben and slowly licked her lips. What would he taste like? Better than Tex, she reckoned. Better even than maple-and-pecan-butter ice cream.

"Let's go dance."

"Sure." Ben reclaimed her hand. "Let's do that."

The bar he chose was just as crowded as the one in the hotel. When April tried to dance, her body ended up plastered over Ben's front. Not that he seemed to mind, or did anything other than draw her even closer, so that she could rest her cheek on his shirt and hear his heartbeat, appreciate the heat and thickness of his cock rubbing against her stomach. His big hand clamped down on her ass, his thumb riding under the hem of her skirt to stroke the soft underside of her buttock.

"Umm...you smell good, honey. Like home."

April looked up and Ben lowered his head and captured her lips, kissed her with a slow lascivious ease that made her instantly wet. When he drew back she simply stared at his narrowed brown eyes and pressed herself closer into the swell of his cock.

His smile was crooked. "I'd *really* like to get in your pants now, but perhaps we should take this someplace else?"

April nodded. She didn't fuck around when Tex was gone, and despite her best solo efforts she was dying to feel a real man, a real cock, and a real wet tongue sucking her breasts and pussy. She frowned up at Ben.

"Do you think I'm shallow?"

"Nope."

"Two hours ago I was engaged to Tex and ready to marry him on Saturday, and now I'm contemplating going to bed with you and Jack."

He looked down at her as they headed off the dance floor. "First off, I don't think you would've gone through with the wedding. You're way too smart for that. And secondly, I think you're doing the right thing. Tex gets two slutty blondes, you get two hot guys. It's kind of like cowboy karma."

April squeezed his arm. "So you don't think I'm using you?"

Ben poked Jack. "Will you feel used if April fucks us?"

"Hell, no." Jack shrugged. "I'd be honored."

"And you won't go around bragging about it?" April asked.

Ben kissed her again, then pushed her back toward Jack, who linked his arms around her hips from behind and held her tight until she realized he was just as hard and ready as Ben. "Stop overthinking it, darlin'. We want to help you, we're willing and if we want to share any details, we can always share them with each other."

There was no sign of Tex in the lobby when they returned, so the journey to the room the men shared was quick and uneventful. April shivered as Ben shut the door and locked it, and then walked toward her.

"You okay, honey? You still want to do this? Because if you don't, you can stay and watch me fuck Jack instead." His smile was full of lust. "Either way, I get lucky."

April put her hands on her hips and shook her head. "Typical selfish male."

His smile died. "I'd prefer it if we both got to fuck you, but I'm trying to be a gentleman, here."

April took a deep breath. Strange that she felt far more comfortable with Ben and Jack than she had recently with Tex, when he'd done nothing but order her around and criticize her sexual performance. "I'd like to be fucked and then I'd like to watch you fuck Jack. I've never seen two men together before."

"Sounds like a plan to me." Jack unbuttoned his denim shirt and removed his belt from his jeans, exposing his lean, muscled chest sprinkled with black hair. Ben did the same, his gaze fixed on April as he revealed his tanned abs and heavily muscled arms. She stared at the two men, felt her nipples harden against the silk of her top. She'd seen them without their shirts before, but somehow in such a small space it felt way more intense and personal. Neither man attempted to remove his jeans or boots as Jack sank to his knees in front of her and Ben reclaimed her mouth.

God, he kissed so thoroughly and possessively that she wanted to moan into his mouth. Jack walked his fingers up the inside of her skirt and urged her thighs to part for him. April gasped as Ben released her mouth and trailed his lips down her throat, latched on to her nipple through the taut silk. Her knees threatened to buckle at the dual assault to her senses, but she couldn't fall, knew she wouldn't fall because they wouldn't let her. Jack's finger circled her clit, delved lower into the thick cream of her arousal.

"She's wet, Ben, so wet," Jack murmured. "You're going to love sinking your cock deep into her pussy." He pushed up her skirt, set his mouth over her clit and sucked and licked her in time to Ben's pulls on her breasts. His arm tightened around her waist as she arched against the pressure of Jack's mouth, fought for the climax she knew was close.

"Take her skirt off, Jack." Ben raised his head long enough to undo the halter ties at the back of her neck. "I want to see her naked."

April allowed herself to be undressed, then sat on the edge of the bed, with Jack on the floor between her spread legs, one finger still moving inside her, his thumb flicking her clit. Ben stared at them both and slowly unbuttoned his jeans, kicked them and his boots off.

"Take my cock in your mouth, honey, make me big for you."

"You look pretty big from here," April managed to croak. His answering smile made her even wetter. He climbed onto the bed and straddled her chest, his weight on his knees. One hand gripped the root of his shaft and he rubbed it against her lips. "Take my cock. I want your mouth on me."

April opened her mouth, but he didn't shove himself deep like Tex always did. He waited for her to suck him in, take him deeper, and explore every thick, hot inch of him. And she took her time experiencing his differences, the things he liked her to do and the things he loved. Jack returned his mouth and tongue to her pussy and it became difficult to concentrate, to maintain her focus under the onslaught of pleasure. She came hard against Jack's tongue, felt Ben's answering groan as she instinctively clamped her teeth around him.

"Hold up, honey, I want my cock in your pussy when I come. I want to feel you coming all around me."

Jack tossed Ben a condom and he covered himself and moved off her to replace Jack between her open thighs. He ran his finger down her slit. "She's soaking, Jack."

"Yeah." Jack moved to sit beside April on the bed and slowly took off his boots and jeans. "She sure is."

April turned her head to look at him. "Don't you mind?"

"Mind what?"

"Ben fucking me?"

"Nope."

"What are you going to do while he does it?"

Jack smiled. "Watch and give myself a good yank. If that's okay with you."

Ben cleared his throat. "Hey, guys? Can we move it along here?"

April tried to ignore the press of Ben's cock against her pussy. "But it doesn't seem fair." She gasped as Ben rocked his hips and pushed in three inches. "Couldn't Jack join in?"

Ben's hands came to rest on her hips. "Exactly where do you want him?"

"In my mouth?"

"God, yes, whatever you want, just do it." He surged forward, grabbed her hips and drove himself deep. April went to scream but found her mouth suddenly stuffed full of Jack's condom-covered cock instead. She closed her eyes and gave in to the pleasure, the thrust and withdrawal of Ben's cock and the thick presence of Jack's shaft grazing the back of her throat. She climaxed and Ben kept going, grunting into each stroke, one hand reaching out to grip Jack's shoulder as he came.

April screamed as Ben's final thrust set her off again, and remembered to release Jack's cock before she could bite through the condom. He collapsed onto the bed beside her as Ben covered her body with his own. For a long moment, no one spoke, until Ben levered himself up on his elbows and touched her cheek.

"There's only one thing I need to know, honey. Were we better than Tex?"

April found herself giggling like a five-year-old, watched as Jack started laughing, too, and then Ben joined in. She was so glad she hadn't run back home to cry and start returning engagement presents. This was way more fun than she had had since she'd agreed to marry Tex. Was Ben right? Would she really have gone through with it on Saturday? She managed to sit up and cross her legs, studied the guys' expectant faces.

"You were twice as good."

Ben frowned. "Is that all?" He glanced at Jack. "We'd better try harder next time then."

April sighed. "You guys are so competitive."

"Tex's loss is our gain, right? If you married him, he'd probably take it as an invitation to fuck around even more. We're glad you dumped him." Ben shrugged. "Not that he'd left much pussy unfucked already."

April glanced from him to Jack. "Tex has really been that bad?"

Ben grimaced. "Hell, that's none of our business, is it? I'm sorry, honey."

She crossed her arms over her chest. "It's okay. I'd kind of worked that out myself. He's a terrible liar."

"Then why did you agree to marry him?"

Jack's quiet question made April swallow hard. "Because last time I caught him with another woman he promised he'd do anything to keep me. I was stupid enough to believe him when he said he wanted to marry me. I'd waited so long, you see, it seemed that if I didn't marry him I'd have to admit I'd made a mistake, and I've never been good at doing that."

Ben reached out and stroked her knee. "Makes perfect sense to me. You've always been stubborn as a mule."

She slapped at his hand before she realized he was smiling, his brown eyes full of warm affection and a hint of something deeper, stronger. She sighed. "I came to Vegas early on purpose. Tex was being so evasive. I'd kind of decided I had to know, for better or worse."

Ben crawled toward her, wrapped her in his arms and lowered her back down onto the bed. "And now you know, so how does it feel?"

"Like I made the right decision for the first time in years."

His stiff wet cock grazed her stomach as he kissed her, and her body responded with more heat than she'd known was possible. When he drew back she was panting.

Ben's grin was full of intent. "In the interests of fairness, will you suck Jack's cock while I fuck him?"

"Yeah, it will be a pleasure."

Jack knelt up facing the headboard of the bed, hand gripping the frame, back arched as Ben positioned himself behind him. There was just about enough room for April to kneel on the pillows in front of Jack's cock, but she waited as Ben kissed Jack's neck, fondled his nipples and rubbed his covered cock against the crease of Jack's ass.

"Do you want it, Jack? Do you want it as much as April?" Ben glanced at her. "Are you going to suck him off?"

"Yeah, but I want to see you..." She waved her hand at his groin.

"You want to see me shove my dick in Jack's ass?"

April could only nod like an idiot as Ben smiled at her. "Then here you go, honey, just for you." He gripped his shaft at the base and rocked back and forth until the crown of his cock disappeared inside Jack. "You want to see me go all the way? See me fuck him so hard he begs?"

"I'm begging now." Jack groaned. "And I'll be screaming for it if April sucks my cock."

Ben started to move, his big hands anchored on Jack's narrow hips. Almost reluctantly, April crawled around to face Jack. One look at his straining cock was enough to make her warm to her task. She licked the heavy crown, opened her mouth wide and took him deep. He cried out, his back arching into Ben's thrusts even as he tried to shove himself farther down April's throat.

"Scoot forward, honey." She barely heard Ben's guttural command before his hand snaked around behind her ass and his fingers pumped into her soaking wet pussy. God, he was so strong, fucking Jack and finger fucking her pussy at the same time, making them both cry out, making them both come for him.

April lay sandwiched between the two guys, more sexually replete than she had ever been before. Her cheek rested on Ben's muscled chest and Jack spooned her from behind, his arm stretched across both Ben and her, his rumbling snores vibrating the hairs on the back of her neck.

"Are you okay, honey?" Ben kissed her forehead, the rough stubble of his beard making her shiver.

"Yeah, I think I'm more okay than I've been for years." She touched his smiling mouth. "Did you really want me right from the start?"

"Yeah." He kissed her fingertips, then drew them into his mouth and lightly bit down. "But it was always Tex you wanted. I'm dumb, but I'm not stupid."

"And if I didn't want him anymore?" April held her breath as he went still. "I know it's too soon and I could just be desperate, or on the rebound, or… Not that I'm trying to say I want to hook up forever or anything, but…"

He brought his hand down and covered her mouth.

"Honey, as I said, I'm not stupid. If you want me, I'm yours—but there's Jack."

She shook his fingers off. "What about Jack?"

He shrugged. "I don't want to give him up."

April raised her eyebrows. "Did I ask you to? Am I not lying here between you both, after just having the best sex of my entire life?"

His smile was breathtaking. "Then I'm yours and so is Jack. If you're planning on rejoining the rodeo circuit next year, Jack and I will make sure Tex doesn't bother you." He kissed her nose. "Do you want me to wake Jack up and tell him the good news?"

"Do you think he'll be okay about it?"

Ben eased her gently away from Jack, who continued to sleep. "I sure do. You've figured in our sexual fantasies for years now. He'll think we're the luckiest guys on the planet."

"You've both fantasized about being with me?"

Ben's thigh slid between her legs and his knee nudged her wet pussy. "All the time. Do you like the sound of that?" His grin was triumphant. "You do, don't you?"

Dammit, he knew her far too well. April sighed as he kissed her, and she closed her eyes. So she wouldn't be getting married on Saturday, but she'd certainly won the jackpot. Two guys who adored her, fantasized about her and knew her through and through. A return to the career she loved and the potential to win big. How good was that? Maybe Vegas was for lovers, after all.

Taking Vows

Kristina Wright

It was too much. The yards of ribbon and tulle piled on every surface; the fifty yellow and white roses chilling in the refrigerator; the silver-foiled Belgian chocolate party favors; the too fancy, too expensive dress hanging on the back of the bedroom door. It was all simply too much. It was suitable for a wedding, perhaps even suitable for a renewing-the-vows ceremony, which this was going to be. But it certainly was not suitable for a couple who were planning to divorce.

Charlotte washed a wineglass for the third time, her mind drifting to the big event the next day. The invitation had read "Charlotte and Oliver Duncan request the honor of your presence as they reflect on their life together and renew the vows they took twenty-five years ago." The first part was accurate—there had certainly been a lot of reflecting lately—but the renewal part was for show only.

The renewal ceremony had been the girls' idea. In typical twin fashion, Sarah and Caitlin had doubled up on her and somehow talked Charlotte into this farce. Meanwhile, their older brother, Matthew, had made some heartfelt speech to Oliver about this being the last time all of them would be together until he got back from Iraq in a year. It was too much and Oliver and she had been helpless in the face of their children's request for a big celebration.

Thankfully, the girls had kept their promise to plan the whole thing, dragging their good-natured brother along in the process. Charlotte just didn't think she had it in her to contribute more than her presence to this event. She had agreed with Oliver that there was no reason to tell the kids about the divorce until Matthew got back from Iraq. It was probably the only thing they agreed on. They had to be separated for a year, anyway, and with Matthew overseas and Sarah getting ready to head off to grad school at Berkeley, and Caitlin transferring to the London office of her advertising agency, there would be no need to tell them anything until the papers were signed and everything was finalized.

A year. Now that they had both agreed to the divorce, a year seemed like an awfully long time to wait to get on with her life. But Virginia law was specific about the terms, and unless one of them wanted to claim abuse or adultery— which neither of them would or could—they were only legally separated. Well, they would be after tonight. They had to spend one more night under the same roof before going off on their "second honeymoon." They had told the kids their destination was a surprise. Charlotte didn't know what Oliver was intending, but she was heading up the coast to Maine. Alone.

She figured she might as well get used to it. At forty-six, she had never really been alone. She'd gone from her parents' house to a sorority house to setting up house with Oliver. It would be strange having no one to answer to. Strange and exciting. *And lonely,* a small voice said, but she pushed it aside. She set the wineglass on the rack to dry next to the others just as the front door opened.

Oliver came in and leaned against the counter, watching her as she washed serving dishes for the buffet. "Where are the kids?"

"Out running errands," she said, fighting to keep her voice even. "They said they'd bring pizza home later."

"It's good to have them all home, isn't it?"

She nodded, feeling hot tears behind her eyelids. "First time in...what? Two years?"

Oliver nodded. "Yeah, I guess. That Christmas before Matthew joined the marines."

"Time flies."

"Twenty-five years went by in a flash," he agreed. "Have you written your vows?"

She stiffened her shoulders. "Not yet. You?"

He took a sip of her iced tea on the counter. "No. Anything I write seems like a lie."

"Sorry it's so hard to think back on the good stuff," she said, her voice sharper than she intended. "I know the feeling."

"Fine. The *decision* was your idea," he said. "Don't forget that."

She whirled on him, smacking a casserole dish hard against the counter in the process. "I haven't forgotten anything, Oliver. I haven't forgotten the nights you worked double shifts or the medical conferences that took you away for days at a stretch or all the soccer games and dance recitals you missed because of work."

He sighed. "Yeah, yeah, I was a bad father and a bad husband. But you liked the lifestyle, didn't you?"

They'd been down this path so many times before, they had worn it into a rut. "I would have liked my husband home. With me."

"And now the kids are grown and they have their lives and

you want one, too." The edge of bitterness in his voice wasn't something she often heard. Oliver was a workaholic and total A-type personality who didn't have time for regrets.

"I want us both to be happy," she said, meaning every word.

Oliver took the glass dish out of her hand and slammed it down on the counter hard enough to shatter it and send glass shards flying. "You don't know the first thing about what I need to be happy," he said, oblivious to the fragments of glass that dropped around their feet. "Make yourself happy, but don't presume to know what I want."

He stalked out of the kitchen, leaving the shattered remains of the dish for Charlotte to clean up, much as the shattered remains of their relationship had been her job to resolve. The front door slammed behind him, leaving her alone. Again. She shook her head, blaming herself for provoking him, and then being angry for assuming the blame.

"I didn't break it by myself," she whispered as she tucked her long hair behind her ears and bent to sweep up the glass.

She finished washing dishes just as a crack of thunder made the lights flicker. Dashing around the house closing windows before the rain came, she caught a glimpse of white tossing about on the wide lawn. The girls had spent the morning making about a dozen elaborate bows to tie around the deck posts and now they were destined for the lake. Charlotte slipped out the back door and took off after the fluffy bows as the wind picked up and sent them fluttering just out of her reach. The sky opened up and let loose with a torrential downpour just as she snatched up the last bow before it could slip down the incline to the lake.

Since it was closer than the house, Charlotte ran down the dock toward the boathouse with her arms full of white fluff.

She was drenched in seconds, her blouse clinging to her and her skirt flapping wetly around her knees. It dawned on her that the boathouse might be locked, but no, the padlock hung open on the door. She slipped inside and slammed the door behind her, piling the bows on a decrepit iron table nearby. The boathouse smelled of decaying wood and motor oil and the musty scent of neglect.

A crack of thunder shook the small wood building and she let out a shriek.

"It's only thunder."

A second shriek followed the first as she whirled around toward Oliver, who was sitting in the rowboat they used to take out on the lake when the kids were off with their friends. He sat propped against some patio cushions that had been relegated to the boathouse, along with a lot of other junk. Lounging there like that, in his golf shirt and khakis, with his sandy-blond hair falling over his forehead, he looked so much like the frat boy she fell in love with that she shook her head to dispel the image.

"What are you doing in here?"

He shrugged. "I needed to be alone."

She saw the bottle propped between his legs. "You're drinking?"

"Sure, why not? Seems like a good occasion to get drunk," he said, taking a slug from the bottle. "A mighty fine occasion to tie one on."

"But...you don't drink."

He gestured at her. "And you don't go barefoot, but here you are. We're two peas in a pod."

"One has nothing to do with the other," she said, wringing out her wet hair and pushing it over her shoulder. "I'm not sitting in a dark boathouse getting loaded. I just didn't have time to put on shoes."

"You always make time to put on shoes before you go outside."

"What, exactly, is your point?" she asked, wondering just how drunk he was and whether it was worth having this argument.

He seemed to consider her question for a long time. "I don't know. Why don't you tell me what my point is? You've always been good at that."

"You're insufferable."

Charlotte considered going back out into the rain, but another ground-quaking roll of thunder, followed by a crack of lightning that lit up the entire boathouse, made her change her mind. She wasn't afraid of much, but she'd always been afraid of thunderstorms.

She expected a retort. The beginnings of yet another fight. Once the divorce was final, there would be no reason to fight anymore. Maybe that's why they seemed to be fighting even more often lately. Time was running out.

But instead of another poke at her flaws, Oliver asked, "What happened to us?"

She rested her head wearily against the door. He had no idea how many times she'd asked herself the same question. With a resigned shrug, she said, "We just fell out of love."

Oliver surged up out of the rowboat quicker than she could have thought possible. He was standing in front of her in a heartbeat, one hand braced on the door behind her head, the other still gripping the liquor bottle. He leaned in close enough so that she could smell the whiskey on his breath and see his green eyes dilated in the gloom.

"Do not speak for me," he growled at her. "Maybe you fell out of love with me, but I never stopped loving you."

Her heart felt as if it was ricocheting around in her chest. She had never seen Oliver like this before. She knew it was just the alcohol talking, but it made her stomach do a little flip-flop to hear him say he still loved her.

She'd been hurt enough and wouldn't fall for it again. "Whatever, Oliver. I didn't have to twist your arm to visit the mediator for the divorce."

"The divorce was your idea."

"And you seconded that emotion, remember?"

He took another pull off the whiskey before setting the bottle on the table covered in bows. "I'm not going to keep you tied to me when you don't love me."

Despite her intentions not to engage him in a fight, she was getting angry. "You don't love me, either."

He leaned into her then, his erection pressing against her lower belly. It was a shock to feel his body against her, at once familiar and strange. It had been so long. She could feel her body responding, softening. She put her hand against his chest, tangling her fingers in the nubby fabric of his golf shirt and feeling the steady, comforting thud of his heart beneath her palm. She wanted to fall into his arms and forget the real world just outside the door; forget the divorce papers upstairs in Oliver's briefcase, just waiting for their signatures.

"Feel that?" he whispered in her ear, his breath tickling the hairs at the nape of her neck. "Don't tell me I don't love you."

She found her resolve then. Flattening her hand against his chest, she gave him a firm shove. "That's not love," she said as he took two steps back. "That's just a hard-on and you just want to get laid."

He wouldn't be deterred. He caught her by the wrist so she couldn't get away—as if there was anyplace for her to go. "How long has it been, Charlotte?"

She knew he was asking because she never forgot anything. Not a birthday or anniversary, not a special event or holiday.

She never forgot a fight and she never forgot a makeup romp between the sheets.

"Eight months. It was last year, right before Thanksgiving."

He nodded. "Yeah, that's the last time we had sex, but that's not what I want to know. I want to know when was the last time you really enjoyed it? When was the last time you were out of your mind with passion for me and not faking your way through it?"

She gasped, a flush of heat creeping into her cheeks. "How dare you denigrate our sex life like that?"

He didn't waver. "How long, Charlotte?"

Pushed to the breaking point, she forgot about taking the high road. "Remember that weekend trip to Charlottesville?"

He cocked his head. "The winery tour weekend?"

She nodded, watching the expressions flit across his face. Confusion, anger, shock. But he'd asked for it.

"That was—what?—five years ago?"

"Six."

He didn't need her to push him away; he rocked back on his heels all by himself. "Six years since I made you come? Six years since you enjoyed being in bed with me? Damn, woman, why didn't you divorce me then instead of being miserable for so long?"

She blinked back tears. He was making it sound worse than it was. Or maybe he wasn't. Maybe she'd been justifying things for too long.

"I wasn't miserable," she said softly.

"You just didn't enjoy sex with me."

She'd hurt him. Maybe that's what she'd intended and what he deserved, but now she wished she could take the words back. She reached out a hand, not quite sure what to do with it, and settled with grabbing the front of his shirt as if she could keep him from falling over the edge.

"It's not about sex," she said. "That was just a symptom of the problem."

"And I had no idea." He shook his head. "What a joke. My memory isn't as good as yours, but I seem to recall some pretty impressive performances of yours."

"I didn't want to hurt you."

"Until now."

"I didn't even want to hurt you now!" She jerked on his shirt for emphasis, which only served to bring him closer. "But you pushed me too far."

He swallowed hard and nodded. "I know. I just wanted…"

She felt self-conscious standing there with her hand balled in his shirt, but she couldn't seem to let go. "You wanted what?"

"I wanted to get some emotion out of you," he said, his voice rough. "Just something to let me know I'm not the only one feeling so fucking raw."

"You're not," she whispered.

A long roll of thunder rumbled over the boathouse, rattling the door at her back. One minute she was pressed to the panel, the next she was in Oliver's arms. Kissing him.

She couldn't have said who initiated it. But twenty-five years of marriage had made them a bit like magnets—at least when things had been good between them. If they stood too close, they just naturally gravitated toward each other, fitting together so naturally and perfectly she had often wondered how they had ever had awkward, fumbling moments.

Crooking her arm around his neck, she brought his face down to hers, deepening a kiss that had started out tentatively and was now spreading like heat lightning through her lower belly. He tasted like whiskey and Oliver, his lips and tongue so familiar and yet somehow different. Different because it had been so long—years—since they kissed like this? Different because he tasted of alcohol? Different because they weren't a couple anymore, not really? She didn't know and she didn't care.

Oliver hauled her up against his body, his erection pressing insistently against her hip as he twisted her long, damp hair around his hand. She hooked a leg around him, shifting so that the bulge between his legs pressed against the softness between hers. She moaned into his mouth, almost embarrassed by this show of wantonness. At least he had the excuse of alcohol. What was her excuse?

Still holding her close, Oliver spun her around and walked her back to the rowboat. She bumped against the solid weight of it and wobbled, steadying herself against his chest. He unbuttoned her blouse and slipped it off her shoulders. Her nipples pebbled under his thumbs as he cupped her breasts and stroked them through the thin fabric of her bra. She threw her head back and moaned, her damp hair trailing down her spine.

She felt as if she was watching the two of them from a distance, knowing she would regret this later. But she didn't have time to change her mind, because Oliver was laying her down on the cushions in the boat. It smelled musty and the cushions were too thin to protect her from the hardness of the hull, but it didn't matter as he pushed her skirt up over her hips. She gasped when he palmed her crotch through her panties, her entire body going rigid with the shock of being touched like that after so long.

"I'm going to make you come," he whispered hoarsely, skimming her panties down her damp legs. "I'm not going to stop until you come for me."

It was a promise. It was a threat. It was Oliver spreading her thighs with his big hands and lowering his mouth to her wetness. It was the tremor that coursed through her body as his tongue flicked her swollen clit for the first time in so long even she couldn't remember the last time. She gripped his hair, hair too long to be respectable for a man his age, a doctor with his prestige, but just long enough for her to tangle her fingers in it. The perfect hair for a lover between her thighs, lapping at her pussy, promising to make her come.

Thunder rumbled around them and rain lashed at the grimy little window above, but Charlotte closed her eyes and gave herself over to the feeling of Oliver's mouth. She raised her hips and pulled his head closer, rewarded when his tongue dipped inside, swirled her wetness on his tongue and dragged it back over her clit. She whimpered low in her throat to encourage him, too quiet for him to hear over the sounds of the storm, but still he licked and swirled, teased and nibbled, driving her higher.

Had it once been like this? she wondered fuzzily, feeling out of control, on the edge of some great explosion. Had he been able to coax her to passion so fast, so easily? She couldn't remember, not now when he was using the flat of his tongue to torment her, dragging it slowly up between her lips and over her clit. Again and again he licked her, until she was arching her back and moaning, thighs clenched around his head. His beard stubble scraped against her sensitive skin, but it only added to her pleasure. She quivered on the precipice of her orgasm, every muscle taut and humming with the need for release.

And then he stopped.

He took his mouth away and she looked down to see why he was denying her, a sudden fear that this was some sort of punishment making her heart pound. He met her gaze, looking up at her from between her thighs. His position was so incongruous she would have laughed if she hadn't been so aroused.

"I promise to make you come every time we make love," he said.

"What?"

He didn't respond because he was busy lapping at her again, bringing her back to that peak that had slipped away. She was there again in an instant, gripping him just as tightly, making sure he didn't stop this time. Not now, not when the sensations were spiraling out from her pussy, her stomach muscles tightening in anticipation.

"Oliver!" she screamed. Just his name. That's all she had time for before her orgasm crashed over her like the thunder shaking the ground beneath her.

He pressed his tongue to her, moving it slowly over her wetness as she came. The constant contact was too much—and not enough. She cupped the back of his head and pulled him into her, wanting more, wanting it to last forever. She rocked against him, feet braced against the sides of the row-boat, clenching her muscles around the tip of his tongue as he slipped it inside her.

The sensations subsided, little aftershocks quaking through her and making her tremble as Oliver kept up his steady pressure. Finally, she lowered her feet to the bottom of the boat and pulled him up by the shoulders of his shirt. He settled his weight on top of her, pressing her deeper into the hard wooden boat. She wrapped her legs around him and rocked against him even though he was still fully clothed.

"I promise to never fake it again," she whispered as she pulled him down for a kiss, tasting herself on his tongue. "Now fuck me."

Oliver rose up and she reached between them, unfastening his pants and palming his erection once she worked the zipper down. Between the two of them, they got his pants down around his knees. She squeezed his cock before guiding it into her, arching her back to take him inside. He groaned as he sank into her, inch by blessed inch.

"I promise not to go eight months without making love to you," he said, his face buried in her neck. "I promise not to go eight days without fucking you senseless."

She wrapped her legs high around his back, feeling him go so deep it almost hurt. It was a familiar feeling, a familiar longing to have him this close, but she'd let herself forget it. They found their rhythm as easily as if they'd just had sex the day before, as if it hadn't been months since the last time and years since it was good. He slipped his hands under her and gripped her ass, pulling her up high on his cock, rocking into her slow and deep, just the way she liked.

"I promise not to forget what this is like," she gasped as he thrust into her. "I promise to tell you how good it is and how much I love you inside me."

He sucked at her neck, no doubt leaving marks on her pale skin. She trembled under him, the emotional sensations nearly as powerful as the physical ones. The rowboat shifted under their weight, banging against the wall of the boathouse and making the whole structure shake.

Charlotte pulled his head up and looked into his eyes, feeling another orgasm building. "I'm going to come again," she said with a gasp as his pelvic bone rocked against her clit.

"Promise me you'll come hard."

She tightened her pussy around him, nodding. "I promise."

He leaned down to kiss her hard, nipping her lip. "I promise not to come until you do."

And then she was coming again, coming with him so deep inside her she felt impossibly full and stretched and whole. She moaned as she strained up against him, going mad with the pleasure as he fucked her just as he had promised. Senseless.

She had made love to him too many times not to know when he was ready to finish. His cock pulsed inside her and the vein in his jaw throbbed in response as he tried to maintain control. She slid her hands down the taut muscles in his back to grip his ass, pulling him into her, her pussy still quivering and tightening around his length.

"Promise me you'll come as hard as I did," she whispered, pressing a kiss to that vein his jaw. "Promise me you'll come right now."

His response was the groan of an animal in pain—or pleasure. He quickened his pace, thrusting into her slick wetness, the boat thumping hard against the wall. She whispered promises in his ear, promises of the things she would do to him later, promises of the things she would beg for from him. That was all it took. He arched up over her, his expression as wild and out of control as the storm outside.

She held on to him and soothed him like a wild thing as he came, thrusting into her again and again. "Yes, yes, yes," she said, an affirmation in response to the look on his face, the feel of his body. "Yes."

He lowered himself on top of her, his cock still throbbing inside her. She wrapped her arms and legs around his still trembling body and held him close, reveling in the smell of his hair and the steady thump of his heart against her chest.

After a while, he pushed up on one elbow and looked down at her. His expression was unreadable and she licked her lip nervously, waiting for him to speak.

"I promise not to let you go," he said.

She nodded. "Me, too."

A smile slid easily into place on his boyishly handsome face. "As much as I liked those other vows we took, maybe we should come up with something more appropriate for tomorrow."

She wiggled under him. "As easy as that? We're...together again?"

He rocked his hips, his softening erection still enough of a presence to make her gasp. "Do you want us to be together again?"

She knew it shouldn't be that easy. She also knew that they had too much to gain not to try. "Yes, I do."

"Then we are. We start over. We begin again. New vows, new promises. You and me."

It sounded good. She cupped the back of his neck and pulled him down for a kiss. She had meant it just as an affirmation of her feelings, but it turned into a long, slow tongue kiss that had him hardening inside her.

"Again?" she gasped as he gave a little thrust.

He smiled, all husbandly pride and masculine arousal. "I promise."

The Wedding Stoppers

Michael Hemmingson

1

The morning of the wedding, they had sex. She showed up at his door at 7:00 a.m. Somehow, he knew she would do this; he knew she would torment him one more time with what he could not have: her body, her touch, her pussy.

"I thought you said no more."

"You know I'm a liar," Chloe said.

She walked past him and into his messy apartment. "Maid didn't come yesterday?"

"So once you're a married woman..."

She put fingers to his lips. "Quiet."

They went to bed.

She said, while he was inside her, "You *had* to come play sloshball that day, didn't you?"

"I should show up *today* and object to your wedding," Gabriel said.

"You wouldn't *dare*. Would you? *Would* you?"

As in: *would you, please?*

2

His name: Gabriel Barnes, twenty-eight years old and in love with Chloe McNamara, twenty-three, who worked in the same office as he did. She was engaged to the son of the woman who owned the company they worked for—a very rich and powerful woman in Encinitas, California: Gretchen Binkowski. Chloe's intended was Gregory Binkowski, who always wore immaculate suits. Gabriel hated him. Gabriel had noticed Chloe at the office—what man didn't—but she was engaged, after all, and at the time he had a live-in girlfriend, Hannah. Everything changed the day of the office sloshball game, considering what happened between Chloe and him. Or maybe it started the day at the Binkowski house, to celebrate the announcement of the wedding day....

3

Hannah Tate: twenty-six years old, aspiring playwright and actress, unhappy about the theater prospects in San Diego. She had come to San Diego when she was twenty-four because the drama department at UCSD had given her a scholarship. She was from Boise, Idaho, where there was no significant theater. One day she met Gabriel Barnes and six months later they moved in together. The problem: she could not be faithful to him. She enjoyed sex too much to keep to one man, no matter how much she loved Gabriel. She preferred variety and she was a playwright; after all, she needed new experiences to write about. The problem: most of the men she had sex with weren't very interesting.

Take, for instance, the day of the announcement party. She was to meet Gabriel there. He had to go because he worked for the woman throwing the event; she had to go because she was his girlfriend and companion. She was late, though, because she was having sex with a surfer guy she'd met two weeks ago at Starbucks.

When she realized she was late, she jumped out of the surfer guy's bed and quickly got dressed.

The surfer guy lay naked on the bed, his cock resting on his belly, and stared at her. "Why the hurry?"

"Wasn't watching the time."

"Who cares about time? Get back here."

"Have to be somewhere. I'm late, I'm late, said the rabbit to Alice. Poop! Where's my other sock?"

She looked around, couldn't locate the sock.

"Oh yeah?" said the surfer guy. "Can I come with?"

"No, you cannot 'come with.'"

"Dudette."

"What?"

"A quickie before you go?"

"Dude," she said, "it's never a 'quickie' with you."

"And that's a bad thing?"

She smiled. He had a point. She said, "Actually, it's your most endearing quality, that innate penchant you have for stride and stamina. It's not like I come here to discuss high literature and string theory with you."

He stood up. She admired his body: tanned and muscular, his cock already hard and ready.

"Come hither, chick-eee."

"I wish I could come hither. Gotta jet, cockmaster."

She found the sock!

She headed for the door.

"Whoa," said surfer dude, "what's so important?"

"Prewedding party thing!"

"Yeah? Yours?"

"Funny," she said, "bone."

4

Gabriel was on his third beer and wondering where Hannah was. She was forty-five minutes late. Everyone at the office was here, plus their various spouses, significant others and friends. The party was in the lavish backyard of Gretchen

Binkowski's home in Encinitas. Home—mansion, with twenty rooms. The event was catered, open bar, with a string quartet playing chamber music on the lawn. There were also a lot of people he did not know, friends and business associates of Mrs. Binkowski's. He counted seventy people when there should be seventy-one.

People were too well dressed for this, the men in their suits and ties and the women in their suits and gowns. He thought this was to be informal. He tried to avoid Mrs. Binkowski noticing his lack of proper attire.

Hannah drove her beat-up VW bug quickly on highway 5 north to get to Encinitas, part of San Diego's north county line. She almost got into three accidents; with a small car, she could swerve adeptly and avoid death.

She was impressed by the mansion, located on a cliff overlooking the ocean. She found Gabriel standing by himself on the grass, holding a beer.

He seemed relieved when he spotted her walking his way. "There you are!"

She took his half-empty bottle and drank. "Sorry I'm late."

"Traffic was a bitch?"

"Rehearsal was a bastard," she lied.

Gretchen addressed the guests at her house. "Ladies, gentlemen, guests, friends, family and coworkers. We are here today to celebrate the official wedding date, one month from now, of my son, Gregory, and his bride-to-be…Chloe, dear, and Gregory…." She waved to the couple. They joined her, fresh drinks in hand, and the three of them raised their glasses and toasted, as did many of the attendees. "To the future," said Gretchen, "to family!"

Hannah raised a half-empty beer. "Rah-rah-rah," she said. She looked at Gabriel and thought about her life, about art, about sex. There was more to life than struggling to be a theater artist in San Diego, a city that was artless and had little interest in serious theater. She had always talked about moving to New York, where real theater was done; no Los Angeles, that was a TV and movie town, and actors and writers viewed theater as a hobby until a TV or film job came through. New York was the answer and she was going to go there.

At home, after the party, Hannah said, "I have to move to New York."

"Um–hmm," Gabriel said. He'd heard it before.

"Will you go with?"

"We've talked about this already."

"And we can talk about it again."

"I'm not going to just quit my job and move all the way across the country...."

"Why not?"

"It's crazy, is why."

"No it's not."

"New York, New York," he said.

"I'm serious," she said.

5

The next day, Hannah went to rehearsal of her play, watching a scene with the male lead. His monologue was not going well and she didn't think the director got her play at all. *This sucks,* she said to herself. The actor held a prop gun in his hand during the monologue, contemplating suicide. Hannah wished it was a real gun so she could shoot him and the director.

Three hours later, she was in the studio apartment of the male lead actor, another one of those twentysomethings with Hollywood on the agenda, not her play. They fucked twice.

He lit a joint and sat back on his futon, watching Hannah—naked—pace back and forth.

"It sucks it sucks it sucks," she was saying.

"What does?"

"You *know.*"

"I think it's going okay," he said.

"That director..."

"He's all right."

She stopped pacing. Hands on her hips. "Yes, he is. That's just it. He's 'all right.' Not good or great or marvelous or fantastic. 'All right.' That's the problem with theater in San Diego—it's. All. Right. So what. Where does that ever get anyone? Would Arthur Miller have made a name for himself in San Diego? Huh? No. Eugene O'Neill? David Mamet? Wendy Wasserstein? Even Whoopie Goldberg had to leave San Diego to become a superstar. I'm in the wrong place at the wrong time. I'm sick of going nowhere. *I'm in the wrong body!*"

She paced again: back and forth, back and forth...

"I like your body," the actor said, watching parts of Hannah jiggle and wiggle.

"I'm sick of being an unknown nobody! I'm tired of everything just being 'all right.' I'm weary of the struggle, don't you understand? It's a snarling one-note performance in this shitty town."

6

Gabriel was cooking spaghetti for dinner. Hannah came home and said, "That sure smells good."

"Your fave."

She watched him cook.

"I know that look. What is it?"

"I have to leave," she told him. "With or without you, I'm going to New York. I have to or else I'm gonna go insane or kill myself. I'm serious."

"Oh," he said, and went back to cooking.

"Do you want to talk about it?" she asked.

"No."

"I think we should."

"No."

"Are you sure?"

"Do we have to?"

"I think we should," she said.

"No," he said.

An hour later, they went to bed and made love. It was slow and nice and tender and sad all at the same time.

Hannah said, "I'm sorry."

Gabriel replied, "Don't be."

"I am. Really."

"No need. Really." A bit sarcastic.

"I *want* to be sorry," she said, because she wondered if she was.

"It's okay."

"*Is* it 'okay'?"

Pause.

"No," he said.

"Look. Just come to New York with me."

"I can't."

"Why not?"

"My wife—life is here."

"Your *wife?*"

"Life."

"*What* life? Your job?"

"Yes. My *job,* for one."

"That job? That's not a career," Hannah said. "That's 'a job.' And you hate it."

"I like my job. I like San Diego," Gabriel said.

"I can't stay here, Gabe. You know that. Moving here was just an experiment, you know that."

"Yeah…"

"My career…"

"I know."

Pause.

Hannah said, "Are we breaking up?"

Gabriel replied, "I don't know. You tell me."

"Listen," she said coldly. "I haven't been faithful. I've had…lovers."

"I know," he said.

"Wait. What do you mean, you *know?*"

"You think I didn't? That I didn't *smell* them on you when you came home? The stench of their sweat, their cum? The smell of fuck."

She was surprised, and angry. "And you never said anything?"

"What was there to say?"

"Are you angry with me?" she asked.

"I'm…sad."

"Why have you stayed with me…if you knew?"

"Because I love you," he said.

7

Three days later, Hannah was packed and ready to go. She had two suitcases. She was traveling light.

Gabriel sat on the couch and looked at the TV, ignoring her.

"I'm going now."

"Okay."

She said, "Tell you what. I'll give it a year. Just a year. If things don't happen with my playwrighting career one year from today, I'll come back. I'll come back and we'll pick up where we left off. What do you say?"

"Okay."

"I mean it," she said.

8

The next day was the office Sunday sloshball game, which had been planned for three weeks. The office played sloshball every summer, or the last two summers Gabriel worked there.

From Wikipedia.org: "*Sloshball* is an unofficial variant of softball…the inclusion of alcohol has been implemented to enhance amusement, while diminishing both mental and physical acuity."

That's what it was, all right. The game started at 10:00 a.m. and by noon, the entire office attendees were, well, sloshed: drunk, snookered, smashed, bombed.

Softballs were pitched, hit, people drunkenly ran and tried to drunkenly get to bases while other drunken people drunkenly try to touch them with the ball.

Gabriel had second base. Chloe was on the other team. She hit the ball and ran, almost tripping, falling. She passed first base. She saw the ball tossed to the cute guy on second base, Gabriel, whom she had hardly ever spoken to. She ran fast, slid, hoping to touch the base before he touched her with the ball. She miscalculated. She slammed into his legs as she slid and he fell on top of her. The two scrambled in the sand, their legs entwined. His hand, with the ball, was on one of her breasts. His other hand was on her bare leg.

They were face-to-face.

"You're out," he said.

"Yeah," she said, her hand touching his crotch. She was

drunk and didn't care. She wanted to know if being on top of her made him hard. He was half-hard. Her touch made him harder.

His hand went from her leg to her ass.

They were again face-to-face.

"Wow," he said.

"I'm sloshed," she said.

Half an hour later, the two were in Gabriel's car and making out, taking their clothes off.

"This is crazy," Chloe said.

"Should we stop?" he asked.

"Hell no," she said.

They fucked in the backseat like teenagers on a wild date.

9

The next day, Monday afternoon, Gabriel and Chloe met in the office supply closet and kissed for five minutes straight, tongues mutually exploring mouths.

Chloe broke away. "Wait."

A strand of saliva connected them.

"We can't," she said.

"We can," he said.

"We can," she agreed.

10

That evening, in Gabriel's bed, after some rigorous sex, Gabriel made a suggestion and Chloe said, "That's preposterous. You realize this. It's absurd, insane, inane and unrealistic."

"No it's not," Gabriel said.

"I'm not going to *leave* him."

"You could."

She held out her left hand. "Look at this diamond ring. I

love it. I am not going to give it back. I dreamed about such an engagement ring ever since I was eleven years old. I'm *not* going to give it back."

"So don't."

She said, seriously, "I am not going to give it back."

"Call it off," he said. "The wedding."

11

Saturday night: Gabriel sat at home, eating Chinese takeout, watching *Star Trek* reruns on TV and feeling depressed.

The doorbell rang. He got up and answered it. Chloe stood there, wearing a long fur coat and high heels.

"Hey," she said.

"Hey," he said.

"May I come in?"

"Please."

She walked in, her heels going *clack-clack-clack* on the hardwood floor.

"This is a nice surprise," he said.

She turned and faced him. "Why am I here?"

"Because you want to be?"

"That's not the answer I'm looking for."

"You need to be?"

"No."

"You were meant to be?"

A small smile appeared on her face. She opened the fur coat and let it drop. She was completely naked. All she wore were the high heels.

He rushed to her, grabbed her, kissed her, put his mouth on her breasts. They didn't bother with the bed. They did it on the floor.

The answering machine picked up and Hannah's voice

said, "Gabriel? Baby? Are you there? If you're there, pick up. I need to talk to you…."

"Who is that?" Chloe asked.

"Nobody," he said, "nobody at all."

Twenty minutes later, they lay spent on the floor. Chloe felt cold and snuggled with her lover.

"Okay. This *really* is the last time," she said.

"I know."

"You don't believe me."

"Of course I do," he said, and kissed her forehead.

"I hate you," she said.

"No. You don't."

"No…"

"You love me."

"No," she lied.

12

The artistic director of a tiny off-off-Broadway space that Hannah had given some of her plays to—and had slept with after—said he wanted to produce a one-act in a festival. He was in his late forties and Hannah wondered why she had sex with him. She didn't even remember what it was like. How many men had she gone to bed with in the past two weeks? She wasn't even counting.

He invited her out to drinks to talk about her play. They sat in a small, dark bar and drank beer.

The director said, "I'll say again…your play is one of the finest I've read in a long time. A long time. So many people think they can be writers, playwrights, screenwriters, poets, novelists, you name it. They think they can sit down behind a computer and bang words out and it's art. The truth—it's shit. It's all shit. Your work, I can safely say, your work—well, it ain't shit."

"Thank you," Hannah said, "for those kind words."

He reached out and touched her face and she let him. "You're so pretty," he said.

He moved to kiss her and she stopped him.

"Anything wrong?" he asked.

"No," she said. "Not here."

He said, "I think we have reached the point in this artistic relationship where it would be wise and advantageous for the two of us, as they say in the vernacular, to have carnal knowledge."

"We already did that."

"Did we?"

She laughed. "Oh, really? How many women do you fuck that you can't remember?"

"You'd be surprised," he said.

"No," she said, "I wouldn't."

While this was happening, on the West Coast, Gabriel and Chloe were relaxing after having carnal knowledge with each other.

Chloe said, "I really do hate you."

Gabriel replied, "Why do you say such a thing?"

"For what you've done to my life."

"'Done'?"

"You're trying to derail it. You're trying to change my future."

"I am? I mean, sure I am."

She said, "It's not going to happen. You're not going to stop me from becoming a wife. Do you hear me?"

"So this is the last time?" he asked.

Chloe screamed in frustration and jumped on top of him—

13

—while in New York, Hannah screamed during sex with the director, but it was not out of pleasure but out of disgust. She pushed him off her. There was a funny, wet *pop* sound when they disconnected.

"What's the matter?" the director asked. "Did I hurt you?"

She sat up, head in hands. "Everything is wrong."

He touched her bare shoulder. "Sweetheart."

She shrugged his hand away. "Don't."

"What? What's the problem?"

She stood up, got out of his little bed and started to dress, picking up her clothes from the floor. "Want to know the problem?" she said. "The endless stream of losers like you. Yes, you heard me. *Like you*. One after the other."

"I don't get it."

"Of course. You guys never do," Hannah said, and paced back and forth as she delivered her monologue: "Okay, you want the blunt truth—I'm not in the mood to have your tiny dick inside me. Don't look so shocked, buddy boy. Let's face it, your cock is small and you're small-minded. You think you're the cat's meow here, the hottest theater director on earth, but you ain't shit, *as they say in the vernacular*. A small fish among many small fish in a giant ocean, Shark Food stamped on your forehead in glittering neon."

He didn't know what to make of these belittling words.

Her voice gradually got louder. "'Sweetheart' this and 'your play is so great' that. To what? To get in my panties? You fuckers. You—*fuckers*. I've been in this city for—what? Three weeks now. Three weeks and what have I learned? It's the same everywhere. Locations don't matter. And to think I left the man I loved—the man who *loved me*—to think I *abandoned* him to just let asinine nobodies like you talk me into bringing you home so you can shoot your semen inside my body. *You make me sick.* The way you talk, the way you direct, the way you smell, the hair on your back and the lack of hair on your head. Your teeth, your eyes, your nose, your lips, I hate everything about you. And your small penis—and the way you touch a woman, it is so slimy, and I just know you're a lousy, awful fuck who probably premature ejaculates!!!"

She walked out.

"Lock the door, will you?" the director called after her.

It was snowing outside. She wandered around in the snow, wondering if Gabriel would take her back….

14

In San Diego, it was lightly raining. Gabriel had been walking around, wondering how he was going to stop Chloe from getting married. He walked into a bar, to get out of the rain and to have a few beers.

At the same time this happened, Hannah was also in a bar in New York. She sat alone, with a beer and tequila shooters. A man in a suit, whose name was Ted, a man in his mid-thirties, Hannah guessed, this man was sitting near her and watching her. She said to him, "Didn't your mommy teach you that staring is bad manners?"

Ted flushed. "Sorry."

"'Tis okay."

"It's not okay."

"People stare at people. It's what people do. Like theater. Ever go see a play?"

"Sure."

"So what do you do? You stare. You stare at the actors. If one of them has a nude scene, you stare at their body parts.

You stare at other audience members. It's the way the world works, if you have eyes and can do it."

"I see," said Ted.

"You do see! Because you have eyeballs. So stare away, but for your sins, you must buy me another drink."

"I can do that."

"And sit over here with me."

"I can do that, too."

"I bet you can."

He sat across from to her, and waved at the bartender for another round. He said, "It's just that you resemble someone I used to know." He added, "That's why I was staring."

"Don't tell me. Your very first love?"

"My long-lost wife."

"Ee-gads," Hannah said, "I need another shot of tequila—now!"

Meanwhile, in San Diego, Gabriel sat at the counter drinking and feeling sorry for himself, and he overheard two people talking in the booth behind him. A man was saying:

"…my wife meant everything to me, the world, the universe, like the song goes, so that day, when she died, I had lost the world, the universe, and while I didn't plan on committing suicide, I just wanted to get away from the earth, the ground, and mortality…."

Gabriel got up.

The bartender asked, "Off to leak the ol' lizard?"

"I have a wedding to stop," Gabriel said.

15

Hannah invited Ted back to her place and they had quick sex. After, they lay in bed, quiet for a long time, and Ted stroked her hair.

"That's nice," she said. "You do know how to touch a woman. You've had experience."

"I don't usually do this."

"This?"

"Sleep with a woman I just met in a bar. In fact," Ted said, "I never have."

"So I'm your first?"

"Seems so."

"It's my pleasure to pop your cherry then," Hannah said.

Neither laughed. It just wasn't that funny, the way she said it: more like sad.

"You're beautiful," Ted said, touching her face.

She asked, "Is it really me or because I look like your dead wife?"

"Dead?"

"Isn't she dead?"

"No."

"You said—"

"Long-lost.'"

"She's not…?"

"Not at all."

"You two are…"

"Separated."

"Oh."

"Maybe I should have said 'estranged.'"

"Maybe," she said.

"Are you okay with this?" he asked.

"I don't know."

"Have you ever slept with a married man before?"

"Not that I'm aware of."

"Then I'm your first. I popped your cherry."

"Very funny."

"Sorry."

"Don't be. It was bound to happen."

"Like I said," he said, "I've never done this before."

"It was bound to happen."

"That's why I have been thinking…that's why I want to thank you."

"Thank me?"

"I know what I must do now," he told her. "I must go back to her and beg. Plead for marriage. To make it work. You made me realize this."

Hannah jumped out of bed and started to get dressed.

Ted said, "I'm sorry if that was the wrong thing to tell you."

Hannah was excited, happy. "It was the right thing," she said. "I have to thank you! Because I know what I have to do now. I have to get on the first flight back to San Diego and do some begging myself!"

16

She had an excuse for being in San Diego anyway: her play was about to open. Not that she cared; she knew it would be awful. The first thing she did was go see a dress rehearsal, which was in the morning. She did her best not to scream and run out. Yes, it was terrible. But she had another reason for being here. It was just an idea. When the director gave the cast notes, Hannah went backstage and stole the prop pistol from the monologue scene. Well, borrowed it. She'd bring it back. She had a feeling she might need it. The wedding was this afternoon.

17

Gabriel stood in front of the mirror in the bathroom and practiced the speech he planned to give:

"Yes, I object—I object to this union. This marriage is all

wrong and I will tell you why...listen to me, Chloe, this man is not who you think he is. He's a whore. Chloe, listen to me...ask your mother...Gretchen, tell Chloe the truth...you talking to me, punk? Yeah, you, Gregory, Greg, the Greg-meister, I know what you are. You looking at me? I don't see anyone else, so you must be looking at me, ya freakin' gigolo...."

18

Chloe was also looking at herself in the mirror, wearing her long white wedding gown. The image looking back at her was beautiful, on the outside. Inside, there was uncertainty and torment. She knew she was doing the wrong thing, but she didn't know how to get out of it. All she wanted right now was to be in Gabriel's arms as he made love to her.

Run, run now, run far away, Chloe thought, but her feet could not, would not move.

A woman appeared behind her: Gretchen Binkowski. Soon-to-be mother-in-law, who looked Chloe over. The woman was weaving. She held a martini in her hand. She was drunk!

"You look wonderful and stunning, my dear," Gretchen said.

Run...

19

Gabriel now had his tuxedo on; staring at his reflection, he winked and made a gun finger, posing like James Bond.

The doorbell rang, and rang, and rang frantically. Who the hell could it be? "Coming!"

He opened the door and standing before him was...

"Hannah."

"Surprise!" Hannah said, and walked in. She looked around. "At least the apartment is still clean. I'm impressed."

To say the least, Gabriel was flabbergasted. "Hannah—*what are you doing here? Why aren't you in New York?*"

She smiled, hesitated. "Well…"

They stared at one another.

She said, "Why are you so dressed up? I've never seen you looking so good. What's with the tux, Gabe?"

"What…why…what are you doing here?"

She hugged him. "Oh! I came back!" She kissed him, looked him in the eyes. "Long story short, I made a mistake, I messed up, I learned my lesson, I ask for your forgiveness, so here I am. Kiss me again, darling!"

"Hannah—wait."

"Kiss me, fool."

He backed away.

"What's wrong?" She looked hurt.

"Why didn't you call?"

"Wanted to be a pleasant surprise."

"I don't understand."

"What's there to understand?"

"Why are you here?"

She threw up her arms. "So we can be together and be in love and everything will be okay, *okay?*" Hannah kept trying to kiss Gabriel but he wouldn't let her. She took offense. "Do you hate me?" she said.

He looked at his watch. "Hannah, I have to go."

"Go?"

"Leave. Or I'll be late."

"Go where?"

"I have somewhere to be."

"Can I come?"

"Absolutely not!"

"What? Why? Why are you dressed so nice?"

He told her, "I'm going to a wedding."

"Whose? Whose wedding?!"

"Mine!" he said.

"Yours? You're getting married?"

"I'm going to a wedding," he said. "I'm in love," he said.

"Love?" She looked at him as if he was crazy.

"When you left...I started seeing Chloe—you remember Chloe?"

"Didn't she get married?"

"Today! And I have to stop it! She's making a mistake!"

Hannah processed this. She was getting it now. "What will you do? Go to the chapel and whisk her away?"

He thought a moment. "In fact, yes."

She laughed. "Who do you think you are? Dustin Hoffman in *The Graduate?*"

He moved past her. "Gotta go," he mumbled.

She cried out, "Halt! Mister!"

He stopped, turned.

She reached into her purse and pulled out the prop gun. She pointed it at his head.

"You're not going anywhere, buddy."

20

I can be a runaway bride, Chloe thought, touching the fabric of her gown. Why not? Plenty of brides got cold feet and split...if only her feet could *move.* She thought she was going to be sick.

I could puke on my dress and ruin it and…

But there was nothing in her stomach. She couldn't eat all day yesterday, or this morning.

21

Gabriel sat in a chair, in the kitchen, as Hannah tied an extension cord around him, a makeshift rope. She kept the gun on him.

He said, "This isn't funny."

"It never is."

"You wouldn't shoot me."

"Think not?" She pointed the gun. She looked serious.

"What the hell happened to you in New York?"

"I discovered who I really I am and where I belong. I belong here, with you. We belong together."

She paced back and forth in the kitchen.

"Please," Gabriel said.

"You'll stay put. Chloe will get married and take off to her honeymoon. Then I'll untie you and we'll have a serious, sober talk about our relationship."

"There is no more relationship."

"Would you stop being so negative, please? You're going to get me down."

They stared at each other for a long moment. He gave up and said, "Okay. Kill me then."

"You can't say that…that's just…"

"What?"

"Horrible."

He said, "Yes, horrible. What do I have to live for if the love of my life marries another man?"

Hannah said, "I'm the love of your life."

"The day you got on that plane for New York, that stopped being true."

"Okay. I hate you now," Hannah said.

"So shoot. Put a bullet in my head and end this mortal misery."

She pointed the gun. He closed his eyes and waited...

She lowered the gun. Defeated, she told him, "I can't. This is a prop gun."

She cried.

He was pissed.

"Goddammit." He released himself from the electric cord. It was easy; he never really was a prisoner.

He moved toward her.

She backed off.

He took the prop gun away from her. "Should I be surprised? It's always been one big show for you, Hannah," he said. "Nothing is ever real, not even your weapon." He dropped the gun on the floor.

She lunged toward him, tried to grab him. She planned to not let go. But he was faster. He dashed out of the apartment and jumped into his car and drove off.

Hannah picked up the gun. She picked up the phone attached to the wall and called Yellow Cab. "I need a taxi, pronto," she said.

22

Gabriel drove as fast as he could without causing a bad accident. He was late, but if he got there just in time...

Not far behind him a taxi was also driving fast. Hannah was in that taxi cab. She knew where he was going; she'd been there that one time....

23

The band played "Here Comes the Bride."

Chloe walked down the makeshift aisle, between the guests, in her mother-in-law-to-be's large backyard. Ahead of her was Gregory, dapper in his tux, and the minister. Best man, maids of honor, flower girl—the whole works.

This is supposed to be every woman's dream, Chloe thought. And here it was: her nightmare.

She strained her eyes to look at the guests. Where was Gabriel? Why wasn't he here?

Gabriel arrived late, of course, but not too late. He pulled into the driveway of the Binkowski residence, his brakes and tires screeching. He jumped out his car and ran toward the back....

A minute later, the taxi cab pulled up and Hannah jumped out....

24

He got there just in time. The minister was saying, "If there is any man or woman present who objects to this union, speak now or for—"

"I do!" Gabriel yelled, out of breath. "I object to this wedding!"

Gasps of shock, surprise, confusion—all bodies turned and all eyes looked on Gabriel.

"What in the hell," muttered Gretchen, standing up from her seat. She was holding a half-finished martini in her hand.

Gabriel walked up the aisle. Gregory stared at him, mouth agape.

"You can't marry him, Chloe," Gabriel said. "You don't love him. You love me."

Chloe looked at Gregory, at her guests and at Gabriel.

"You're right," she said.

She dropped the bouquet and ran to Gabriel, clutching him, hugging him and kissing him, right there in front of everyone.

"What in the hell is this?" Gretchen cried.

Hannah arrived, prop gun out. "Hold it right there!"

More gasps, more shock, more awe.

"Stop kissing him!" Hannah yelled at Chloe, pointing the gun.

"Oh my God," said Chloe.

"It's okay," Gabriel told her.

"You!" Hannah said to Chloe, and ordered: "You let go of him and get back up there and say 'I do' and get married."

Chloe didn't know what to do.

"Someone do something!" cried Gretchen.

"The gun isn't real," Gabriel said.

"I've had enough of this!" Gretchen stomped toward Hannah, martini in hand.

Hannah was shaking. "Stop..."

"You want to shoot? Shoot!"

"That gun isn't real," Gabriel said.

Gretchen tossed her martini into Hannah's face. Hannah was blinded by the vodka and vermouth. She dropped the gun and clutched at her eyes. "Ouch," she said.

More gasps...some laughter.

Gregory watched, and he was amused.

The minister was not amused. "See here, is there to be a wedding or not?" he asked.

"Beats the hell out of me," Gregory said.

"Yes, there is!" Gretchen said. "Chloe!"

"Some wedding," Gabriel said.

Chloe said, "We need to get out of here before some other crazy thing happens."

She grabbed his hand. The two of them ran out of the yard, fast.

The two lovers on the run...

"Come back here!" Gretchen screamed.

"Ouch," Hannah said.

Someone helped her to a seat. A man.

"You all right?" the man asked.

The man was Gregory.

Her eyesight was coming back...a handsome man. "I think so," she said, and smiled.

He smiled back.

Not bad, she thought.

25

Gabriel and Chloe drove away from the scene in his car, laughing. She threw off her veil, letting it float into the wind. She got out of her dress and tossed the dress out onto the road. They laughed.

She was wearing only panties and garters now, in white.

"Wow," Gabriel said.

"Is it honeymoon time?" Chloe said.

He parked his car by a cliff overlooking the ocean and... well, you can guess what they did there. People driving by noticed a woman's two bare legs up in the air.

✑ about the authors ✑

Janine Ashbless likes unconventional weddings: she was once best man for a male friend and she herself got married in secret…which really upset her new mother-in-law. She has written five erotic books for Black Lace and her short stories appear in anthologies by Black Lace, Cleis (including *Best Women's Erotica 2011*) and—starting with *Alison's Wonderland*—Harlequin. She lives in the UK and blogs at *www.janineashbless.blogspot.com* where she enthuses about mythology, Victorian art and minotaurs.

By day, **Jax Baynard** is a financial investment advisor. By night, she makes her own (and her clients') fantasies come true. This part-time dominatrix's short fiction has appeared in *Pleasure Bound*, online, and in several literary journals. Her favorite weddings are the ones you never think will happen.

Cheyenne Blue combines her two passions in life and writes travel guides and erotica. Her erotica has appeared in several anthologies, including *Best Women's Erotica, Mammoth*

Best New Erotica, Best Lesbian Erotica, Best Lesbian Love Stories and on many websites. Her travel guides have been jammed into many glove boxes underneath the chocolate wrappers. She divides her time between Colorado, USA, Australia and Ireland, and is currently working on a book about the quiet and quirky areas of Ireland. Her favorite type of wedding is an Irish one with black pints and singing. Visit her at *http://www.cheyenneblue.com.*

Rachel Kramer Bussel *(www.rachelkramerbussel.com)* is an author, editor, blogger and reading-series host. She is senior editor at Penthouse Variations, wrote the Lusty Lady column for *The Village Voice,* and has contributed to *Cosmopolitan, The Daily Beast, New York Post* and other publications. She's edited over twenty-five anthologies, including *Bottoms Up, Spanked, Yes, Sir, Yes, Ma'am, The Mile High Club, Do Not Disturb, Rubber Sex, Dirty Girls,* and is the Best Sex Writing series editor. Since October 2005, she has hosted New York's In The Flesh Reading Series, featuring everyone from Susie Bright to Zane. She cries at weddings but doesn't anticipate walking down the aisle herself.

Heidi Champa was married on a hot, humid August day eleven years ago. The wedding started with thunder and lightning and ended with a brilliant pink sunset. Her husband has always encouraged her to write, believing her dirty mind should be put to good use. Her work appears in numerous anthologies including *Tasting Him, Frenzy, Playing With Fire* and *Girl Fun One.* She has also steamed up the pages of *Bust Magazine.* If you prefer your erotica in electronic form, she can be found at *Clean Sheets, Ravenous Romance, Oysters and Chocolate* and *The Erotic Woman.* Find her online at *heidichampa.blogspot.com.*

Portia Da Costa is a British author of romance, erotic romance and erotic fiction, who loves writing about sexy, likable people in steamy and wickedly scandalous situations. Her many novels have been translated into languages such as German, Spanish and Dutch, and she's had well over a hundred short stories published in magazines and anthologies. A passionate believer in matrimony, Portia has been married more years than she cares to count, but she still remembers feeling like a princess on her wedding day. She and her prince live in the heart of West Yorkshire with their cats.

Bella Dean was always the one dodging the bouquet. And she still is. But that doesn't mean she's not making eyes at the sexy groomsman or flirting with the caterer. She figures when the right guy comes along, she'll go straight for the garters. Skip the bouquet. Bella's work has appeared in *Alison's Wonderland, Pleasure Bound, For the Girls* and *Afternoon Delight,* among others.

Erastes lives in the UK. She writes gay historical romance and believes that marriage is for everyone. Her second novel, *Transgressions,* was launched in March 09 as part of Running Press's seminal gay romance line, targeted at both men and women. Her website, which includes many excerpts of her work, can be found at *www.erastes.com.*

ADR Forte is the author of erotic short fiction that appears in numerous anthologies from Cleis Press, Circlet Press and Black Lace, including *Hurts So Good* and *Pleasure Bound,* also edited by Alison Tyler. She once considered wedding cake design, but after a few notably disastrous attempts with the icing and food coloring decided to stick with writing instead. Visit her at *www.adrforte.blogspot.com.*

Lana Fox has published erotic stories in *Alison's Wonderland* and several Xcite anthologies, including *Naughty Spanking 1* and *Sex, Love and Valentines*. Her other short fiction about sexuality has appeared in numerous lit mags. Lana was taught that sex before marriage is sinful, so she had lots and lots of it before getting hitched in white. She is currently working on a collection of erotic stories about sex and magic. You can find her online at *http://www.lanafox.com*.

If **Shanna Germain** was a wedding cake, she'd either be red velvet with cream cheese frosting or a bite-size gypsy tart. When she's not dreaming of new things to put in her mouth, she's writing. Her award-winning work can be read in places like *Best American Erotica, Best Bondage Erotica 2, Best Gay Romance, Best Lesbian Erotica, F is for Fetish, Playing With Fire, X: The Erotic Treasury* and on her website, *www.shannagermain.com*.

P. S. Haven is from Winston-Salem, North Carolina. He began writing dirty stories as a way to turn on his girlfriend. They've been married for twelve years, so he did something right. His style is heavily influenced by the works of Hugh Hefner, Henry Ford and David Lee Roth. Haven's stories have been published in *Best American Erotica Series, Playing With Fire: Taboo Erotica, X: The Erotic Treasury, B is for Bondage, Frenzy: 60 Stories of Sudden Sex* and many others. He blogs about writing and lots of other stuff at *pshaven.blogspot.com*.

Michael Hemmingson's first feature film, *The Watermelon,* is out on DVD and Blu-Ray, and ends in a possible wedding-on-the-verge: that is, the hero gets the girl. His novels include *Wild Turkey, The Comfort of Women* and

The Dress, along with a collection of erotic stories *Sexy Strumpets and Troublesome Trollops.*

Kristina Lloyd is the author of three erotic novels including the controversial Black Lace bestseller, *Asking for Trouble.* Her short stories have appeared in numerous anthologies and her novels have been translated into German, Dutch and Japanese. She has a master's degree in twentieth-century literature and has been described as "a fresh literary talent" who "writes sex with a formidable force." The last wedding she attended was in Duras, the French town associated with Marguerite Duras. For more visit *kristinalloyd.wordpress.com.*

Nikki Magennis is a Scottish writer of erotica and erotic romance who has a habit of falling over at weddings. You can find her short stories in many anthologies including *Alison's Wonderland* from Harlequin and the *Mammoth Book of the Kama Sutra.* Her novels, *Circus Excite* and *The New Rakes,* are published by Virgin Black Lace. Find out more at *nikkimagennis.blogspot.com.*

Sommer Marsden made her own wedding cake. And then the cat ate it. A lovely friend made her second so she didn't have a nervous breakdown. Even though her original cake did not survive, her marriage is still going strong. She's been with one very patient, sexy man for a baker's dozen years (and counting). Sommer is the author of *Lucky 13, Double Booked* and *The Mighty Quinn.* Her work has appeared in dozens of anthologies, including *Alison's Wonderland, Best Women's Erotica 2009* and *2010, Liaisons,* and *Sex and Satisfaction.* According to Ashley Lister (ERWA), she is "renowned for her style of combining exquisite sex with well-realized situations and credible characters." Visit her at *sommermarsden.blogspot.com*.

N. T. Morley thinks the happiest marriages start out with strippers at the weddings, not just the bachelor and/or bachelorette parties. Morley's many novels include *The Parlor, The Limousine, The Appointment* and *The Visitor,* as well the trilogies *The Castle, The Library* and *The Office,* and a double anthology, *MASTER/slave.* More can be unearthed at *www.ntmorley.com.*

Kate Pearce was born into a large family of girls in England, and spent much of her childhood living very happily in a dream world. Despite being told that she really needed to "get with the program," she graduated from the University College of Wales with a master's degree in history. A move to the USA finally allowed her to fulfill her dreams and sit down and write that novel. Along with being a voracious reader, Kate loves trail riding with her family, "Western style" in the regional parks of Northern California. Kate is a member of RWA and is published by Kensington Aphrodisia, NAL, Ellora's Cave, Cleis Press and Virgin Black Lace/Cheek.

A veteran of many friends' too-elaborate weddings, **Thomas S. Roche** hopes the next time he wears a tuxedo, he'll be accepting his first Oscar or dispatching Russian agents. The most romantic wedding he ever attended was inside a rusted-out gun emplacement overlooking the Golden Gate Bridge. His widely published short stories have appeared in such venues as the *Best American Erotica* series, the *Best New Erotica* series and many other best-of anthologies. He can be found at *www.thomasroche.com.*

Sophia Valenti loves married men—well, one in particular, who she has adored since their wedding twelve years ago. She thinks the best part of being married is living with your best friend—and having someone strong in the house to open jars. Her erotica has appeared in the Harlequin Spice anthology *Alison's Wonderland* and the Cleis Press books *Afternoon Delight, Playing with Fire* and *Pleasure Bound*. Visit her at *sophiavalenti.blogspot.com*.

I.K. Velasco is a corporate slave by day and a slave to her passions at night. She tries to come off as hardcore, but is really a big softie. She's a bit chagrined to admit that she's had her dream wedding planned in her head since the age of six—raspberry and chocolate-brown color scheme, pink hydrangeas and a gaggle of bridesmaids, oh my!

Saskia Walker *(www.saskiawalker.co.uk)* is an award-winning British author whose short fiction appears in over sixty anthologies. Her erotic novels include *Along for the Ride, Double Dare, Reckless, Rampant, Inescapable* and *The Harlot*. Saskia lives in the north of England close to the windswept Yorkshire moors, where she happily spends her days spinning yarns. Saskia once attended a wedding on the arm of a horned demon. Saskia was dressed as a cobweb-covered ghoul. The bride and groom were vampires, and the guests included all manner of paranormal creatures. Even the registrar was wearing witch's garb. The date? All Hallows' Eve.

Rita Winchester has multiple hideous bridesmaids dresses and nary a bridal gown in sight. But she never says never and she figures the bridesmaids gowns come in handy for Halloween...or witness protection. Her work has appeared in *Mammoth Lesbian Erotica, I is for Indecent, Tasting Her, Pleasure Bound,*

Never Have the Same Sex Twice and *Frenzy,* among others. You can drop her a line or a rope at *rita_winchester@yahoo.com.*

Kristina Wright *(kristinawright.com)* is an award-winning author whose erotica and erotic romance has appeared in over seventy-five anthologies including *Bedding Down: A Collection of Winter Erotic, Dirty Girls* and the collections *Seduction, Liaisons* and *Sexy Little Numbers.* She is also the editor of *Fairy Tale Lust: Bedtime Stories for Women.* Her writing is inspired by her own happily-ever-after tale: she married her soul mate after a whirlwind six-month long-distance relationship. Twenty years later, she is happy to say she would do it all again.

❧ about the editor ❧

Called a "trollop with a laptop" by *East Bay Express*, a "literary siren" by *Good Vibrations* and "erotica's own superwoman" by the *East Bay Literary Examiner*, Alison Tyler has made being naughty a full-time job. Her sultry short stories have appeared in more than a hundred anthologies including *Sex for America, Liaisons* and *Bedding Down*. She is the editor of fifty erotic anthologies, including *Alison's Wonderland, Naked Erotica* and *Naughty Fairy Tales from A to Z*. Her twenty-five novels include *Tiffany Twisted, Melt With You* and *Something About Workmen*.

Ms. Tyler is loyal to coffee (black), lipstick (red), and tequila (straight). She has tattoos, but no piercings; a wicked tongue, but a quick smile; bittersweet memories, but no regrets. She believes the rain won't fall if she doesn't bring an umbrella, prefers hot and dry to cold and wet, and loves to spout her favorite motto: You Can Sleep When You're Dead. She chooses Led Zeppelin over the Beatles, the Cure over the Smiths, and the Stones over everyone—yet although she appreciates good rock, she has a pitiful weakness for eighties hair bands.

In all things important, she remains faithful to her husband of fifteen years, but she still can't choose just one perfume. Her favorite anniversary gifts to date have been the ones for her third anniversary (a leather riding crop), her eleventh anniversary (regulation steel handcuffs), and her fifteenth (a crystal dildo). Who says "traditional" has to equal "boring"?

Find her on the web at *www.alisontyler.com*.

ALISON'S WONDERLAND

ALISON TYLER

Over the past fifteen years, Alison Tyler has curated some of the genre's most sizzling collections of erotic fiction, proving herself to be the ultimate naughty librarian. With *Alison's Wonderland,* she has compiled a treasury of naughty tales based on fable and fairy tale, myth and legend: some ubiquitous, some obscure—all of them delightfully dirty.

From a perverse prince to a vampire-esque Sleeping Beauty, the stars of these reimagined tales are—like the original protagonists—chafing at unfulfilled desire. From Cinderella to Sisyphus, mermaids to werewolves, this realm of fantasy is limitless and so *very* satisfying.

Penned by such erotica luminaries as Shanna Germain, Rachel Kramer Bussel, N.T. Morley, Elspeth Potter, T.C. Calligari, D.L. King, Portia Da Costa and Tsaurah Litzsky, these bawdy bedtime stories are sure to bring you (and a friend) to your own happily-ever-after.

> "Alison Tyler has introduced readers to some of the hottest contemporary erotica around."—*Clean Sheets*

www.Spice-Books.com

SAT60545TR